Praise for
RACHEL LEE

"*The Crimson Code* is a smart, complex thriller
with enough twists to knot your stomach and keep
your fingers turning the pages."
—*New York Times* bestselling author Alex Kava

"Incredibly complex and blood-chillingly plausible in
the current global political climate, this story grabs
hold of the imagination and heart and never lets
up for a second. Top-notch."
—*Romantic Times BOOKreviews* on
The Crimson Code (4 ½ stars)

"A highly complex thriller…deft use of dialogue…"
—*Publishers Weekly* on *Wildcard*

"Lee offers a timely, harrowing peek into political
machinations on several continents, beginning what's
certain to be a fascinating series."
—*Romantic Times BOOKreviews* on *Wildcard*

"A suspenseful, edge-of-the-seat read."
—*Publishers Weekly* on *Caught*

"Rachel Lee is a master of romantic suspense."
—*Romantic Times BOOKreviews*

THE JERICHO PACT

RACHEL LEE

ISBN-13: 978-0-7783-2416-4
ISBN-10:   0-7783-2416-8

THE JERICHO PACT

www.MIRABooks.com

Printed in U.S.A.

To Rolf Winkenbach, whose tireless assistance, constant patience and willingness to travel with camera and share things we might never have otherwise known about Europe have made so much possible.

To our editor Leslie Wainger, whose belief never flags and whose suggestions always help. To her assistant Adam Wilson, whose patience exceeds Job's.

To one another, for having survived this book on speaking terms. Barely.

Part I: *MIßTRAUENSVOTUM*
(German: A vote of no confidence)

Prologue

Paris, France

Hami Khadir did not hear the noise at first. He was both excited and troubled as he sat at a table in the café within the Grande Mosquée de Paris.

On the one hand, his mother and sister would be arriving tomorrow from Algiers. He was looking forward to the visit and to showing them his new apartment in the twentieth *arrondissement*. For two years he had lived in student housing at the Sorbonne, where he was working toward his doctorate in urban planning. But while it had been pleasant enough in most ways, and while there were Islamic student groups at the university, the student quarters left him feeling cut adrift. At the end of the day, he found himself longing for the sights and sounds and smells of his native culture.

The Belleville district of Paris, where he lived now, offered a pleasant alternative. For decades it had been a haven for artists and immigrants of all stripes, and its Arab quarter felt as close to home as Hami could feel while still continuing his studies.

He had turned down a flat in the Clichy-sous-Bois, not wanting to live in the seething cauldron of anger and discontent that characterized the Islamic community there. Paris would never be his home, but neither did he wish to perceive himself as an exile while living there. As Hami saw it, contentment was something one made for one's self, and he was determined to find it in every day.

It was for this reason that he had come to the Grande Mosquée tonight. Even in Belleville, the tension in the streets had been palpable as Parisian youth, disgusted and disheartened by stifling unemployment, vented their anger on their Muslim neighbors. Hami had been spat on as he had walked from the Arab market to his flat, and rather than respond in anger, he had steeled himself to attend evening prayers and turn his thoughts to the words of the Prophet.

For it was the Prophet—peace be upon him—who had set the example that Hami strove to follow. Tradition held that a woman had spat upon the Prophet every day as he was walking to the marketplace in Mecca. But Mohammed neither chastised her nor permitted his followers to lift a hand against her. Indeed, when the woman was not there one day, he went to her home to see if she was ill and to pray for her recovery.

It was this spirit that Hami chose to emulate, both as

a matter of faith and as a matter of simple survival. To meet violence with violence would surely cost him his seat at the Sorbonne, if not his life itself. To wipe spittle from his face was a small price to pay for the opportunity to complete his studies and return home to help build a better Algiers.

Yet the affront still burned in his stomach as he sipped the rich Turkish coffee. He had done nothing to the young man who had spat on him. As he looked up at the beautifully painted ceiling of the café, he wondered if the Prophet had even felt the anger that Hami felt now. Was it more holy to feel and suppress the anger or not to feel the anger at all?

Hami had learned from earliest childhood that *jihad*—the struggle—was the duty of every Muslim. However that word had been perverted by some, to Hami it meant simply the struggle to conform one's life to the teachings of the Prophet and the will of Allah. If that were true, he reasoned, then perhaps there was no sin in the anger he felt. For if he felt no offense, if he did not care that someone he did not know and had never spoken to would spit in his face, then how could he struggle to overcome those feelings?

It was this that he had discussed with the mullah after evening prayers. While the mullah had shared Hami's anger, he had counseled Hami against retaliation. Indeed, Hami was pleased to note, the mullah's reasoning had been much the same as his own. Hami's duty was not to remain devoid of anger, for no man could expect that of himself. Rather, his duty was to transform that anger, to find in that pain a reason to draw nearer to Allah and, ultimately, to allow Allah to judge both the grievous and petty slights of men.

The dull echoes of voices slowly filtered into Hami's thoughts, and for a moment he thought perhaps they were the voices of angry young Muslims arguing with the mullah and elders in the mosque. Such arguments were increasingly common, and he could understand the young men's desire to lash out and reclaim a measure of dignity. However much the mullahs might say otherwise, Hami knew there were times when these young men felt as if life offered no choice but to fight if they wished to retain their manhood.

As Hami listened more closely, he realized the shouts were not coming from within the mosque but rather from the street outside. He rose from his chair and walked toward the door. If there were more demonstrators in the streets, he might need to plan another route home to avoid any more confrontations.

He had just opened the door when he saw the bottle flying toward him, tumbling through the air, the flame at its neck creating a spiral of orange light that seemed to fix his concentration.

He felt the crack as the bottle hit him and was vaguely aware of lying on the floor of the café, once more looking up at the ceiling, before the searing heat of the flames penetrated his fogged awareness. Now the world seemed to tumble as he felt himself rolling, the pain growing ever deeper, until finally, mercifully, the nerves surrendered and there was only peace.

He would soon be in the arms of Allah. This he knew, and nothing else mattered. Not even the dull gray pipe in the hands of the man who stood over him, dimly reflecting the orange glow of the surrounding fires before it arced down toward his eyes and crushed him into blackness.

1

In the warehouse where Office 119 hid itself, Lawton Caine stood in a walkway between cubicles, absent-mindedly juggling a round football between his feet as he watched a bank of television monitors on the wall. He wasn't much of a footballer, having grown up in the United States, where football was an entirely different sport and what he now practiced was called soccer, but he had decided to adopt the European name for the sport. It was, he realized, symbolic of a deeper change within him. He no longer thought of himself as a former FBI agent who had disappeared into the rabbit-hole world of Office 119: He was no longer an American living in Rome. This was home now, and learning to appreciate football as it was played in Europe was a way of connecting himself to this new stage of his life.

Nearby sat his colleague Margarite Renault, formerly

of the French *Sûreté*. She, too, had left an old life behind, although the change had not been as radical for her. She was still on her native continent, if not in her native Paris. But she seemed even more uncomfortable than he felt, for it was the rioting in her native city—and the burning of its historic mosque—that dominated the news broadcasts.

They were waiting for a speech by the president of the European Union, Jules Soult. Except for light from the bank of monitors, the offices were dark. The other agents were either gone for the day or off on missions somewhere. Even *El Jefe,* the chief, had bailed, remarking that he had a dinner date that could not be postponed.

Margarite and Lawton had joked about whether a woman was involved, but neither believed it. Their existence in and service to this ultrasecret UN organization required them to be invisible to the world and dead to everyone in their past lives. Relationships would not only complicate their mission, relationships could put all their lives in jeopardy.

"You know," Lawton remarked to Margarite, trying vainly to master a step-over while he watched the images of the burning mosque, "there's something missing here."

She looked at him. "What would that be, apart from your appalling balance?"

He smirked. "Give me a break, Margarite. I'm still learning. This wasn't my game before."

"That's more than apparent," she said, her face dead-pan for a long moment before she finally smiled. "But you weren't talking about your footballing skills. So what's missing, *mon ami?*"

"Where are the pictures of young men in handcuffs, being led away by the gendarmes?"

She nodded, her eyes scanning the broadcasts from all over Europe plus the international news networks. "What do you mean?"

"Surely you don't think the Paris police aren't making any arrests. In every riot there are three kinds of pictures: buildings and cars burning, the rioters and the police making arrests. They're showing the mosque burning. They're showing the blood-stained and charred bodies of Muslims being taken into ambulances. They're showing the French youth rioting. But no arrests."

She nodded. "The commentators are calling these riots an *intifada,* Lawton. The Muslims are starting them. The French are only defending themselves. Perhaps the police see no reason to make arrests."

He looked at her. "No reason?"

"*Oui,*" she said. "It is…how do you call it in English when it is okay for hunters to shoot rabbits?"

"Open season." He frowned, scanning the endlessly playing views of violence. "You're saying the French government is going to stand by while people kill Muslims?"

Margarite shrugged. "Perhaps it is time for that. Why should French citizens stand by while Muslims take to the streets and burn buildings? Is there any proof that the Muslims did not start the fire at the Paris mosque?"

Lawton's gaze was intent. "What are you saying?"

"You *do* understand that one of the primary objections to the EU Constitution was that the EU might accept Turkey as a member, yes? That would have permitted unrestricted travel to Arabs coming in by way of Turkey. Surely you know the anger we Europeans feel toward Spain for accepting so many immigrants from Morocco, because once they are in Spain, they can fan out through the entire Union."

"How do *you* feel about that?"

Margarite shrugged that irritating Gallic shrug that seemed to say she was above it all, when she wasn't above anything at all. "It would be dangerous to allow any more Muslims into Europe. I agree with that. We had enough of terrorism with the Red Brigade and Black September. If we are xenophobic, then perhaps there is good reason for it."

Lawton felt startled. There was an undercurrent in her words that he hadn't expected. "What exactly are you saying?"

"I am saying that we would not be having these problems if we hadn't allowed so much immigration from countries that do not share our cultural and moral viewpoints. How can there not be problems when there is such a divide, and the Muslims make every effort not to cross it? How can there not be a divide when we have London,

Madrid, Black Christmas and Prague to show us that we are allowing dangerous people to live among us?"

"They're not *all* dangerous."

"Of course not. But enough of them are, and how are we supposed to know who is who?" She pointed to one of the screens, where young Muslim men were throwing rocks at the Paris police. "Do you think words or naive feelings can stop this? The Muslims come here to work and make money, and then they refuse to accept our way of life. They create tensions. Then some among them go out and kill others. Why do they do that, Lawton?"

He opened his mouth to reply, but swallowed the words when he realized that he couldn't answer her question.

"We are infidels to them," Margarite continued. "As far as they are concerned, we are not human."

"I'm sure that's not what the *Qur'an* teaches."

She shook her head. "The Bible teaches many things that we do not heed. Why should Muslims be any different? My country is secular. We long ago threw off the yoke of the Catholic Church. Yes, there are still Catholics in France, still priests and churches, but most of us have moved beyond that. And one thing I know for certain. All of us believe that government should be secular. But the Muslims do not share this view. They do not like our secular society."

"So you tell them they can't wear veils to school? You make them violate *shari'a?*"

Again she shrugged. "Live like us, or go somewhere else. That law also limited the size of a cross a Christian may wear to school. It was not discriminatory."

"You don't think so?"

"No, I do *not*."

Lawton gave up and returned his attention to the ball at his feet. He could see Margarite's point of view, though he didn't agree. But he knew he wasn't going to change her mind, and their mission in Office 119 was difficult enough without manufacturing rifts between agents.

Margarite sighed at the silence and looked to the television. "Despite what I think about all this, I can see that this event will be used. And I fear how President Soult will use it."

"How so?"

"That mosque was built with funds donated by the French government in gratitude for the service of Algerian Muslim soldiers in the First World War. When the Nazis took Paris, the mosque hid over two hundred Jews from them in its basement. Now they've burned it down. Soult will use that crime to justify his ambitions."

"Don't you agree with his plans for a more united Europe?" Lawton asked. "He seems to say a lot of the same things I hear you saying."

A long silence passed between them. Then Margarite said, "I can agree with his goals and disagree with his methods, Lawton. I know what he did in the army, in Chad. He is ruthless, and he will not shrink from violence. A lot of innocent Europeans will get caught in the crossfire."

"Including a lot of innocent European Muslims," Lawton said, hearing the edge in his voice, no matter how he tried to curb it. "Many of them have lived here for generations. They are Europeans, too, Margarite."

"A nice sentiment," she said. "But a bit naive, my friend. Muslims are a quarter of the French population. Many people see them as fifth column agents for a Moorish invasion. We remember our past, Lawton. Never again will we surrender one hundred virgins a year as tribute."

"Your memories are too long," Lawton said.

"Perhaps," Margarite replied. "But the Muslims also remember. They remember the Crusades and the attack by the Mongols. We are not like you Americans, who seem to think that history began the day you were born. The attacks of 9/11 surprised you only because you persistently forgot all that had come before. We do not forget, so we are not surprised by what is happening now. We have been fighting Muslims for centuries. We cannot simply wish that conflict away."

"You're saying there will be war."

"Perhaps," she said. "Perhaps there is no other way."

Lawton shook his head and drove his instep into the ball, releasing his frustration in the thud of its impact on the wall, then softened his foot as the ball rebounded so that he could settle it gently at his toe. "There *must* be another way, Margarite. We can't meet force with force forever. If everyone takes an eye for an eye, the entire world goes blind."

"Keep your hips forward as you strike the ball," she replied. "You will get more accuracy and power. We can only do so much, *mon ami*. The key is to do it well."

2

Berlin, Germany

Fatigue pulled at Karl Vögel's shoulders like the pack he had once carried on endless marches in the *Bundeswehr*. As Chancellor of Germany, he now carried a briefcase rather than a field pack—refusing to let his aides carry it for him was a mark of pride—and he was no longer required to trek all night over rocky trails in the *Schwarzwald*. Yet he felt more exhausted tonight than he had then.

"*Sie sind fertig,* Herr Bundeskanzler," Johannes Grauberg said.

Grauberg was Vögel's *Kanzleramtsminister*—chief of staff—and one of his oldest friends. A skilled lawyer and politician, Grauberg chose his words carefully. As always, they were rich with subtle meanings. In the colloquial, he had said *You are exhausted.* But the literal meanings—*You are spent,* or *You are finished*—might well be just as accurate.

"*Ja,* Johannes. That I am." Vögel leaned down to lock his desk, another long-standing habit, even though his was perhaps the most secure office in all of Germany, and walked toward the door. "Please, walk with me."

Grauberg looked into his eyes for a moment, as if trying to read his thoughts, then nodded and took his coat from the rack.

The cabinet meeting had been long and difficult. When he had campaigned, Vögel was convinced he could solve at least some of the problems that nagged at Germany. Three years into his term, he was much less confident. Perhaps the German people would be better off with someone else at the helm. Or perhaps no one could fix the problems.

Nearly two decades had passed since *der Wende,* the change, the reunification of Germany. On 3 October 1990, the future had looked gloriously bright. An artificial separation pitting brother against brother over the harsh concrete of the Berlin Wall had come to an end. The last vestige of Germany's punishment for Hitler's evil was gone. Across this ancient land, hearts were filled with hope.

But full reunification proved to be a difficult task. The problems in the East were legion. Unemployment hovered at nearly twenty percent. The Eastern economy continued to grow slower than the West, increasing the gap between them. All in all, the West-to-East subsidies amounted to four percent of Germany's gross domestic product, more than her annual rate of growth. Each year, she fell further behind.

If all that weren't enough, there were Jules Soult, the horrors at the Paris mosque and the growing sense that the EU was spiraling out of control.

"Too much," Vögel found himself repeating under his breath.

"You're doing all that you can, Karl," Grauberg said.

As was their custom, they switched to first names as they strolled along the spiral walkway inside the glass dome of the Reichstag. At nearly eleven o'clock at night, the dome was silent, lacking the usual bustle of government office workers and tourists.

The two GSG-9 security agents dropped back a few steps, giving Vögel and Grauberg some minimal measure of privacy. That in itself was a small comfort. Too rarely was he simply "Karl" now. With nearly every word he said going into the public record, too rarely could he simply speak as a man to a friend.

"Am I?" Vögel asked. "Are we really doing all we can for the East?"

"Yes," Grauberg said. "Remember Bayern, my friend. After the war, they needed subsidies for forty years. Now it is one of our most productive states."

"But can Germany afford that again, Johannes?"

"The German people will do what they must, Karl. They are a good people. And in the end, it is them upon whom we must rely. Never forget that there are two ways to build a ship. The first is to lay out detailed plans for everyone to follow."

"And the second is to create in their hearts a dream of the sea," Vögel said, smiling at the poetic hope embodied in the ancient German proverb.

As was so often the case, the old wisdom held true. A man could manage, or he could lead. Vögel had chosen to be a leader rather than a manager, campaigning on his vision, his dream of a prosperous Germany leading Europe into a new age of peace and prestige in the world. The German people—enough of them—had approved of his vision. He owed it to them to keep the vision bright. Yet now he was faced with a choice more vexing than any in the past sixty years.

"And what about Soult?" he asked.

What about Soult? That question had lain over the cabinet meeting like coal dust, blackening and fouling every other issue. The new President of the European Union had become the bane of Vögel's every thought. Soult's latest legislative proposals—purportedly offered to "pacify and protect" European Muslims—were nothing short of evil.

It could become a new Holocaust.

"Germany cannot participate in what Soult proposes," Grauberg said. "We have worked too hard to cleanse the stain of Hitler. Now Soult proposes that all of Europe defile itself again. You are right, and you know you are right. And the German people will know you are right, Karl, when they learn the details. They will follow you."

Grauberg broke step and faced the chancellor directly. He lowered his voice. "Karl, you cannot think it even remotely possible that the German people will stand aside while an ethnic group is forced to board trains to go to these so-called protection zones."

Vögel's sigh was pained, heavy. "There are those who would like nothing better."

"But they are a minority. Most Germans remember the past and have learned from it. They will support you."

The chancellor looked his friend in the eye. "Even if we must withdraw from the European Union in protest?"

"Yes. Even then."

Vögel frowned deeply, resuming their walk down the ramp. "I have no desire to see the Union fail. Too many have worked too hard to build it."

"Perhaps it is too soon for unity, Karl. The French and Dutch voted against the constitution. And there have been protests all along."

"And you know why." Vögel glanced at his friend. "Fear of the outsider. Fear of the immigration that Europe *needs* to maintain a viable work force. Our population is shrinking. If we are to remain economically viable, we *must* accept and welcome immigrants. Soult and people like him would 'purify' Europe, only to watch it stagnate and die. Yet I will be blamed for destroying the EU."

"We will be a beacon," Grauberg said firmly. "We must stand for what is right."

Grauberg paused, and Vögel paused with him, looking out over the lights of Berlin. Even at night, the city bustled. Unlike what Vögel had seen in his many visits to the United States, most German cities slept at night, dark, quiet and peaceful. In his hometown of Freiburg, on a clear night, lovers who walked out into the darkness could look up at millions of stars. Not so in Berlin.

The sound was faint at first, musical and yet not, a single pitch riding on the air, barely at the threshold of hearing. Vögel raised an eyebrow for a moment and glanced around. The huge, open dome was empty save for Grauberg, the two security agents and Vögel himself.

Grauberg hesitated, cocking his head to one side. "What is that sound, Karl?"

Vögel shook his head, looking around inside the dome. "I don't know."

The whine had grown louder, almost the sound of a child blowing across the top of a bottle, but firmer. The two GSG-9 agents had also heard it and were edging closer to them.

"It sounds like air blowing across an open window," Grauberg said, "but there are no open windows here."

"None that we know of," one of the GSG-9 agents said, lifting his wrist to his mouth. He spoke into a cufflink microphone. "Give me a security check on all windows and doors in the dome."

"We need to get you out of here, Chancellor," the other agent said.

Vögel was about to nod when he felt as if an electric shock jarred through his body. He gasped, trying to catch his breath, but it was as if the air had been sucked from the room. He tried to reach out for Grauberg, but his arm would not obey this most simple of commands.

As he began to sag to his knees, he saw snow falling around him. But as the snow landed on him and opened rivulets of blood, he realized it was not snow.

It was falling glass.

Rome, Italy

Renate Bächle did not want to hear the ringing of her cell phone. At that moment, she wanted nothing but the body of Antonio Lazio, a man she barely knew, but still a man. Her sex ached with need and pleasure, glowing with a warmth she had not felt in years, as Antonio thrust into her. He was masterful, first plunging fast, then slowing, constantly varying the pace to keep her at the peak of desire, all the while sprinkling kisses over her neck, her shoulders, her breasts. Raw, animal lust drove her muscles in reply, her hips thrusting up to meet him, her inner muscles clenching tight every time he withdrew. The world was miles away, and there it should stay for this night. Because right now she felt like a woman at her most basic level.

But the phone was insistent, not only ringing but clattering across the nightstand, the buzzing vibration reverberating through the wood. As fully as her fluttery contractions had built, they evaporated even more fully, leaving her feeling more dissatisfied than when she had begun.

"*Ja*, Bächle," she snapped as she brought the phone to her ear. "What is it?"

"Renate, it's Lawton. You need to get in here now. Something has happened in Berlin. Chancellor Vögel has…he's collapsed. And part of the Reichstag, too. His assistant and security detail were also injured."

Office 119 had taken everything from her. She had lost her best friend. She had lost her parents. She could not even manage an orgasm. No, she told herself. That wasn't true. Her parents and her friend had not been killed by Office 119 but by a shadowy banking cabal known as the Frankfurt Brotherhood. Office 119 had recruited her after the death of her friend, a death that had been reported as her own. The woman she had been—Gretchen Zeitgenbach, a skilled forensic accountant for the German *Bundeskriminalamt,* or BKA—was no more. She was now Renate Bächle. And Renate Bächle knew all too well that duty trumped everything else, including a sex life.

"*Scheiße!*" she swore, anger fading into resignation. She used one hand to push Antonio none too gently off her. "I'm on my way."

"No," Antonio said. *"Non andare via."* No. Don't go.

Renate tried to smile. She did not love Antonio. She had no room in her life for love. Moreover, she knew he did not love her. This was a liaison of convenience, nothing more. But neither did she wish to hurt him.

"I have no choice," she said, touching a fingertip to his nose. While she didn't feel deeply for him, she didn't want to offend him. In the days ahead, she might want to seek him out again. "It is my job. I must go."

"What an awful job that would tear you from my arms in this moment," he said.

She could not disagree. Office 119 didn't even allow her time to be a woman.

Berlin, Germany

Doctor Ulla Viermann tried to ignore the weight of the moment and focus on her patient. He was dying, and it was her task to prevent that. Nothing else—not even that he was the Chancellor of Germany—mattered in this moment.

But a part of her knew otherwise. Already the hallway was filled with security and government officials, and she knew the hospital lobby would be mobbed with reporters from all over the world. Her every action, her every thought, would be picked over in detail, not just today or this week but for years to come.

The patient's seizures had begun while he was in transport to the hospital, and he had twice fallen into respiratory arrest. Ulla had pushed the oxygen rate to one hundred percent, and still she could not stabilize him. Worse, he did not look like a man in respiratory distress. He was not cyanotic—his fingertips and lips were not blue—and yet his body was acting as if he were suffocating.

Cyanotic.

"Draw venous blood," Ulla said. "I need venous versus arterial oxygenation. Now."

The nurse worked quickly, drawing a vial of bright red blood from the patient's vein, and Ulla did not need to see the test results to confirm her diagnosis. Arterial blood was bright red because it carried oxygen. Venous blood, while not the blue shown on the charts in school biology classes, was visibly darker. The blood in the vial should be almost purple.

"You are sure you drew from a vein?" Ulla asked.

The nurse nodded. "*Ja*, Frau Doktor."

"Cellular asphyxia," Ulla said aloud.

The patient's lungs were working fine, transferring oxygen into the red blood cells for transport throughout his body. But his tissues were not receiving the oxygen, and thus his venous blood was still rich with vital gas.

"Venous O_2 is sixty em-em," the nurse said, watching the blood oxygenation readouts. "Arterial O_2 is sixty-five. Almost the same."

Ulla knew there were only three culprits. She ruled out carbon monoxide; the Reichstag dome was far too large to be filled with it in sufficient concentration to cause these symptoms. She ran to the door and grabbed one of the GSG-9 agents who had come in with the patient. The man was still on duty, despite the rivulets of blood flowing from a multitude of cuts from falling glass.

"Did you smell rotten eggs before the chancellor collapsed?" she asked.

He gave her a quizzical look, pausing for a moment.

"I need to know," she said, shaking him. "Did you smell rotten eggs?"

"*Nein,* Frau Doktor. *Nein.*"

"*Danke,*" Ulla said. That ruled out hydrogen sulfide, leaving only one possible culprit. She turned to a nurse. "Cyanide kit. Now."

Time was critical. If this was indeed acute cyanide poisoning, her patient had only minutes to live. The nurse had the cyanide kit in hand, and Ulla gave the orders.

"Push three hundred milligrams sodium nitrite over five, then twelve-point-five grams sodium thiosulfate IV over ten."

"*Ja,*" the nurse said.

"Keep O_2 at one hundred percent. Tap a vein and give me constant venous O_2 stats."

"*Ja.*"

Ulla glanced up at the blood pressure monitor. While less deadly than cyanide, thiocyanate was still toxic and could cause the patient's blood pressure to drop quickly.

"Hang blood and have it ready," she said.

She shone a penlight into the patient's pupils but found no response. The soles of his feet and palms of his hands were equally unresponsive to pressure. His central nervous system was shutting down. They were losing the battle. He was dying.

"Hydroxocobalamin now," she said.

"Frau Doktor?" The nurse arched an eyebrow.

Although hydroxocobalamin had performed well in clinical trials, the government had not yet approved its use for treatment of cyanide cases. At this point, however, Ulla could not worry about such details. They had only minutes.

"You heard me," she said. "Hydroxocobalamin, four grams IV. Now!"

"Blood pressure is still falling," another nurse called out. "Sixty over forty. Pulse irregular."

"He's going into cardiac arrest," Ulla said, ripping the patient's shirt wider to expose his chest fully. "Prep the paddles. Charge two hundred."

"Charging two hundred," the nurse said. "Charged."

"Clear!" Ulla yelled as she placed the paddles to his chest, one in the center and one below the armpit.

"Clear!" the nurses said in unison, confirming that they were not touching the patient.

Ulla pushed the buttons, and a two-hundred-joule current coursed through the patient's chest. She looked up at the heart monitor. There was no change. "Charge three hundred."

"Charged at three hundred."

"Clear!"

She pushed the buttons again, and the patient almost rose off the table as the electricity seized his body. Still the heart monitor showed a flat line.

"Blood pressure fifty over thirty and falling," a nurse called out. "We're losing him fast."

"Charge three hundred!" Ulla said, not yet willing to concede defeat.

"Charged at three hundred."

"Clear!"

Again the nurses stood clear as she pressed the buttons. And again there was no response.

"Frau Doktor," the nurse said, reaching for Ulla's hands, shaking her head. *"Exitus."*

He is gone.

Only then did Ulla taste the blood in her mouth. She had bitten her lip hard enough to break the skin. Already the bottom of her mask felt damp. She looked around the room, taking a silent poll of each face. There was neither question nor dissent.

"Time of death: 23:57 hours."

Three minutes before midnight.

3

Renate walked into Office 119, hardly glancing around as she made her way to her desk.

"Where the hell were you?" Jefe demanded.

Like Lawton, Jefe had once served in the FBI. Now he was simply *El Jefe,* the Chief. In their previous lives, Lawton Caine, then known as Tom Lawton, had known him as John Ortega. But now, neither Lawton Caine nor Jefe spoke of that. For, like Tom Lawton, John Ortega was officially dead.

"I was having sex with a man I met at a bar," Renate snapped. "Your timing is abysmal."

Jefe's jaw dropped. Even Lawton seemed embarrassed by her blunt reply. Margarite's reaction, however, was purely European. "My sympathies. Maybe you can finish your workout later."

"Workout?" Jefe repeated, eyes pinched. "What…?"

Renate dropped her pager on her desk, letting it bounce as she sat. "You Americans sell cars by leaning half-naked women across them, yet you get all upset when women talk about sex as a normal part of life. I will never understand you."

"Well, don't blame us for the timing," Lawton said, something lurking in his tone that annoyed her even more. "We didn't kill Chancellor Vögel."

"He's dead?" Renate asked, forcing her anger into the background. There was no room for the personal here, not Lawton's ill-concealed jealousy, not her own frustration and sense that she was losing important parts of herself. Here there could be only business. She had violated the code by announcing where she had been. "You said something about the dome collapsing. What happened?"

"We don't know yet. The news is still spotty, beyond reports that part of the Reichstag dome has collapsed. The hospital and the government are sitting on the story until they know more. But our source says Vögel is dead. What's more, it was probably murder. Cyanide poisoning."

"Cyanide! But how? Why would cyanide make the Reichstag dome collapse?"

Margarite's reply was sarcastic. "*Merde*, are those not the same questions we have been asking while we awaited you? Was he good?"

"He was Italian," Renate answered, annoyed anew by Margarite's tone and question, and by the cringe she saw in Lawton's eyes.

"Not bad," Margarite said. "My countrymen are good, but sometimes a little hot-bloodedness…" She smiled, clearly aware that she was discomfiting the men.

Something in Margarite's eyes softened Renate's anger. There was more there than mere playfulness at the expense of the men. There was a hint of…approval, as if Margarite understood what Renate had been searching for when she had gone to that bar.

"Yes," Renate said to her, ignoring Lawton's look of distaste. "Sometimes we need to feel the blood rush in our veins, to feel our hearts pound and our legs quiver, just to know we are alive."

"Enough," said *El Jefe,* obviously as uncomfortable as Lawton with the subject. "Let's get back to business. We don't know much, but we know something is wrong. Renate, we have a BKA source, but it's secondhand from Washington. The news is only saying that part of the dome collapsed and the chancellor has been injured. The German government hasn't announced it yet, but they know it was cyanide poisoning."

Renate nodded. She was not surprised that her old colleagues at the *Bundeskriminalamt* were investigating so quickly. They knew that the first hours were the critical ones, and that trails quickly grew cold. It bothered her that Office 119's knowledge of what was happening within the BKA was limited to what they received from Washington, however. Secondhand information was always suspect.

"Who is our contact in Washington?" she asked.

"Miriam Anson," Lawton said. "After the mess with Phillip Bentley, President Rice made Grant Lawrence his National Security Advisor. Miriam is now Director of National Intelligence. Chief Spook."

"And she knows where we are," Renate said, suspicion in her voice. "We're supposed to be invisible, or did that change while I was out this evening?"

"Okay," said *El Jefe,* the one English word that was the same in every language the world over, "everyone calm down. We all have contacts, Renate. And as contacts go, Miriam Anson's as good as anyone could hope for. Let's look at what we have instead of quibbling over where it came from. Whatever is going on here, I don't think we're looking at a lone gunman."

"Vögel publicly renounced Soult's proposed legislation about security zones for the Muslims," Renate said. "*My* sources say he was going to pull Germany out of the EU if it came to that."

"You think Soult did it?" Margarite asked.

"You know he's capable of it," Renate replied. "He wants an ethnic cleansing, and Chancellor Vögel was standing in his way."

"'Ethnic cleansing' is a strong term," Margarite said.

"So dress it up with a different euphemism," Renate replied, her voice dripping sarcasm. "Call it whatever you want. His Europa Prima Party is blatantly racist. Blame the bad foreigners for all of your problems. All they're missing is the swastika."

"Oh, we *are* in a mood," Lawton said.

Renate turned to him. "The Chancellor of Germany is dead. Your friend Miriam says it was murder. Soult is going to tear Europe apart. Paris is burning. And yes, you dragged me out of a warm and pleasant bed to get this news. What, exactly, am I supposed to be cheerful about?"

"Nothing," Lawton said. "But venting your spleen on us isn't going to change anything. I'm sorry I interrupted your liaison. But we have a job to do here."

"Yes," she said bitterly. "The job. Always the job. So what *do* we know?"

"Too damn little," Jefe said. "And that's the problem. Get in touch with your sources in Germany, Renate. We need to know what they know and what they suspect. And I'd like to be ahead of the curve on this one, instead of constantly playing catch-up."

Renate drew a breath and forced herself to relax. Lawton was right. It was wrong for her to snipe at the people in this room, when the trouble was happening out there. She let the breath out slowly and nodded. "What have we heard out of Frankfurt?"

"Assif has a team working decryption around the clock," Jefe said.

Assif Mondi, formerly of the Indian national police, was the computer wizard who had masterminded the Office 119 bugging of the communications network of the Frankfurt Brotherhood, the international banking cabal that Renate had first discovered during her time with the

BKA. It had been intelligence from Frankfurt that had enabled Office 119 to capture the terrorist who had tried to bomb the EU Parliament building in Strasbourg.

That attempted bombing had catalyzed Jules Soult's political career, after he had led EU security forces in finding and disabling the bombs. Most of Europe thought him a hero, but Renate suspected he had planned the entire event himself. She had no firm evidence beyond her gut-level revulsion at Soult and the policies he espoused. But bitter experience had led her to trust those instincts.

"Margarite," Jefe said, looking at a yellow legal pad on which he had been scribbling, "I want everything you can get about Jules Soult, as well as this mess in Paris. Lawton, we need whatever Miriam knows or even thinks she knows. Get to work, people. Full reports in two hours."

Rome, Italy

Father Steve Lorenzo was dining in a small restaurant with Monsignore Giuseppi Veltroni, his mentor and friend. Though he had been back in Rome for a while now, Steve was still having trouble adjusting to the change.

He had gone from Savannah, Georgia, to the jungles of Guatemala with little sense of culture shock. Now, having spent two years fleeing both the government and the rebels, hiding in the jungle with his small flock of villagers, he found it almost impossible to return to the First World.

Perhaps, he thought, life at its most basic, the life he

had lived in Guatemala, felt more comfortable, more real, to the mind, heart and soul than white linen table-cloths and sparkling crystal. Certainly he had felt purer there than here.

"Steven," Veltroni said, "you're ignoring your pasta."

"It's more than I am used to eating, *Monsignore.*"

"And you look like it. We must fatten you again, at least to some semblance of health."

"I am healthy."

Veltroni leaned back in his chair, putting down his fork and spoon. His dark eyes studied his protégé with both concern and intrigue. "You have changed."

"It's hard not to change when you see innocent people gunned down and their families chased through the jungle, almost to the point of their extermination. It's hard not to change when you are stripped of everything save one set of clothes someone has given you, and when each day is a search for survival. One learns what is truly important."

"I quite agree. I hope faith was among those important things."

Steve nodded. "Yes, *Monsignore,* it was. The women made tortillas for the Eucharist. I blessed rainwater rather than wine. Every day. It was the closest I have ever felt to our Lord, and I know many with me felt the same."

Veltroni nodded, his gaze fixed on the younger man. "That's an amazing story of spiritual heroism, Steve. Yet you will not move into the apartment I have secured for you in the Vatican. You will not take up the post the

Stewards of Faith have found for you. Have you any idea how much good you could do in the Vatican? So many could learn from your experiences, as I do."

"Could I?" Steve Lorenzo looked down at his plate, mounded with pasta, and shoved it away, trying not to think how many villagers it could feed in Guatemala. "I am not ungrateful."

"What, then? What is going on in your head?"

"My head? Perhaps it is in my heart, *Monsignore.*"

The *monsignore* leaned forward, lowering his voice confidentially. "Tell me. I place the Seal of Confession on the rest of this conversation." Veltroni was truly worried. He loved Steve Lorenzo as a son.

Steve glanced out the window at the rainy evening, watching as people hurried by beneath umbrellas or tucked deep within raincoats. Then he looked again at Veltroni.

"I am a Steward of the Faith."

"Yes," Veltroni agreed. "You are. You are pledged always to protect the Faith, and so far you have done an exemplary job."

"But what is 'the Faith,' *Monsignore?*"

Giuseppe Veltroni leaned back in his chair and frowned deeply. "Do you doubt your faith, after all that you have seen and done?"

Steve's expression grew even more somber. "I do not doubt my faith, my friend. But I wonder what the Stewards are protecting. What is the Faith—to you, Giuseppe? The Church? Or the Word?"

"Why are you asking this? What is it that troubles you? Please explain so I can understand, Steve."

"It's very simple. I've given you a short account of what I endured in Guatemala, what my people endured, what I found and how it was lost. But now that I am back, I find myself remembering things from the Church's past, things that trouble me."

"For example?"

"You recall, I'm sure, when Pope Paul VI denounced so-called 'liberation theology.' He ordered socially active priests in South and Central America to stop speaking out against the atrocities of their governments. Those priests were demanding change, yet the Holy Father spoke of it as 'fomenting rebellion.'"

"Of course I remember. He was concerned lest the Church be evicted from those countries, and the people thus denied the grace and sacraments of their faith. The Church cannot minister long distance, Steve. We must be on the ground, in a place, to offer the Eucharist."

"I understand that," Steve said. "But I ask you this. Did Jesus worry about offending the local authorities?"

Veltroni drew a breath.

Steve smiled faintly. "It makes you think, doesn't it? Jesus spoke out for the oppressed in every instance. He was willing to die to save all those people who weren't allowed to set foot in the Temple because they were deemed unclean. The Church did not decry the Holocaust when it was happening. I hear nothing from the

Holy Father about Soult's proposals for the Muslims living among us. And I suspect the reasons are the same
as they have always been—those in the Vatican deem it
more important to preserve the Church's presence than
to fulfill its moral duty to the weak and the voiceless in
need of a strong voice. So again I ask you, am I pledged
to protect the Word or the Church?"

It was an old and vexing question, and Veltroni took
a moment before responding. "Some consider the Word
and Holy Mother Church to be one and the same."

"And you, my friend? What do you think?"

"Of course they are not the same, Steve. The Church
is, for better or worse, an institution of human beings.
We pray for spiritual guidance, and I believe that much
of what the Church does and has done has indeed been
led by the Spirit. But we are still human beings, prone
to errors of fact as well as errors of motive."

Steve nodded and once again looked out the window.
"That's why I can't move into the Vatican apartment or
take the job you have so kindly offered me. I am not re-
jecting my Church, *Monsignore*. She will always be my
Church. But, for a time at least, my heart tells me that
my duties here lie on a different path."

Veltroni remained silent for a long time, not moving.
Steve waited patiently.

Finally the *monsignore* spoke. "Take our food home
with you. Give it to the hungry you meet along the way."

"I will, thank you."

"But, Steve—" and here Veltroni's voice carried a wealth of concern "—please be careful. I can see the light of your soul in your eyes now. You have been purified in a way that I can only envy, were that not a sin. But please remember…those who become saints are often called to lives of horrible suffering. And while that might glorify our Lord, it would rend my heart."

"I'm no saint!" Steve actually laughed.

"Then let me put it to you another way. There is darkness in the world, forces against which Holy Mother Church is perhaps the only steadfast bulwark. It is far easier to protect the sheep who are within the fold and very difficult to protect the one who must, for whatever reason, take his own path. Beware the wolves, Steve."

Veltroni watched Steve leave with two nearly complete dinners. The food would not feed many, Veltroni knew. But the grace of feeding the multitudes had not been given to Steve or to him. They had to feed one man at a time and pray that the Lord would lead others to feed the rest.

Still, as Veltroni sat on the tram riding back to the Vatican, he thought about what Steve had said. What Jules Soult was proposing—however well-intentioned it might seem—was surely a spiritual abomination. It was a return to an Old Testament God, a God of wrath and war and separateness, a God in whom men could find orders to slay every man, woman and child in a Canaanite village.

And yet Christ's first missionary had been not only a woman but a Samaritan woman, forgiven her sins and sent back to her village to spread the word of forgiveness and hope. And one of the most famous and beloved of all the parables was that of the Good Samaritan, the man who did not pass by in selfishness or fear, but who instead stopped to care for a wounded traveler.

While the Samaritans were of Jewish descent, they had different beliefs, and for those differences they were cast out, set apart, spat upon and reviled. Were not Muslims also children of Abraham? And were they not about to be cast as the Samaritans of this time, a maligned Them against which to judge the righteousness of Us?

Steve was right. The Word would not have stood by and watched this happen. And if the Church was indeed grounded in the Word, then it must follow His example, whatever the temporal cost.

Veltroni saw his own path illuminated in the light of Steve Lorenzo's eyes. But could he walk that path? That, as always, was the deepest and most difficult question.

And one for which he had no answer.

As Steve approached the place where he now lived, he did not find it difficult to give the food away. In every city of the world, on the streets, often seen only at night, were the forgotten souls, all too many of them children.

They were the people no one wanted to see and no one seemed to know how to truly help. They were the people among whom Jesus would have walked.

Steve passed out the food as best he could. The restaurant portions were overly generous, and each could feed the hunger of more than one child. When he was finally empty-handed, he ached with a desire to do more, much more. But he had no money, and his stipend had not yet resumed, most likely because he had refused the job he had been offered. Either it would resume soon or he would be on the streets himself.

In a town so overflowing with priests, Steve would not have been surprised if the so-called rabble had treated him with disrespect as he walked among them. Instead, many darted out of darkened alleys and doorways, often seeking no more than a blessing, a tangible symbol of a loving God who had not forsaken them. For each, he drew the sign of the Cross on their foreheads with his thumb and murmured words of encouragement. It was a small thing, and yet for so many it seemed everything.

His small hotel room in a run-down area of Rome was hardly luxurious, yet after Guatemala, it was so comfortable that he almost felt indulgent in staying there. He and his de facto aide, Miguel Ortiz, had spent most of the past two years living in the most primitive conditions imaginable. Many were the nights that he had slept on the wet ground, tossing and turning to relieve the incessant irritation of a stone or a tree root. Now he slept in a bed, warm and dry and safe, while the villagers he had led remained behind, fashioning their homes in a secret valley deep in the heart of the jungle.

Such thoughts had cost him sleep in the first days of his return to civilization. He had even slept on the floor until the patent absurdity of that practice made itself painfully apparent in the form of a persistent backache. God had not found a home for the people of Dos Ojos and then borne Steve Lorenzo safely to Rome so he could torture himself needlessly by sleeping on a hard floor.

But now he was thinking about his vow to the Stewards, an oath to protect the Faith at whatever cost. That oath had taken him to Guatemala, but it was another oath that had returned him here. That was something he spoke of to no one, not even Veltroni.

For Steve was also a Guardian of the Light, and while he didn't know the full extent of that pledge, neither did he doubt the purity or worthiness of that cause. He felt between worlds now, between oaths and realities, and needed time to sort himself out. Needed time for God to clarify his understanding of his path.

But not only God sought him out in the quiet hours of the night as he studied and waited for his heart to be filled with answers. The Guardians sought him, as well. And they came in his dreams.

Ur of the Chaldees,
c. 3500 B.C.E.

"Avram, my son," Enlil said to the man who stood before him, "you have served me well, though it has not been easy. Now I must ask you for a greater sacrifice."

Avram bowed to the terrifying but beautiful being before him. "I live but to serve."

"It is a terrible thing I must ask. But you have seen how my fellows have taken advantage of many of the *adama* we have created."

Again Avram bowed. Though he did not know the full story of creation, he knew that *adama*, known to some as Adam, were the race of men created from the earth and the breath of the gods.

"It is wrong that my kind have relations with your women," Enlil continued. "The Nephilim are an abomination in my sight and a threat to all the *adama*. If their numbers continue to grow, they will destroy the *adama*.

"What is more," Enlil continued, "there are troubles among us, a war in the heavens. It is time I take my rightful place and my own path. You will take the path with me, Avram."

"Yes, my lord."

"So obedient you are, my servant. Hear me now. You must abandon your granaries and all that you have achieved here. No longer will you be counselor to kings. But you and yours will be safe."

"My lord?"

"As long as you serve me, Avram, and no others, I will keep you and your descendents close. From them I will create a great nation. But for now you must gather your wife, a few servants, a small flock, and only what you can carry. You must head toward the setting sun, toward the land I am preparing for you."

"Yes, lord." Avram quivered but hoped the all-seeing eyes of his lord would not perceive it.

"Go, Avram. And take upon yourself the new name of Avraham, as you will be father of a new race. But remember, Avraham, honor no other lord before me!"

The implied threat was perfectly clear to the newly named Avraham, descendent of the first *adama,* as were all his kind. "So it will be."

"It is well." Enlil stepped close. "After you have left Ur, I shall bestow a gift upon you. It will be a new language, Avraham, the language of creation. I will give you a secret book that you must keep and pass along as your birthright, for in it will be great power. This book we call the Kabbalah. I will tell you later how I wish you to use it, but for now let none know you possess it."

Avraham shivered. "Yes, lord."

"But before you go, I will give you something equally precious, something you must guard for me with your life."

At that, Enlil gestured to a plain box lined with gold. Except for the lining, it might have been any wooden crate used for transport. "Come and see."

His knees feeling weak, Avraham moved tentatively toward the box. As he approached, four shimmering gems stunned his gaze. Ruby, emerald, sapphire and diamond, they glistened as if light resided within them. They were shaped a little like the ziggurats the *adama* built to adorn their cities, but flatter and with smooth sides. Indeed, he could see that all the sides were equal.

The light shining from them dazzled him and filled him with much wonder.

"These," said Enlil, "are the most precious stones of creation. They contain the power that gave life to the *adama,* and much more besides. They also contain the power of great destruction, if handled wrongly. The book I spoke of, the Kabbalah, is the key to all the power and knowledge these contain."

Avraham swallowed hard.

"You will take them with you so that none can use them in the coming war. You will be the guardian of their light, Avraham, and upon your shoulders will rest the protection of your race, for if you let these come into the wrong hands, you and your kind will vanish forever."

Avraham dared to look at his lord Enlil, his mouth open with both horror and astonishment.

"Be obedient to me always, and I will watch over you. That is my promise to you and yours. But you must keep your bargain, Avraham."

"I will. I swear I will."

"Then it will be as I have said for you. I will forever watch over you. But never forget that I am a jealous master."

Avraham was still shaking as he left the presence of the Lord Enlil. He could not grasp all that was happening, but he was clear about what he must do. And he would obey.

4

Nathan Cohen did not like to remember his past. To this day, every night, he said the prayers of repentance for his many missions into the West Bank, the Gaza Strip, Lebanon, Syria, and even Europe, where his orders had been to infiltrate, identify, terminate and escape undetected. He had been very good at his job.

But his job had been evil. At the time, he had told himself he was serving the greater good, eliminating threats to his homeland and his people. He had believed that by killing some, he was saving many others. These beliefs had enabled him to press detonator buttons, pull triggers, slip knives under ribs, snap garrotes around necks.

He had long since abandoned such self-serving platitudes. He had been a killer, no more and no less. The stain of every victim lay on his soul, and only God could decide whether what he had done in the years since was worthy of mercy.

His transformation—what he hoped was his redemption—had begun in the rugged foothills of Mount Etna, on the island of Sicily, in a small town called San Fratello. He had been dispatched to assassinate an Iranian scientist who, he had been told, was a key figure in Iran's nuclear program. Publicly, the scientist had been on holiday with his family in Sicily. Privately, he had been meeting a Russian expatriate who was training him in the theory and techniques for producing weapons-grade plutonium.

Nathan had planned carefully, expecting the scientist to leave his wife and two children in the hotel and slip away for his nightly assignation with the Russian woman. Thus, he had not activated the car bomb until sunset, when he saw the lights in the vacation cottage wink out.

Instead, the scientist had opted for a late-night drive to show his family the impressive glow of a volcano venting the energy of the earth into the night sky.

It was not the first time Nathan's actions had killed innocents. Indeed, he might have steeled himself against it that time, had he not spent the day in the guise of an automobile repairman, chatting with the man's son about whether the Iranian national football team could earn a spot in the World Cup finals. As they had chatted, the boy's face had lit up with hope for his country. For him, the world was no bigger than a football, twenty-two pieces of leather stitched around a rubber bladder, yielding magic at the touch of skilled feet.

It was ironic, Nathan had thought at the time, that the boy's father was equally transfixed by the geometry of a football, albeit for a far different reason. For it was that same geometry, fitted together in high explosives around a radioactive core, that created a darker magic: the cruel power of a nuclear bomb.

That night, as Nathan watched helplessly, unable to deactivate the car bomb as he saw the Iranian scientist and his wife and son laugh as they climbed into the car, the true horror of his profession slammed into his soul with the fiery force of three kilograms of plastic explosive.

Nathan Cohen had not killed since. And, if there was indeed a merciful God, he would never kill again.

Now, spurred by the news that poured from the television before him and the bank of four laptop computers on his desk, Nathan opened a small leather pouch and dipped his finger into the fine white powder within it. Touching the powder to his lips, quietly mouthing the sounds of a series of Hebrew letters, he reached out into the minds of Steve Lorenzo and the other Guardians of Light.

It was a risk, but a risk that must be taken.

For Nathan Cohen knew how Karl Vögel had died.

Rome, Italy

The Rome night had turned blustery and wet. Pavement, some of it dating to the reign of the Caesars, glistened under streetlights. In this part of the city, at this time of night, the few people who were out paid no attention to Lawton Caine. Out here, he was just a warehouse worker, strolling along in worn pants and a battered jacket, seeming but one step away from the homeless who slept under lean-tos and in alleys.

A few streets further on, there were more lights and a different kind of person strolling. Through windows he saw people sitting at tables, sipping wine, laughing, some eating the late meals that were so common in Mediterranean cultures. Finally he came to the piazza, where he could use his cell phone without the signal being traced back to the warehouse in any way. The call to Miriam clicked through in less than seven seconds.

"Anson," she answered briskly.

"Are you on your way home yet?" he asked.

"Not likely," she said. "I just finished a briefing. Maybe in a couple of hours."

"How good is your source in Germany?"

"I couldn't ask for better."

From Miriam Anson, that was high praise indeed. Lawton knew her personally, for she had been his mentor at the FBI. He had watched her career blossom after missions in Guatemala and then, at his bidding, in Idaho.

He also knew, from other contacts, that her skill and tenacity were the stuff of whispered legends in the U.S. intelligence community. He was not surprised that she had risen to the post of Director of National Intelligence.

"I'm supposed to find out what you know," Lawton said.

"Chancellor Vögel had enemies," she replied. "Some he made just recently. I've heard rumors that he'd threatened to pull Germany out of the EU. But you're closer to that than I am."

She didn't need to ask the question directly. Lawton knew she was expecting him to share, as well. "We've heard that, too. Nothing confirmed yet, however."

"Lawton?"

"Yeah?"

"We're getting chatter, a lot of it. It's not solid, and we can't trace it to sources, let alone confirm it. These people have gotten much better at hiding their tracks on the information superhighway. But what we're hearing suggests things there are about to get worse. Much worse."

"Wonderful news."

"Remember what you used to say when it was your turn to talk to school kids? The warning you always gave?"

"I do," he said. *If a man is frightened enough, he will sell his soul for even the illusion of safety.* "Is that what's going on here?"

"Like I said, I can't confirm anything yet. But the chatter we're getting, what we can read of it, is talking about preparations for major outbreaks of violence. And it's odd."

"Odd how?" he asked.

"It doesn't read like the preparations of street fanatics," Miriam said. "It's more organized. The tone is almost...bureaucratic."

"Government?"

"Not quite," she said. "But not far from it, either. Like I said, it doesn't fit any of the known players, and we can't source it. Maybe that's what bothers me most of all. It's something new."

"Why is it that 'something new' is almost never a good thing in our business?" he asked with a bitter laugh.

"I don't know, but you're right. Stay safe, Lawton."

"I'll do my best," he said.

Then she was gone.

A chill passed through him. Miriam's tone left no doubt that she believed this was much bigger than a single assassination. Vögel's death was the opening salvo. But to what end?

Shaking himself to ward off the feeling of evil that was trying to creep into his bones, he headed for a *trattoria* that the office often used for takeout. The minute he showed his face, they would start packing the boxes, smiling, talking in sputtering, mixed Italian that Lawton was only now learning to follow, knowing exactly what he and his colleagues preferred.

It didn't matter a damn to Lawton that they were

Muslim. They made good food at a reasonable price and never tried to overcharge him. What did their religion matter? And why couldn't sensible people grasp that?

Riyadh, Saudi Arabia

"We can find nothing," the doctor said as he stepped into Ahmed Ahsami's office with the last of the MRI films. "I wish I were as healthy as he was when he was examined."

"But not as dead as he is now," Ahmed said.

"No. Not that."

Ahmed Ahsami sat in the predawn darkness, lit only by the pale light of his dimmed computer screen. The news out of Berlin had gone sparse after the confirmation that Vögel was dead. No official cause of death had been given, nor did Ahmed expect one in the next several hours. Had the cause of death been obvious and innocent—a heart attack or stroke—it would have been announced when the spokesman had confirmed the news. No such announcement had been given, which meant that an autopsy was probably under way at that moment.

As the operational director of *Saif Alsharaawi*, the Sword of the East, a group formed to bring unity and stability to the Middle Eastern nations, it was Ahmed's job to know what was happening in the world's halls of power, especially if it might impact Muslims. In the past months, French-born European Commission President Jules Soult had made it clear that Europe would not remain a benign-if-neglectful haven for Muslim immigrants. In the wake of train bombings in Madrid and London, and the ricin gas attack in Prague and a wave of reprisals by angry Europeans, Soult had proposed the forming of "pacification zones" throughout Europe.

While Soult spoke of protecting innocent Muslims from the increasing mob violence, Ahmed had no illusions as to Soult's agenda. The Islamic pacification zones—within which Muslims must live and work in exchange for increased police protection for their homes and businesses—would be ghettos at best. And they might well set the stage for something far more sinister.

A minor prince in the House of Saud, gifted with a keen intellect and groomed for leadership from an early age, Ahmed Ahsami was an educated man. He had earned a law degree at Oxford, an MBA at Stanford and a fellowship at the prestigious *Institut d'études politiques de Paris*. But his education had not ended with his formal schooling. Ahmed was an avid student of history, both eastern and western, which he believed was the most reliable lens through which to view the present and predict the future. It had forced him to look past the Wahhabist Sunni tradition in which he had been raised and that sometimes put him in a tenuous position.

"This is not good news," Ahmed said. "Vögel was our hope. Now there will be chaos."

"Perhaps you are too much a pessimist?" the doctor asked. "Chancellor Vögel was but one man."

"And so were Gandhi and Hitler," Ahmed replied. "One man can enable great good or great evil. All of Europe used Nazi Germany as a means to shed its Jews, both during the war and after, in the creation of Israel."

"The state of Israel was an act of guilt and mercy after the Holocaust," the doctor said.

Ahmed laughed bitterly. "That is the common myth, my friend. The truth is that Europe's leaders also wanted a dumping ground for those few Jews who had survived. They were solving their 'Jewish question' as much as assuaging their guilt."

"And to do so, they violated the will of Allah," the doctor said.

"Westerners do not read the *Qur'an,* Dr. Massawi. Those who do, read it only as literature, without faith. They do not care that the Prophet forbade the existence of non-Islamic states in Islamic lands."

"But were the Palestinians not partly at fault for that, Ahmed? After all, they welcomed Jewish immigrants under British rule. They approved the partition agreement. Should they not have objected then?"

"Perhaps," Ahmed said. "But they believed the British withdrawal would leave the Jewish territory a protectorate, under an Islamic Palestine. A sovereign protectorate, to be sure, but a protectorate nonetheless."

The Prophet had been clear as to the rights and privileges of such peoples. So long as they paid their taxes and lived peaceably, the Jews would have been free to practice their religion, allowed to govern themselves and entitled to full citizenship in the Islamic state. Islam was a faith born in the harsh desert, and the duties of host to guest were strict and sacred. The Prophet as well as ancient tradition decreed that to shun a guest who came in peace—to refuse food, water, shelter and protection for his family and livestock—was a grave sin.

"But the Jews demanded more," Massawi said. "As they always do."

"Do not judge too harshly, Doctor."

Ahmed had spent enough time both in the West and in Israel to understand why such an arrangement would have been a slap in the face to the Jewish settlers. Although they would not have been compelled to observe *shari'a*—Islamic law—neither could their government or its courts have directly violated the law of the Prophet.

"Palestine is the home of three great faiths," Ahmed said. "None would lightly bear the yoke of another."

Massawi shook his head. "Then there is no choice but the extermination of Israel? I cannot accept that, Ahmed, and I know you do not accept it, either."

"No," Ahmed said. "I do not. Now the burden lies with enlightened and merciful *imams*. They must reinterpret the words of the Prophet—peace be upon him—so that even a Jewish state is entitled to protectorate status, so long as the Israelis foreswear making war against their Arab neighbors."

"And do you think Israel would offer this?"

"Yes," Ahmed said. "I do."

Long since worn raw by the Palestinian *intifada*, and scolded by the Western world for the brutality of its most recent incursion into Lebanon, Israel seemed willing to make and honor such promises. Ahmed believed the Islamic states—including his own House of Saud—would be foolish not to respond in kind.

"The Jews are an industrious people," Ahmed continued. "We are cousins under Abraham. We should be working with them to build a prosperous and humane Middle East, instead of spilling each other's blood."

"You are always the dreamer," Massawi said with a sad smile. "The Israelis do not trust us. They and their Western supporters see us as little more than wild dogs."

That was sadly true, Ahmed knew. After sixty years of nearly constant war, most often begun by attacks from their Arab neighbors, the Israelis were justifiably suspicious of Arab promises of peace, even if the Arab nations had the united will to offer them. Worse, such a united will did not exist.

Oil, the envy of the rest of the world, was the bane of the Islamic states. For the profits from oil were enough to allow Arab rulers to maintain lavish lifestyles with little need for, and less allegiance to, their own people. The gap between the people and their rulers had yawned into a chasm over the past century.

Worse, the rise of Wahhabism and the even more extreme Salafism in Sunni Islam, coupled with the ascendancy of the Shi'a in Iran and Iraq, had turned the Islamic world into a powder keg. Ahmed often thought the differences between the sects were no more than the differences between Catholicism and Protestantism, but like those two religions in the past, the conflict between Shi'a and Sunni Islam had provided a dangerous flashpoint for thirteen hundred years.

And that was where oil created an additional problem. The Shi'a were a majority—often a substantial majority—in many of the region's most oil-rich areas: Iran, southern Iraq, eastern Saudi Arabia and Bahrain. Yet until the American invasion of Iraq, only in Iran were the Shi'a allowed a political voice. In the rest of the Middle East, the Shi'a were either an excluded minority or—worse—an oppressed majority.

The Americans, with their naive ideals of spreading democracy while ignoring ethnic and sectarian differences in local populations, had ripped the scabs off age-old wounds.

In such conditions, the seething cauldron of Muslim violence was all but inevitable. And every time a Muslim triggered a roadside bomb, strapped *plastique* to his chest before boarding a bus in Tel Aviv or dispersed deadly gas in a subway tunnel in Prague, the world shook its head and concluded that Muslims were genetically incapable of living in peace.

"We need a Pan-Islamic council," Ahmed said. "One that can speak for all Muslims. One that can mediate between Shi'a and Sunni, Saudi and Egyptian, Sudanese and Indonesian. And one that can speak to the West with a firm and united voice, to secure for our people a safe and prosperous place in the world."

"That is what *Saif Alsharaawi* was born to create," Massawi said, smiling. "That is your dream. But it is an impossible dream, Ahmed. The Shi'a have not accepted a caliph since the eighth century. Why would they do so now?"

"Not a caliph," Ahmed said simply. "A council that includes both Shi'a and Sunni voices, from the Middle East, Africa and Asia. A council with religious and political legitimacy throughout the Muslim world."

"In sh'Allah."

"I wish," Ahmed said, "that Allah's will were clearer."

Massawi smiled ironically. "When has it ever been so? Too many mullahs and imams think they know and tell us to do things I wonder about, but the only will we know for certain is in the *Qur'an*."

"I feel quite certain that these 'removals' of which the president of the EU speaks are not Allah's will."

"Of course not. We are Muslim."

It was Ahmed's turn to smile, though he felt no humor or joy. "You know the story of the Jewish Holocaust."

Rachel Lee

Massawi tapped his head. "How could I not know? It has torn Palestine to shreds. Had it not happened, matters would have taken a different turn there, no?"

"I don't know, Massawi. What I do know is that Soult's proposals sound very much like Hitler's final solution to the Jewish problem in Europe."

Massawi fell silent, a deep frown creasing his handsome face. He was Persian, not Arab, which made his life difficult here in Saudi country, as it had in Iraq. Ahmed often thought that Massawi knew far more about persecution than he himself could imagine.

"They say Muslims in the zones would be protected. Do you believe that, Massawi?"

Slowly Massawi shook his head. "Perhaps at first."

"Exactly. My sources say the Germans will protest."

"Even though their chancellor has died?"

Ahmed's lips twisted bitterly. "You remember the English saying about the cat and the hot stove? Germans are like that now at any suggestion of religious persecution. I will not absolve them of it completely, of course. All of Europe is suffering a tension because of the conflict of our culture with theirs. Many Europeans feel they will lose their culture to ours. I do not say whether this is good or bad. But they *do* feel threatened, Massawi, and a threatened man is a dangerous man. But the Germans…for sixty years they have born the stain of the Holocaust. Any suggestion of such a thing now makes them all jump like cats on a hot stove. That is why

Vögel objected, and why I think Germany will continue to object."

Massawi nodded. "May you be right."

"Vögel was a voice of reason," Ahmed said, thinking aloud. "My sources say he had the support of the Americans and was close to President Rice. Germany's army numbers a quarter-million men, and there are still over one hundred thousand American troops, civilian employees and dependents living in Germany. An attack on Germany would be an attack on the United States. Not even Soult is that crazy. Vögel would have prevented this new purge."

"But might not Soult simply let Germany withdraw and continue with his plans?" Massawi asked.

"He cannot," Ahmed said. "The German economy is too integral to the European Union for Soult to merely bid the Germans *adieu*. An EU without Germany would be an empty shell. Soult would go from the captain at the helm of a ship of state to the figurehead at the prow of a dinghy. His pride could not bear such an insult. No, Chancellor Vögel had stalemated him."

"And now Vögel is dead," Massawi said.

"Yes," Ahmed said. "And you are certain it could not have been from natural causes?"

Vögel had received his annual physical examination only a month earlier. Ahmed's contacts in Germany had secured the records of that examination, and Massawi had spent the last three hours poring over the chancellor's MRI films, EKG tapes, blood profiles and examination notes.

"I cannot be certain of that," Massawi said. "But I can say that, one month ago, Karl Vögel was healthier than most men half his age. He had no circulatory, pulmonary, neurological or skeletal disorders, save for a small measure of arthritis in his fingers and knees, and even that was less than most thirty-year-old adults. He was on no long-term medications. He had no tumor, no lesion, no latent aneurism or infection. There was nothing that would hint of pending collapse and death."

Ahmed shook his head. "I do not believe this is mere coincidence. Allah would not grace the plans of Monsieur Soult with such serendipity."

That was why Ahmed had dragged Massawi from his bed in the middle of the night. And that was why he had sent a flash message to his network of contacts in Europe: *Find out what happened in Berlin.* If Vögel had been murdered, Ahmed had to know why and by whom.

For Ahmed knew his brethren had the most to lose.

Then he sighed and shook his head. "I must go to Europe."

"But why? You would only be forced to go to a protection zone."

Ahmed shrugged as if it didn't matter, but his eyes told Massawi otherwise. "Sheik al-Hazeer has said I must go to observe and report."

At that, Massawi's head jerked. "No."

"It seems we have a divide beginning within the organization, Massawi. Since you are Shi'a, I would suggest that you, like others, take advantage of the first opportunity to slip away into a more private life."

"But this is what you built *Saif* to fight against."

"Sometimes we must live to fight another day, my friend. Take your family, go to some other place. I will do what I can. But right now, Massawi, no Muslim is safe in Europe. And no Shi'a is safe in this country."

That tore his heart worst of all.

5

Strasbourg, France

Jules Soult, President of the European Commission and leader of the European Union, sat in a cool, windowless conference room adjacent to his office in the *Institutiones Européens*, the European Parliament complex. To this day he still sported the soldierly bearing and close-cropped hair of a general in the French army. No one who knew him well doubted his determination—or his ruthlessness. When he faced his advisors, they almost invariably looked away. He found this profoundly satisfying. Had it not been said of Napoleon that his gaze was so intense that no mortal could long bear it?

At first glance, except for the flag of the European Union behind him at the head of the table, the conference room might have been in any office building in the world. Only an alert and practiced eye would note the discreet pods on the walls, ceiling and floor, sensors that continuously swept the room for electronic surveillance. Not even the most practiced eye could see the copper mesh that was built into those same walls, ceiling and floor, TEMPEST shielding that masked transmissions from the computer and telephone equipment in the room. No cameras or recording devices were permitted, and beside the door a heavy duty shredder stood ready to receive any notes that might be taken.

Soult had directed the upgrading of security because he had needed a meeting place that was beyond the reach of any but the most trusted eyes and ears. And even those people knew they were watched regularly, their home, office and cellular telephones monitored, even their mail opened and screened at random. They were his inner circle, yet should any hint of what was discussed in this room reach the outside world, he would root out and dispose of the leaks with ruthless finality. And he made sure none of them doubted that fact.

Insofar as Soult had been able to determine, the operations in Paris and Berlin had gone off flawlessly. The news bore no hint that the burning of the mosque had been a carefully calculated act; instead, it was being cast as yet more street violence brought on by the actions of Muslim extremists. They would not know, tonight or ever, that the men at the front of the firebomb-throwing mob in Paris had been mercenaries acting under Soult's orders.

Moreover, at that moment, he knew, frustrated doctors were sharing looks of confusion, having found only trace levels of cyanide in Vögel's bloodstream. Already they would be asking each other if Vögel were somehow more sensitive to the minute amounts of the toxin that were present in the body of every adult European, absorbed from tobacco smoke, automobile and factory exhaust, and other common environmental sources. Already they would be arguing that no, cyanide was not the sort of toxin to which one body was more or less vulnerable than another body was. Already they would have confirmed that neither of the other known cellular asphyxiants—hydrogen sulfide and carbon monoxide—accounted for his death.

Nor would they be able to explain how such a substance could have been administered without affecting the others who'd been with Vögel. The broken dome of the Reichstag would distract them for a while, a long while, as none would realize it had been merely a side effect.

They would know that Herr Bundeskanzler Karl Vögel had indeed died of cellular asphyxia. But they would not know, tonight or ever, how that had happened. And that, Soult knew, was the genius of his plan.

For Vögel's death would be a chilling warning to anyone who dared to oppose Jules Soult. While there would be no evidence that Soult had committed the assassination, neither would there be any doubt in the shadowy corridors of true power, among those who whispered of ancient secrets that had long since been lost to the sands of time.

Those secrets were *not* lost, however. And Jules Soult alone possessed the knowledge and the means to apply it. The men who needed to know would understand that, any time, in any place, their lives could be forfeit at the will of one man. There was no security that could protect them. They must obey or pay the consequences.

That Vögel's death also cleared the way for a more reasonable government in Berlin, one willing to recognize and join in the twenty-first-century clash of civilizations that would be Soult's passport to power, was the proverbial icing on the cake. Just as many argued that the use of the atomic bomb in 1945 was only peripherally motivated by the need to defeat Japan, with its principal objective to cow the Soviet Union and the rest of the world into abject submission, Soult's primary objective in Berlin had been, to borrow an American catchphrase, "shock and awe." The technology he possessed was every bit as shocking and awe-inspiring as any missile or bomb. And it was his alone.

The ruby pyramid that gave him his power sat locked inside a hidden safe in the wall behind him, brought from his country estate so that he would always have it at hand. He thought of it now and smiled in private satisfaction. The power that had brought down Jericho, that had built the pyramids, that had parted the Red Sea, was now his and his alone.

His by birthright. Sometimes he wished he could just use its full power and bring these matters to conclusion immediately, but there were warnings in his family's history and records, warnings of what could happen to the too-ambitious when they used the pyramid. Willingly or not, he was forced to treat the ruby pyramid with the respect and caution it demanded.

The question before him—and before the man who sat across the conference table—was whether and where to apply it next, and how to use it to marshal a still-too-spineless Europe toward its ultimate destiny.

Colonel Hector Vasquez, Soult's security deputy and the only man Soult had kept beside him through this long night, broke the silence. "And what about Schlossman?"

Albert Schlossman had been Vögel's vice chancellor until he had been awakened in the dark of night. Just two hours ago he had taken the oath of office as chancellor.

"Do we make another example of him?" Vasquez asked.

Like most European democracies, Germany was a multi-party state with a parliamentary government. For decades, power had shifted between two coalitions, the liberal Red/Green bloc of the Social Democrat and Green Parties, and the conservative coalition built around the Christian Democratic Union and its Bavarian cousin, the Christian Social Union.

However, when Social Democratic Chancellor Gerhard Schröder's government had collapsed, neither the left nor the right had secured a parliamentary majority. After weeks of political wrangling, the Grand Coalition had been forged, a unification of the Social and Christian Democrats. No one had expected this arrangement to last, for there had long been far too much friction between left and right. It had come as no shock when the Grand Coalition ruptured in the next round of elections, and once again the familiar left-right blocs defined the German political landscape.

Karl Vögel was a Social Democrat, but his party had not won enough seats to form a majority government. As had his predecessors, Vögel had turned to the Green Party for the necessary support. This time, however, the price had been to name Green Party leader Albert Schlossman as his vice chancellor.

"He will not yield on Vögel's policy toward us," Vasquez continued. "If anything, he is worse, for there are Green Parties across Europe. They have seats in our own EU Parliament."

"And they are a minority everywhere," Soult said, growing impatient. "Even in Germany, their sole power lies in their capacity to build a coalition with another near-majority party. Germany will not retain a Green Party chancellor."

"You leave too much to the machinations of the German *Bundestag*," Vasquez said. "We should eliminate Schlossman, as well, and guarantee a new government."

Colonel Hector de Vasquez y San Claro, like Soult,

was a member of the Order of the Rose. Like Soult, Vasquez had a royal bloodline tracing back to the child of Jesus Christ and Mary Magdalene. And like Soult, he longed for a return of the rightful European government under a new Merovingian dynasty and had worked to make that happen. Vasquez had invisibly orchestrated the al-Qaeda attacks on the Prague subway, and it was his operatives who had carried out the burning of the Grande Mosquée.

After the attempted bombing of the EU Parliament building—another operation overseen by Soult and Vasquez and funded by their Frankfurt allies—Soult had emerged as a European hero and ridden that tide of public support into the new EU elections. His Europa Prima Party—proclaiming European cultural solidarity while it was in reality the political arm of the Order of the Rose—had easily won a majority in the European Parliament, and it in turn had elected him president.

None of this would have been possible without Vasquez and the mercenaries he had secretly paid with money Soult was given by the EU Department of Collective Security. But now, Soult saw, Vasquez had developed an impatience that, if not tightly reined, might well undermine all they had built thus far.

"And if we kill Schlossman?" Soult asked. "Do you think the Germans will passively accept our candidate for chancellor?"

"They will know they have no choice," Vasquez argued.

"Oh yes, my friend. They *will* have a choice. They will choose war before humiliation, and this is not a war I mean to fight at this time."

Vasquez shook his head. "With the power of the codex, we would prevail. Europe has beaten down Germany twice in the last century. Do you doubt she could do it again?"

"You forget the Americans!" Soult said, slamming his fist on the table. "They will not stand by while Germany is crushed. They have troops there, with their families. Not even the codex can stop a rain of cruise missiles!

"No," Soult continued, taking a breath to calm himself, "we must do this by legal means. We have allies in the *Bundestag*. They will put up roadblocks at every turn and make Schlossman appear unable to lead. Then, and only then, will Germany be ready to accept our leadership. Once we have Herr Müller in the chancellery, the Hamburg operation will convince the Germans to join in our plans."

"I hope it will be enough," Vasquez said. "I do not like to place my faith in politicians."

"But I am a politician now," Soult said, his voice and face devoid of emotion. "Do you still have faith in me?"

Vasquez paused. "I have faith in the Order."

It was a correct answer. It was also the worst answer Vasquez could have chosen. For with that sentence he signed his own death warrant. But not yet. The man was still useful.

"We have argued enough," Soult said, offering what he hoped would appear a conciliatory tone. "Now, Hector, tell me about our preparations in Hamburg."

Rome, Italy

Renate's face was pale as she hung up the telephone. Like a distant observer watching a speeding train approach a stalled auto, she could see the impending mayhem. And she could do nothing to stop it.

"What is it?" Lawton asked, as if reading her thoughts on her face.

"That was my contact at the Charité," she said. After his collapse, the chancellor had been treated at the most renowned hospital in Berlin, one of the finest in all of Germany. It had not saved his life, and now not even the most skilled pathologists had any clue how Vögel had died. "Miriam's source was half-right. Vögel died of cyanide-like poisoning, but there were only trace levels of cyanide in his system. They're doing more tests now, but they have no idea what poison was used, or how it was administered. Some are saying it must be related to the collapse of part of the dome, as if he were shot with some kind of poisoned dart or bullet and the wound hidden in those caused by the falling glass. But you know how strong that glass is. Few bullets would penetrate it."

"Shit," Lawton said simply.

Renate merely nodded, a faint, strained smile on her

face. "Despite your American gift for vulgarity, you're right. This is very bad."

"So we know it was murder," Margarite said, stepping over to Renate's desk. "Lawton's source, Miriam Anson, gave us the same information."

"Yes, she did. And it probably was murder," Jefe said, also joining them. "But how can anyone prove that without knowing what the toxin was?"

"Be reasonable, Chief," Lawton said. "Even if it were some bizarre compound, why would it kill Vögel and not his security people or anyone at the hospital? It's too well-targeted to be an environmental toxin. Nothing else makes sense *except* assassination."

"I agree with you, Lawton," Jefe said. "But there's what we know intuitively and then there's what the German police can prove. They're not going to unravel this on the basis of speculation, however rational. They'll need hard evidence to get at whoever did this."

"Why do I smell an assignment coming?" Lawton asked.

"Because you're not the dullest knife in the drawer," Jefe said, producing two airline tickets from a file. "You and Margarite are off to Berlin."

"But…" Renate began.

"Don't even start," Jefe said. "You're far too well known in Berlin. And even if none of your old friends at the BKA knows you're still alive, the Frankfurt Brotherhood does. The last time I sent you to Germany, they nearly killed you."

"They tried," Renate agreed, remembering the attack at the Rome train station on her way back from an operation in Frankfurt. She also remembered how quickly and brutally she had dispatched her attacker, and the rage she had felt afterward. At some point that, too, had joined the rest of her feelings in a frozen vault. "But they know I came to Rome. I'm no safer here than anywhere else."

"You're also my best, my *only*, German agent," Jefe said, ignoring her point. "Most of what we get is going to be in German, and I don't want this operation to fail over a mistranslation. I need you here, where you can give me context and subtext in addition to plain meaning. That's how it's going to be."

"My German is improving," Lawton said. "But it's still spotty."

"*Ich spreche fließend Deutsch,*" Margarite said. *I speak fluent German.* "I studied it both in *lycée* and at university."

"Her German is more than sufficient for your needs," Renate said. However much she wanted to be part of the operation in Berlin, Jefe had made his decision, and she knew she had to support it. "And I will tell my people you're coming. But be careful when you approach Ulla Viermann."

"Who is she?" Lawton asked.

Renate handed him a slender file. "She's the doctor who treated the chancellor. We don't have much on her yet. But she has an excellent reputation, and right now it looks as if they are setting her up as the scapegoat."

"How could she know Vögel was going to collapse during her shift?" Jefe asked.

"Oh, they're not saying she caused his collapse, or even that she murdered him," Renate replied. "They're saying she misdiagnosed him, and her treatment killed him. Apparently she pursued an unorthodox method when the usual steps failed. My source says that as soon as she heard what was being said, she stopped talking to the *Polizei.*"

Lawton shook his head. "Let me get this straight. The chancellor collapses when the Reichstag dome does and arrives at the hospital near death from an unknown cause."

Renate nodded. "Right."

"And because she *couldn't* save him, they're accusing her of causing his death through malpractice?"

"They need someone to blame, Lawton," Margarite said through a cloud of smoke. "Until they know who caused his collapse, the doctor who couldn't save him is the only convenient target for people's shock and outrage. I don't blame her for refusing to talk. They can't charge her with anything, but they could strip her of her license." She stubbed out her cigarette. "Poor woman."

"That's usually how it goes," Renate said. "Are you surprised?" She was looking at Margarite.

"Someone has to take the blame," Margarite said, shaking her head. "Right now, the idiots in the BKA can't find anyone else. So let us go find someone else for them to blame."

Rome, Italy

The dream came over Steve Lorenzo slowly, as if he passed through layer upon layer of mist before he arrived in the otherworldly plain. Even in his dream, he found it strange that the place felt so familiar. Featureless, nearly colorless, yet everything was visible as if light were coming from everywhere, yet there were no shadows. And beyond the place where he and the guardians stood, there was the inkiness of nothing.

For the first time in these dreams, he sensed that the plain beneath his feet and the physical appearance of the others were more for his comfort than any kind of necessity.

"Welcome," Nathan said. "You were slow to answer tonight."

"I have been tired."

"You have been worrying. I am sorry to tell you that before this night ends, you will worry more."

Steve wanted to sigh. Life had been so much simpler in Guatemala.

"Yes, it was," Nathan said, clearly reading his thoughts. Steve felt unnerved. "It was simpler, but your mission there was accomplished. Now you have a more important one."

"And that is?"

"When you awake in the morning, you will hear of the death of the German Chancellor, Karl Vögel. He was assassinated, though they do not yet know how. You will have to show people how it was done."

Nathan stepped forward. "Leave your church behind for a while, as it will only hinder you. Find the codex. You will see its trail in recent events and in some yet to come. It must be recovered, whatever the cost."

"Wait," Steve said as Nathan's figure began to fade. At once it came into clear focus. "What does the pyramid have to do with any of this?"

"Find the pyramid and you will find the murderer of Chancellor Vögel. But more importantly, you will find the source of great troubles to come."

"What do you mean?"

Nathan hesitated. "The pyramid was used to murder the chancellor."

This was too much for Steve. "You expect me to believe that? How could it possibly do that? And who could make it do that?"

Nathan sighed. "I will not tell you everything. The only way for you to answer your questions and clear your doubts is to learn for yourself. Go to the library in Toulouse. Investigate the Merovingians. Read about the Cathars. Follow the trail."

Slowly the dream dissolved into mist, and a short while later, Steve opened his eyes to a bright dawn. Moments later his clock radio clicked on, and the shocking news poured out into the quiet morning air.

Chancellor Vögel had died during the night, possibly from poisoning.

Steve sat bolt upright, the last of the effects of sleep wiped away in an instant. He had known in the dream. He had known. And to him that could mean only one thing. Throwing back his covers, he rose and reached for the jeans and sweatshirt he had recently purchased secondhand. Then he went out to get some strong coffee.

6

Vatican City

Pablo Cardinal Estevan frowned at Monsignore Veltroni. "I don't understand. Why can you not persuade Father Lorenzo to take the apartment I have had prepared for him? There is hardly a priest on this planet who would not be thrilled to have a sumptuous Vatican apartment and a high position in the Congregation for the Defense of the Faith."

"Father Lorenzo," Veltroni replied, ignoring the glass of fine Irish whiskey the cardinal had placed at his elbow, "is not that sort of priest."

Estevan's frown deepened. "He has seen and touched the codex. We cannot simply let him wander all over, doing as he pleases."

"His pleasure, at present, seems to be caring for the poor. You must understand, Eminence, that Father Lorenzo spent the last two years in Guatemala running for his life. He was living in the most primitive of conditions, where even the day's succor was not assured. He watched people die, people he knew and who had come to trust him. Culture shock after such experiences is quite common. One has only to look at the reentry problems of soldiers returning from war to understand his state of mind."

Estevan waved a hand. "Father Lorenzo was not a soldier, and he can readjust to civilization as well here in the Vatican as out there in the warehouse district. Besides, *Monsignore,* we have only his word for it that the codex was stolen from him."

"Surely you don't think…" Veltroni was absolutely aghast. "Steven is as honest and righteous a man as I have ever known."

"Power can corrupt even the purest soul."

Oddly, Veltroni found himself suddenly thinking that it might have corrupted Estevan, a possibility he had not considered before. "Not Steven Lorenzo," he said firmly. "He told the absolute truth when he said the codex was stolen. Our own sources tell us the Hunter was after him."

"Yes, but the Hunter has vanished, and Lorenzo might well have hidden the codex from him."

Veltroni shook his head vigorously. "Had that been his purpose, he would tell us where to find it."

"So sure, Giuseppe?"

The *monsignore* hated it when Cardinal Estevan called him by his first name. It implied an intimacy they did not share, and it always preceded an unpleasant order. Once again, that proved the case.

"I want Lorenzo watched at all times. Assign personnel from the Stewards who are practiced in such matters. He must never be out of sight of the Church."

The order gave Veltroni an immediate case of dyspepsia, which he hoped didn't show on his face. The burning in his stomach would ease, but his anger wouldn't. "I think that may be a bit extreme," he finally said.

"I don't." Estevan waved a hand in a way that said as clearly as any words that no argument would be heard. "Trust me, Giuseppe, you have no idea of the importance of that codex."

"And what is its importance?" Veltroni asked. For the first time in all his years as a Steward, he began to wonder if the group had another purpose, apart from simply defending the faith. "Why is the church so worried about this artifact?"

"You have no need to know. All you need to know is that that codex could present a serious problem for the Church. We must possess it to protect the faith."

Circles and more circles, and very little in the way of answers. Veltroni steepled his hands, inwardly offering a little prayer. He must not let Cardinal Estevan suspect in any way that he might be having doubts.

"Very well, your eminence," he said, his face smooth. "I will see to it immediately."

And he most definitely would, since Estevan would

certainly know if spies were not sent to keep an eye on
Steve Lorenzo. Still, that did not mean that Monsignore
Veltroni could not let Steve know the situation. As long
as he did so carefully.

Estevan smiled. "You are a good servant, *Monsignore*. I have no doubt that your rise among our companions will continue."

"I am most grateful."

Like hell, Veltroni thought as he walked away from Estevan's apartments a short while later. It was a phrase he
had learned from Steve, one for which he had developed
a fondness. "Like hell," he said aloud, savoring the words.

First to alert Steve, then to set the spies. Then...per-
haps a visit to the Trevi Fountain. It just might be that
his old friend Nathan Cohen would show up. The man
had an amazing way of doing that. And right now, Veltroni felt a strong need for a different perspective.

Berlin, Germany

Of all the traveling companions to have on his first trip
to Berlin, Margarite would not have been Lawton's first
choice. The Second World War had been over for more
than sixty years now, but for Margarite, whose parents had
been mere babes at the time, it was as fresh as yesterday.

Lawton understood that war left bitter scars, and that
Europe had been so rent by the two world wars that the
history was bound to feel fresh.

It would, he supposed, have been possible to see mostly the new Berlin, the city that had risen from the ashes of the war to become a great economic and political power in Europe and the world. But it was impossible for him not to look with a sharper eye and note where old buildings still bore the creases hewn by bullets and bomb fragments, where some that were new had been cobbled together from the rubble of those that had been destroyed.

But for all that Margarite frowned sourly, as if the revival of Berlin offended her, even she paused with wonder before the new Reichstag. The old one had burnt in 1933, and although reconstruction had been attempted at one point, it wasn't until after the reunification of Germany that it was fully restored by Norman Foster, a British architect. Foster had added the symbolic and beautiful glass dome that had become one of the most popular tourist attractions of the city.

The dome contained two inclined walkways that circled the inside, offering panoramic views of the city from different angles, and at the top one could peer down through a large pane of glass as the *Bundestag* sat in session. The symbolism of the openness seemed to quiet even Margarite's disgust. Unfortunately, they were not allowed within. The part of the dome that had broken was covered with thick black plastic, and every entrance to the building was marked *Verboten.* Do Not Enter.

"Just behind the Reichstag building," Margarite said, "used to be The Wall."

She spoke the words as if they were capitalized, and Lawton supposed they ought to be. It horrified him at some very deep level that any country should build a wall to keep its citizens inside. Not to keep an enemy out, but to keep its own citizens from leaving.

"Well," she said, placing her hands on her hips and tipping her head back to view the broken dome, "I wish we could see a bit more of the damage."

"I wonder if the local press managed to get photos."

"If they did, the police probably seized them as evidence. I am not certain that they would wish, this early in the investigation, to have such photos out before the public."

He nodded. "Yeah. Why give some malcontent ideas?"

She gave him an amused smile. "I think the malcontent already had his idea. And if there is another one, he already has that idea, too."

"But the attention can induce copycats."

She arched a carefully shaped brow. "I forget you were with the American FBI. You make much of their vaunted profiling, *oui?*"

"Only when it works."

She laughed and for once looked pleasant. "I hate this city. It is so…German. Have you been to Paris?"

"Not yet."

"You will like it. We have a great deal of charm there. Even Hitler considered Paris to be a jewel worthy of protection. When the Allies neared the city in 1944, he ordered it to be declared an open city."

"So there's one thing the Germans did right?"

First she frowned, then pursed her lips. "Are you mocking me?"

"Merely thinking that most of the people here and now had little if anything to do with the last war."

She waved a hand. "It is the German temperament."

"I doubt it. At least not anymore. The ones I've talked to seem to have learned the evils of war to their very bones."

"Perhaps it is so." She shrugged. "Europe must have peace. We have spent too long tearing one another apart."

"On that we most definitely agree." He looked up again at the dome, shaking his head. "I'm not sure the collapse of the dome is relevant to our investigation."

"What do you mean?"

"The glass broke at the same time the chancellor fell. Isn't that what the informant said?"

Margarite opened a notebook and scanned notes written in her own private shorthand. "So it seems, but the timeline is not perfectly clear, owing to confusion."

"Okay, so they happened about the same time. But it wasn't the shattering of the glass that killed him, nor were his companions hurt, apart from falling glass. Now if some kind of poison had been delivered through the shattered opening, it would have affected everyone inside to some extent."

"Unless it struck him only."

"But there is no residue in his blood that would support that. And I'm trying to think of who could shoot through that dome with such accuracy…" He shook his head. "It's like shooting into water, Margarite. Unless you are looking straight through, the light bends and you miss your target. And the thicker the glass, the more refraction you get. Plus, any projectile heavy enough to penetrate that glass would have done more than administer some poison. There would be a puncture wound, at least."

Her eyes widened a shade; then she nodded. "So maybe the two are not directly related."

"Sometimes things are just coincidence." Lawton had a suspicious mind, one that had led him to notice an almost insignificant paramilitary organization in Idaho and thus unravel the attempted assassination of then presidential hopeful, now National Security Advisor, Grant Lawrence. But he could see no connection here.

He turned from the dome, allowing his thoughts to percolate before they tried to talk to the physician who had treated the chancellor. His gaze fell upon a row of slate plates, all free-form, set on end in the ground in a neat row. There must have been nearly a hundred.

"What are those?" he asked, pointing.

She shrugged. "Berlin is not a city of pleasant memories, and here less than anywhere. I wish they had salvaged none of the look of the original Reichstag."

Suppressing annoyance at her persistent bigotry when no wrong had been done to her, he walked over to the row of slates, thinking that from one angle they almost looked like the opaque ribs of a tunnel through time. Then he found the plaque that identified them.

After a moment he looked back at Margarite. "You should appreciate this."

"Why so?" she asked, looking bored.

"Because this is a memorial to the ninety-six Reichstag members who were killed by the Nazis in 1933. One plate for each member."

Margarite drew a sharp breath. Then she looked from the memorial to the dome and back again. "It seems they may have learned."

"Indeed, so it does."

Lawton hoped they had learned enough, and that the rest of Europe could learn from them.

Before it was too late for them all.

Rome, Italy

Monsignore Veltroni had chosen an out-of-the-way café for his meeting with Steve Lorenzo. It was not in a place any of the Stewards of Faith were likely to come. Not even remotely. As he sat awaiting Steve, he felt his conscience twinging mightily. Loyalty, he thought, could be a very difficult thing. Right now his long loyalty to the Stewards was warring with his loyalty to Steve, placing him on the famous horns of a dilemma.

But he had chosen, he decided. He had chosen the moment he had summoned Steve so he could talk to him before setting the spies on him. He told his conscience to hush, but it insisted on pricking him anyway.

All of a sudden he remembered Steve's question about whether they were protecting the Faith, the Church, or the Word of God. They should all be the same, and he had believed so for a long time, but now, after Cardinal Estevan's directive, doubt had begun to plague him. For the first time he began to think there was more to this ruby codex than proof that Jesus had sired a son. Estevan was not the kind of man who would require spies on a priest who had merely seen the thing if that were all it was.

Sighing, Veltroni sipped his espresso and wondered what was taking Steven so long. Maybe *he* had some answers for all this perplexity.

Just then the little bell over the door jingled and Steve entered, raindrops glistening all over his cheap wool jacket. He stood just within the café, shaking himself a bit to shed some of the wet, then smiled at Veltroni and came to join him at the small table. Immediately another espresso appeared, this one at Steve's elbow. He seemed glad to lighten it with a little cream from an enamel pitcher and swallowed it hot.

"Ah," he said with a smile of pleasure. "Just what I needed."

Veltroni chuckled and waggled his fingers, indicating that the waiter should bring two more. "Are you hungry?"

"A little."

"Then let me get you a small pastry. You need the calories so you can walk home."

Steve's smile deepened. "I'm worrying you."

"More than a little bit. But I need to talk to you. Something is going on, and perhaps you can shed some light."

"Me?" Steve arched an eyebrow, then turned to thank the waiter who brought two more coffees. "What could I possibly know? I've been in the jungle for the last two years."

"That's why you may know something. But first…" Veltroni hesitated, aware that he was about to break a vow of obedience. Years of submission to his church made that a difficult thing to do, even though it was not the first time. "Pablo Cardinal Estevan. You remember him?"

"Yes, of course. He heads up the Stewards now, doesn't he?"

"Yes, he was elected after you went to Guatemala."

"I haven't met him yet."

"Better," Veltroni said heavily, "that you don't."

Now both of Steve's eyebrows lifted. The waiter brought a plate of *pasticciotti* that was far bigger than a "little" pastry, but Steve merely lifted a fork and helped himself to a bite of the delicious lemon-filled pastry puff. "All right," he said, when he had swallowed a few mouthfuls and the sugar met with the caffeine, energizing him. "Tell me what is worrying you."

"Estevan is not sure you will hunt for the codex. In fact, he's not certain that it was ever stolen from you."

Steven toyed with his fork, and his expression did not reassure Veltroni. "Trust me, it was stolen."

"I believe you, Steve. Even if you find it, Estevan also does not believe you will turn the codex over to the Church. He has told me to have you followed and watched."

Steve took another bite of the sweet and sighed with obvious pleasure. "All right. Thank you for telling me."

Veltroni leaned forward. While he believed Steve, he was unhappy with the sudden sense of doubt that assailed him. Why did Steve seem so unconcerned that he was to be watched? "Tell me, Steve. What is it about this codex? Why should Estevan be so concerned that the Church should possess it if it's just a shard of history?"

"It's more than that," Steve said. He put his fork down and sipped his espresso. "Far more. If it contains the information I was told to search for, I cannot say. I certainly could make neither heads nor tails of it."

"Then what is Estevan hoping for?"

Steve hesitated, turning his head and looking out the window at the rainy afternoon, as if weighing something. Finally he looked at Veltroni. "I don't understand it myself, Giuseppe. Honestly. But I know there are those who believe it wields great power. The Quiche *curandera* who passed it on to me warned me that it would be terribly dangerous in the wrong hands. Then it was stolen before I could do more than look at it."

Veltroni nodded and waited, but when Steve didn't say any more he asked, "What is your opinion? What do you suspect?"

Steve tugged at his earlobe, then used a cloth napkin to wipe his mouth. "What I *know,* Giuseppe, is that there are people who believe this codex has the power to create Armageddon."

All right, Veltroni thought later, as he walked back to the Vatican, taking his time because the moment he arrived, he would have to set the spies on Steve. All right.

Armageddon. Many wanted to see it, fools that they were. That people should actually have the hubris to believe they could force the second coming by setting the Apocalypse into motion often stole his very breath. As if God would allow his hand to be forced in such a fashion.

But those people could create a living hell on earth regardless of whether the Lamb chose to return as the Lion.

Armageddon. He wondered if Estevan was aware of that possibility, of the power Steve claimed was inherent in the ruby codex. He wondered if the person who held it now believed that and was trying to use it.

Just a few days ago Veltroni would have said the safest place for such an item would be in the hands of the Mother Church. Now he was no longer certain.

Perhaps the best place for it was in the deepest part of the ocean. For certainly such a thing would never be harmless in the hands of men.

7

Berlin, Germany

Frau Doktor Ulla Viermann didn't wish to speak to anyone. That much soon became apparent to Lawton and Margarite when the doctor didn't answer her phone or her door while she was at home. Finally they had to wait outside the hospital and snag her when she walked to her car.

At first it looked as if they would have a screaming fight on their hands, but speaking quickly, Lawton said in awkward German, "We don't believe you were in any way responsible for the chancellor's death. And we want to prove it."

The shout for help that had been about to emerge from the doctor's throat died. She hesitated, hugging her coat tightly around herself, and stared at them through the soft drizzle of rain. "Who are you?" she demanded.

"Friends," said Margarite in German. "Better friends

than any others you have right now, because we think the chancellor's death was an assassination, and that you did your best save him. Only an idiot would think otherwise."

"There seem to be many idiots," Ulla Viermann said slowly, her gaze still suspicious.

"We aren't among them," Lawton said. "Please. Meet us at the café around the corner. We'll share a pastry and hot chocolate, and tell you more."

After a moment the doctor nodded and went to her car.

"Do you think she'll come?" Lawton asked Margarite.

Margarite shrugged. "Who knows? If not, we try again."

Really, Lawton thought, he sometimes wanted to shake this woman for her studied indifference. It was worse than Renate's ice, for it was a pose, not a matter of self-defense. "She could think we're trying to set her up."

"Stop worrying until we have something to worry about."

He couldn't argue with that, he supposed. Together they walked around the corner to the bakery. Ulla Viermann already awaited them at the door.

A good sign? He certainly hoped so.

"One of the things I love about Germany," Lawton said, trying to break the ice, "is all these little bakeries where one can go inside and have coffee and a pastry. We have nothing this nice where I come from."

Ulla smiled reluctantly. "No, you have the McDonald's,

ja? You see?" She pointed up the block to where the famous symbol hung from a second-story window. "It seduces our youth, as well. Burgers and fries." She shook her head. "The sweets may not be better for me, but they are certainly more civilized."

They certainly were, he thought, for inside the bakery they sat at a table covered in white linen. Their hot chocolate, made from scratch, was thick and creamy, and topped with whipped cream. The pastries were fresh from the oven.

"When I die," Lawton said, "heaven had better have a few of these bakeries."

Ulla laughed, and some of the tension escaped her posture and expression. "Your French friend here will tell you they do it better in France." Apparently she had quickly picked out their nationalities.

"Indeed we do," Margarite agreed.

Ulla smiled. "Your people make wonderful pastries, Madame. I do not deny it. But these are fine also, *oder?*"

Margarite gave in and smiled. "They are wonderful."

"So." Looking satisfied, Ulla reached for a second pastry. As thin as she was, she no doubt could afford it. "You want to know what I know about the death of Herr Vögel. You say you do not believe I did anything wrong. I know I did not. But why should I talk to you? Especially when the police have already told me I must talk to no one about it? I should not even be here."

Lawton nodded. "I know you are in a very difficult

position, Frau Doktor. But while we are not police, we represent…" He paused, looking for the words he wanted. "A larger group."

Ulla smiled and spoke in flawless English. "If you are going to lie to me, Mr. Caine, it would be better if you do it in your own language. You would certainly find it easier, and I could then say—should I ever need to— that I must have misunderstood your American idioms."

Lawton nodded to her and, with relief, switched to English. "We're concerned that this investigation might settle for a scapegoat—you—and conceal the real cause and real culprit. You are aware that Vögel had threatened to withdraw Germany from the European Union if President Soult pursues his plans for pacification."

Ulla Viermann snorted. "Pacification. What an ugly word that is. It has been used for centuries as an excuse to commit genocide." She sipped her hot chocolate and paused, looking out the window at the people who hurried by in the darkening evening. "We tried for a while to evade our past. For many years we taught our youth nothing about Hitler or the Holocaust. Then we realized that history forgotten is history repeated. For over twenty years now, every German child has learned what happened here."

Lawton nodded. "History forgotten is history repeated. That is exactly what we fear."

She looked at him, her watery blue eyes shot with the red of weariness. "We have faced our past here, and spared ourselves nothing of its ugliness and horror. Oh, there are those who do not believe it, who place their hands over their ears and eyes because they cannot conceive any German could do such things. But they are a minority, Herr Caine. Most of us have faced the past and determined never to repeat it. Any of it."

"So Vögel's position had popular support?" Lawton asked, studying her intently.

She nodded. "Just so. We became concerned several decades back when the German youth rioted against Turkish workers. Among those of us who had studied the matter, we heard echoes of *Kristallnacht,* the night when Hitler's goons stormed the streets all over Germany, smashing and burning Jewish-owned shops and businesses, even murdering their owners. When our youth rioted, some heard the echoes of that past and recognized that it was time to reeducate our people."

Lawton nodded. "That was a very brave move."

"It was necessary. You will notice that despite the bombings in London and Madrid, and the ricin attack in Prague, the German people are not rioting. We are not burning mosques." Ulla glanced at the Frenchwoman with a slight smile, to soften the implied insult. "There is tension, of course, but we choose not to begin a problem that will only grow. Always there are those who disagree, but Germans will not support another Nazi regime, no matter the name. Europa Prima? Does he think that fools us?"

Margarite stiffened, and Ulla appeared to realize the second barb had sunk deeper than she intended. "I do not speak ill of you or your people, Madame. It is not only Frenchmen who elected Monsieur Soult to his post."

Margarite nodded, her face remaining expressionless.

Ulla looked thoughtful. "These are difficult times. We are so anxious to avoid any appearance of religious bigotry that we allowed a radical mosque to develop in Hamburg, and out of it came the horrors of September eleventh. Yet when we talk about that, we back away quickly, because to try to eradicate or control any religious sect might lead us once again in the wrong direction." The doctor shook her head. "It appears that any answer holds dangers."

"But the chancellor," Lawton said, anxious to get back to the point. "From what we have learned, it seems there is no clear cause for his death."

"In that you are wrong," the doctor said. "The cause of death is very clear—cellular asphyxiation. The means by which it occurred are another matter."

"There can be no doubt?"

"None whatsoever." Ulla Viermann licked her thumb and forefinger, then reached for her napkin to finish the job. "It is not an everyday occurrence, but any emergency room physician with experience has treated cyanide poisoning. There is a cyanide kit in every emergency room. Cellular asphyxia, usually caused by cyanide poisoning, can easily be confirmed by looking at blood oxygen levels. If the venous blood is nearly as oxygen-rich as the arterial blood, then something is keeping that oxygen from bonding with the iron in the red blood cells and moving into the patient's body. I performed that test on Chancellor Vögel, and the treatment notes confirm that."

"But why did you treat for cyanide?" Margarite asked. "Surely there are other chemicals that could cause this. *Is* it possible that your misdiagnosis and the antidotes for cyanide were the cause of death?"

Ulla bridled a bit, then visibly calmed herself. Under the table, Lawton gave Margarite a warning nudge. Things were bad enough without being antagonistic.

"Forgive my associate," he said quickly to the doctor. "She's French."

For that he received a small laugh from Ulla and a poke in the ribs from Margarite, but at least the tension evaporated.

Ulla spoke. "I have answered that very question countless times since the event. I will answer it once more for you." She looked pointedly at Lawton. "There are three known cellular asphyxiants," she said. "They are carbon monoxide, hydrogen sulfide and cyanide. The circumstances of the chancellor's collapse ruled out carbon monoxide. There was simply no way the Reichstag dome could have been filled with a sufficient concentration of that gas. I ruled out hydrogen sulfide because the chancellor's security agents denied smelling it at the scene. Hydrogen sulfide has a very power-ful odor of rotten eggs, and it could not have been pres-ent in a lethal concentration without the agents having smelled it. That left cyanide."

"Or, obviously, something else," Lawton said.

"As I said before, there are three *known* cellular as-phyxiants," Ulla said, once again looking defensive. "Even now, nearly a week later and after hundreds of blood assays, they do not know what toxin killed the chancellor. But even if I had not treated him for cyanide poisoning, the chancellor would be dead."

"And you're certain you performed the right treat-ment for cyanide?" Margarite asked. "Comparatively few murders are committed with cyanide. It is a con-trolled substance. Surely you do not treat cyanide poi-soning very often."

Ulla sighed. "Clearly you are not doctors," she said after a moment.

"No," Lawton agreed. "I'm sorry if we offend you. That is not our intention. We are simply trying to ensure that we understand everything."

She appeared to accept this. "I said that every mod-ern emergency room is equipped with a cyanide kit. There is a reason for that. Cyanide is a common chemi-cal, used in or produced by many commercial processes. We see cyanide poisoning more often than you would think. Most are workplace accidents. The diagnosis is not difficult, and the treatment protocol is clear and well-known. Most patients survive, unless the dose was massive or they do not receive treatment in time."

She reached for another pastry. "My patient's dose was not so massive that he died in minutes, although he was very near death by the time he reached the hospital. We followed the standard treatment protocol. When he did not respond to that, I ordered hydroxocobalamin. While it is not approved for cyanide poisoning, neither is it a lethal toxin. It is vitamin B12, the same substance found in every multivitamin pill on the market. It, too, had no effect, and the patient died." She looked at them. "I had barely confirmed the time of death when they swept him away to autopsy."

Lawton shook his head. "And now they suspect you, because they have no other explanation. Surely they do not think you could have diagnosed an unknown toxin?"

She sighed and looked down at her plate, white ceramic now dusted with white powder from the pastries she had chosen. "I don't know what they think, Herr Caine. All I know is that I treated the chancellor in the best way that my training and experience allowed. And I failed."

"We're not blaming you," Lawton hastened to assure her. "And we're not going to stop our investigation. It will help no one to bury the truth."

Ulla Viermann seemed to study him for a long moment before she replied, as if she were trying to decide whether he could be so naive. "Oh, there you are wrong, Herr Caine. Burying the truth will help *someone*. It will help the person or persons who murdered Chancellor Vögel."

Egypt
c.1300 B.C.E.

Jacob preferred to live among the Hebrew community to the north of where his son Joseph now served as Grand Vizier to the Pharaoh. He was proud of Joseph's accomplishments. His brothers had sold him into slavery, but Joseph had risen far, and now Joseph's daughter, Tiye, was to marry the Pharaoh. It seemed that the Lord's bounty knew no limit.

But Jacob's years were catching up with him, and he knew it was time to pass along the knowledge that had so long ago been entrusted to Avraham. He had, of course, educated all his sons in the knowledge of the Kabbalah, including Joseph, and even a few of his daughters, for it was important that the knowledge not die. But now it was time to pass along the instruments.

He had debated for a long time, since there were four of them, one ruby, one emerald, one sapphire, one diamond. Should they all be given to one son, or should they be divided?

In darkness and solitude, he opened the chest where he kept them and lifted out all the old blankets that concealed them. They glowed so that he could see them even without the assistance of an oil lamp. Gently he touched each one.

He found it symbolic that there were four, and all

were the same shape as the three huge, awe-inspiring pyramids on the plain of Giza. The people of Egypt related that the pyramids had been there since a time long lost in the mists of memory, and Jacob had no difficulty believing it. These gemstones, into which one could look and see the mysteries of the universe, along with the accompanying scroll that contained the mystical alphabet of letters that held the sounds that had created the world and now were being incorporated as a way to write the old, sacred Hebrew tongue, also came from a time no one clearly remembered.

It had been told to Jacob from his fathers that the Lord, El, had given these gifts to Avraham. But it was also said that the glowing pyramids had been created by Seth, at the behest of El. The scholars argued whether Seth was the son of the first *adama,* or if he was a god himself. The Egyptians likened him to a god and called him Tahuti, who was revered by the scribes as the creator of all writing…which would go along with the scroll of strange writing and the moving symbols within the pyramids.

But Jacob was now past worrying about the answers. If he had been meant to have answers, El would have provided them. Instead, El had told him that he would be the father of a great nation, that his children would number as many as the grains of sand, and so had named him Israel. Jacob still found that name uncomfortable to bear, although most of his sons and their sons now went around calling themselves the sons of Israel.

He touched the pyramids again, and watched the light within them shift and change as symbols and signs floated around. He had looked deeply into one once, and El had warned him away, advising him to stick with his study of the scroll. The knowledge in those pyramids was not meant for him.

He wondered what it must have been like for Avraham to be able to stand face to face with El and accept the charge to move into Canaan. Would being face to face make it any easier than having to rely on dreams?

Yet, Jacob admitted, his dreams had never misled him, not even when he had fled after stealing Esau's inheritance. He sometimes remembered his misdeed and wept, but still El had favored him. Or cursed him. He would have been happy to remain in Canaan raising his goats, but no, he had been summoned to Egypt, where he had watched his children and his children's children turned from herders into laborers. They were not far from slaves now, and he suspected that once Joseph died, slavery would become their lot. Tiye, beautiful and strong woman that she was, would not be able to save her people from the scorn of their Egyptian landlords.

El must have his reasons, Jacob reminded himself.

All he could do was remain a good servant, as Avraham had promised so long ago. El said he had great plans for Avraham's descendents. Jacob sometimes wondered why it was taking so long, but then he reminded himself that the affairs of the Lord were beyond his ken.

"Every sword," his beloved Joseph had once said to him, "must be tempered in fire."

So perhaps this was the tempering of the sons of Israel.

Shaking his head, Jacob once again piled the old blankets, still smelling of goat, onto the pyramids and closed the chest. He would give the sapphire pyramid to Joseph, he decided. The ruby and the emerald... He hesitated as he thought about it. Tiye, he decided. He would give the emerald one to Tiye. Then she could pass it down the line of her royal daughters and bring them to the will of El.

As for the others, he had numerous sons who he loved. That decision could await another day, he decided. Somewhere deep inside he felt that it was time for the pyramids to be scattered, no longer kept close together.

There was safety in that, his heart said. Safety for everyone. For together, these pyramids could change the whole world.

8

Rome, Italy

Monsignore Veltroni sat on a bench near the Trevi Fountain as the predawn sky began to lighten. Pigeons cooed to one another, waking to another day of pestering tourists for scraps. So far the tourists had not begun arriving. Only a few people were about, hurrying to open shops that would provide food and thick coffee to those on the way to work later in the morning.

The fountain was as quiet and peaceful as it could be, except perhaps at three in the morning. The water rushing from Neptune's rising steeds filled the entire piazza with its soothing sound.

As he had hoped, in that seemingly magical way that filled Veltroni with both awe and fear, Nathan Cohen suddenly appeared around a corner and walked toward him. Today the man looked like a laborer on his way to work at a construction site. When he sat near Veltroni, he pulled a bag from his pocket and began to toss bread-crumbs to the pigeons.

"Do you come here often?" Veltroni asked, trying yet again to find out whether Cohen somehow knew when Veltroni would be here, or whether he simply passed by here as part of his routine.

"As often as I need to," Cohen answered. "I like the pigeons and the company."

"It is a lovely fountain."

"It speaks to a time older than much of Rome," Cohen replied. "Though it is itself not that old."

"Meaning?"

Cohen looked at him, the creases by his eyes deepening as he smiled. "Must there be a meaning to everything?"

"I am beginning to think so. You reassured me once that my friend Steven was still alive when he had vanished into the jungle in Guatemala."

"True."

Veltroni looked at him. "Do you know who he is?"

"He is an important man, your Father Steve. Am I to gather the Church itself has begun to realize it?"

"Parts of the Church have."

"Ah. Your little organization."

It always unnerved Veltroni that Cohen seemed to know so much about the Stewards, a group that did not exist in any Vatican record. He wished he had Cohen's sources, and his resources. Finally Veltroni merely nodded and watched Cohen scatter some more crumbs.

Presently Cohen spoke again. "Father Lorenzo is more widely known than you might imagine, *Monsignore*."

Veltroni opened his mouth to question, but Cohen had already risen and was emptying his entire bag of crumbs on the ground.

"Set your spies, my friend," Cohen said. "But do not be surprised when they fail. And do not worry if you lose contact with him. I will keep him safe for you."

Then he strolled away, whistling a tune that sounded vaguely Eastern. After a half-dozen steps, he stopped and looked back. *"Monsignore!"*

Veltroni stood and waited.

"Please attend to the news from Berlin and Strasbourg. Events of great importance are being placed in motion. You have a role to play in them. An important role."

Mouth drawing into a tight line, Veltroni watched Cohen walk away. Then, feeling suddenly paranoid, he turned to see if he was being watched. But no one seemed in the least interested in what had passed between him and Cohen, and there were few enough people about, in any case.

It was then that Veltroni realized Cohen's last statement had been spoken in flawless Latin.

He strolled quickly back toward the Vatican, his thoughts percolating as he stopped at a newsstand and glanced at the front pages of the Rome newspapers.

While the specific headlines differed, all had the same theme as *La Repubblica:*

Soult—'Pacificazione'

Was that what Cohen meant? He had not paid attention to European politics of late; the Vatican was more global in its outlook, and the policies of the European Union were rarely of religious import. But of course he had heard of Jules Soult's election and was vaguely aware that Soult was offering some new policy to quiet the street violence in Europe. Something surely needed to be done to stop the violence and save lives.

The wizened old man who operated the stall tapped the newspaper with a yellowed, twisted fingernail. "You should read that, *Monsignore.* You were not alive under Mussolini, but I was. I recognize the signs."

Veltroni looked at him. "Signs?"

"Read it and see, *Monsignore.* It is not my place to tell such a learned man as yourself what is in the paper."

Veltroni tossed him a coin, took the newspaper and read it as he walked, growing more uncomfortable with each step. The vague and innocuous notion of pacification had taken concrete form in a set of legislative proposals Soult had offered to the European Parliament. While some might laud Soult's intentions, Veltroni could find no comfort in their proposed expression.

If the legislation was enacted, each member of the

EU would be required to declare one or more "protection zones" for its Muslim inhabitants. While Muslims would not be required to live in these zones, the EU would subsidize additional security measures to protect those who did.

The word "ghetto" crossed Veltroni's mind more than once as he read the article. Long before he had reached the Holy City, he had decided it would be in order to call his friend Ahmed Ahsami. If Nathan Cohen saw handwriting on this wall, his advice was not to be ignored.

Rome, Italy

"Explain it again, please?" Jefe said, looking at the complex diagram Renate was displaying on a computer monitor. "A Mis-whatever-it-is…that's like an impeachment, right?"

"Not quite," she said. "A *Mißtrauensvotum* is a vote of distrust, the German equivalent to the English vote of no confidence. For Americans, it would be more similar to replacing the Speaker of the House of Representatives."

"But this isn't the Speaker of the House," Jefe said, holding out the newspaper whose front page proclaimed that the German *Bundestag* had proposed a vote of no confidence against the current chancellor, Albert Schlossman. "Your Chancellor is like our President."

"In some ways, yes," Renate said. "In America, the President is both the head of state and the head of the government. The head of government does the day-to-day leadership, while the head of state is a more ceremonial position. In England, the head of state is the Queen, but the head of government is the Prime Minister. In Germany, the head of state is our President, but the Chancellor is the head of government."

"I see," Jefe said.

Separating the two positions made no sense to him, but then again, he hadn't grown up under a parliamentary government, which was why he'd asked Renate to explain the significance of the *Mißtrauensvotum.* She knew the inner workings of German politics better than anyone else at Office 119, and he needed her expertise.

"Our Chancellor," she explained, "is elected by the *Bundestag,* the senior house of our federal legislature, like your Senate. In effect, he is chosen by the party or coalition of parties that holds the majority of seats in the *Bundestag.* Chancellor Vögel was the leader of the Social Democrat Party. But the Social Democrats did not hold a majority. They formed a coalition with the Green Party to secure that majority. As part of that coalition agreement, Chancellor Vögel chose the leader of the Green Party, Albert Schlossmann, as his Vice Chancellor. That is how Herr Schlossmann—the leader of a small, minority party—became Chancellor on Vögel's death."

"But that coalition still has a majority," Jefe said. "So they will defeat the *Mißtrauensvotum,* and Schlossmann stays in office. I don't see why this is a big deal."

"The Social Democrats will back out of the coalition," Renate said. "Chancellor Schlossmann is pushing his new *Gründgesetze,* his Green laws. These are environmental laws that would tighten our already severe limits on emissions from coal-fired power plants. The Social Democrats cannot afford to lose the support of the coal miners' unions."

"So Schlossmann should drop those laws," Jefe said.

Renate shook her head. "Chancellor Schlossmann would lose the support of the Green Party, and they would replace him as party leader. He is in an impossible position."

"I understand," Jefe said. "Schlossmann will be voted out. Then what? New elections?"

"Apparently not," Renate said. "The proposal is what we call a constructive vote of distrust. If it passes, and I'm sure it will, then one of three things will happen. First, the Social Democrats and the Greens might make a new coalition agreement, with the new SPD leader as chancellor. Second, the Social Democrats and the Christian Democrats might attempt another Grand Coalition as they did under Chancellor Merkel, but this time the Social Democrats have more seats, so the SPD leader would be chancellor. I don't think the Christian Democrats would approve that. It gains them nothing."

"This *Mißtrauensvotum* was proposed by the CDU— the Christian Democrats," Jefe said. "Surely they wouldn't do that just to replace Schlossmann with an SPD chancellor."

"Surely not," Renate agreed. "That means there is a third coalition deal, one they have not yet announced to the public. The Christian Democrats would need at least two of the minority parties to join with them. Their usual allies, the Free Democratic Party, do not have enough seats to give them a majority. I cannot imagine them making an alliance with the Left Party."

"No," Jefe said. "The Christian Democrats are the conservative party, aren't they? Like our Republicans in the United States?"

Renate laughed. "Even conservatives in Germany would be liberal in America, but yes, you are right. The Left Party is far too liberal for the Christian Democrats. And that leaves only one group to tip the balance."

"Oh, shit," Jefe said, looking at the chart again and doing some mental calculation.

"Yes," Renate agreed. "Soult's Europa Prima Party. In coalition with both the Free Democrats and Europa Prima, the Christian Democrats would have a majority. This is why I am so concerned. This would give Monsieur Soult a lot of leverage, and he is not one to waste political capital. So what was his price for this coalition?"

Jefe lowered his head to his hands for a moment before looking up. "This is going to be bad for Germany."

"Not just Germany," Renate said. "This is going to be bad for the world."

9

Hamburg, Germany

The Moorburg district in Hamburg was not featured on most tourist maps. On the southwest edge of the city's huge port facility, it was a place of commerce with a largely transient population of seamen and dockworkers on short-term contracts. As such, it was the ideal staging area for Paxti Lezeta and his three companions.

Lezeta had more than once wondered at the ironic twists his life had taken. His given name—Paxti—was the Basque equivalent of Francis, and its Latin root, *pax,* meant peace. It was, he thought, about as close to peace as his life had ever come.

His father and two brothers had been active in the Basque Fatherland and Liberty group—*Euskadi ta Askatasuna* or ETA—the separatist movement seeking independence from Spain. But when it had come time for Lezeta to make his stand and join with them, he had not only declined but had become an informant. He had seen too many attacks planned over the dining room table of his family's home in St. Palais, a village on the French side of the border, where they had lived just beyond the reach of the Spanish police. Sooner or later, he knew, his family would be implicated, and he would be swept up with the rest to rot in a cell.

He had been willing to sacrifice his father and brothers for his own freedom, and he had gained far more than that. His treachery had come to the attention of a Spanish colonel, Hector Vazquez, and with that attention had come a life that, if ugly, had been the stuff of spy thrillers.

For Lezeta had been sent back into the Basque community as the sole surviving member of a martyred family, pretending to be bent on avenging their deaths. Over the next four years, information he provided led to the arrests of dozens of ETA members, always after he had made arrangements to cover his tracks and retain his standing in the movement.

That many of the men he had turned over were now lying in unmarked graves, having refused to provide information or having tried to escape, did not bother him. As Lezeta saw it, he had not killed them. They had killed themselves by casting their lot behind a hopeless cause. In the end—after it had been mistakenly blamed for the Madrid train bombings in 2003—even ETA had recognized the futility of continued armed struggle. In March of 2006, the group had declared a permanent ceasefire and announced its intention to pursue the Basque cause solely through legal means.

Thus, Lezeta did not see himself as a traitor to his family or his people. In the end, he believed he had done more to ensure the future of the Basque people than had all of the bombings, kidnappings and murders. As for those who had died, their blood lay on their own hands.

However, he had in the process learned many skills that were essential to his current mission. Along with other members of the cell he was infiltrating at the time, Lezeta had traveled to a training camp in Syria, where he had learned the theory and practice of preparing shaped charges and remote detonation.

During his time in Syria, he had also met the two Lebanese men whom he had recruited six months ago to join him on this mission. They were, he knew, unafraid to die as martyrs in their twisted world of *jihad.* And Lezeta was more than willing to help them meet their god. It was vital that their fingerprints and their faces—not his—be linked to the destruction that would happen this night.

Lezeta did not think of his role in their deaths, any more than he thought of his role in the deaths of the men in Spain and France. They were nothing more than misguided missiles destined for self-destruction, if not tonight at his hands, then surely on some other night and at some other's hands. Blinded by their messianic vision of a utopian world under Islamic law, they were already among the casualties in this war of civilizations. It was only a matter of time until their deaths moved from foregone conclusion to established fact, and this night was as good a time as any.

Thus, while he was supposed to be waiting in a Zodiac on the bank of the Köhlbrand River, ready to gather the two men and spirit them across to the safety of a waiting van, in fact he already had slit open the boat's pontoon sides and driven back to the safe house, leaving them stranded in the deadly inferno they were about to create. At this moment, they were at the port's huge chemical storage facility, attaching shaped demolition charges to two underground tanks, each of which was filled with two hundred thousand tons of liquid nitric acid.

An ordinary explosion might dent or even puncture the Teflon-coated, stainless steel roofs of these tanks. But most of the explosion would be dissipated upward and wasted. Thus, Lezeta had used shaped charges, with hollow, trumpet-bell bottoms that would fit snugly to the surface of each tank. These would not only puncture the tanks, but also concentrate the explosive energy into thin streams of superheated plasma, igniting the highly volatile acid into fireballs that would spew clouds of caustic gas.

Lezeta had chosen his targets carefully. Nitric acid, while extremely corrosive at liquid concentrations, was, in gaseous form, rarely more than a severe irritant. It would give the people of Hamburg—and the people of Germany—a well-deserved shock, as hundreds or thousands would stream into hospitals with ragged coughs, only to be told that the symptoms would pass in a few days.

Public health officials would then breathe a hearty sigh of relief, while knowing in the pits of their bellies that they had been lucky, that the casualty toll could have been much higher if the terrorists had chosen to attack other tanks holding more deadly chemicals. The media would then take up the call, first wondering how terrorists had slipped past the Hamburg River Police who handled security at the chemical storage facilities, and then issuing dire warnings that Europeans could not dare hope that the next such attack—and there would surely be more, expert after expert would declare with somber conviction—would cause so few casualties.

Lezeta's reverie was interrupted by the ringing of his cell phone. "Yes," he said in accented English.

"All is ready," Mahir Abood said. "We are at the river. Where are you?"

But Lezeta was already dialing a second cell phone. "I am not there," he said as he pushed the send button.

Less than a second later, Lezeta saw the flash through his apartment window, and moments after that the shockwave rattled the glass and shook the walls of the building. He watched only long enough to see the twin fireballs rising into the night sky, then nodded and picked up the suitcase he had packed a half hour before.

"Vaya con su dios," he said as he closed the apartment door for the last time. *Go with your god.*

He climbed into his small rented sedan and headed south on the E45 Autobahn. In six hours, he would cross the Dutch border and would be sitting in the lobby of the Schipol Airport in Amsterdam. There a contact from Vasquez would meet him with a package of information for his next assignment.

Lezeta was going to Berlin.

Rome, Italy

Ahmed Ahsami watched the television news reports, biting his lip until blood flowed. It was all he could do not to slam his hand down on the table, which would have done nothing except attract unwanted attention in the small café where he was sipping coffee. Instead, he rose from his chair and walked toward the rear of the room, as if he were going to the restroom, then ascended the stairs to the deceptively ramshackle room above.

A pair of televisions and three laptop computers on a creaky wooden table gave no clue to the true importance of this room. It was, in fact, the European headquarters of *Saif Alsharaawi*. It was also Ahmed's new home base.

"How did we not know this was being planned?" he demanded angrily.

"It was *Hezbollah*," said Abdul al-Nasser, an Egyptian who was station chief here. "The identities of the bombers have not yet been released, but their fingerprints were uplinked to Interpol twenty minutes ago. I ran them through our own database. Both were Lebanese."

"Why would *Hezbollah* attack in Germany?" Ahmed asked, quickly scanning the data screen. "Such an attack does not fit their profile."

Hezbollah had begun as a collection of local Shi'a militias in southern Lebanon, crystallizing during the twenty-year Israeli occupation. Its aims and operations had always been local, preserving Shi'a dominance against Sunni and Druze Christian militias, resisting the Israeli occupiers, and carrying the battle into Israel itself after the formal occupation ended and southern Lebanon was left a desiccated and mine-strewn wasteland. A strike in Germany would do nothing to advance their interests in Lebanon. It made no sense.

"*Hezbollah* work for Iran," al-Nasser said, as if that were answer enough. "They are Shi'a."

Ahmed shook his head. He had opposed recruiting al-Nasser from the Muslim Brotherhood in Cairo, and had also opposed al-Nasser's appointment as European station chief. The Muslim Brotherhood, with its virulent Wahhabist-Salafist message, was in Ahmed's view emblematic of the problem in Islam, rather than the solution.

"People still act for reasons," Ahmed said. "I cannot see what either *Hezbollah* or Iran could gain from this."

"Attention," al-Nasser said. "Remember that with all that is happening in Europe, the world is once again seeing the plight of true Muslims."

"I have bad news for you, my friend," Ahmed said. "The world does not distinguish between Persian and Arab, Shi'a and Sunni. To them, we are all the same, the same enemy. When Iran seeks to develop a nuclear program, the West asks how long it will be before Iran gives nuclear weapons to al-Qaeda, as if the Shi'a in Iran would consider giving such power to fundamentalist Sunni terrorists."

"Yes," al-Nasser agreed. "And Westerners ignore the fact that your country and mine fear a nuclear-armed Iran more than the West does. We know what the Iranians would do with such weapons, and it would not be to attack Israel. No, they would first blackmail Sunni nations into accepting Shi'a rule. Only then—once they had an oil monopoly and the political leverage that goes with it—would they turn their sights on Israel."

Ahmed thought al-Nasser's nightmare scenario unlikely, but this was not the time to argue the issue. "What do we know about the travel of these two *Hezbollah* operatives?"

"I am checking now," al-Nasser said, his fingers flying over the keyboard. "Here. They flew from Beirut to Hamburg a week ago."

"So who were they working with?" Ahmed asked.

This was not the kind of operation that could be mounted in a single week. Someone must have been in Germany ahead of them to perform the reconnaissance on the target and work out detailed plans.

"Like I said, they work for Iran," al-Nasser said. "I will check on the known activities of Iranian nationals in Germany. My guess is that we will find a port employee or an Iranian student attending university there. Or someone in the Iranian intelligence service. Someone who was too valuable to waste on a suicide mission."

"Perhaps," Ahmed said, remembering how his erstwhile allies in Europe had betrayed Black Christmas and funded the attack in Strasbourg. "But don't limit your search. It would not be the first time Islamic strings were pulled by others."

And regardless of al-Nasser's protestations to the contrary, Ahmed did not think this was an Iranian mission. No, this had a rancid smell that he knew all too well. He made a mental note to double-check all of al-Nasser's work on this project. If the Egyptian would not turn over the right rocks, Ahmed would do it himself.

Benjamin watched his nephews run around the edge of the Nile, where a pool had been formed near the Pharaoh's palace. He was an old man now, enjoying the heat of the sun for the way it eased his aching joints, enjoying the day because he had so few left.

His niece Tiye's sons, Joseph's grandchildren, scampered around in loincloths, full of the vigor of youth, chasing one another in and out of the pool. The elder of them would be pharaoh soon, for often sons ruled beside their fathers even before they were men full grown. The younger, Moses, would serve his brother for the rest of his days.

Perhaps. Of late Benjamin had been troubled by dreams, a failing or a blessing, depending on one's point of view. It certainly seemed to run in the family of Israel. Joseph's dreams, often seeming to mock his brothers, had caused the brothers to sell him into slavery. Benjamin, who had barely been born at the time, had no part in the treachery, but he had certainly heard of it.

How many times had Jacob said, "El works in mysterious ways." For was it not true that Joseph had risen from slavery to become the Pharaoh's most trusted right hand? Had not Joseph saved the sons of Jacob and their families from starvation? And had not Joseph's beloved, beautiful daughter married a Pharaoh?

Matters were not going as well for the sons of Israel as once they had, but hope played before him in the pool near the reeds of the Nile. Those boys were their hope.

But the dreams...the dreams. Benjamin closed his eyes, ignoring the giggling laugh of Miriam as she dashed by her brothers, and the wail of Aaron from his reed cradle.

The dreams. With his eyes closed, Benjamin could feel the darkness that hovered over the two playing boys. Their future would be troubled, of that he was certain. Another part of El's plan would play out with those two at the center of it.

But all Benjamin could do was teach them all he could of the Kabbalah and what it meant to guard the Light. The boys received the wisdom with eagerness, even if they did not fully understand it. Amenhotep, the elder, seemed particularly enthralled by the idea of a single god. Moses, on the other hand, seemed to think it could be no other way. But Amenhotep had always been a deeper philosopher than Moses, who seemed more ready to simply accept. Amenhotep took each idea the way a bird receives a seed, as something to be carefully pecked open for the meat within.

Yet despite their differences, Benjamin's dreams told him that both had pivotal roles to play in the plan of the One God. And that neither would achieve joy because of it.

"Uncle?"

He opened his eyes and found Amenhotep standing beside him.

"Are you all right?" the heir to the throne asked him.

"I'm an old man," Benjamin said with mock sternness. "I need my sleep."

Amenhotep grinned. "You were not asleep. You were talking under your breath."

"Merely the voices of my dreams."

The boy, already showing signs of an unusual face and build, laughed. "I want another lesson."

"Then tell Moses to come while I get my scroll."

"I'll run and get it," Miriam chirped. "Then I must take Aaron back to Mother, for he is growing hungry."

Amenhotep watched his young sister run toward Benjamin's house, a modest dwelling nearby. "I should marry her."

Benjamin shook his head. Pharaohs married their sisters often, but Benjamin was certain that Amenhotep's father had other ideas. "I think you are meant for another, my nephew. Later you will choose others, but by then Miriam will be wed within the family of Israel."

Amenhotep nodded. Whatever he might dream and wish, he had long since adjusted to the fact that few decisions were yet within his power. Moses, still dripping from the pool, joined them. Powerfully built, he was more inclined to action than study.

"A lesson?" he asked, correctly intuiting Amenhotep's presence beside Benjamin.

Amenhotep nodded, expecting no disagreement and receiving none. They both knew their positions.

Miriam returned rapidly, carrying the proper scroll, then scampered away with her baby brother. The boys sat at Benjamin's feet.

For a few seconds he closed his eyes, feeling the slithering foreboding of his dreams slip over the beautiful day. To be in a position of destiny decreed by God offered little solace to those who must endure the difficulties.

But these boys had no idea their paths had already been set, and Benjamin would not be the one to tell them.

Let God tell them. It would be *His* doing after all.

Part II: *TARHĒL*
(Arabic: *Removal*)

10

Hans Neufel was almost asleep as his Leopard II tank pulled into the platoon's protective *laager* for motion. Road marches were always grueling, and a march through the *Schwarzwald*—with its steep hills, twisting roads and oppressively thick forest—was ever more so. There was a reason this was called the Black Forest. In the summertime, the sun seemed unable to penetrate the dense foliage, even at the height of noon. The rugged terrain and the carpet of dead leaves combined to warp and deaden sound to the point that one could barely hear something close by and yet could clearly discern a sound from a distant hillside. Small wonder that this place was ripe with legends of monsters.

More than once in the past twelve hours, Hans had been forced to drop down into his turret to avoid low-hanging branches. In the past hour, with the forest

gloom growing truly black in the waning light and ex-
haustion overtaking him, he'd given up trying. Goggles
and his crew helmet protected most of his face, and the
few scratches he'd taken were, he thought, the closest
thing to battle wounds he was ever likely to suffer.

Neufel had served in the *Bundeswehr* for nineteen
months of his two-year commitment. Most of his classmates had elected to do their requisite national service in
the public sector, working for charitable or civic groups.
He had decided to follow in his father's footsteps, for in
his father's day army service was mandatory for able-
bodied young men. Hans hadn't minded his time in the
army. The food was palatable, his officers reasonable, and
while the German military was no longer as culturally re-
spected as it had once been, there was no shortage of
young women who still flushed at the sight of a uniform.

Moreover, he had discovered an aptitude for army
life. Where others chafed under the regulations and discipline, he found a logical sense of order. He could rely
on his tank crew to respond to his commands, and they
could rely on him not to issue pointless orders simply
for the sake of asserting his authority.

His father had begun to warn him about his looming
transition to civilian life. He would be aghast at the lack
of respect his university classmates showed for profes-
sors and office colleagues would show for their manag-
ers. Hans had listened to his father's words with a mix
of bemusement and impatience. He had, after all, been

a civilian for most of his twenty years. Surely he had not changed so much that he wouldn't fit in anymore.

These thoughts usually occupied his mind during the maintenance chores that accompanied the end of a road march. Even in the twenty-first century, the old ways of the cavalry still applied in armored units: first the horse, then the saddle, then the man. Their panzer was their home as well as their weapon, and their first priority was to make certain that its engine was in working order, fluids replenished, tracks clear and undamaged, crew compartment emptied of the day's detritus. Only then could they turn to the tasks of feeding themselves and setting out bedrolls for much-needed sleep.

But on this night, he could not wander his usual mental paths. Otto Schulingen, his loader, was suffering from severe heat rash. If that were not enough to make Schulingen cranky, there was the news out of Berlin that the *Bundestag* had joined the European Union in enacting the *Muslimschutzgesetze*—the Muslim Protection Laws—in the wake of the terrorist bombing in Hamburg.

Schulingen was from Hamburg; he had talked about little apart from the poison gas attack for the past two days. It had shaken all of Germany, but with his parents and his sister having gone to the hospital, it had shaken him deeply and personally. Perhaps that was why he'd been lax in bathing and applying the antifungal powder to combat the heat rash.

"You must see the medic for that," Neufel said as

Schulingen stripped out of his tanker's coveralls with a pained wince.

"*Ja, Stuffz,*" Schulingen said, trying to scrub away the inflamed skin with a damp towel.

Yes, Sarge. There was no disrespect in Schulingen's use of the colloquial, and Neufel took none from it. He scrubbed his loader with an intensity that made Neufel wince, and finally he put his hand on Schulingen's shoulder.

"I mean it," he said. "Go see the medic, Private. There is no need for you to suffer this way. It will not make your parents or sister better. Only time will do that, the doctors say."

"Damn Muslims," Schulingen said softly. "What did my ten-year-old sister ever do to them?"

"Nothing," Neufel said. "Nothing at all."

"They deserve to be in pens like animals," Schulingen said. "I cannot believe the government is going to pay them compensation for relocating them."

"That is only just," Neufel said. "Most of them are good citizens, fellow Germans who want nothing at all to do with these terrorists."

Schulingen huffed. "Do you really think so, *Stuffz?* If so, pardon my disrespect, but you are a fool. You cannot make them German. They do not want to be German. And we should get them out of Germany."

Neufel nodded. He did not wish to argue politics, and especially not with a member of his crew. Such disputes could easily undermine the effectiveness of the team, and he took great pride in his crew's performance.

"Perhaps you are right, Private," Neufel said. "I am no politician. But I am a German, and I have grandparents. I do not wish to explain to my grandchildren the very same mistakes that my grandparents had to explain to me. So we must all be careful, no?"

"Ja, Stuffz," Schulingen said, obviously taken aback by the firmness of Neufel's tone. "I apologize. I am worried about my family."

"Of course. Now see the medic, Private."

Schulingen sighed. "I am sure it will go away."

Neufel studied him for a moment. "What is wrong, Private? Why are you not taking care of this?"

After a long moment, the loader sighed. "The way she looks at me. It makes me feel...unclean."

Neufel chuckled quietly. That would explain it. The company medic was a young woman from Frankfurt. More than that, she was exceptionally pretty. Schulingen obviously had a crush on her, not unheard of among men and women in uniform, but exquisitely embarrassing if the man was a tanker with a flaming red rash in his crotch and the woman the medic who would treat it.

"Has she said anything to you?" Neufel asked.

"Only that it is caused by the heat and that the powder will make it go away," Schulingen said. "But it is not what she says, *Stuffz.* It's...I wish she were not seeing me there at all, not that way."

Rachel Lee

Neufel smiled and shook his head. "Well, Private, I cannot resolve your love life. But I need you healthy and fit in my tank. So somehow you must put aside your fears and see the good *Frau Sanitäterin*. That is not a request. It is an order."

"You are a hard tank commander," Schulingen said.

"Yes," Neufel said. "I am. Now go, before I have to put you on report."

Neufel briefly checked on the other men of his crew, ensuring that they had finished their assigned tasks and were settling in for the night. But he could not sleep yet, for as tank commander, he had additional duties. Once he had seen to his own tank, he reported to the platoon leader for the daily debriefing. With quick, clipped sentences, Neufel reported on the condition of his vehicle and his men.

After each of the tank commanders had reported, Bräuburger gave them the customary dressing down for the day's myriad mistakes. The platoon had been a half hour late leaving its position that morning, owing to a thrown track on the number three tank as they were forming up. The lieutenant gave his men a lot of slack on many things, but he gave no leeway on vehicle maintenance.

Bräuburger turned his attention to the commander of the number one tank, who had twice lost visual contact with the trail vehicle of the platoon ahead of them. While it seemed a small thing in a training exercise, in combat such a mistake could leave the company staggering piecemeal into a battle, and dying piecemeal, as well. The digital network technology used by the *Bundeswehr* was second only to the Americans', but even the best electronics could fail. War was and would always be an intensely personal affair, and there was no substitute for direct visual contact with the other members of one's unit.

Still, as a training march, it had gone about as well as could be expected. Hans could count on his fingers the number of field exercises he had participated in during his tour of duty. Field training was expensive, dangerous and inevitably destructive of civilian property. It was also essential. Computer simulators were good, but they could not replace the inherent chaos of five hundred men and sixty vehicles attempting to move from one place to another in the real world. Hans considered himself a professional soldier, and his crew were capable and disciplined. Still, he wondered how his unit would perform if it faced combat.

Fortunately, he thought, he was unlikely ever to know. The horror and devastation of the Second World War and the birth of the European Union had signaled the end of the major power wars in Europe. Hans Neufel was, and would probably always be, a peacetime soldier.

And he liked it that way. To be ready to defend one's homeland was a noble calling. To actually face an enemy, to fire his tank's twelve-centimeter cannon in anger, to confront the stark choice of killing or being killed, was not a prospect he sought. Others might long for the adrenaline rush of combat, but he was not among them.

He would finish his tour, attend university and move on with his life. Just like his father.

Rome, Italy

Although he had come to Rome to be Steve Lorenzo's bodyguard, Miguel Ortiz spent most of his time alone. In the course of his daily ministry, the priest rarely faced any threat more dire than a hungry child. Most of Miguel's day was spent watching from a discreet distance, looking busy enough not to attract attention without actually being engaged in anything that would distract him if he were needed.

Miguel also tried to avoid attention for another reason. While Miriam Anson had reported him dead upon her return from Guatemala, he knew the murder of the American ambassador there—a murder he had participated in—was still unsolved. Should anyone recognize Miguel, they might wonder why a dead man was still among the living. So he had gained some weight from regular meals accompanied by pasta and had cut his long *indio* hair to a more European style. He'd even had it tightly permed and was often mistaken now for a Moroccan or Arab, not an advantage in the current climate, but still a form of anonymity.

The treatment he saw Muslims enduring picked open

memory scars like the thorn bushes in his native jungles. He had seen, firsthand, what people will do when they feel the boot of oppression and live in constant fear. He was beginning to wonder if Europeans were incapable of living with anyone, including themselves. The more he pondered, the more he concluded that the human race was its own worst enemy, and far less civilized than it believed.

He looked up as the door to the small *ristorante* opened and Padre Steve entered. The priest wore what he called his "mufti": jeans, a windbreaker and a T-shirt that read *I'd rather be golfing*. He looked like an American tourist, but Miguel knew *el padre* was no tourist in Italy. He had obviously lived here before and was as fluent in Italian as he was in his native English or his adopted Spanish.

Steve, as the padre insisted Miguel call him now, sat down across the table and smiled. Moments later he ordered a meal that Miguel knew was far more than he would eat, but Steve would take away the leftovers to give to the poor he encountered on his way back to his room.

While Miguel had gained weight, Steve seemed to have lost even more than the jungle had sweated off him. He didn't exactly look gaunt, but he looked…purified, Miguel thought. The air of a prophet or a shaman seemed to clothe him now, something more than even his priesthood.

"I need your help, Miguel."

"Always."

Steve smiled a little wryly. "Our new task will be dangerous. I am being followed."

Miguel nodded, listening and enjoying his pasta. If he ever went back to Guatemala, he was going to miss eating pasta with every meal. "I have already noted that. I was waiting to tell you until I identified them. They are from the Vatican, *Padre.*"

"I know."

"Why should your own people follow you?"

"Because of the codex. They think I know where it may be. And while they are not exactly correct, it remains that you and I have a dangerous task. We must recover it. But we must not let it fall into other hands."

Miguel paused with a forkful of linguine halfway to his mouth. His dark eyes met Steve's, and he saw certainty there. This was no joke.

"How are we to find the codex?"

"My friend tells me the trail is in France."

"Since I have never been there, I will enjoy at least some of this journey."

The smile returned to Steve's eyes. "I hope so. It may be our last."

"It will be as God wills. As you have taught me, *Padre,* we only get into trouble when we try to bend God's will to our own."

"Very true. However, I will be honest with you, Miguel. I am not certain about God's will in this matter."

It was Miguel's turn to smile. "Somehow, Steve, I have a very strong feeling that God is guiding you on every step through your life."

"That would be wonderful if it were true, but I have my doubts. I'm only a man, after all, and I can be misled as much as any other."

Miguel leaned forward, keeping his voice low. "This codex. Paloma taught us that it is very powerful. Whether that power comes from the heavens or somewhere else, it is not my place to know. But what I do know is that given its power, it must not be in the wrong hands. God would will that we recover it if for no other reason than that it will be safe in *your* hands."

Steve shook his head. "You can't know that."

"Yes, I can. Because it was to you that Paloma passed it. She knew all would be well if you held it. I need no more proof."

Steve looked uneasy, but Miguel let it go. The food was good, the mission ahead frightening, and he could do nothing except live in the moment until he needed to do otherwise.

At last Steve rose, most of his meal packed to take with him, and tossed money on the table to cover the bill. "Tomorrow," he said. "At the main station at nine."

"I will be there." A train ride to France. Not everything in life was bad.

Renate waited for the takeout meals she'd purchased for Jefe and herself, and watched the two men, one older, one considerably younger. She was troubled by the feeling that she had seen them before and told herself she had probably seen them right here, dining. She certainly came here often enough.

The past six weeks had been a whirlwind of activity that had led her nowhere. Worse, most of the action had been focused in Germany—the still unexplained death of Karl Vögel, the vote of distrust that had deposed Vögel's successor and brought Harald Müller into office, and the bombing in Hamburg—and Jefe still stubbornly refused to let Renate go there to investigate.

Lawton and Margarite were excellent agents, but they were not German. Lawton's German was improving but still spotty. While Margarite spoke the language fluently, she was not a native and was likely to miss subtle subtexts that Renate would catch. Renate knew she ought to be in Germany. She was willing to take her chances at being recognized, and she chafed at being forced to sit on the sidelines in Rome.

Worse, she knew her old companions at the BKA were botching the investigation in Hamburg. The River Police had recovered a slashed Zodiac, surely the intended means of escape for the two bombers. That it had been slashed meant that someone else had been involved in the bombing—someone who wanted to make sure that the two Lebanese men were killed at the scene and their bodies found. But the BKA, eager to soothe a frightened populace, had focused on the bombers and their known links to the virulently anti-Zionist *Hezbollah* movement.

As Renate walked through the darkened warehouse district, she could already see and hear the bitter fruits of that sort of easy investigation. The Italian government had designated this district as an Islamic protection zone. For the past week there had been steady traffic as non-Muslims moved out and Muslim families moved in. Some of the new arrivals seemed pleased at the prospect of creating a community that would reflect their ethnic and religious sensibilities. Others resented having lost nicer homes in the city and its suburbs in exchange for the promise of greater protection from the *Polizia di Stato*.

Neither they nor Renate had noticed any increase in police presence. Renate was happy enough for that; the founders of Office 119 had chosen this warehouse for its headquarters because this district was loosely monitored and their presence would attract little attention. But that would change if there was trouble.

It wasn't until she was almost back at the warehouse that she realized why she had recognized the younger man in the restaurant. In the office, she quickly passed the bag of food to Jefe and sat down at a computer, calling up old files.

"What's going on?" Jefe asked.

"I think I just saw someone the FBI was looking for."

"It's not our job."

"It is if it satisfies my curiosity. It goes back to the first case I worked with Lawton, the shooting of Grant Lawrence. I just saw a man who was involved somehow."

"Was he one of the planners?" Jefe asked.

"I'm not certain. Maybe I am wrong, but I trust my instincts. As I recall, this man was reported as killed."

A few minutes later, she sat back in her chair, perplexed. "It was this man."

Jefe leaned over her shoulder and looked. "Miguel Ortiz, one of the rebels who killed the U.S. Ambassador to Guatemala. He *was* reported dead. By Special Agent Miriam Anson." The photograph of Miguel was a mere snapshot, taken by a tourist as the assassination unfolded. "Miriam Anson was in Guatemala when they tried to capture Ortiz in the village of Dos Ojos. She saw him die. Are you sure this is the man you saw?"

Renate bit her lower lip. "Time has passed. The man I saw today was heavier. His hair was different, too. Not long and straight but short and very curly, almost African. I'd have placed him as Semitic."

"So maybe there's just a similarity. They say everyone has a double. Think about it, Renate. Miriam Anson is widely regarded as the best of the best in a field where people aren't prone to saying that."

Renate stared at the photo and shook her head. "I could swear I saw him in Rome once before—before the change in hair and weight. He was with a priest."

"Well, that's a likely combination."

She heard the humor in his voice, but she wasn't smiling when she looked up. "It's the same man. I need to let Frau Anson know he's in Rome. Something's going on."

11

Miriam Anson recognized the voice immediately, although she had heard it only once, years ago in a motel room in Montana. Renate Bächle.

"Miguel Ortiz is in Rome."

She sat back in her chair and for a long moment almost couldn't catch her breath. Her investigation in Guatemala had left her with a few lingering scars, not the least among them the memory of that awful day when she and Miguel Ortiz had ambushed and killed a rebel patrol in the jungle. She still had nightmares of paper targets blowing in the breeze, only to watch them turn to men while her bullets shredded their bodies.

She had shot and killed a man who had had a rifle trained on Grant Lawrence. She had shot and killed men in Idaho, in a firefight between a right-wing militia leader and his men and the FBI SWAT team that had been there to stop their escape from the country. But on both of those occasions, the men she had shot had been shooting back at her, or at least intending to shoot someone she was charged to protect.

In Guatemala it had been different. While she had seen these rebels kill without mercy, none had time to so much as lift his rifle during that ambush. She had shot them where they stood, their faces frozen in surprise and the awful realization of impending death.

When she had first arrived, her Guatemalan police translator and driver had said, "You will not have happy memories of Guatemala." She'd watched him die only a few weeks later, caught in the crossfire at Dos Ojos. His words had been all too prescient.

"Miguel Ortiz is dead," Miriam said quietly.

"No, he is not," Renate replied. "I saw him this morning. He is traveling with an American. And your voice tells me you are not surprised by this."

Miriam didn't answer immediately, and the fact that she hesitated spoke volumes about how her outlook had been changed in Guatemala. Yes, the U.S. Ambassador's murder was evil. But she'd also seen what the Guatemalan army, operating at the behest of the U.S. government, had done to the villagers of Dos Ojos, whose only crime had been to give birth to one Miguel Ortiz. Those same villagers had sheltered her and treated her wounds, and carried her to safety with them.

Nor were the rebels any less evil. After the raid on

Dos Ojos, the rebels knew that the government was looking for Miguel Ortiz. And Miguel knew far too much about them to be allowed to fall into police hands. So the rebels, too, had come to Dos Ojos, killing men and women and babies, pursuing the villagers through the jungle, until Miriam and Miguel had killed them in the ambush.

The only ray of hope she'd seen was Father Steve Lorenzo. God bless that man, she thought. Although Miriam was not Catholic, Father Steve had heard her confession and given her absolution. What was more, he had listened to her pain and guilt, neither justifying nor condemning her for having killed men in cold blood but simply recognizing the awful necessity of that act at that moment. No one else, except for her husband, Terry, had listened that way. The Bureau's shrink certainly hadn't seemed to understand.

Even now, sitting at her desk in the White House complex, Miriam couldn't find it easy to think of Miguel as a criminal. The murder of the U.S. Ambassador had been more an act of war than a crime, an attack on a foreign invader, for the people of Guatemala had lived with civil war for half a century, instigated by a Cold War-era CIA that saw other countries as mere pawns on a chessboard.

She shook her head. Did she really have to deal with this decision again?

Hell yes, she thought. Good God, the things she'd learned in the last few years were enough to shake bedrock. The Miguel Ortiz who had killed in Guatemala City had been a mere boy whose father had been killed by the army of his country. Grief and rage had driven him into the arms of the rebels, and with them he had struck at a symbol of the American legacy in his country.

Did she really want him in jail? Or executed? No. She had no evidence that he was engaged in anything illegal at present, and no motivation to see him punished for what had happened in the past. She had arranged for his escape then, and she saw no reason to change her mind now.

But what was he doing in Rome? Was he being set up yet again by the shadowy powers? Or hiding from them? How had he come to be there?

Steve Lorenzo.

If Miguel was in Rome, he was with Steve Lorenzo. Miriam was certain of that. But what was it Father Steve had told her in the jungle? He'd warned her about an impending religious war. He'd gone so far as to use the word "Armageddon." Steve had gone to Guatemala to look for some ancient text that, if revealed, would set off a war beyond imagining. And he didn't seem the type to give up on a quest. If the text existed, and if Steve was back in Rome, then he'd found it.

"No, I'm not all that surprised," Miriam finally said.

"Should I ask?" Renate said.

"No," Miriam replied. "Miguel Ortiz is not a threat. You have my word on that, and that is all you need to know about him."

"Too much is happening here," Renate said. "I need to know why an assassin from Guatemala has entered the scene."

The German woman was nothing if not persistent, Miriam thought. And reasonably so. But there were confidences she could not give up, and this was among them. "He is not an assassin. Not anymore. I'm sorry, but I can't say more than that."

"I understand," Renate answered.

"How is he?" Miriam asked, suddenly struck by the fact that it was Renate and not Lawton calling her.

"A few years older and a few kilos heavier," Renate said. "He looked healthy."

"Not him."

"Oh." Renate paused. "He was fine when we spoke this morning. He is on assignment."

There was something in Renate's voice. Longing? Yes. Renate missed Lawton.

"I'm sure he'll be home soon," Miriam said, trying to conceal her smile.

"It is not that," Renate said, too quickly. "And now it is I who cannot say more. Operational security."

"I understand," Miriam said. Renate's response had more than confirmed Miriam's intuitive reading. And, she thought, perhaps that was good. Lawton had been alone for far too long. "Take good care of him."

"Thank you for taking my call," Renate said.

"Stay safe," Miriam replied.

Hanging up the phone, she glanced up at the muted television screen. As it had been for the past week, the news was filled with images of European Muslim families piling their belongings into cars, pickups or trailers and heading for the protection zones. In far too many cases, people in the streets pelted them with eggs or worse as they drove away. The bombing in Hamburg had been the last straw. The city had been spared a catastrophe of ghastly proportions only because the terrorists had blown up comparatively harmless nitric-acid tanks, but no European leader was willing to pin his hopes on the terrorists making that mistake twice.

The Europeans had decided to solve their "Muslim problem," and European Union member states were implementing the new solution with chilling efficiency. On the one hand, Miriam could understand people's fear and anger. But what she saw now sickened her, calling to mind horrific images from grainy newsreels.

How much time did they have? she wondered. How long until the Islamic world struck back in force? And how long after that until the West reacted with terrifying finality, leaving mushroom clouds in its wake? They had come to the brink of that less than a year ago, when Harrison Rice was within a single word of launching a nuclear strike on an al-Qaeda base in Pakistan.

Rice had been acting under duress, pushed into the decision by a National Security Advisor who had been an agent of the banking cartel that had organized the shooting of Grant Lawrence and catapulted Harrison Rice into the Oval Office. Now Grant Lawrence held that post, and Rice seemed to have grown the kind of backbone that even Miriam could admire.

Yet did she feel safer today than she had on that afternoon in the Oval Office, when she and Grant had stared down Phillip Bentley and stopped a nuclear war?

No, she didn't. If anything, open and escalating warfare seemed more likely now than it had then. If she knew anything at all for certain, she knew that Steve Lorenzo would be on the side of peace. And he would not stand there alone.

She rose from her desk, once again feeling that steely, almost predatory resolve that made her at once admired and feared by her peers. People stepped aside as she strode through the tunnel that ran beneath the Ellipse from Building Seven to the West Wing. Someone had to calm the waters, before the whole world exploded in fire.

"Grant," she said, stepping into his office and closing the door behind her. No one except his wife had this kind of access to the National Security Advisor, but Miriam did not shirk from that. "We need to talk."

"Please, have a seat," Grant said, his blue eyes and chiseled features every bit as Redford-esque as they had been when he was running for President. "What's going on?"

"Europe is about to explode. What's more, I don't think any of this is mere coincidence."

Grant leaned forward and braced his elbows on his desk. "Tell me more, Miriam. Tell me everything."

Berlin, Germany

"We're getting nowhere," Lawton said to Margarite as they sat in the *Vorgarten* of the *Galeriecafé* Silberstein, across the street from the Judicial Centrum. Much as he loved the *Maultaschensuppe* at this café—a rich chicken broth with spinach ravioli and leeks—he had only sipped a little. Frustration was not good for his appetite. "We know those bombers weren't working alone in Hamburg. We know *Bundeskanzler* Vögel was murdered. But whoever is behind this is…*sehr sauber.*"

Margarite laughed softly. "*Oui.* Very tidy."

"Why do you laugh?" he asked.

"You're starting to think in German," she said. "I find it charming and admirable, especially as you are an American."

Lawton shook his head. He was sure there was a compliment buried in there somewhere. "And that means?"

"Most Europeans know at least two languages," she explained. "Almost all European children learn English in school, but most also study other European languages, as well. A German visiting Paris will probably massacre our beautiful language, but he will at least speak it. Too many Americans know only English."

"Well, America is a much bigger country," he said.

"You could spend your entire life traveling and never leave the U.S. In Europe, your countries are much smaller, and more people cross national boundaries more often. You need to know each other's languages."

"That is probably true," Margarite said, nodding. "Still, the reputation—fair or not—is that Americans cannot be bothered to learn the languages of others, yet expect others to learn English. And not only English, but American English."

"It's a fair criticism," Lawton agreed. "Most American children have to study a foreign language in high school or college, but only for a year or two. I took Spanish, and for a while I thought I was pretty good. Then I had an undercover assignment in L.A., and I learned just how little I knew."

"You've studied no German?" she asked.

He shook his head. "Not in school. I've used the language software at the office, of course. But most of what I know I've learned from Renate, or from getting by during my assignments here."

"Then I *am* impressed," she said.

"I still miss more than I catch," he said with a shrug. "If you weren't here, I'd be lost."

Margarite shook her head. "I doubt that."

"Regardless," Lawton said, "we're still stuck. I talked to Renate this morning. Jefe wants us to pack up and come back to Rome."

She nodded. "But?"

"I don't want to go back empty-handed."

"What do you propose?"

Lawton watched the pedestrian traffic on the Oranienburger Straße. Across the street, protesters marched in front of the Centrum Judiciaum. Some were objecting to the *Muslimschutzgesetze,* while a smaller but louder number demanded an end to the subsidies for Muslims moving into the protected zones. The atmosphere was charged with tension, and only the firm if restrained hand of the *Polizei* had thus far kept the two factions in check.

"It can't last forever," Lawton said.

"What?" Margarite asked.

"This tension," he said, nodding across the street. "Sooner or later, someone will do something. Then…"

He didn't have to finish the thought. Nor did he get the chance.

Through a crowd of antisubsidy demonstrators, he saw the flicker of flame in the instant before the Molotov cocktail arced up and over the police line, into the crowd of mostly Muslim protestors.

"Lawton, no!" Margarite cried, but too late.

He was already out of his chair, neither running nor quite walking, eyes focused on the green-striped shirt he had seen nearest the origin of the firebomb. While the crowd was surging forward, this man was casually backing away, as if content with what he had begun and looking to avoid further attention. And he *had* begun it. Of that, Lawton was certain.

The man spotted Lawton approaching and broke as if to run, but he was far too late to escape. Lawton accelerated quickly, his muscles remembering his days as a four-hundred-meter runner in college, his stride eating up the distance between them. When the man saw that he could not escape, he reached around, beneath the back of his shirt, and into his waistband, and Lawton spotted the flash of blue-black steel emerging.

Like most American boys, Lawton had played sandlot football, and now he lowered his shoulder and drove it into the middle of the man's back. The man's breath rushed out with a grunt, and Lawton heard the satisfying *crack* of a rib giving way under the impact.

Lawton's legs still churned, powering his body weight forward, his arms pinning the other man's arms against his sides, as their bodies surged together for one more stride before balance gave way to gravity and they crashed against the pavement.

Another *crack* emerged from the man's torso as Lawton landed atop him, and the arm reaching for his pistol seemed to lose its focus, now twitching as Lawton rose to his knees and wrenched the weapon from the limp hand.

Lawton did not hear the cries of "Halt!" as he twisted the man's other arm behind him. Out of instinct, Lawton reached for handcuffs he no longer carried, and he cursed as his quarry kicked weakly beneath him. Only when he looked for something with which to disable the man did Lawton see the German police officers coming toward him, their sidearms drawn, their mouths moving.

"Halt!" they said again.

Between them, he saw Margarite approaching, looking around as if searching for witnesses who might stand ready to defend what he had done. But he knew that was a vain hope. If anyone had seen what his captive had done, they were up the street, trying to force their way through the beleaguered police and add to the fray that was erupting. It would be his word against the word of the man pinned beneath him. But that man had been armed.

Lawton raised his hands, expecting the man beneath him to resume the fight as soon as he was released. But he lay there, eerily still save for weak, sucking twitches that finally attracted Lawton's notice. Carefully watching the police, Lawton moved off the man and grasped a shoulder to roll him over, but a weak scream stopped that action as soon as it was begun.

Minutes seemed to stretch like hours as Lawton knelt beside the man, trying in nerve-wracked German to explain what he had seen. The police, having heard the man's cry when Lawton tried to roll him over, made no attempt to move him. By the time the ambulance arrived and the paramedics turned him over, the man's glassy eyes merely confirmed what Lawton already knew.

He was dead.

"*Serienbruch,*" the paramedic said. Then, seeing the confused expression in Lawton's eyes, he added, "Series break. Two ribs…*nebeneinander*…adjacent. The chest wall failed. He could not inhale."

"*Er hat die Bombe geworfen,*" Lawton said, over and over to the policemen. "*Und er hatte eine Pistole.*"

When an English-speaking detective arrived, Lawton repeated it. "He threw the bomb. And he had a pistol. Why would he carry a pistol if he didn't intend to start something?"

The detective looked at the man's identification and then at Lawton. "Of course he had a pistol, Herr Caine."

"He did," Lawton insisted.

"I saw it also," Margarite said, stepping forward. "Herr Caine tackled and disarmed him."

"Oh, I believe he had the pistol," the detective said. He held out the man's identification. "But he did not throw the bomb. He was an agent for the European Security Service. You have killed a police officer, Herr Caine."

12

Rome, Italy

Although Renate took the call, Jefe saw the look of shock in her eyes. He picked up another telephone and keyed in his security code to pick up the line. He could plainly hear the anxiety in Margarite's voice. "What's going on? This is Jefe. Start at the beginning."

"Lawton has been arrested," Margarite said. "There were demonstrations at the Judicial Center. One of the anti-Muslim demonstrators threw a firebomb. Lawton thought he saw who did it and gave chase. The man tried to draw a pistol. Lawton knocked him to the ground, like in American football."

"Tackled him," Jefe said.

"Lawton was running very fast," she continued. "He broke two of the man's ribs. Lawton did not know this, and he knelt on the man's back, trying to subdue him. The man could not breathe and died."

"What aren't you telling me?" Jefe asked.

"The man was a European Security Service agent," Margarite said. "Lawton had the wrong man. He killed a police officer."

"Shit," Jefe said.

"What exactly did Lawton say?" Renate asked.

"He said the man threw the bomb, and that he had a pistol," Margarite said. "He kept repeating it."

"He actually saw the man throw the bomb?" Jefe asked.

"I'm sure he thought he did," Margarite said. "But we were across the street, and the man was in a crowd. I am not sure Lawton could see it clearly. I tried to stop him from interfering, but he was already running."

"Did *you* see the bomb thrown?" Renate asked.

"*Non.* I was sitting with my back to the street. By the time I turned, Lawton was already crossing the street, chasing the man."

"Lawton didn't get the wrong man," Renate said. "He is too good to make that mistake."

"*Oui,* he is very good," Margarite said. "But we are all human. The man Lawton saw could have been next to the man who threw the bomb. It would be impossible to be certain in a crowd."

"Yes," Renate said, "but if the man were an ESS agent and standing next to the bomb thrower…"

"I see where Renate is going with this," Jefe said. "What was the man doing when you first saw him?"

"I think walking away from the protesters who were

fighting," Margarite said. "I am not sure when I first saw him as an individual. I did not know who Lawton was after for a moment. Then this man saw Lawton and began to run."

"Toward Lawton?" Jefe asked.

"*Non*. He ran away. Always away from the protesters. When he saw that Lawton would surely catch him, he reached for a pistol. He did not have time before Lawton hit him."

"Where is Lawton now?" Renate asked.

"We are at the Section Thirty-Two police station," Margarite said. "They are holding him here. Interrogating him, I think. They will charge him with *Totschlag*. In English you would call it manslaughter. Killing without intent."

Jefe heard voices in the background. Margarite spoke quickly. "Wait, please."

"It doesn't make sense," Jefe said to Renate.

"No. Why didn't the ESS agent arrest the bomb thrower? Why was he first walking and then running away from his duty?"

"He might have been frightened," Jefe said, knowing as he said it that the answer was flimsy at best. "Perhaps he was going to call for backup."

Renate shook her head. "If that is the case, then the ESS chooses very poorly in hiring its agents. If he were BKA, he would have had a radio on his person. And he would have taken down the bomber immediately, before the suspect could disappear into the crowd."

"Any FBI agent would have done the same," Jefe agreed. "Something smells wrong here."

"Lawton did not make a mistake," Renate said firmly. "I have worked with him. He would not have relied solely on believing he had seen, from across the street, the act of a single man in a crowd. He must have seen something more or he would not have focused on that suspect."

"I am back," Margarite said. "He will appear before a judge soon for charging and his bond hearing. Then they will take him to jail. They ask if I am his attorney."

"Tell them yes, for the time being," Jefe said, grateful that Margarite had attended law school before joining the *Sûreté*. "Stay in contact. Hourly."

"*Oui*," she said. "I will. I am sorry…."

"Save the apologies for later," Jefe said, realizing immediately that his words sounded harsher than he'd intended. "Look, what's done is done. You didn't do it. Lawton did. Now we have to figure out what to do next. So stay sharp and keep us informed."

"*Oui*. They are saying I can see him now. I will call back soon. *Au revoir.*"

Jefe hung up and looked at Renate. Her pale blue eyes had faded to a frightening shade of icy gray. "Renate…"

She did not allow him to finish. "I must go to Berlin. He needs me, Jefe."

He put a hand up. "Renate, you're not a lawyer. Margarite is."

"Does she understand the German courts?" Renate

asked. "Is her German good enough to understand the intricacies of German legal speech and writing?"

"Let me think on it. You can't leave right this moment, regardless," Jefe said. Part of him knew she was right. Part of him knew she would almost certainly be recognized, her cover blown. And then, as one thought led to another, his stomach dropped. "Damn it!"

"What?" Renate asked.

"We have a bigger problem," Jefe said. "They will certainly take Lawton's fingerprints. When they realize he is American, they will send those prints to the FBI."

Renate gasped as the implication set in. "And as a former agent, of course the FBI has his fingerprints on file. Except that he is supposed to be dead."

"Miriam Anson," Jefe said, nodding. He had met her twice when they were at the Bureau, though he had never worked with her. He hoped she would remember him. "You were just on the phone with her. Get her back. Now."

"I'm on it," Renate said.

Toulouse, France

Steve Lorenzo shifted in his seat, trying to force himself to concentrate on the pages spread open in his carrel. It was difficult, however, with so much grandeur surrounding him. The Bibliothèque de Toulouse was a library in the grand gothic style, from its gleaming marble floors to the soaring dome above. Seemingly everywhere there was some detail, some niche, to catch and hold the eye and the mind.

"You are tired, Steve," Miguel said. "You need rest."

Steve nodded. "Yes, I am. And I *will* rest. But not yet, my friend. There is much to do."

Were he not so tired, Steve thought, it would not be nearly so difficult to focus. But his journey from Rome had been a two-day adventure involving three city buses and two subway trains—to shake off the surveillance—then a seven-hour bus ride to Milan, and finally a thirteen-hour train ride to Toulouse. Steve had caught only brief snatches of sleep on the train. He had arrived in Toulouse with his head foggy and throbbing in a way he hadn't felt since his one and only hangover after an all-night party in college.

Still, he felt too wired to sleep, so he had come directly to the library after finding a room at a tiny but clean inn. Morpheus would claim him tonight, but until then, he felt he must press on. There was so much he needed to learn, and with what he had read in the newspapers during his journey, he was working against a relentless and very threatening clock.

"Are not these same books in the Vatican library?" Miguel asked, pointing to the stack of volumes at Steve's elbow.

"I'm sure they are," Steve said. "The Vatican library is one of the finest in the world. But the information I need would be locked away in volumes that could only be viewed with special permission. I would have to make a formal application, and the Vatican librarian would have to investigate my *bona fides*. I can't risk that kind of scrutiny at this time, my friend."

"Why would this information be held secret? These books were on the public shelves here."

Steve smiled. "The persecution of the Cathars was not a shining moment in the history of the Church."

"What happened to them?" Miguel asked.

Steve drew a slow breath, trying to gather his thoughts. "The Cathar, or Albigensian, heresy was put down in the thirteenth century. Nearly ten thousand were slaughtered in 1209 when Simon de Montfort led the storming of Béziers. Thirty-five years later, another two hundred followers were thrown into a fire at the castle of Montségur. It was a brutal purge."

Miguel shook his head in astonishment. "But why?"

"There were religious reasons, of course," Steve said. "The Inquisition was founded to destroy the Albigensians. They did not believe in the Eucharist, or in the duality of Christ's nature. They contrasted the loving God of the New Testament and the stern God of the Old, and concluded that the Old Testament God was actually Satan. And, of course, they rejected the papacy."

Miguel nodded.

"On top of that," Steve said, "the Cathar theology venerated life. They exhorted their followers to adopt lives of poverty and charity, to share all they had with those in need rather than amassing personal wealth.

And they rejected both capital punishment and war, without exception. Teachings like that stood in stark contrast to the excesses of the Church at that point in history."

"They made the Church look bad," Miguel said.

Steve nodded. "Sadly, yes. Then there was simple greed. Pope Innocent the Third issued a proclamation that declared all Albigensian property forfeit. That is, anyone who captured Cathar land could keep it for himself. Many of France's northern nobles saw that as an opportunity to enhance their own holdings by aiding in the slaughter."

"So all of the Cathars are gone now?" Miguel asked.

"Yes," Steve said. "The last were killed over seven hundred years ago."

Miguel leaned forward. "Then why do we search here? Why do you read about them if they are all so long dead?"

"There was another mystery involved," Steve said. "It was widely believed that the Albigensians venerated the Magdalene as the bride of Christ. And contemporary writers spread rumors of a hidden Cathar treasure. That treasure was never found."

"Where did it go?"

"The better question, my friend, is what was it?"

Miguel nodded. "So? What was it?"

"No one knows for sure," Steve said. "There are some modern writers who believe the treasure was documentary evidence that Jesus of Nazareth and

Mary of Magdala had married. They believe there was no way the few fleeing Cathars could have carried away a hoard of gold or jewels. And of course this fits with pet theories that they advance in their books."

"You don't believe this?" Miguel asked.

"I've no idea," Steve said. "But I very much doubt that a document purporting to be a first-century marriage license would have been taken as proof by either side. I'm not even certain such things were documented back then. I doubt it, actually. So, no, I don't believe that was the Albigensian treasure. In fact, I don't believe they had a treasure."

"I don't understand," Miguel said. "You say the treasure is why we are here, but you do not believe it existed?"

"Look at it this way," Steve said. "If you were a French noble, the papal proclamation would play to your greed, yes? If your army captures Cathar land, you get to keep it."

"Right," Miguel said.

"But what does that mean to the ordinary French peasant who would serve in that army? *He* wouldn't get to keep any land."

Miguel's eyes widened as he nodded. "I see. So you make up a story of a treasure and tell the peasants they can keep whatever they find."

"Exactly," Steve said. "But you can't make these things up out of whole cloth. There has to be *some* basis, some local legend, which the peasants will hear repeated as they marched through Cathar lands to keep their dreams of wealth alive."

"So we are here to learn the local legends about the treasure?" Miguel said. "A treasure you believe was only legend. This still does not make sense to me."

"What if the treasure was a codex?" Steve asked.

"Like the one you found in my country?"

"Yes," Steve said. "But not *like* that one. I think it *was* that one."

"That cannot be," Miguel said, shaking his head. "Our stories tell of that codex being in my country far longer than that. It was given to us by Kulkulcan."

Steve nodded. "I doubt the Albigensians ever actually had a codex, but they had stories. Stories passed down for a thousand years, dating from the time when there *was* a codex in these lands. The codex that Mary of Magdala brought with her when she fled Palestine after the death of Christ. The codex that she gave to her daughter Sarah, and that Sarah gave to her son before he fled across the sea."

"Kulkulcan?" Miguel said.

Steve nodded. "Yes, exactly. If the Mayan histories are true, it fits."

"So you are looking for the stories of the codex, passed down to people who never had the codex," Miguel said. He shook his head and shrugged. "Why are we not looking for the codex itself?"

"The Guardians have told me that the codex was used to murder the German Chancellor," Steve said. "I am not sure whether to believe them, and they know that. They sent me here to find the proof for myself. Even if they had not, I wouldn't go into this blind again. I was sent to Guatemala to look for a document, and it turned out that I had not been sent to find a document at all. Perhaps if I had known what the codex was, and what it could do, I might have made different decisions. Perhaps Paloma might still be alive."

"Don't," Miguel said, reaching across to squeeze Steve's forearm. Miguel knew that the death of Paloma, the village *curandera* and previous keeper of the codex, still haunted his friend. "Don't blame yourself for my mistakes. You did not bring the army down upon my village. I did that. You were not the reason the rebels chased us into the mountains. I was. And you were not the one charged with protecting Paloma. That was my job, and I failed."

Steve sighed. "You blame yourself too much, as well, my friend. Regardless, I do not wish to go looking for the codex again until I know more about it. The Guardians hint that it can kill a man. To search for it now, knowing so little about it, would be like trying to defuse a bomb while blindfolded."

"So that is why we are here," Miguel said. "And you understand these books?"

Steve lifted a shoulder. "Some. It's been too many

years since I studied Latin, and even more since I studied French. But the more I try, the more starts to come back."

"Are any of the books in Spanish?" Miguel asked. "Perhaps I can help."

"Yes, one of them," Steve said, sorting through the stack. "Let me find it. But it's not modern Spanish."

"And you didn't study medieval French, I am sure," Miguel said, smiling. "So we must both…how would you say? Get up to speed?"

Steve smiled and passed Miguel the book. The library was open for another three hours. They would press on until then. After that… He tried not to think about what lay ahead. Thoughts of sleep would only distract him, and what tomorrow might bring was beyond his control.

For the moment there were these books and the mysteries they held. Mysteries he must understand if he was to play his role in the events unfolding around him.

Jericho,
c. 1200 B.C.E.

Jericho stood before the Hebrews who had fled
Egypt so many years before. If the land of Canaan was
to be truly theirs, this city must be taken. Everyone
who had been part of the original flight had died, including Moses, who had been denied even the sight
of this land by the Lord God.

Joshua had been chosen by the Lord himself to replace Moses as leader, and while he was not a weak
man, he still trembled at the memory of the day in
the tent when the column of fire had spoken first to
Moses and then to him, charging him with the sacred
duty of bringing these people to the promised land
of milk and honey despite their errors.

He bore that charge as a heavy yoke, never letting
it slip from his shoulders for even a moment. And the
Lord had been proved right, for already among the
people there were those who had chosen to worship
other gods and disobey the laws that Moses had set
down for them, even though they had seen the Ark
divide the waters of the Jordan for them.

But just now he had weightier matters on his
mind. The Lord had given him orders, and only his
faith would maintain him through this day. For
though the city of Jericho was virtually besieged by
the presence of the Israelites on the plain around it,

still the city was barred to them. The Lord had ordered Joshua to destroy the city and place a doom on it, so that never would a city arise here again.

But before that, he must take the city, and for this he also followed the orders he had received, odd as they sounded. For Joshua had long since learned never to doubt the Lord's word.

He summoned the priests to him and told them, "You must carry the Ark around the walls of the city seven times. And walking before you must go seven priests with rams' horns. For thus it has been decreed by the Lord."

Odd indeed. He passed the order among the camp and watched as the people prepared themselves. He warned them to make no noise until he commanded it; then they were to shout.

The priests performed a sacrifice of a white goat and burnt its blood upon the altar in the tent where the Ark was concealed. Joshua felt a twinge of relief that he was not needed in there, for he had seen the power of God and the power of the Ark, and he preferred to purify himself at a distance.

He also knew the contents of the Ark, for Moses had told him. Within it, along with the scroll of the law, were the *thummim* and *urim*, small pyramids of emerald and ruby. Only the purest of the priests could safely approach the Ark, because, Moses said, within the Ark the *thummim* and *urim* never slept.

Joshua hoped they were not sleeping as his priests marched boldly forward, the Ark shouldered by six of them, led by the seven trumpeters.

As commanded, the priests walked around the walls of the city, blowing the rams' horns.

Before long, however, Joshua heard the sound of another horn. Deeper, darker. Not like the rams' horns. It seemed to him to rise from the Ark itself, a sound not unlike what he had heard when he spoke with the Lord in the pillar of smoke and fire.

As the sound intensified, he saw the guards on the city walls begin to collapse. And then... And then, as the rams' horns blew loudly and the seventh circuit was completed by the priests, he lifted his hand, calling upon all his people to shout. The people obeyed, raising a deafening din until the walls of the city themselves began to shake and tremble and crack.

Before Joshua's amazed eyes, the city of Jericho began to tumble into ruins. And amidst the din, only he heard the soul-shaking sound of the trumpet from within the Ark.

Joshua, son of Nun, pulled his sword and motioned for his army to follow him. His last order must be carried out now.

"The Lord," he called to his soldiers, "has doomed this city."

And that meant only one thing: no man, woman or child would be left alive. Not even the gold and other wealth would leave this spot.

Jericho's existence would be marked only by blackened, bloody earth and tumbled stones.

For so it was ordered.

13

"Anson," Miriam said, hesitation in her voice. Her assistant had put the call through to Grant Lawrence's office, saying only that her friend was calling back. That meant Rome. Grant had ushered her into a private anteroom where she could talk.

"Is this line secure at your end?" the voice said.

"Give me a minute," Miriam answered.

She pressed a series of buttons, and the line exploded into a deafening squeal for a moment as the voice-scrambler technology sent cues across the line, then quieted as the two systems synchronized.

"I'll need a new ear now," the voice said.

"Sorry," Miriam said. "You wanted secure. So who am I talking to? This isn't Renate. And how is the weather in Rome?"

"They call me Jefe," the man said.

"Chief," Miriam said. "So you're the boss there."

"I am. And I need your help."

"Get in line," Miriam said. "With all that's going on in the world, everyone seems to want my help nowadays."

"This concerns Lawton. He's been arrested."

"No," Miriam said, her heart sinking. "What for?"

"It's a mistake, I'm sure," the man said. "But we won't get a chance to prove that once the German government faxes his fingerprints to the FBI and your people run them. Once the Germans find out they're holding a dead man…"

He didn't finish the sentence. He didn't have to. Miriam could see how those cards would play out. Lawton's cover would be blown. There would be no way to mount any legal defense without revealing his role in Office 119, and that would blow the entire organization.

"You need me to change the identification on his fingerprint file," Miriam said. "We have stock identities for undercover operators. I could swap one in."

"No can do," the man said. "We have no way to brief Lawton on a new identity. It would all come unhinged."

She had to concede the point. The stock identities were very detailed and fully documented, so much so that any government agency would find it all but impossible to crack the shell. But agents needed days of intensive study and quizzing to be confident of the details.

"What do you suggest?" she asked.

"Let the print request come back blank," Jefe said.

"Then he can stick to the identity he's using. There's no reason his prints would have to be on file."

"Passport control," Miriam said, shaking her head. "All new passports have fingerprints on them. He'd have to be on file."

"Only if he has a U.S. passport," Jefe said. "And he doesn't. He's traveling under an EU passport issued in Italy. His cover identity has dual citizenship—Italian and American—and has been living in Italy for twelve years. We have the Italian side covered. So long as the U.S. fingerprint check comes back clear, they'll assume he was never fingerprinted."

"Yes," Miriam said. "That ought to work. But it's still risky at this end. I can't expunge an FBI file and not leave tracks. At the very least, it leaves a big hole in the database. If anyone has a reason to look up Tom Lawton—and people in the Bureau will, even just in following up on his old cases—they're going to wonder why he's suddenly gone."

"You can reinsert him once this blows over," Jefe said. "What are the odds that anyone will go looking for him in the next couple of weeks?"

"Pretty slim," Miriam agreed. "So are you going to tell me what's going on?"

"Here's a number where I can be reached," Jefe said. Miriam copied it down quickly as he continued. "It's a secure line. Get back to me once you've pulled his file. We'll have time for explanations after I know he's safe."

"Yes, of course," Miriam said. The man's tone was curt, even peremptory, but she could understand the stress he was under. "I'll get back to you within the hour."

She hung up and explained to Grant that she had an urgent task, then went to her office and retrieved a map of Building Seven of the White House complex, lest she get lost en route from her office to the computer center in the basement. She had worked in this building for months and still had a hard time finding her way around. But this was not a job she was going to entrust to whoever picked up the phone downstairs. She wanted to handpick the geek who did this, because she was going to have his balls in a vise if any hint of it leaked.

Whatever Lawton had done, whatever he was up to, it had better be worth the risk.

Berlin, Germany

Lawton Caine had been in jails many times—visiting his father and later visiting suspects as an FBI agent—but he didn't know what to expect when two guards came to get him. While it was his experience that Europe was highly civilized and very conscious of human rights, he still couldn't help but remember flashes from old movies where the Gestapo interrogated a prisoner.

He knew he was being ridiculous, but he also knew how rough life could be in the U.S. for someone suspected of killing a police officer. Legal or illegal, batons had a way of slipping; prisoners had a way of falling....

It was something of a relief when he was ushered into a small room where Margarite awaited him.

"I'm your lawyer," she said in English. "For the moment, anyway. You'll have to go before the judge before the end of the day tomorrow, since you were arrested without a warrant. By then I'll have found someone well-versed in German law for you. The judge will determine whether a warrant will be issued. If not, you are free."

Lawton smiled sourly. "That doesn't look likely."

Margarite's sigh was moderately exasperated. "I *told* you not to get involved." She leaned forward, keeping her voice so low that he had to lean toward her to hear. "That is *not* our job. You are not John Wayne anymore. You are not a law enforcement officer. You have risked our entire unit with your actions."

Lawton leaned back. For the first time in his life, he felt an impulse toward violence against a woman. But he was honest enough to know that the urge rose mainly from an acute awareness that she was correct and he had been wrong. Very wrong. Impulse, however justified, had gotten him suspended at the Bureau, and impulse, however justified, had gotten him arrested in the death of a European security officer. He suspected that, without proof, it was going to matter very little that he had seen the man throw a Molotov cocktail. He might not get a murder rap, but he would probably get the next best thing.

"Do not look at me that way," Margarite said sharply. "I wasn't the one who tried to play Superman."

"I thought it was John Wayne?"

"You Americans. *Merde!* You believe your own cinema. Every man is the cavalry riding to the rescue."

"Come off it, Margarite."

"Why should I come off it, as you say? Look where you are sitting. You did not use your brain."

He couldn't exactly disagree with her. His response had been instinctive, honed by his FBI training, not the considered and careful reasoning of an intelligence agent.

"So here is how it will be," she said firmly. "Tomorrow I will bring you an able Germany attorney, so you will have proper representation. You will say you saw the man throw the petrol bomb, but you have no proof. The *Haftrichter* will most certainly decide that this case must be further investigated. He will issue the warrant."

"And then?"

She shrugged. "You can be held up to six months before trial."

"Six months!"

"Next time, think before you act. It will save us all a lot of trouble."

"That's it? That's all we can do?"

She hesitated. "I have a thought, but I must discuss it with someone who knows German law more intimately than I do. While there are many similarities between French and German law, there are of course variations. So I must speak to the expert who will represent you."

Lawton swallowed a sigh, unwilling to give her the satisfaction. "Anyway, once they look at my fingerprints, they'll find out—"

"Shh," she interrupted quietly. "They will find out nothing. Jefe is dealing with that. We *do* have resources, Lawton."

He took little comfort in that, especially since they didn't have the resources to spring him from this place. "That man was running away from the explosion. I saw him throw the bomb. What true policeman would run *away* from something like that?"

"One who was doing something he should not have been." Margarite shook her head. "But it appears you are the only one who knows that."

"Didn't you see him running?"

"You forget," she said. "I don't exist. I am already too visible. I cannot testify."

Lawton figured he could be excused for feeling very little optimism about that point. In the end, all that mattered was that he had acted on long-honed instinct, and, through mischance, instead of merely capturing the subject, he had killed him. While the death had been accidental, that didn't excuse him. He might not deserve a murder conviction, but he sure as hell deserved one for manslaughter.

He sighed and looked at Margarite. "I'm not going

to walk out of here, and you know it. It wasn't murder, but my actions led to the death of that man. There's no way around that."

She met his gaze head on. "One must never be too sure of an outcome."

But he was.

Margarite felt far more concern than she wanted to admit. She couldn't help but be troubled by the identity of the man Lawton said had thrown the bomb. Even if he had been mistaken about that part, it remained that he had chased a man who was running from the scene. That man may have been running to escape the bomb and ensuing violence. But it was not what one would expect of EU security. Lawton was right about that much.

On the way out, she stopped by the desk and said politely, "Please ensure that my client is well cared for."

The officer at the desk looked offended. "Why should we do otherwise?"

"I know that it is hard for police to deal with someone accused of harming a police officer."

The man shook his head. "The same rules apply to everyone."

"Yes, I'm sure. And in this case, there was absolutely no way for my client to know he was chasing a security officer. Indeed," she continued pleasantly, "it is surprising that a member of EU security should be fleeing such a scene."

The desk officer shifted a bit uncomfortably. "There have been many questions," he admitted.

Margarite was pleased to hear someone finally admit it aloud. "Yes," she continued pleasantly. "There are *many* questions. I am certain you are investigating."

"We have a task force."

"Excellent. Throwing a petrol bomb into a crowd is a dangerous thing. And there is one thing I am certain of: my client did not do that. I was standing beside him when it happened. So that leaves the question of why my client was so certain that the man he chased was the one who threw the bomb. And if he is correct..." She trailed off and shrugged.

The desk officer nodded. "We are required to investigate his claims of innocence as thoroughly as the claims of the officers who arrested him. Nothing will happen to your client, Madame. If you would like to bring him a change of clothes and his toiletries, you may do so. He may also have books and magazines to read. He is not guilty of any crime yet, so he is not treated as a convict in our jails."

"Of course not. I knew this. I have great faith in the professionalism of your organization."

Still smiling, she walked out of the station and onto the street. Once there, her smile faded. A few minutes later she was seated in a busy café, in a corner away from the view of most other patrons. It was then that she pulled out her phone and called Jefe.

Washington, D.C.

Dealing with the computer nerd had been easy, Miriam thought as she headed back to her office. He was well-versed in the requirements of security, and when someone in her position asked someone in his position to erase something from the records because an agent was involved in a highly covert operation, he was only too eager to oblige. In fact, he'd blushed and been downright thrilled to be part of something so important and out of the ordinary.

She'd leaned against his desk while he made the erasure and asked, "You guys get ignored a lot, don't you?"

He shrugged as if it didn't matter. "We're supposed to be invisible."

"Until there's a crisis of some kind."

At that his face lit up. "There are times when we have people breathing down our necks to acquire information faster. Sometimes it even gets exciting for *me*. But basically we're just a communications node. The big agencies do the work."

"But a communications node is essential," Miriam said, watching his nimble fingers dance on the keyboard. "The President relies on you to keep information flowing. Heck, so does my agency. Think how much time we'd waste without you, having to send couriers back and forth. No, you're at the very heart of America's security."

He'd puffed up a bit at that and grinned at her.

Then she'd added, "No one but you knows about this, and if it gets out, an agent's life could be endangered." She hadn't needed to say another word. He had squared his shoulders and nodded his understanding. Under Harrison Rice, no one would dare to compromise the identity of an undercover operative.

Lawton's fingerprints had disappeared from the national database within seconds. The geek had the clearance to do darn near anything he wanted, and removing fingerprints had been a surprisingly easy thing to do, compared to some.

"It's easy," the young man said, "because no one thinks anyone would do it. From our side of the wall, security is actually minimal, mostly designed to prevent accidental erasures. On the other side of the wall, it's as impenetrable as we can make it." He went on at some length about how things were set up to protect the national fingerprint database, while still making it possible for someone with his clearance to modify that database, all of it revolving around covert operations and a whole bunch of computer terms Miriam didn't pretend to understand.

Still, she had stood there nodding and listening with every evidence of total attention until he assured her that Tom Lawton's prints were gone. Completely. Not simply protected from access, but utterly erased.

Then she had patted his shoulder, told him that she was impressed with his expertise and would put in a good word for him.

Still, when she finally sat at her desk again, her stomach was in knots. She had acted out of necessity, but she had no doubts what would happen if anyone ever found out what she'd done. She might have violated the law. She wasn't sure, and she wasn't sure she wanted to know.

She still struggled sometimes with the greater secret threats facing her country and her world. Even after all she had learned, a part of her wanted to return to her old view of how global power worked. But she knew she couldn't, and that was why she had erased Lawton's prints, which would be replaced later with some other man's. It had been justified. But she still felt queasy. Never in her life would she have imagined manipulating a national database without explicit authorization.

She drew a steadying breath and looked around her office, reminding herself of her position. A year ago, if she had received direct authorization from the Director of National Intelligence, that would have been enough. Now she *was* the DNI. Her position authorized her to protect Lawton. He'd been a highly valuable asset to the United States even after his faked death had ended his FBI career. He had helped her to crack the plot to kill Grant Lawrence, as well as to stop Phillip Bentley from maneuvering the President into a nuclear war. She was not only entitled to protect him, she was obligated to do so.

But butterflies still twittered uncomfortably in her belly.

Finally she sighed, trying to release the tension, and punched the intercom that connected her to the assistant outside who was her gatekeeper, guardian and dexterous right hand. "Jacob? Please ensure that I'm undisturbed for the next ten minutes."

"Yes, ma'am."

Then she picked up the secure phone, switched on the scrambler and called the man she knew only as Jefe.

"It's done," she said without preamble when he picked up the phone. "Now, tell me what's going on."

14

Berlin, Germany

Seven years away was long enough to make Berlin feel both familiar and strange. Renate strolled the street toward the general area of yesterday's riot, her blond hair carefully hidden beneath a dark wig, her eyes invisible behind sunglasses, although the day's light was watery and pale, filtered through clouds.

Berlin was a large city, and in theory she should have been able to walk these streets anonymously, even without a disguise. But the Frankfurt Brotherhood knew she was still alive, and she couldn't afford to rely on simple measures.

That led her to the sunglasses and wig, and her uncharacteristic dress: an American ballcap, a red sweatshirt proclaiming her a fan of some team called the Buccaneers, battered jeans and jogging shoes, and a backpack that seemed to be one day short of the trash heap. Gretchen Zeitgenbach would not have dressed this way, and neither would Renate Bächle.

As that thought filtered through her brain, anger and frustration began to choke her. Spying a bench, she sat on it, fists clenched, trying to regain her self-control. Self-control was all that was left to her, that and a sense of mission. But right now both deserted her, and her throat tightened with all the feelings she couldn't ordinarily allow herself.

Her best friend had died in an accident intended to kill her. She would never have a friend like that again. No one to whom she could turn with a thought or feeling and see immediate understanding. She couldn't afford that kind of closeness anymore. When the Brotherhood had killed her friend, they had killed her, too, in a way. They had killed an ordinary future that involved friends, marriage, children. They had truncated her humanity and her womanhood, and left nothing but ashes in her soul.

She hated them for that. Hated them for killing her family in the Black Christmas bombings in an attempt to draw her out. As the hate filled her, overruling every other sense, her vision darkened and her surroundings retreated into some distant place, leaving her with only the black crater inside herself.

At that moment she couldn't have said who she hated more: the Brotherhood or Office 119, which had caused her to sandwich herself into an impenetrable box of calculating cool in order to perform an unquestionably important mission. The emotional amputations had wounded her as much as the personal losses.

Several trams passed by, at first only a distant noise and bustle as people boarded and descended nearby. But eventually her surroundings returned to clear focus, and the rage settled into the cold place inside her, the place that would never be warm again.

Drawing a deep breath, she tipped her head back and closed her eyes, wondering if returning to Berlin had triggered this reaction, or if something else had.

Then Lawton Caine's face popped into her mind, reminding her that she had come here for a reason. He was in jail. Much as she had tried to tell herself he was just a colleague, apparently that wasn't the full truth.

She was afraid of losing another friend.

Shaking her head, she rose to resume her walk.

At Centrum Judiciaum on Oranienburger Straße, she paused near a café and looked across the way at the area where the riot had occurred only yesterday. Police tape still marked off the area where the Molotov cocktail had struck, marked by broken glass and a black spot on the pavement. Dark, coppery stains and tape marks left no doubt what had happened after the bomb had exploded. Seventy meters away, another taped outline marked the end point of Lawton's pursuit. She forced herself to note all the details clinically, even though objectivity kept trying to desert her.

And still there were protesters. Some were protesting the relocation, others the subsidies, and others the violence of the protests themselves.

Little, she found herself thinking, ever really changed. She distrusted the *Muslimschutzgesetze,* and while she was not surprised that some Germans supported them, she was disappointed that they were bold enough to show their bigotry on a public street. She considered that she might be unfair in this judgment, that some of those protesting in favor of the laws were sincere in their belief that this was the only way to end the cycle of violence, and that once things calmed down the Muslims would be allowed to move freely again through Europe.

But it ought to have been obvious, she thought, that this would not be the case. For those who relocated were not only giving up their homes but often their jobs, as well. In a pattern common to immigrants, many had opened small shops and other businesses, which they were now being forced to abandon. Even if the protection laws were lifted, they would have nothing to go back home to. No matter how much Soult might talk of it being a temporary measure, it was a permanent upheaval for those involved.

And then there was the stigma of belonging to an ethnic group singled out for special "protection." Muslims who had lived and worked for years with non-Muslims were now unavoidably cast as "others." Once having made that distinction, it would be all but impossible to return to being simply Hans and Ibrahim, two men who worked at the same factory, lived in the same neighborhood, ate at the same restaurants and cheered for the same football clubs.

Renate understood the late chancellor's willingness to pull Germany out of the EU. While the new administration was offering housing subsidies, she knew there was no way to compensate for the other losses that German Muslims would endure in the relocation. This was not a solution.

Still, she was torn. She was a German by birth and by heritage, and whatever had happened in her life, she would always be German. Yet she believed in the ideals of the EU and did not want to see it torn apart. But her first loyalty was now to Office 119 and the United Nations, which thus far had characterized Soult's plans as "an unfortunate but temporary response to growing civil unrest."

Glancing at her watch, she discovered she still had time to get to the courthouse before Lawton was scheduled to appear before the judge. At a café, she stopped to order coffee and a roll before she continued her stroll east to Littenstraße and the Amtsgericht Mitte, the courthouse for the *Mitte* district of Berlin.

It would be nice, she thought as she sipped the familiar German coffee, if she could expect to see both Margarite and Lawton emerge from that building, but she suspected only Margarite would appear. Lawton's position was too difficult to allow for easy resolution.

She frowned down into her cup and tried to ignore the sinking sensation in the pit of her stomach. It frustrated her beyond description to be unable to help Lawton, and it seriously concerned her that Jefe had asked Margarite to stand in as Lawton's lawyer. A German lawyer had since been called in, but Margarite could still muddle things if she was not careful.

For reasons Renate had never been able to pin down, she had never liked Margarite. Nor did she like the way those feelings were magnified by Margarite's involvement in this mess with Lawton. Or maybe they were magnified by Lawton's involvement with Margarite.

She understood full well that she couldn't afford to have personal feelings in this business, beyond collegial friendship, but Lawton had somehow struck a chord in her that was different. She was not in love with him. That would be both impossible and dangerous. Still, she felt a special bond with him.

And something about Margarite irritated her to death. The two of them tried to pass it off as a joking tension between a German and a Frenchwoman, but at some level it was more than that.

Sighing, her appetite totally destroyed, she left her half-finished coffee and untouched roll on the table, and paid the check. Moments later she was walking toward Littenstraße with the easy stride of someone who loved to spend her vacations hiking in the mountains. Two kilometers. If she wanted to, she could run that distance without getting out of breath.

She eased past the demonstrators, noting that police were keeping the groups well separated, then increased her pace again. Everyone had a point, she thought as their chants and cries followed her down the street. They were all right, and all wrong, in their own ways. Only one thing was certain. The violence must end.

Margarite introduced Lawton to Horst Wieberneit just before the hearing. Horst was a tall, lean man with graying temples and bright, youthful eyes. "Herr Wieberneit will be representing you. He and I have discussed a small plan, which may work."

"A plan for what?"

Margarite looked at Wieberneit, who nodded to her. She turned again to Lawton. "Under the law, you were arrested without a warrant, yes?"

"Yes."

"Under the same law, *anyone* can make such an arrest if he witnesses a crime occur. Herr Wieberneit will argue that you were attempting to make an arrest of a person you believed responsible for throwing the petrol bomb. What happened thereafter was purely accidental."

Wieberneit nodded, then spoke in gently accented English. "The judge will, I am certain, take the argument under consideration before he issues a warrant. However, he will not dismiss the case today, and you will probably not receive bail. For you see, you have no domicile here. You are clearly American. You will be considered a flight risk because of that and the nature of the crime of which you are suspected."

"So you think the judge will issue the warrant?"

"Yes, and he will remand you to custody. But once we make this claim in your defense, the prosecution must then investigate it and must disprove it before you can be convicted. And German jails are better than yours, so you will be comfortable."

"Oh, really?" Lawton tried to keep the sarcasm from his voice and wasn't sure he succeeded.

"Most certainly. Until you are convicted, you are not a prisoner. You are simply a suspect awaiting trial. You are entitled to have a cell to yourself and to make it comfortable, within reason. You may wear your own clothes."

"I was wondering when I was going to get the orange jumpsuit," Lawton said.

"That will not happen unless you are convicted," the attorney said. "And given your reasonable belief that you were attempting to arrest a criminal, I believe we should not worry too much about that just now."

But Lawton *did* worry. He'd killed a cop. In any country, in any language, in any justice system, that was not a charge one simply walked away from.

Rome, Italy

Ahmed Ahsami watched the telecasts of the riots all over Europe, accompanied by heartrending film of Muslim families being moved to "safe" districts. Europeans hailed the move as a solution to the violence, insisting they did not have enough police to protect Muslims who were scattered everywhere. An interesting rationale, especially given that most of the Muslims in Europe already clung together in closely knit communities, most often because they felt so unwelcome in society at large.

Was he the only one who could see the dangers here? As directed by his superior, who was already on the phone, he started a conference call to Monsignore Veltroni. He did not tell Veltroni that Sheik al-Hazeer was also on the line. "Must I take action?" he asked.

For a few beats the *Monsignore* didn't answer. "That depends on what you're talking about and what kind of action you intend. Violence only begets violence, my friend. You know that as well as anyone. At the moment, there is far too much violence."

"I am not speaking of violence. I can see there is enough of that. I also see the beginnings of concentration camps. I see Western commentators suggesting that Islamist extremists were behind the death of the German chancellor, when Mr. Vögel was perhaps the last, best friend we had in Europe. European broadcasts show only Islamic youths rioting. Yet on Al Jazeera I see the Muslim neighborhoods under attack."

Veltroni sighed, a heavy sound that crossed many miles of phone line and satellite. "Allow me to say that you are wrong about one thing, my friend."

"And what is that?" Ahsami snapped.

"Chancellor Vögel was not the last, best friend you had. There are others. Many others."

"Please introduce me to them," Ahsami said. "I see crowds cheering the warehousing of Muslims in ghettos. I do not see friends."

"And yet you called me," Veltroni said.

"Your church stood by while one Holocaust happened," Ahsami said. "Why would you not do the same again?"

"Do not believe every wild accusation you read," Veltroni replied. "Even if the Church did not do everything it could to protect the Jews in the last century, there were many priests and church leaders who *did*. And we have all learned the lessons of inaction. Even now, many of our parishes are opening food lockers and stores of clothing and furnishings to help Muslims who are being forced to move. And have no doubt that there are many of us who wish to speak to the Holy Father about this. Remember that he is a German who saw the Holocaust happen at his doorstep. I myself am going to Germany to learn more about the situation."

"You cannot ask me to sit and do nothing while my brethren are herded into filthy slums," Ahsami said.

"Then perhaps it is time for you to come out of the shadows, my friend," Veltroni said. "Let the world know who and what *Saif Alsharaawi* is. If you wish to speak with a voice of peace for all Muslims, you cannot continue to do so in whispers."

"I wish it were that simple, *Monsignore*."

"There is much that you are not telling me."

The tenor of Veltroni's voice left an unspoken question but also made clear that he did not expect an answer. Nor could Ahmed afford to give him one. No, he would have to work first on his own people. Veltroni was right. Sooner or later, *Saif Alsharaawi* must speak not in whispers but with a clear and certain voice.

"Yes," Ahmed said. "Please accept the thanks of all Islam for what your churches are doing on our behalf. And I beseech you to exhort your leaders to do all that they can. People who feel they have nothing to lose become most dangerous. We do not want that to happen."

"Of course," Veltroni said. "These are difficult times, my friend. For all of us. The Lord be with you."

"*In Sh'Allah,*" Ahmed replied. Then he cut the connection to Veltroni, leaving himself alone on the line with the sheik.

"You handled that well," Sheik Youssef al-Hazeer said. "Perhaps it will hurry them along. Now, tell me the status of our preparations."

"We have teams standing by in Vienna, Rome, Marseilles and Barcelona," Ahmed said. "They are prepared to respond to any attacks in the Muslim neighborhoods. But you know I believe that such a response would do more harm than good. We will do nothing but prove to those who hate us that we are a fifth column in their midst."

"We cannot stand by while our European brethren are oppressed," al-Hazeer said. "If *Saif Alsharaawi* will not come forward in their aid, then what is our purpose?"

"As you say," Ahmed said.

In truth, he had doubts abut the sheik's true agenda. *Saif Alsharaawi* had been founded as an instrument of peace, a means by which to both resist Western oppression and also curb the excesses of fanatics who twisted Islam into an excuse for hatred and murder. Now, it seemed, al-Hazeer was trying to encourage those very factions.

"We will have to rely on the Roman Church for help," Ahmed said. "They are our best allies right now."

The sheik made a negative sound. "In the end, my friend, we cannot depend on the fidelity of infidels. We must stand ready to defend ourselves, wherever they may strike."

Ahmed rose from his chair. *"A'Salaam Aleikum."*
"Aleikum salaam."

Ahmed hung up the phone, wondering if Sheik al-Hazeer really meant to wish Allah's peace upon his Islamic brothers. The phrase of greeting and parting was more than mere ritual. It was a prayer, a fervent wish that Allah would bring all Muslims together in a world of peace and light.

For all that Westerners, and far too many Muslims, misread the words of the Prophet—peace be upon him—true Islam was a discipline of the self, a bending of one's own will to the will of Allah, a willingness to sacrifice one's earthly whims, and even life itself, in order to be a fitting servant to the One True God. The *Qur'an* stated that if a man killed another, except as punishment for murder, it was as if he had killed all of mankind. And if a man saved a single life, it was as if he had saved all of mankind. To surrender one's own life to save that of another was to guarantee for oneself an eternity in the arms of Allah.

After the Black Christmas bombings, Ahmed had recruited Sheik al-Hazeer. At the time Ahmed had been worried about the betrayal he had experienced from outside financiers and wanted Arab money he could count on. Al-Hazeer had readily signed on, providing any necessary sums of money, and had seemed to agree with Ahmed's goals.

Too much of what Ahmed had attempted to accomplish had been undone by others. His carefully laid plans for a bold declaration of strength and peace had been turned into the horror of Black Christmas. And his every attempt to rescue that situation by bringing the betrayers to justice had been usurped by others, denying *Saif* the clear, unambiguous victory it needed to step forward and claim its place on the world stage.

Now, as the money man, al-Hazeer was running *Saif*. Worse, al-Hazeer was a Wahhabist Sunni. And while he was not as extreme as some in that sect, he had lately made it clear that in his mind, the Shi'a ascendancy in the Middle East, and not the treatment of Muslims in Europe, was the greatest danger Islam faced. For decades, Middle Eastern Sunnis had kept the Shi'a in check with a firm and even brutal hand. It was only to be expected that, as the Shi'a had asserted political power in Iran and now Iraq, they would look for revenge on their former oppressors. That cycle of violence—too often ignored by Western media who lumped all Muslims into one pot—now threatened to flare up into a regional conflict in which Sunni and Shi'a battled for dominance.

If al-Hazeer saw this conflict as the primary threat, and if his Wahhabist beliefs conditioned him to see a more forceful crackdown on the Shi'a as the only solution, then he was working an agenda that left little room for Ahmed to maneuver in Europe. Or anywhere, for that matter.

But Ahmed didn't see any easy options. *Saif* remained invisible largely because al-Hazeer provided much of its funding out of his own very deep pockets. Without that funding, Ahmed knew, *Saif* would have to go to a more public well. Twenty years ago, his organization could have raised money in local mosques across Europe and the U.S. without attracting attention. Nowadays, if a father in Cairo sent a wedding gift of a few hundred dollars to his son in Los Angeles, both the U.S. and Egyptian intelligence services would know it, and the transaction would be pored over down to the last detail.

No, there was no way to depose al-Hazeer in the *Saif* hierarchy. As Ahmed watched the unfolding ugliness on his TV, he knew he would have to outmaneuver al-Hazeer, to retain his support without allowing him to pervert *Saif*'s holy mission.

Of course, if he could think of this, al-Hazeer could think of it also. At this same moment, al-Hazeer was most certainly calculating how he might outmaneuver Ahmed.

And that made the game all the more dangerous.

15

"You're sure it was this table?" Renate asked, watching the traffic on Oranienburger Straße.

"I am certain," Margarite said. "He was sitting in the same chair you are sitting in right now."

It had been a week to the hour since Lawton's arrest, and Renate and Margarite had come to the *Galeriecafé* Silberstein, trying to assess Lawton's story. From the *Vorgarten,* Lawton would have had a clear view of the demonstration in front of the Centrum Judiciaum, apart from pedestrians and, of course, the street traffic. While there was no tram line along Oranienburger Straße, there was bus service, and the traffic was steady, if not heavy.

"We cannot be certain that Lawton saw the right man," Margarite said. "A bus or van or panel truck could have blocked his view at the key moment. Even if it did not, he had to pick out a single actor in a crowd."

"I can see the problems." Renate's voice was thick with impatience, especially since Margarite, in typical fashion, was criticizing Lawton's observational abilities as if he were just some man on the street instead of a trained law officer. "In the end, it doesn't matter if you believe Lawton saw what he claims. We are not neutral parties here. We *must* develop evidence that he acted with good reason, even if we think he may have been mistaken."

"Yes, of course," Margarite said a bit testily. "I am not ignorant of our aims, Renate."

"*Es tut mir leid,*" Renate said, hoping she sounded as if she meant it. *I'm sorry.* "It's just that...."

"You are worried for Lawton," Margarite said. "As am I. But for you it is...different."

"What are you saying?"

Margarite shrugged. "You fancy him. It is not surprising. He is a handsome man."

Renate shook her head in disgust. She hardly needed Margarite to tell her what she already knew. She wasn't sure if she was more angry at Margarite for saying it—or at herself for being so transparent.

"Yes, Lawton is a good man," Renate said. "I brought him into Office 119, and I feel a certain responsibility there. But I have no designs on him. Such a relationship could never work in our organization."

"*Pfft,*" Margarite uttered with a wave of her hand. "You are a woman. He is a man. The two of you obviously connect at many levels. What cannot work?"

Renate rose and dropped a ten-Euro bill on the table. "I don't need this, Margarite. We must focus on the case."

"And what, exactly, is the case?" Margarite asked, following her. "Lawton and I came here to find out what happened to Chancellor Vögel. We still don't know. Now Lawton's in jail. Do we focus on Vögel? Or on Lawton?"

They walked along the street, and Renate lit a cigarette. She'd quit smoking years ago, while she was recovering from the auto accident that had killed her best friend. That accident had also led to her being reported as dead and her new life at Office 119. She felt no urge to smoke when she was in Rome, but whenever she was back in Germany, the old cravings arose again. She knew she would never spend more than a few days at a time in her homeland, so she did not resist. Margarite also lit up, and they walked together in silence for a moment.

"You trust Lawton, don't you?" Renate asked.

"I am French," Margarite answered with a shrug, as if that explained every mystery of the universe.

"It's not going to work, is it?" Renate said, drawing on her cigarette.

Margarite's brow furrowed. "What do you mean?"

"The European Union," Renate said. "The UN. Even Office 119 and its assumption that stateless, 'dead' people will have no allegiance besides the agency. You answer personal questions with 'I am French,' and here in Germany I know that, for at least a few days, I am back home. They were accidents of birth. You were born in France and I in Germany. But everything that happened afterward—all of the cultural indoctrination—that was no accident. And we could no more change that than we can transform ourselves into eagles or fish."

"That is true," Margarite said. "But consider how far we have come. Seventy years ago, our conversation would have been colored by the certainty that our nations would soon be at war again. Now we share a common currency and an open border, a common declaration of human rights and a hope for the future."

Renate nodded. "Perhaps. And yet the French voted against the EU constitution."

"Not really," Margarite said. "We voted against our government. You read the newspapers, Renate. You know what our unemployment rate is, especially for our young people. Many of our brightest have simply given up. They feel hopeless, and the French government hasn't helped. The government supported the EU constitution, so we voted against it, just to tell them we were angry with them."

"Knowing that the *non* would not change anything," Renate said with a faint smile.

"Exactly," Margarite agreed. "That draft constitution simply collected into a single document the agreements that already existed under separate treaties. Those treaties still exist. The Union still exists. The vote did no harm except to the prestige of our own leaders."

"I wonder if the vote would be different now that Soult is President of the European Commission."

"*Oui,*" Margarite said. "Of course it would. Many of my countrymen are still very parochial. They would gladly support a unified Europe if they were certain France would be always at its head."

Renate stopped and turned. "Always." She repeated the world slowly.

"What?" Margarite asked.

"I said the vote might be different because Soult *is* the European president. *Is* as in *now*. Present. But you said 'If they were certain France would *always* be at its head.'"

"What are you thinking?"

Renate shook her head, hating the feeling that something was hovering just out of reach. "I'm not sure yet."

She walked on, smoking absently, barely aware of Margarite or the traffic around her, allowing the swirl of vague thoughts in her mind to congeal into something she could wrap words around. When the thoughts finally began to settle, she and Margarite were at a *Straßenbahn* station.

"Where are we going?" she asked, realizing she'd been following alongside Margarite while lost in her reverie.

"We're going to see Frau Doktor Ulla Viermann again," Margarite said. "I know where your thoughts are turning."

"Please tell me," Renate said with a short laugh. "I need all the help I can get."

"Should Germany provide the *Leitkultur* for Europe?" Margarite asked.

Renate shook her head as they boarded the tram. The Nazis had tried to establish a single guiding culture for Europe, an attempt both misguided and evil. "No, of course not. Europe does not need a *Leitkultur.* I think our many cultures make us stronger, more colorful, and give us more opportunities to learn from each other."

"You attempted to impose a *Leitkultur* during the war," Margarite said.

It sounded less like an accusation than a historical assessment, and a correct assessment at that. Much as part of her was tempted to bristle at the criticism, Renate saw the truth and simply nodded. "Yes, we did. It didn't work well—for anyone."

"*Oui.* And I suspect most Germans would agree with you, Renate. But in France…we are *La Grande Nation.* We have the finest food, the finest wine, the finest literature, the finest culture."

Renate was unsure if Margarite was being sarcastic, so she simply nodded in agreement, letting the other woman continue.

"I am not saying that France should rule Europe," Margarite said. "But I was taught to believe that all of Europe would benefit from being a bit more French in its outlook. I still believe that, in many ways."

"The arrogant French," Renate said, trying to soften the words with her tone.

Margarite shrugged. "It is a fair criticism in many ways. We *are* perhaps more arrogant. Our culture is more centralized than most others in Europe. We were a united country, with a king in Paris, when Germany and Italy and even Britain were still broken into regional city-states. We came to see Paris as the height of culture, the center of the world, the ideal to which all should aspire."

"Yes, that's true," Renate said. The idea she couldn't quite reach was at last beginning to take shape. "And now we have Soult talking about a unified Europe standing together against the Islamist menace. But he speaks more often in Paris than in Strasbourg, and always in French."

"Keep going," Margarite said, nodding, appearing to understand that Renate was reaching for an idea beyond their present conversation.

"Germany was standing in his way, under Herr Vögel. He refused to implement the *Muslumschutzgesetze.* Then Herr Vögel is killed and the laws are enacted."

"Convenient for Monsieur Soult, *non?*" Margarite asked. Now her voice expressed an undercurrent of excitement. "And why is Soult, a retired general with no prior political experience, the President of Europe?"

"Strasbourg," Renate said. "He was the hero who saved the institutiones européens. He put his own life at risk, carrying the pipe bomb out of the building."

"Yet he was only barely injured when it exploded in his hands," Margarite said.

"Ja, ein Wunder." Yes, a miracle.

"Or so we were told by the press afterward," Margarite said. "Remember the headlines? 'Soult saves EU Parliament from bomb attack.' But we know the truth. Kasmir al-Khalil was paid by the Frankfurt Brotherhood. The same people who paid for Black Christmas. The people with him—the people who were supposed to kill him after the attack—they were Europeans. You said that the early rioting against European Muslims was a *Kristallnacht.*" Margarite's words now came so rapidly they nearly tripped over one another. "Renate, if that is true, then what happened in Strasbourg was the equivalent of the Reichstag fire."

At that, Renate's thoughts came into clear focus. "Soult *knew* the bombs were going to be there. He knew the cameras would be there. He knew which bomb to pick up. He knew he wasn't going to be injured by the blast. He was swept into office on a tide of public adoration, with his Europa Prima Party at the helm. But the violence doesn't stop. The Paris mosque is burned. Herr Vögel is killed. In case that was not enough to ensure the cooperation of Vögel's replacement—a man whose election was guaranteed by the support of Soult's party—two chemical storage tanks are blown up in Hamburg."

"Which kill only a handful of people but terrify

everyone," Margarite said. "The television experts talk of how much worse it might have been. But it wasn't."

The two women stood face to face now, ideas jumping back and forth between them like lightning.

"And of course there are two dead Muslims right at the scene, to ensure the blame is placed correctly."

Margarite nodded. "But no mention is made of why they were stranded there, with their getaway boat ruined."

"It was Strasbourg all over again," Renate said. "A Muslim face on which to pin the blame, but the strings were pulled elsewhere. From the beginning, this has all been...orchestrated."

"All to justify the Muslim protection zones."

Renate shook her head. "No. To what end? What do the Muslim protection zones accomplish?"

"Ethnic cleansing," Margarite said. "Did Milosovic need another reason? It's the dirty little secret of the post-colonial age. People use the opportunity to settle old scores. It happened in Rwanda. It's happening still in parts of Africa."

"*Das stimmt,*" Renate said. *That makes sense.* "But it doesn't fit here. What old scores do we have to settle?"

"Munich. Air France. New York. Bali. Madrid. London. Black Christmas. Prague. Need I go on?"

"Black Christmas, Prague, Strasbourg and Hamburg were staged, though, if we are correct." Renate paused for a moment, thinking. "Let us assume you are correct.

Soult is not simply reminiscent of Hitler. He is *consciously* following Hitler's script."

"*Oui.*"

"Hitler needed the Jews as *die Andersartge*." She searched for an easy translation. "The different ones. The others. Someone to blame for the problems in Germany. Then he could institute new laws to 'protect' Germany from that alleged threat. People accepted the new laws because they were applied against *die Andersartge*. But once the laws were in place, he could turn them against anyone he wanted. And anyone who might have considered resisting remembered what was being done to the Jews. Power through fear, and then through intimidation."

Margarite nodded. "It makes sense. Soult is using European Muslims the way Hitler used European Jews. And it is even easier for Soult, because Islamic extremists *have* committed so many heinous acts. People are ready to blame Islamic terrorists whenever something awful happens. And all the while, the people grow accustomed to the yoke of a government that, it says, is only trying to protect them. It is like the frog in the pot of warming water."

Renate bit her lip, angry that she had not seen this pattern before. Many critics had likened Soult to Hitler, and even she had seen some parallels, yet she had missed the purposeful planning within those parallels. They were not mere coincidence nor the inevitable byproduct of a man with ambitions of dictatorship. It was intentional.

Soult had searched through history for a pattern to follow in taking over Europe and found one. Then he had begun to follow that pattern, step by step. And so far it was working.

"There's a missing piece," Renate said, gnawing her lip as she thought. She turned over the dusty vaults of history she had studied through her life. "Hitler could not have risen to power without Ernst Röhm."

"He was the leader of the Brownshirts, yes?"

Renate nodded. "The *Sturmabteilung*. Storm troopers. It was a private militia. Hitler used the SA as a pawn to organize the early violence against the Jews, as well as to intimidate or kill political opponents, without directly involving himself and without having to cut deals with the army generals."

"So who is Soult's Ernst Röhm?" Margarite asked.

"Exactly. Who were the men in Strasbourg that day? The men we killed in the park? Who was this Lezeta, the man Lawton said threw the firebomb outside the Centrum Judiciaum? We need to dig into their pasts. If our theory is right, there will be a connection. And that connection will be Soult's Röhm."

Margarite hesitated. "You know how insane this sounds?"

Renate nodded grimly. "As insane as the fact that the man who threw the firebomb into that crowd turned out to be a member of the European security service."

Margarite gasped. Renate could almost see the pieces

click into place in her fellow agent's eyes. Any lingering doubt vanished.

"We must find Soult's Röhm," Margarite said. "If we find him, then we will have Soult."

Béziers, France
1209 C.E.

The old *bonne femme* worked alone, by the flickering light of candles. Her task was an important one, and she hadn't much time to complete it. Soon, all too soon, the Catholic army would storm the city. Her days had been long on this earth, and she carried secrets that she had never whispered to another. But those secrets could not be allowed to die with her.

The city of Béziers ought to have been secure against attack, and it would have been, but for the small crystal pyramid carried by the enemy commander, Simon de Montfort. Tomorrow, if her dreams were true, Montfort would turn to Arnaud Amaury, his papal legate, and ask how he could tell the faithful from the heretics once he entered the city.

"Kill them all. God will know his own," the legate would reply.

Montfort would lift the crystal pyramid, and the guards at the city gates would begin to suffocate even as they drew air into their lungs. Their deaths would horrify those who witnessed them. With that, the same faint trumpet sound that had shattered the walls at Jericho would shatter them here. Then the massacre would be underway.

The *bonne femme* had never seen the pyramid. Her ancestors had once possessed a similar pyramid, over a thousand years ago, but the legends told that it had been carried across the sea, far from the hands of those who would use it to destroy. Perhaps it might be found someday. Perhaps not. As she thought about what was to happen on the morrow, she wished that the four pyramids had never been handed down to man. For man was not ready for such power. Yes, that power could be used for great good. But it could also be used for great evil, and it was the nature of man to find evil long before he even thought to search for good.

She had to confess a certain excitement. For thirty years she had searched the sinuous fibers of time and space for the pyramid that was now less than a league beyond the city wall. Her search had been shaped and guided by the *gardiens rêveurs*. She called them "dream guardians," for never had she met any of them face to face. Yet they had shaped her life far more than the other *bons chrétiens*—good Christians—with whom she lived. Her life had been committed to both causes—to creating a purer society in the model of the Magdalene, and to learning and preserving the ancient secrets of the *gardiens*. If she had given more to the latter than to the former, it was because they were fewer in number and had greater need of her efforts.

Yet on this night, the two causes stood in stark opposition. She could speak to the city commanders with authority, assemble a raiding force to sally out beyond the walls, and perhaps even seize the pyramid before Montfort could lift it to destroy her city. In so doing, she could save her own life and the lives of her fellow citizens. But she would reveal a secret she had sworn to keep unto death and perhaps loose on the world a greater horror than the one she prevented. For while her companions in the city were indeed *bons chrétiens,* she had no doubt that they could be as perverted by power as the men in Rome.

And so she chose fidelity to the *gardiens.* In time, a just and loving God might forgive her choice, for surely He could see the greater good in what she must do. She must preserve these secrets, weaving them subtly into a diary that perhaps no one would ever read, although she had been assured that, in the fullness of time, there would come one who would read her words and grasp their significance.

She filled the pages with riddles and allegory, knowing that to most they would be only the ravings and fears of an old woman who knew that her death was at hand. Only the one who knew what to look for would see through those riddles to the truth she was passing on. And he would need that truth, in his own time, to shatter an evil greater than the one that stood outside her city.

The candles were guttering by the time she finished. Already the sky lightened in the east. It would be her last sunrise, and she stepped out onto her roof to watch it. It was a cruel sunrise, painted in shades of blood and gold and flickers of bile. And yet it was what was given her, and she felt an obligation to find beauty in it.

She heard the sound of a horn, at once distant and as close as if it were echoing in her mind. She turned to look at the city gates, where already the guards were clutching their throats, sinking to their knees, shuddering as muscles clenched in a pain that would be imprinted onto her last thoughts. This was the power of the pyramid she had sought for so long.

She was happy that she had never possessed it.

Now the cries of men and the tramping of feet replaced the sound of the horn, the gates already quivering before the impact of the rams that shattered them as if they were glass. The men came through like a horde of locusts under the banner of the cross, swords held high and men hewn low, the streets slick with blood and bile, the men's eyes set on the gold.

The gold that they would never see, for it lay in the riddles of her diary.

16

Steve Lorenzo's breath caught in his throat as he read the words. He must not have knocked enough of the rust off his Latin and French in these past days. Surely he must be mistaken. And yet, even after double-checking his grammar, there seemed to be no other way to read it.

The final pages of the diary described dreams, written in riddles, and on his first pass he had assumed they were nothing but the delusions of an old, dying woman. But the words were there: *gardiens, pyramide en crystal.* And the power displayed in the woman's dreams was the same power that had felled Karl Vögel in Berlin. It could not be mere coincidence.

"Padre," Miguel whispered, excitement and concern in his eyes. "You have found something."

Steve nodded slowly.

"You are not happy."

"It was true," Steve said, his voice hollow.

"What was true?" Miguel asked.

"I can't believe he said the words, and yet he must have," Steve said. "'Kill them all. God will know his own.' The Church has always maintained that Arnaud Amaury never uttered those words, although they were documented by contemporary witnesses. Yet here they are, in the dream of a woman who died on that day. I am…ashamed."

Miguel put a hand on Steve's arm. "*Padre,* you knew the history of the Church is not pure. The Church is made up of people, and people will do evil as well as good. We can only hope that the Church learns from her mistakes. And I think she has."

"Has she?" Steve asked. "If this account is true, and I feel in my heart that it is, the Church once possessed a jeweled pyramid like the one we seek. And it was used for a terrible evil. Now the Church asks me to find another. Do you believe they would use it only for good now?"

Miguel seemed to ponder the question for a long time before answering, and Steve changed the question. "Have we become better, Miguel, in eight centuries? Is mankind more prone to do good and shun evil? Are we more enlightened than the people who came out of caves to slay the people in the next village? Or are we simply more efficient, more able to rationalize our evil as good?"

"You already know that answer, *Padre,*" Miguel said. And he *did* know the answer. But that did not mean he had to like it. Steve Lorenzo had committed his life to his Church. *His* Church. For all its foibles, he firmly believed that his faith was not only a means to salvation and eternal life, but the best way of creating a heaven on this earth. Yes, people made mistakes. Sometimes, Steve was willing to concede, those people wore cardinatial red or even the white vestments of the Pope. But the central core of his faith—the miracle of the Eucharist and Christ's message of love—was beyond question.

Yet it was obvious that the pyramid was a power not even his Church should possess. Nor was he at all certain that the Guardians—of whom he still knew far too little—were fit to control such a power. In the end, it came down to an issue of personal conscience.

Steve nodded. "Yes. Someone has already shown us that, in Berlin. We must find that codex, Miguel. And we must hide it somewhere so that no man will ever touch it again. For so long as man has the power to do evil…"

"He will do it," Miguel said. "But where do we look for this codex?"

"We look for the man who took it," Steve said. He drew a slow breath. "The man in Guatemala. You saw him. Can you draw a picture of him?"

Miguel nodded. "I think so."

"Do you remember Miriam?"

"The American policewoman? Yes."

"If you can draw it well enough, she might be able to identify him."

"You will call her?"

Steve shook his head, smiling sadly. "No. She is no longer in the police but high in government. But I can get the drawing to her through Monsignore Veltroni and our Papal Nuncio in Washington, I think."

Miguel smiled. "Yes. Your Vatican contacts should not go totally to waste."

"I hope she remembers me," Steve said.

And, he thought, he hoped Miriam had forgiven him for abandoning her in the jungle.

After Miguel had drawn the man's face, Steve took the drawing to an Internet café. They had a scanner, and for only a few euros he was able to scan the drawing and send it to Veltroni's private e-mail address.

Steve had appended the words "God will know his own" to the drawing. He hoped Miriam would figure out the code and find him in Béziers. For he had decided that would be the next stop on his journey. Somewhere in that ancient city must lie another clue to the *bonne femme*.

A prayer, he decided, might be a good thing right now.

Rome, Italy

"This sounds far-fetched, Renate," Jefe said.

"I know it does. It probably is. But believe it or not, this is the *least* far-fetched of the ideas Margarite and I kicked around today."

Jefe chuckled. The least far-fetched, huh? He

wasn't sure if that strengthened her speculation or was merely evidence that two of his best agents were losing their minds and in need of some leave time. In the end, his decision was constrained by the fact that he had no one to replace them. And since he couldn't give them leave, it was better to consider that they just might be right.

"Okay, let's say I think this isn't totally nuts," he said. "How can we verify it?"

"We killed three men in Strasbourg when we took down Kasmir al-Khalil," Renate said. "They were European, not Arab. Then there's Paxti Lezeta, who Lawton killed here in Berlin. He was a European security agent, except Lawton swears he saw Lezeta throw a Molotov cocktail into the Muslim demonstrators. Get identities on the Europeans we killed in Strasbourg and run their backgrounds against Lezeta's. If Margarite and I are right, there will be a nexus."

"And that nexus will be someone very close to Jules Soult," Jefe said. "We can get into Interpol's database. But that will only help if these guys had criminal records. Any idea where this Lezeta is from, in case we need to get into national databases?"

"Hold on," Renate said. After a muffled conversation, she returned. "Margarite says it sounds Basque to her. That narrows it to southwest France or northeast Spain. She has a contact in the French Interior Ministry who can search their records if we need to."

"Hold off on that," Jefe said. "Let me try it through Interpol first. I'd rather leave as few tracks as I can."

"*Das stimmt,*" Renate said.

Jefe laughed and shook his head. "Sorry, Renate, but unless you know Spanish, you'll need to stick to English or pidgin Italian with me."

"*Es tut mir leid,*" she said. "*Ich habe mit dir übereingestimmt.*"

"Y'know, Renate, sometimes you're a pain in the ass."

"With Lawton out of touch, I figured you needed one," she said. In his mind's eye, he saw the briefest flicker of a smile on her face. When she spoke again, it was in English. "And by the way, all I said was that I agreed with you."

"Let me get busy here. Call me tonight."

"*Ja,*" she said. "*Bis heute Abend.*"

That much he understood as *until this evening*. He'd never considered Renate as having a sense of humor before. In fact, as he thought about it, he realized that, in the years they'd worked together, he'd never seen her joke. A blissfully ignorant man would have taken her humor as a sign that she was fine. But Jefe was neither ignorant nor in a state of bliss. He'd learned not to ignore it when people acted out of character.

Something was wrong. He scribbled a note to talk to Margarite later, at a time when Renate would not overhear, then walked over to the data room. He found Assif Mondi, one of the best computer minds in Office 119, hunched over a terminal and muttering in Hindi.

"That doesn't sound positive," Jefe said.

"Positive," Assif said, "would be the Frankfurt Brotherhood sending me decrypted copies of their e-mail. This, Jefe, is called reality."

"I have some more reality to dump in your lap."

"I'm standing," Assif said, without looking up. "No lap. Sorry."

"Then I'll dump it on your back," Jefe said. "This is a no-shit, get-it-done job, Assif."

Assif straightened, meeting Jefe's eyes for the first time. For a moment the young Indian man seemed angry, then inscrutable. Finally he smiled. "Okay, boss. Sorry. I'm just frustrated. There's been a ton of Brotherhood traffic in the past forty-eight hours, and they've updated their encryption software. I hate knowing those bastards are up to something and not knowing what it is."

"Then a break will help you," Jefe said. "This ought to be easy by comparison. I need to get into the Interpol database."

Assif let out a sigh of relief as he moved to another data terminal. "You're right, that *will* be easy. I still have a Trojan listening to a socket on their firewall from when I worked for the New Delhi police. I just run my t-exec to telnet in and I'm on at the root."

"Doesn't anyone speak English anymore?" Jefe asked.

"That *was* English. What I said was—"

Jefe put up a hand. "Don't bother. Just do it, please. I need to know the identities of three men we took down in Strasbourg. And I need everything you can get on the man Lawton killed in Berlin, Paxti Lezeta. Margarite and Renate think there's a connection. I need to know if they're right, or if we're chasing wild geese. And I need it in two hours."

"Now you're doing reality again," Assif said. "These things take time."

Jefe shook his head. "Not this one. I wasn't kidding when I said it's a no-shit, get-it-done job. We have an agent in jail, Assif. Make it happen."

Assif nodded, already typing at the keyboard. "It will go faster without you standing over my shoulder."

Jefe gave the man a pat as he left, realizing that Assif was doing the best he could in a job where his every action was probably illegal. Jefe knew that, and usually he handled these things better.

Maybe it wasn't Renate who was going out of her mind. Maybe it was him.

17

Posing as Lawton's cousin, Renate gained permission to visit him. The visitors' room was tiny, just enough space for the two of them to sit at a table. There was no sign of cameras or listening devices, nor should there have been. Until convicted of a crime, a prisoner in Germany was treated with every courtesy.

"We have a theory," she said. "Jefe's checking out some connections. Suffice it to say, your encounter with the security guard, as unfortunate as it has been for you, has proved a valuable piece of information."

He nodded. "I need to get out of here." The warrant had been issued by the judge yesterday, as he had expected, and since then he had begun to look drawn. Captivity did not at all agree with him.

"We are working on it. Believe me." Forgetting all the rules about collegial relationships, she reached out and covered his hand with hers. "I feel responsible. I brought you into this."

"You weren't the one who went off half-cocked."

"You were only acting as you were trained. I cannot criticize that."

"Margarite sure has."

"Margarite would find something to criticize in the color of the sky."

At that he cracked a half smile. "She told me to stop acting like John Wayne."

Renate actually smiled. "John Wayne is one of the things many Europeans like about Americans. Remember, the French preferred Jerry Lewis."

At that he genuinely laughed, as she had hoped he would. "So what is this theory?"

She hesitated, trying to think of a brief way to sketch it for him without getting into a full-blown discussion that could, if someone happened to overhear, reveal too much.

He seemed to understand her concern, for he nodded and glanced toward the door. It was closed, but she knew that just because no one should be attempting to listen, in reality...

"The man you attacked worked for EU security."

He nodded. "Everyone knows that."

"Well, that is the clue I mentioned. The hint. Being American, you may not know much about...historical events in the 1930s. Here in Germany."

"I've done some reading."

"Do you remember the Brownshirts?"

Now his eyes narrowed, and she could see that he was thinking very hard. "I see," he said finally, his voice heavy.

She nodded. "We think Soult may be using EU security forces in this way."

He closed his eyes and leaned back in his chair. His hand slipped from beneath hers, and she regretted the loss.

Finally he opened his eyes. "What does Jefe say?"

"He thinks we are crazy and fears we may be correct. He is researching persons of interest."

"I hate to think this may be true." He shook his head. "I'm an American, Renate. Like most Americans, I'm rather proud of my country, but I also feel somewhat envious of European sophistication."

Renate shrugged. "The Margarites of the world would very much like it if you continued to feel that way. But our sophistication is born of the many terrible things we have done and experienced. And so-called sophistication does not prevent us from repeating our mistakes. We hold up the EU as a beacon of hope for the future, yet we could not agree on a constitution for it. That would be the easy part, would you not think?"

"Well, it was a complicated issue."

"Yes. It attempted to enshrine business and economic arrangements in the same breath as human rights. But that is beside the point. Look at us now, Lawton." She glanced down briefly. "We—the sophisticated Europeans, with our vaunted EU—seem poised to unleash another Holocaust."

"I thought you were *for* the EU?"

"I am for peace and justice. Herr Vögel saw that Soult's path would bring neither."

"A good reason to get rid of him."

"*Ja.* For all her weaknesses, Germany's economy is stronger than that of France. If she were to withdraw from the EU, many would be angry."

"And Vögel had threatened that," he said.

She nodded. "Now Germany has a chancellor who does Soult's bidding, but still he has angered many by insisting that those who are moved must be compensated. And twice this week there have been fights at train stations. Today Chancellor Müller said he may suspend the relocations."

"So he's not Soult's puppet."

"Not entirely," Renate said. "Every day there are more Germans in the streets protesting the relocations and fewer marching to support them. I do not think Herr Müller can remain loyal to Soult and retain his position. And if he breaks with the EU, there will be repercussions."

"And all that is tied up in my case," Lawton said.

Renate nodded. "When you tackled Paxti Lezeta, you peeled back the curtain on something that could be very embarrassing to whomever sent him. There are powerful forces who would like to keep that truth buried."

"You mean keep *me* buried," Lawton said.

"Perhaps," she said. "But once it is established that you are an ordinary citizen, it will benefit those same persons to see you freed without a trial. The German justice system requires that your claims in your own defense must be investigated as thoroughly as the charges against you. I think those behind Lezeta will not want that kind of deep investigation. So you may be lucky."

"I don't feel lucky at all." He sighed, then fell silent for a long moment. When he spoke again, his voice was quiet. "I killed a man."

She knew how he felt too well. But unlike her own experiences of killing, Lawton had not acted in cold blood. "Lawton, it was an accident. You *did* see him commit a crime, and he *was* reaching for a gun when you were chasing him. What were you supposed to do? Wait for him to draw it and shoot you?"

She could tell he didn't like what she was saying. Nor did she. Ever since she had discovered the activities of the Frankfurt Brotherhood while working as an agent of the BKA, she had lost a great deal of innocence. She had lost even more when they tried to kill her and had instead killed her best friend, and still more when they murdered her parents. With each day, it seemed, she lost more and more of the goodness within her.

Like it or not, the corridors of true power in this world were hidden from public view. When people wondered at the way events played out, all they needed to do was look at the money. Always follow the money. But money was not simply a motive. It was also a means to cover one's tracks, to make one's enemies disappear. She had followed the money, and it had struck back…hard.

A heavy sigh escaped Lawton, and he shook his head. "You shouldn't even be here in Berlin, Renate. The Brotherhood knows you're still alive." He managed a weak smile. "But I must admit, you look great with dark hair."

She considered the compliment, wondered if it was mere humor or something more, and decided to let it pass. "I won't be in Germany long. But you needed me."

He was silent for a long moment. "Damn, I feel so helpless."

"This is Germany. No swearing."

He smiled again. "Sorry, I keep forgetting."

"Under the circumstances, I'll overlook it." She had brought him a cake, and now she edged it across the table toward him. "You will like this. It is not too sweet."

"Thank you. Does it contain a file?"

For an instant she missed the allusion, but then she caught it and laughed. "That won't be necessary, Lawton. You'll see."

Rome, Italy

"This is madness!" Abdul al-Nasser said.

Ahmed Ahsami could not disagree. As he watched, three more buses pulled up, loaded with Italian Muslims being relocated to this already crowded neighborhood. The people climbed from the buses and gathered what few belongings they had brought with them. Then the buses pulled away, having deposited the people at the curb like so much human refuse.

The sight sickened him to his soul.

"We must strike back at them," al-Nasser said. "Our people cannot go quietly, like Jewish sheep."

Ahmed turned to his companion. "And what, exactly, will we accomplish by such a strike? Do you think if we kill enough innocent people, the Europeans will decide we are fit to live among them?"

"There are no innocent Europeans," al-Nasser said. "Not when they stand by while this happens."

Ahmed nodded. "Perhaps that is true. But if it is so, then there are no innocent Muslims, either, not when we have stood by while the most rabid among us have murdered in the name of Allah. Collective guilt flows both ways, my friend."

"You have spent too much time in the West," al-Nasser said. "It has polluted your thinking. Surely you can see the difference between a holy warrior and an infidel?"

"What I can see," Ahmed said, again looking at the

crowd in the street, "is misery and death, paid one for
the other, back and forth, until all is misery and death.
It is our duty, as good followers of Allah, to end this
cycle."

Al-Nasser's lips were tight. "Oh yes, we will end it.
We will teach the infidels the price of oppressing Allah's
people. Then they will cower before us."

Ahmed shook his head and walked out of the restaurant. He could not waste time arguing with al-Nasser.
The most he could do was to keep the man—and the
many other young men in this neighborhood who felt
as al-Nasser did—firmly in check. The idea that Europeans would ever cower before Muslims was laughable. Camels would fly first.

He began to move through the crowd, seeking out fathers, the traditional heads of households. In his hand,
he carried a sheet of paper upon which he had compiled
a list of available lodgings in the area. It was slow work,
for he spoke little Italian and many of them spoke almost no Arabic. Yet he pressed on, trying to match families with flats and men with jobs, trying to ensure that
these new arrivals—like those who had come yesterday
and the day before that, and those who would come tomorrow and the day after—would have places to live
and ways to feed their families.

It was largely thankless work, and not at all what he
had envisioned four years earlier, when he had first
begun to build *Saif Alsharaawi*. His lofty aspirations of

a pan-Islamic institution were collapsing into sectarian war in Iraq and a looming Holocaust in Europe. He felt less a mediator, less a spokesman, and increasingly a fireman rushing from one blaze to another. He was not acting, only reacting.

And yet he found a certain kind of peace in the work he now did. The Islamic traditions of hospitality were as old as the deserts in which they were born, and while Rome was not a sandy wasteland, this neighborhood must seem equally inhospitable in the eyes of those being shuttled in here. Many of the jobs Ahmed helped to distribute were being created by and for the relocation itself. They were neither glamorous nor lucrative, but as the mass of people grew, so, too, grew the need for streets to be kept clean, for food, clothing, medicine and other essentials to be gathered and distributed, for children to be watched and taught, for those with special skills to be matched to those with needs.

He was, he realized, helping to create a city within a city, with all the administrative headaches that attended such a task. If *Saif Alsharaawi* was ever to achieve his dream, it would be because of work like this, because of matching resources with needs in a way that ensured the safety and security of those involved.

The *tarhēl*—the removal—was madness, yes. But in the madness, Ahmed knew, lay the seeds of what *Saif* must become.

18

Mannheim, Germany

Monsignore Giuseppe Veltroni rode the tram standing. He had forwarded Steve Lorenzo's message to a trusted aide to the Papal Nuncio in Washington. He had to trust that the aide would get the message to Steve's friend, Miriam. In the meantime, he had other work he must do.

His mission troubled him sorely, not because of the men he was to meet, but because of the mission's very cause.

The Sultan Selim Mosque in Mannheim was widely known as the "glass mosque" because of its open-door policy. Opened in 1995 to serve some nearly 2,500 Muslims in the area, the mosque practiced a tradition of remaining open all night in order to act as a museum, welcoming the curious to a tour and an explanation of Islam and the prayer services conducted there. While the government had originally been reluctant to permit its construction, and some had decried it as the end of the western world, the mosque and its members had done much to foster cultural and religious understanding in the local community.

Part of him wished he had been invited into the mosque. He felt it would make his position much clearer if he set foot inside, but the men he was meeting all felt that the adjacent church would be a safer meeting ground.

After he exited the tram, it was impossible to ignore the extraordinary number of *Polizei* on the streets approaching the mosque and the nearby church. This was a protection zone, and the *monsignore* was twice asked to produce his identification. Hesitation on the part of the police lessened when he explained he was going to meet Herr Pfarrer Stoll, the local parish priest. Still, he could feel their eyes on his back as he continued to walk toward the church. Not good, not good at all.

The mosque rose across the street to the left of the Liebfrauenkirche, Church of our Lady, which was fronted by the traditional medieval Marktplatz. Each building occupied a corner, either a friendly juxtaposition or a gulf, depending on one's point of view. The church was an old and elegant building, painted white, with contrasting dark brown ornate woodwork. The mosque was huge and modern, yet no less beautiful in its own way. Veltroni had looked at pictures of the interior on the Internet, and he had been impressed by its beauty. No expense had been spared to create a serene place of worship.

The mosque reminded him that Jews and Muslims were in many ways closer in their practices than were Jews and Christians. Jews had a ritual bath for cleansing, and the mosque had a washing room, with a beautiful fountain where all who came to pray washed their faces, hands, forearms and feet. For the Catholic Church that cleansing had been reduced to a baptismal font and holy water for blessings. In the mosque there were no graven images, just as in a synagogue, while the Catholic Church reveled in its statues and paintings.

What many failed to understand was that the Church's use of statuary and paintings had begun in the dark ages, a time when few could read, even priests. Lessons had been taught with tableaux of art, and the statues themselves were meant only as reminders. Certainly none of them were worshipped.

At the curb he paused and looked upward. The minaret and steeple seemed to vie with each other to reach the heavens. For an instant Veltroni thought of the Tower of Babel, though he understood the purpose of these towers was quite different. The one called the faithful to prayer with a bell, the other with a muezzin.

He sighed and reminded himself that he wasn't making this trip to remember the past or to study architecture. He was here to prevent the past from repeating itself.

Just inside the narthex he found *der Pfarrer,* the priest, Hans Stoll, and two other men waiting for him. All three wore suits, although Stoll had not abandoned his clerical collar. The second, Veltroni thought, must be the rabbi, to judge by his sidelocks and hat. And the third, also bearded and wearing a knit cap, must be the imam.

"I'm sorry I'm late," Veltroni said, shaking Stoll's hand.

"Only a little," Stoll answered with a smile. "Gentlemen, this is Monsignore Veltroni from Rome. *Monsignore,* please meet Rabbi Lev and Imam Zekariah."

Veltroni smiled and shook hands warmly with the two other clerics. Together they strolled through the church and across the grounds to the small parish rectory. Stoll ushered them into the front room and poured them very strong coffee. For a few minutes the three Germans observed the customary niceties, chatting generally about their duties, their congregations, even the weather. Veltroni listened intently, though he said almost nothing about himself.

But then the cups were set down, and the priest looked at Veltroni, encouraging him to lead the conversation.

"This removal," Veltroni said, "is a dangerous thing."

The three men nodded. The imam, Ismail Zekariah, sounded almost relieved to have a chance to speak his mind. "I am sorely troubled by it. My brothers and their families are moving here from all over southern Germany. There is not enough room. They are being forced to share dwellings with several families. Yet they are afraid not to come."

"Ja," Lev said. "It is bad."

"But at least here," the imam said slowly, "they are protected by police, as they are not in other places. As difficult as this is, as angry as it is making our young people, most of those who come are grateful for the safety. Europe has become a very dangerous place for Muslims."

Lev sighed. "It is true. The ugliness is appalling."

"It is without excuse," Stoll said flatly. He refilled their cups. "I preach against it at every Mass. But…few enough Germans practice their Christianity any longer." He turned to Veltroni. "And too many of my fellow priests remain silent, as well."

Veltroni nodded. "The Vatican is aware of that. This is why I am in Germany, and why I will go to every country in Europe, if need be, to visit the bishops and make clear that the Church cannot allow this to continue. There is no justification for what is happening. None."

"None?" the imam repeated. "You do not agree with those who believe that we are a threat to Europe? Islamist terrorists have done awful things, Herr Monsignore. Even I cannot deny that."

Veltroni smiled. "*My* prophet says one must turn the other cheek. Besides, the few do not represent the many. They never have. And as you have so deftly phrased it, the terrorists are *Islamist* and not *Islamic*. Their faith is a far cry from the many good Muslims I have come to know. It is the same among our people: some are Christian, some I would call Christianist. They don the mantle but ignore the teachings."

The imam nodded. "So sad and so true."

"Always it is thus," said the rabbi. "There are always those who would misuse the power of faith."

"But," said the imam, "in fairness, I must speak well of the German government and people. The government seeks to repay our financial losses, and a surprising number of the German people have raised their voices against this removal."

"We have learned," Stoll said with a shrug. "Most of us, at least. Unfortunately, while objections are growing in this country, they are not growing elsewhere."

The others murmured agreement. "But," said Stoll, turning to Lev, "you said you had a concern you wanted to talk over with us."

Lev paused, clearly gathering his words.

"I thought on my way here that I should perhaps have written down the things that are occurring to me, but…" Lev shrugged. "Perhaps it is wisest not to write some things. You know I come from Russia. The words that occurred to me as I rode the tram were these—I am an old Jew, and I can smell a pogrom in the wind."

The imam's face creased with concern, and he looked at the priests. Both Stoll and Veltroni frowned.

Finally Stoll said, "But, Avner…this is only temporary."

"So they say." Lev again sipped his coffee. "There were times when my people would know of a pogrom only when the armed men came riding into our villages.

Without warning they would come and kill everyone they could find. But other times…" He laid a finger alongside his nose. "Other times, my friends, you know it is coming. You hear it behind the words that are being spoken. You read it in the eyes. It will not end here."

Veltroni leaned forward. "Are you certain of this?"

"Yes," Lev said. "*Monsignore,* they say they do this to end the violence. But why do they not protect Muslims wherever they are? Instead, they must move. It is the law. 'Take what you can and go to the safe zone.' Even if they are compensated, as the German government promises, it is no different. And other governments are not offering any compensation. My people have seen this before. The Muslims of Europe are being gathered the same way one gathers a herd."

"Perhaps your predictions are too dire, Avner. It is, after all, easier to protect those who congregate in one place, rather than trying to protect individuals everywhere," Zekariah said.

Lev shook his head. "It is also easier to persecute those who are congregated in one place. Now I hear talk that Muslims should be expatriated to Muslim countries, rather than allowed to remain in Europe."

"It is true," Stoll said, bowing his head. "I heard this today, but I thought it merely the half-baked notion of some politician looking to win votes."

"So far," agreed Lev, "that is all it is. But neither of you needs me to remind you how hard it has been for

Muslims to gain acceptance here. I do not have to remind you of the riots in Germany over Turkish workers. Or how the imam and his people had to fight to gain permission to build this mosque. It is strange, but I, a Russian Jew, am more welcome here, perhaps because they feel guilty about us. So now the hatred transfers. *Ach.*"

He waved his hand and sat back in his chair. "I'm getting old. Perhaps I remember too much. Perhaps I am imagining that it could happen again."

"It?" said Zekariah.

Lev's blue eyes settled on him. "A Holocaust."

For a long time silence lay between the four clerics, each lost in his own unhappy thoughts. Veltroni was the first to speak.

"What do you suggest, Rabbi?"

"Prepare," said Lev. "Men of faith cannot be as the lamb when a wolf stalks among us. We must be as the lion."

Zekariah looked down. "Avner, there are not enough Muslims to be the lion. We would be crushed, just as we were in Serbia and Bosnia, just as is happening to us in Chechnya. And when we fight back, it merely confirms the worst that people think of us. The Prophet, peace be upon him, taught us to respond to an attack with love."

Lev nodded unhappily. "I understand. And there are not many of my people, either. But…" He turned to the *monsignore.*

"Yes," Veltroni said. "We are many. Right now we

stand by and watch as Muslims are put onto trains. Fine trains, to be sure. Not cattle cars. So far, it is all with great courtesy. But it will not always be thus. I fear the rabbi is right."

Lev offered a smile of acknowledgement. "Thank you. So what will the Lions of Rome do? And will the millions of European Catholics follow?"

"That is always the question, is it not?" Stoll asked, looking at Veltroni. "You know Rome does not have the firm hand it once had, not here in Germany, not in France. It is good that Rome will act, but we must act in concert or it will be for naught."

"Be ready," Veltroni said. "Rabbi Lev has convinced me that my suspicions were correct. And, Ismail, while I understand and agree with your exhortations that Muslims must remain peaceful, neither can you stand by while your people are gathered for a slaughter. Be ready to act."

"What will you do?" Zekariah asked.

"I will speak with the Holy Father when I return to Rome," Veltroni said. "I will see him personally, even if I have to climb into his bedroom to do it. He is a wise man. He will find a way out of this. Pfarrer Stoll, I will call you personally when I have an answer. I trust that you can contact our friends here."

"I can," Stoll said.

Veltroni looked at Zekariah. "You are not alone, Imam. Never forget that. You are not alone."

19

Béziers was awash in history, including having once been a killing ground during the Albigensian Crusade. Miriam Anson strode quickly to the Place de la Madeleine, map in hand, thinking how much she would love to spend a week or two here. Around every corner there was another surprise for anyone interested in architecture or history. Roman remains. Churches built in the dark ages and others built in the Middle Ages with their slender, rising architecture. A bridge that had survived since the first century and was still in use.

Since receiving the drawing from the Vatican envoy in Washington, Miriam had been busy. She had, as requested, run the photo through the CIA's face recognition software, hoping for the best but not expecting to find a hit. She had been surprised. Apparently whoever had drawn the face had both an excellent memory and a skilled hand, for she had received back an eighty percent match.

At first she had thought to send that information back through the channels from which she had received it. But the name that matched the face had given her pause. He was not a criminal, but rather a contract security agent for the European Union. The more she thought about that fact, the more it gave her pause.

Ultimately she had gone to Grant Lawrence with what she had and explained that she needed to go to Europe to check out the lead for herself. After the usual lecture about how she was a cabinet secretary and no longer a field agent, he had assented. The simple fact was, there was no one else she trusted with this contact. She'd made promises to Steve Lorenzo, and she intended to keep them.

She'd fed Steve's code—"God will know his own"—into an Internet search engine, and out had popped the city of Béziers. Taking this as a clue to where Steve wished to meet, she'd booked a flight to France and had her sources perform a hotel search of the city. Only one hotel had an American tourist accompanied by a "dark foreigner," and she had left a message for Steve at that hotel.

Now she had to hope her message had indeed reached him, and that he would meet with her.

In the meantime, she herself was little more than a tourist. The age of the buildings here was astonishing. "Old" in the United States meant at most a couple hundred years. It gave her chills to walk on a piece of pavement that dated back to the first century, to see a wall built by Roman hands. To walk on the very ground where the Cathars had died so long ago.

Then there was the Madeleine. An all-white church built of limestone from the sea, it had stood since the tenth century, although from her brochure she gathered it had needed some repair after the crusaders attacked the city. It had been built by a viscount for his personal use. She could hardly imagine a nobleman building such an edifice for his own chapel.

She stared up at it with awe, then looked around the gardens filled with potted olive trees and rose laurel. The fragrance invited one to step within, so she did.

Madeleine, her brochure informed her, was the Magdalene. Many churches in southern France were dedicated to her, because, as the story went, she was believed to have fled to this area from Judea after the crucifixion. Her daughter had become Saint Sarah, another very popular saint in this area. Some claimed that the Cathar heresy—which denied the divinity of Christ—traced to these old local legends.

Whether it had or not, their teachings had been positive otherwise, for according to her brochures, the Cathar leaders—the *perfecti*—practiced poverty and love of one's neighbor to an extreme degree. They owned nothing and shared everything. Miriam could easily see how that had arisen from Christ's teachings, and how it would have stood in stark contrast to the medieval Church, with its focus on earthly power and treasure.

Perhaps it was that, more than anything, which had made the Cathars such a thorn in the Church's side that a crusade had been announced to eliminate them, though that wasn't exactly what Miriam thought of when someone spoke of the crusades: Christian against Christian.

She found a limestone bench in the garden and sat, watching as a tour group moved through. They'd lowered their voices almost reverentially, barely disturbing the peace of the garden.

Then one man, clad in jeans and a sweatshirt, separated from them and walked toward her.

Steve! She almost said his name and leapt to her feet but caught herself just in time. Two strangers might admire the garden from the same bench, and an observer, if there was one, would think little of it.

He sat on the end of the bench without acknowledging her and snapped some photos of the area with a disposable camera. Then he turned to her with a charming smile and asked her to take a photo of him in front of the church.

Of course she agreed. Smiling, she accepted the camera and felt a slip of folded paper pressed into her palm along with it. Still smiling, she took a couple of photos of him, then passed the camera back with her other hand.

He waved and headed back to join the tour group.

Miriam resumed her seat, picking up her map and brochure and studying them for a few minutes before she tucked them, along with the paper Steve had given her, into her coat pocket.

Then she wandered inside the church, no longer drinking in the beauty of her surroundings. Her senses stood on high alert for any suspicious movement. Judging by his behavior, Steve thought he was being followed.

Walking slowly, pausing when appropriate, she toured the church. When she stepped back out into the sunshine, her eyes hurt for a moment and she had to stop, blinking.

Not until she was safely away and tucked into a corner inside a café did she bring out the papers from her pocket. The map she placed on the tablecloth, the historical brochure on top of it. Then her hotel room key and a few receipts, which she spread out as if reviewing her expenses.

Then the paper Steve had given her.

I must ensure I am alone, he had written. *Tonight. Late. Your hotel room.*

She balled it up with the receipts, and ordered coffee and pastry. It appeared she would get at least a small part of her wish: for the next several hours, she needed to play tourist.

She smiled at the young woman who brought her food, all the while wondering if she might be too old or too rusty for what lay ahead.

Berlin, Germany

Renate and Margarite went to the train station to-gether, although only Margarite was leaving. Renate still had leads to follow up in Berlin, but Margarite had decided to get in touch with one of her sources in Paris to see what he might have picked up.

"You are confident of him?" Renate had asked at least three times, echoing Jefe's concern.

"Very. Will you please stop asking me that question, Renate? I know my job."

Renate had clamped her jaws shut. For some reason, the minute anyone expressed that kind of confidence, her doubts began to grow. "Be careful," she finally said. "You know what is at stake."

Margarite didn't bother to answer.

The Hauptbahnhof, or Central Station, displayed many of the same earmarks of Germany's other newer stations, although it was itself both the newest and biggest. As they ascended the escalator toward the east-west platforms, they rose into a glass-and-steel lat-tice covered tunnel, designed to maximize daylight and the surrounding view. Atop the southern tunnel, photovoltaic cells gathered power to support the sta-tion's operations.

Many Berliners weren't very fond of the new sta-tion and called the tunnels the glass sausages. Renate didn't blame them. The scourge of uniformity that came along with modernity threatened the charm of the past far too much.

Suddenly Margarite murmured, *"Merde."*

Renate looked up from the top of the escalator and followed Margarite's stare to the next platform over. It was crowded with people, and at first she thought only that it looked more like an afternoon commuter crowd than a midday group.

But as she stepped off the escalator, the reality penetrated. Most of the women wore the *hijab*, the head scarf required by some Muslim sects. Some wore slacks or jeans, but many observed *shari'a* with long shapeless dresses, mostly black, a few colorful and exotic. They stood by themselves at one end of the platform, with the young children. Older boys and men stood at the other end, and around them all were suitcases. None, except the smallest children, looked happy about this state of affairs.

"A removal train," Renate murmured.

"Oui." Margarite stared openly.

"It is an abomination," Renate said.

Margarite shook her head. "Perhaps. Perhaps it is only people doing what people do. It is so easy, after all, to simply pack the bad people away. You did it once before, and, sadly, it worked. Those who survived the camps fled Europe after."

"I didn't do that," Renate said, bristling. "I was not yet born."

"Your people," Margarite said with her characteristic shrug. "Germans."

"And your people, and the rest of Europe, packed your Jews on those trains," Renate replied.

"But who built the camps?"

"So am I to apologize for being German?" Renate snapped. "What do you want?"

Margarite turned to her. "Yes. Apologize for being German. Even better, *stop* being German."

"I have *nothing* to apologize for, Margarite. I was not even born when the Holocaust happened!"

"I am not talking about that," Margarite said.

"What, then?" Renate asked, puzzled. "Is my hair too blond? Are my eyes too blue? Do I mispronounce your holy French *that* terribly?"

The Frenchwoman sighed, sitting on a bench and lighting a cigarette with trembling hands. Renate realized there was something more going on here. She drew a breath and sat beside Margarite, trying to calm her own anger. "Talk to me. What have I done to hurt you?"

Margarite smiled wanly and shook her head. "You really have no idea, do you? You have not hurt me. You owe me no apology for who you are. You should apologize to Lawton. You should apologize to yourself."

"What do you—"

"You asked," Margarite said, cutting her off. "Now shut up and listen. Do you know why Jefe sent you to America to recruit Lawton?"

"I was already in Guatemala, investigating the murder of the U.S. ambassador," Renate said. "I was the closest agent to the scene."

"Merde!" Margarite said. "Any of us could have been in the States as quickly as you could from Guatemala. No. Jefe chose you because *you are the best.* He knew it. I knew it. Everyone at Office 119 knew it."

"So I should apologize for being good at my job?"

"Oui! You should! You are so damn good at being German that you've forgotten to be *human.* You terrify us, Renate. You are brilliant, skilled, utterly dedicated and utterly ruthless. Whatever else the bastards in Frankfurt did, they turned a woman into a machine. No, not even a machine. A predator, brutally efficient and remorseless. A predator that feeds on evil. But you can eat only so much evil before it consumes you, Renate. And somewhere, lost in what you have become, is a woman who cannot or will not see what makes the rest of us *ache* when we look at you.

"You need to *love,* Renate, and to *be* loved. You cannot go on forever living on hate and anger and revenge, or they will consume you. You are the perfect stereotype of a German: dutiful, logical and efficient. You could be more than that, but you crush the rest of you as ruthlessly as you crush your prey. If you do not let it up soon, if you do not let it breathe soon, you will have nothing left of the woman you were. And then you will be no better than the prey you hunt."

Renate felt the words cut through to her core and fought the urge to cry. "Damn you, Margarite."

Margarite put a hand on hers. "I am sorry, *mon amie.* But I must care for my friend, *non?* When you get Lawton out of jail, and you will, take some time with him. The rest of us can chase the bad guys for a few days. Be a woman again, Renate. Before it's too late."

They looked at each other for a long moment, and then Margarite rose. "My train is here. *Au revoir, mon amie.* I will see you in Rome."

After Margarite's train pulled out, Renate headed for the escalator. She glanced again toward the crowd on the next platform and saw that their train was just arriving. Moving with heavy reluctance, they began to lift their suitcases.

But just then a squad of *Polizei,* uniformed but not armed, appeared and moved through the crowd. The Muslims looked confused at first, some still moving their suitcases onto the trains, until the *Polizei* began to take the suitcases off. Renate wondered if they were now being stripped of the last of their belongings and walked over to one of the policemen.

"Was ist passiert?" she asked. *What's happening.*

"The Muslim Protection Laws are suspended," he replied.

"Chancellor Müller has seen the light?" Renate asked.

"Nein," the officer said, smiling. "Bürgermeister Kohl."

The mayor of Berlin had chosen to defy the federal

government, the officer explained. There would be no more removals in this city.

Renate nodded, whispering *"danke"* to the heavens before helping the Muslims to retrieve their luggage. Perhaps the tide was turning. Perhaps there was hope.

Rome, Italy

"You are a physician, yes?" Ahmed asked.

Hassan ibn Hassan nodded. "I am. Or I was."

"You still are," Ahmed said. "We have need of a physician, especially in the…Shi'a district."

Hassan visibly seethed. "Shi'a district? Are we now segregated from within as well as from without?"

"Please," Ahmed said, holding up a hand. "Trust that I do understand your anger. This *tarhēl* is an abomination that must end soon. And I believe Shi'a are just as Muslim as Sunni."

"I suppose I should say thank you?" Hassan asked, anger still dripping from his words.

Ahmed shook his head. "No, you should not. That your inclusion in the family of Islam is even in question is a shame on my brother Sunni."

"We agree on one thing, at least," Hassan said. "Yet still you have established a Shi'a district."

"I have," Ahmed said, nodding. "We have not that many Shi'a families here. I thought—perhaps in error— that you would be more comfortable living together…

having a neighborhood that is yours alone. If I am wrong in that, I apologize."

Finally Hassan's face seemed to soften. "No. I can understand your decision. And yes, with all that has happened, perhaps it is better we have a neighborhood of our own. So…you need a doctor."

"Yes," Ahmed said. "We have only two for the entire district. They are overworked. You will be busy."

"What about my son?" Hassan asked. "Ali is eighteen, and he…needs to be busy, too. Otherwise I fear he may fall in with the wrong crowd. It has…happened before."

Ahmed nodded. This was a request he faced far too often. Many Muslim youth, disenchanted by their treatment in Europe over the past years, had largely abandoned school and work for lives of "activism." Much of the time, that had translated into the kind of violence that had given Islam a bad name. It wasn't enough to hold back his *Saif* operatives. There was a generation of disgruntled youth waiting for a spark, and the *tarhēl* was a ready excuse.

"I will find work for Ali, I promise," Ahmed said. He lifted a hand toward the door. "In the meantime, allow me to show you our clinic. It is a bit…primitive…but we have petitioned the government for more equipment and a wider array of medicines."

"So this is what we have come to," Hassan said. "We are reduced to begging for basic human rights."

Ahmed nodded, his heart tearing. "Yes, my friend.

At least for a time. But let us make the best of what we have at hand, no?"

As he led Hassan to the clinic, Ahmed looked around him. Already, young boys and men were standing idle, with too few skills and too little motivation to be productive. He could feel the anger building. It was not a matter of whether this neighborhood would explode.

It was simply a matter of when.

Paris, France

Jules Soult crumpled the sheet of paper and hurled it across the room, startling the aide who had brought it. At least the man had the good sense to back out of the room.

Merde! The mayor of Berlin had chosen, on his own, to defy the removal laws of Germany. Germany, Germany, always Germany. The bane of his existence.

He picked up the telephone and stabbed in numbers, feeling the pain in his fingertip, a pain that helped him to focus his righteous rage.

"This is President Soult," he said when the phone was answered. "Put me through to Chancellor Müller at once."

"The Chancellor is in conference," the woman said.

"Then get him out of conference!" Soult said. "This is an issue of European security. Do it now."

Two minutes later, Müller was on the phone. "What is it, Monsieur Soult?"

"I am calling about the situation in Berlin," Soult said. "What are you going to do about it?"

"Federal lawyers are reviewing the situation now," Müller said. "It seems we may have drafted the Muslim Protection Laws in such a way that local officials have some leeway in implementation. As of now, I am led to believe that the Bürgermeister is acting within his lawful authority."

"Then change the laws!" Soult said.

"We are discussing whether that may be necessary."

"It *is* necessary," Soult said. "Don't forget, Germany is an EU country. You are bound by EU laws."

"Do not lecture me, Herr President," Müller said. "I am well aware of my responsibilities regarding the European Union. I am also aware of my responsibilities to Germany. Have no doubt as to which I give precedence."

"It had better be the Union."

The phone was silent for a moment before Müller spoke. "I will see to my office, Herr President. I would suggest that you see to yours. I am sure you have heard that one of your security agents was killed here. Witnesses say it was he who threw the firebomb that began the riot outside our Centrum Judiciaum."

"That is rubbish," Soult said. "The witnesses lie."

"Perhaps," Müller said. "Perhaps not. That will be for our courts to decide. But if it is even possible that the witnesses are correct, your own organization has some…bad apples, no?"

"I will look into it," Soult said, shaking his head. "And you fix this problem in Berlin."

"We will both address the problems we see," Müller said. *"Au revoir."*

Soult hung up the phone, not even remotely mollified. So this was how Müller viewed loyalty? Was it not Soult who had secured the Chancellorship for him? How dare he?

The removal was working well in the rest of Europe. Ordinary citizens craving security could be made to follow almost any law, especially when that law appeared to exempt them and their loved ones. All over the continent, people were helping in the containment of what some now called "the Muslim menace." And because the violence was indeed abating in many places, some commentators—especially those whose pay was supplemented by Soult's agents—were pointing to Soult as the man who had saved Europe.

Until this morning, he could scarcely believe how well the plan was working. Then one stubborn Berliner took it upon himself to make decisions, and it appeared that Müller would let it stand. What if other German officials decided to follow the path of Berlin's mayor? Would Müller put his foot down, or would he allow Germany to rebuff the European Union and its lawful edicts?

Soult began to suspect that, like Vögel before him, Müller was too German to be Chancellor of Germany.

But he could not risk another assassination. Given enough dots, even frightened people would make connections. No, this was a time for public action.

He picked up the telephone and dialed again. This time he did not encounter a rude secretary, for no French soldier would be so impertinent. In seconds, not minutes, he was through.

"Colonel Vasquez," Soult said. "We may need to activate contingency plans for Germany. What is the status of our negotiations with the French armed forces?"

"They will be at our disposal if we have cause," Vasquez said.

"Fashion a cause," Soult snapped. "Germany cannot be allowed to defy us."

20

It was nearly two in the morning when Steve Lorenzo finally tapped gently on the door of Miriam Anson's hotel room. He had waited until late to leave his own lodgings so that it would be easier for Miguel to spot anyone who might be following him. Only when Miguel signaled the all-clear did Steve finally enter Miriam's hotel and make his way up to her third-floor room.

When she opened the door, he saw that she had not been sleeping. The bed was still made, and she still wore the touristy clothes she had had on earlier at the Place de la Madeleine.

"Come in, Father," she said with a warm smile. "It's good to see you again."

He nodded silently and slipped past her into the room, taking a seat in what looked to be an antique armchair as she closed and locked the door. "I'm sorry," he said when she joined him.

Miriam arched an eyebrow. "What are you sorry for?"

"For leaving you in Guatemala. I had no choice. I had to protect my flock, and we had to move quickly. More quickly than you could, given your wound. Still, I abandoned you. I'm sorry."

She shook her head. "Do you imagine that I'm angry with you about that? Father, you made sure I could get to safety and return to the United States. I knew why you did what you did. I would have done the same, in your situation."

He looked at her, searching for signs of deception and finding none. She put a hand on his arm and continued.

"Father, you have nothing to apologize for. You are the *only* good thing that happened to me in Guatemala. If not for you and the things you said to me there, I think I'd have gone crazy thinking about what I'd done. So no, you shouldn't be sorry. *I* should be sorry that I didn't let you know that before tonight."

In a world where it seemed that no one was truly what he or she appeared to be, Steve thought, Miriam Anson was the exception. He was proud that his country could find and recognize people like her: true diamonds in a bed of self-promoting, self-serving glass.

"Thank you," he said. "I *am* surprised to see you here, however. I would have been satisfied with an e-mail in response."

That," she said, "wasn't going to happen. Not once I found out who this man in Guatemala was working for."

Something in her tone made his stomach tighten. "Oh?"

"He was a contractor, working for the European Union," Miriam said. "It's more complicated than that, but that's the short version. He had served under Jules Soult, in the French army, and then went to work for a Spanish firm that Soult had hired to handle EU security."

As the news sank in, it felt as if the bottom fell out of Steve's world. "Oh, my."

"Yes," Miriam said. "Oh, my. Because that means Jules Soult has what you went to Guatemala to find."

Steve nodded. It made sense. The Guardians were right. Jules Soult had murdered Chancellor Vögel.

And he had no way to prove it.

Paris, France

Margarite settled into a chair at a table outside *Le Rive Gauche* café and allowed her pores to soak up the gentle civilization of the Left Bank. Leafy trees lined the narrow street, the buildings whispered of elegance, and she could order a *café au lait* exactly the way she liked it. Every time she came home, she realized how much she missed Paris. There were other beautiful places on this earth, but none quite like this city.

Certainly not Germany, she thought with a little shudder, and then scolded herself. She forced herself to acknowledge that she hadn't really looked for beauty in Germany, in part because she visited only on business, and in part because of lingering resentments. Yet after the conversation with Renate at the train station in Berlin, and now having heard that several mayors had joined the mayor of Berlin in suspending the relocation laws, she was prepared to see Germany and Germans in a different light.

She settled back in her chair, awaiting her coffee, smiling as she drank in the atmosphere. Around her, voices chatted in a familiar language for a change, and the air smelled of trees, cigarettes, wine, fresh bread and food being prepared. She sank into the wonderful familiarity as she might have settled into a favored chair.

Perfect.

Except for the tourists, of course. *Le Rive Gauche* was bound to attract them, and it did, but she forgave them. At least they were civilized enough to seek out this beautiful place.

The gray day smelled of coming rain, but the red canvas canopy overhead would shelter her if necessary. When her coffee arrived, she raised it to her nose and inhaled the wonderful scent. *Home.*

Then she glanced at her watch and wondered where Michel was. That he was late should not, she supposed, be surprising, given that he worked for the *Sûreté.* Things happened when one was a *gendarme,* even one as high-ranking as Michel.

A gentle rain had started to fall by the time he arrived, a tall, lean man with gray-dashed dark hair, a beakish nose and a wide smile.

"Margarite!" he said delightedly, seizing both her hands to bring them to his lips. "It has been too long. How do you like working in Italy? Much sun, yes?"

She had cultivated Michel as a source for the past three years, and he knew that her apparent employment as an antiquarian was cover for her job with an international police force. He assumed she was with Interpol, and she let him. Twice she had aided him in stolen art cases. That, and their casual romantic interludes, had cemented their relationship. But they preserved the surface illusion that she was an antiquarian because it also protected Michel.

"I suppose it *is* sunny there, but I have been working in Germany." She made a moue of disgust.

"Ma petite pauvre," he said with mock sympathy. "Was it worth your while?"

"Some items of interest lack provenance."

He shrugged. "The war. The background of some pieces will never be recovered. Pity."

"Barbaric," she said flatly. "Extremely so. Now they are herding Muslims together."

His mouth tightened, and he looked around. "Please, *mon amie,* not too loudly."

"Why not?" she asked, both curious and surprised by his reaction.

He shrugged. "Most people favor it. And sometimes they favor it very—shall we say—heatedly?"

In that instant Margarite realized that a new wind truly had begun to blow. Here, of all places, on the Left Bank of the Seine, free speech and thought were treasured. Now Michel, himself an inspector of police, was worried that she had spoken disparagingly of the removal?

"Michel, what is going on?"

"Nothing. Truly."

"The burning of the mosque...*abominable!* Are you telling me anyone condones that?"

"*Non.* Of course not." He waved for the waiter and ordered two more *cafés au lait* for them, along with a basket of pastries. "Forgive me, Margarite. Matters are so tense here, I feel as if I am sitting on a powder keg all the time. I am perhaps too sensitive."

She would certainly say so, but instead she merely smiled. "I am sorry. I should have guessed, given current events."

At that he seemed to relax, and when the pastries arrived, he tucked in with the appetite of a man who hadn't eaten recently.

"So what brings you to Paris?" he asked. His eyes smoldered into a smile. "Pleasure, I hope."

A part of her wished that she could abandon herself for a few hours with him. But there was work to be done. "I am afraid not, Michel," she said, her voice tinged with sadness. "Business. Always business. But I would rather do business here than in Germany."

"Ah." He dabbed his mouth with a napkin. "At least it gives me an opportunity to see you again." He raised his coffee cup as if in toast and sipped.

"I have missed you, Michel." And that was true. But the situation rendered that irrelevant. Duty first, and duty required that she elicit more information. Perhaps a ruse was in order. "If you think from what I said that I object to the removal, I have misrepresented myself."

He arched an eyebrow.

"Something must be done to end the violence, *non?* But why do you look so tired? I would have thought you were receiving aid from the EU security force to catch those involved in the rioting."

Something in him stilled, and she did not miss it. After a moment, she leaned forward. "Michel?"

"What?"

"When I was in Germany…" She leaned forward even farther and lowered her voice. "I heard something that distressed me."

"Oui?"

"I heard that a man had been arrested for killing an EU security officer. But he is claiming that the security man threw a firebomb into a crowd of demonstrators."

"I have heard that story, as well."

"I need to know…" She hesitated.

He understood their relationship as well as she. "What is it?" he said finally. "If I know, I will tell you."

"Is it true? Is this just a crazy man lying in order to avoid prison, or are EU security people really involved in these riots?"

He frowned then, a very deep frown. "That is a serious charge."

"I am charging no one, Michel. I am merely curious."

"No, you are not merely curious. I have never known you to ask a question for which you did not think you knew the answer before you asked." He dropped his partially eaten pastry on his plate and dabbed his lips with his napkin. "We have helped each other much over the past few years."

"*Oui.*"

"I am grateful to you, *mon amie.*"

"As I am grateful to you."

He smiled. "We have been a good together, have we not? We both need our special sources."

Why was he hedging? she wondered. It was almost as if he were saying farewell. But then she brushed the thought aside. It was too ridiculous.

"I do not know if this supposition has any basis," he said. "Even EU security agents have personal opinions and may act on them."

She nodded.

"You obviously have some confidence in these rumors. I will sound things out quietly and let you know if this was an isolated incident." He shrugged. "I would like to know myself. I had not been thinking along those lines."

"I wouldn't have, except for what happened in Berlin. The witnesses may be wrong. In times of stress, people are often mistaken in their observations."

"That," said Michel, "I believe. But I will check out the other possibility and let you know."

"Merci."

Again he shrugged and dropped his napkin on the table. "Are you certain you cannot stay for a while?" His smile, as always, sent a shiver of raw desire running through her.

"I wish I could. I miss our *cinq-à-sept,"* she admitted, referring to the traditional hours of illicit liaisons. "Next time."

"Most definitely next time. Now I must go to a meeting." He looked disappointed as he rose and bent to kiss her cheek. "Come back soon, *chéri."*

She sat on for a while, reluctant to leave, because when she did, she would have no idea how soon she might return. Michel, in his usual way, had left money on the table to cover the coffee and pastries.

The rain continued to fall gently. She ordered another coffee. Then, realizing she could only wait now, she called for the bill for her second coffee.

Michel would send out feelers. It might be days or even weeks before he actually knew anything certain.

But of one thing Margarite had no doubt: If Soult was at any level involved in this mess, Michel would sniff it out.

Then, sadly, she began to walk away from the café. Tonight she would return to Rome.

She never noticed the man who rose from another table, tossed a few euros down, tucked a newspaper under his arm and joined the flow of people on the street behind her.

Nice, France

Etienne Duchamps stood at the front of the rail car, looking back at row upon row of men facing him from their seats. Given the expressions on their faces, he was happy to be carrying an automatic rifle.

The removal train had left Nice Ville, the main station in Nice, fifteen minutes ago, promptly at 6:00 a.m., every seat full of Muslims. The women were in separate cars at the front of the train, the men at the back. That was the first thing Duchamps objected to. Why didn't the men stay with their families to watch over them? No man worth his salt would leave his wife and children alone at such a time.

But there were other things he did not like. France had welcomed these people for more than ninety years from places that were both poor and backward. In return, what did France get? Riots. Bloodshed. Terror.

But that view he kept to himself. His job was to ensure that these people made it from Nice to Toulon. Not a long trip. Some removal trains traveled a lot farther.

These people would resettle only two hours away. And Toulon had the advantage of having a naval base, which he was sure would protect both the Muslims, as if they were worth it, and the local inhabitants. Nor should these passengers complain too loudly, considering what Muslim *jihadists* were doing to Europe.

But Etienne Duchamps belonged to the European Security Force, so here he stood, guarding people who by rights ought to be sent back to Algiers. His orders were clear: He was not here to protect these people as much as he was to here to ensure they went to Toulon peacefully.

The whole of France felt as if it were sitting on a bomb. The bloody street rioting was bad enough, but the burning of the mosque in Paris had unlocked something dark and ugly. Etienne, who held no great interest in other cultures or politics, was sure of only one thing: There would be retribution for the burning of that mosque, but it was not going to happen on *his* train.

He again scanned the rows of seats as the train slid over the rails. Many of the men had begun to read and murmur among themselves. Among them were boys, one as young as eight. Etienne was sure these men would attempt no violence while their young sons were with them. Nor with their women and daughters in the other cars.

But then he realized he was assuming there were no fanatics among them. Those *jihadists* could not be relied upon to behave as normal men. So he scanned the car again, hands tightening on his rifle.

One row away from him sat a boy with huge brown eyes. The boy stared at Etienne with fascination. Etienne shifted uncomfortably and frowned, hoping to make him look away. The child continued to stare.

The man beside him spoke. "Forgive my son, *monsieur.* He has never seen anyone holding a rifle before except on television."

"Non?" Etienne shrugged. "It is for your protection."

"So we are told. Do you know where they plan to put us in Toulon?"

"I have heard something about the North African Quarter, but I am not certain. It is merely my purpose to ensure you arrive."

"We are grateful for your protection," the man said.

Etienne thought that statement sounded more sarcastic than genuine, but he could not be certain. The man's face, clean-shaven, remained placid.

"I am more fortunate than many," the man said.

"How so?"

"I am not leaving behind a business or a house. I worked for a banking house, and we lived in an apartment. I have been assured that I will have a job awaiting me in Toulon."

"If you are allowed to leave the protection zone."

"I have also been assured I can work on my computer at home."

"What do you do, exactly?"

"I analyze investments. Primarily public bonds. It is mostly research. One does not need an office for that."

Etienne nodded. This man was very successful, he guessed. More successful than he was himself. Part of him begrudged that, and part of him accepted that as a citizen of France, the man had simply earned his way, unlike the young people today who, regardless of religion, couldn't seem to find or hold jobs.

"The youth," Etienne said. "It is the youth who cause much of the problem."

At that the man smiled. "Part of it, at least. But that is because they are not occupied. Or because some pour poison in their ears. All kinds of poison flow from tongues these days."

Etienne couldn't deny that. *"Madrassas,"* he said, referring to the mosque schools that often turned out militants and *jihadists.*

The man nodded. "We had no *madrassas.* I would not allow my son to attend one."

"Why not?"

"Because it is a school of one sect, Wahhabi. They believe Islamic countries should be theocracies, ruled by religion."

"And you do not?"

"I think religion and politics can become very messy when joined. The French realized that long ago, *oui?"*

It was true. *"Oui."*

"Only look how ugly matters have become here."

Another man spoke. "Be quiet, Khalil. You were always soft."

The man called Khalil turned and looked at his fellow passenger. "Soft on what, Binyamin? I am not soft on the practice of my faith."

"You cannot see the wrong that is being done to us with this removal."

"Oh, but I can. Still, there is violence enough. If this is how it must be ended, then so be it."

Binyamin snorted. "Every time we get treated this way, the risk of violence increases. The people who thought up this plan will learn before long. Do you think the *jihadists* will allow this to go on without retaliation? I assure you, they won't. The world will be in flames because of this."

Etienne's grip tightened on his gun, and he remembered his orders. "Enough," he barked.

Without warning, the brakes began to screech. The jolt of the emergency halt knocked him against the wall and down to the floor, though he managed to hang on to his rifle.

Then all hell broke loose.

21

Rome, Italy

"It's going to blow."

Margarite had barely stepped into Office 119 before Jefe's words greeted her.

"What is?"

"This whole situation." He was sitting before a bank of monitors, scanning news stations, his arms folded over his chest. "This relocation is going to backfire. Listen to the Arabic news stations. Then listen to the European ones."

"I didn't know you understood Arabic."

He rolled his eyes at her. "Try the English-language version of Al Jazeera. But the words are unnecessary. All you need is to watch the way the film clips are being chosen and shown. If someone doesn't come to his senses soon, this mess is going to make the Crusades look like a sports competition. What did you learn in Paris?"

"Nothing yet. My source has not heard about the EU being involved, but he will check and get back to me."

"How soon?"

Margarite frowned. "Soon. As soon as he can."

"You're sure he can be trusted?"

"How many times do I have to answer that question?"

"As many times as I ask it."

Margarite's frown deepened. Jefe was clearly suffering from a choleric mood today. "Lawton?"

"Still warming a cell."

"Renate?"

He cocked an eyebrow at her. "When did you start caring about Renate? She's still in Germany. Stubborn, as always. I've called the rest of the teams in."

Margarite registered shock. "Why?"

"We know this all traces back to Soult. The three men we killed in Strasbourg were private military contractors working for a Colonel Hector de Vasquez y San Claro."

"Mercenaries?" Margarite asked, her thoughts suddenly in freefall as she tried to rearrange pieces.

"Private security, at least," Jefe said. "It turns out this Paxti Lezeta also worked for Vasquez for years. He was an informant against ETA. Apparently got some of his own family killed in the process."

Margarite nodded. "What does this tell us?"

"Soult started as Director of Security for the EU after Black Christmas."

"I remember."

"He served with Vasquez in NATO. They did some ops together in the Balkans. Then Vasquez went private, set up a company called *Protección Ejecutiva Atiende.* Executive Protection Services. PEA started with the usual security stuff, protecting corporate bigwigs and their families. He hired former military, exclusively. Remember when those two Swiss kids, the son and daughter of a banker in Zurich, were kidnapped by the FARC in Colombia, three years back?"

Margarite nodded.

"It was a PEA team that got them out," Jefe said. "Killed six of their kidnappers in the process and pretty much made a hash of the FARC base where they were being held. Tough guys."

"Lezeta was one of them?" Margarite asked.

"He worked for PEA, but he wasn't on that op, so far as I know. He seems to have been working in Lebanon at the time. God knows there was enough work to do there."

"How did he end up in EU security?"

"That's the curious part," Jefe said, smiling. "When Soult took over security for the EU, guess who he hired?"

"PEA?"

"Bingo," Jefe said. "Then, when Soult was elected as President of the European Commission, who moves into his old job as security director?"

"Vasquez," she said, her heart speeding up. "And the PEA contractors become EU security."

Jefe nodded. "I also got a message from Miriam Anson. One of the guys we took out in Strasbourg was in Guatemala back when she was there. May have been part of the killing of the U.S. ambassador there, or may have been privately hunting the people who did it. She's not sure. But she's sure he was there. Then he shows up in Strasbourg, trying to take down Kasmir al-Khalil."

"Could they have been legitimate?" she asked. "It sounds like they've been working with the good guys. They rescued those kids in Colombia, were probably hunting for the assassins in Guatemala, then trying to arrest al-Khalil in Strasbourg."

"I'd think so," Jefe said. "But we know who paid for the training of the rebels who killed the ambassador in Guatemala, and we know who was paying al-Khalil."

"The Frankfurt Brotherhood," she said.

"Exactly. And guess who funded Soult's Europa Prima Party when it was getting started?"

"The Frankfurt Brotherhood." Margarite pulled out a chair and sat, her mind awhirl with the possibility that she and Renate had put the picture together correctly. There were too many connections to ignore.

"That puts Monsieur Soult right in the middle of this mess," Jefe said.

"Vasquez is Röhm," Margarite said quietly.

"Röhm?" Jefe asked.

She quickly outlined the discussion she'd had with Renate in Berlin, which had led to the theory Jefe had originally found far-fetched. As Margarite talked, his stomach rolled over.

"If Vasquez is Röhm," he said, "then Soult is…"

He let the sentence hang there, but she finished it.

"*Oui.* Monsieur Soult *voudrait devenir notre meneur.*"

Jefe shook his head. "In English, please?"

"He wants to be our leader. It translates better into German. The word is *Führer.*"

"Shit."

"*Oui. Merde.*"

He closed his eyes, running a hand through his thick, dark hair. When he looked up, the TV was showing a view from a helicopter. A train. On fire. With dead bodies. With bullet holes.

He turned up the sound.

Rome, Italy

Ahmed's face tightened as he watched the news from Nice. The images were coming from a news helicopter, and the blackening cars of the French relocation train looked like dismembered segments of a fiery, dying serpent.

But it was not the dying train that drew Ahmed's attention, nor did it hold the attention of the cameraman in the helicopter. Instead, the camera focused on the bodies laid out liked pale logs alongside the tracks. A few were charred, curled into fetal position, hands clenched in the "boxer's pose" common to burn victims. More seemed simply asleep, apparent victims of the toxic smoke as the train burned. Too many, far too many, were stitched with the telltale red blotches of bullet holes.

They had been shot while trying to escape the inferno.

The burn and smoke victims, he might have understood. Tragic accidents could happen, after all. But this tragedy had been compounded intentionally. This was no mere accident. This was nothing less than murder.

"We must strike back," Abdul al-Nasser said firmly.

Ahmed shook his head. "At whom? It is one thing to wish to strike back, Abdul. It is something else again to strike back effectively. We have no responsible target at which to strike."

"Then let us burn one of *their* trains!" al-Nasser said. "Surely you are not simply going to let this pass?"

"Do you really believe they would let an unescorted Muslim anywhere near a passenger train now?" Ahmed asked. "They will know we are angry. The police— everyone—will be on heightened alert for any hint of retaliation. If we try to strike now, all that will happen is that *Saif* operatives—good and brave Muslims—will be captured or killed. Worse, it will only salve people's consciences over this tragedy. They will think those poor Muslims got what they deserved."

"You are weak," al-Nasser said. "Small wonder that you were sent here, far from the battle in our homelands. The Europeans send Shi'a to live among us, serving them up as lambs to the slaughter, and do you take the chance to rid Islam of these heretics? No. You give them a district of their own, allow them a mosque in which to shame Allah with their infidel words. Now good and brave Muslims are slain by the hundreds, openly, for the world to see, and *still* you refuse to act. Sword of the East? You carry no sword, only your limp idealism. But the world cares nothing for your ideals, Ahmed Ahsami. Nothing! They will kill us all, or we will kill them all. They give us no other choice."

"There is always a choice!" Ahmed said, his jaw tight with rage. "And always, *always*, those who would make the wrong choice claim they have no choice to make. We cannot win a war of annihilation against the West, Abdul. They have nuclear weapons. We do not. In such a war, it is we who would be annihilated."

"Allah would never permit that," al-Nasser replied. "You should have more faith."

Ahmed's face nearly touched al-Nasser's as he replied. "Oh, I agree that Allah would not permit it. Because Allah will not permit people like you to bring destruction down on us all. *Never* question my faith, al-Nasser. It was my faith which birthed *Saif Alsharaawi*."

"Perhaps that is so," al-Nasser said, "but, Allah be praised, it is not your kind of faith that will sustain *Saif Alsharaawi*. No, it will the faith of stronger men, men who will not shirk their sacred duty. I will contact Riyadh. They will authorize action, even if you will not."

"Do not go over my head," Abdul warned. "Do not test my patience."

"Patience?" al-Nasser said, his face twisted in a bitter smirk. "Patience is all you have. But we need no patience now. Now is a time for strength. And strength is what you lack."

Abdul watched as al-Nasser stormed up the stairs. For a moment Abdul thought about following him, restraining him if necessary, before the hot-headed young man set off a fire that could not be quenched. Then he paused.

No, he would let the sheik handle this. The sheik would see the folly of al-Nasser's plan and set him in his place more firmly than Abdul could do. Let al-Nasser fashion his own noose.

Then Abdul would let him hang himself in it.

Strasbourg, France

"This is not good," Vasquez said to Soult. They were sitting in Soult's inner sanctum, watching the unfolding story of the relocation train, listened to the word *massacre* being used over and over like a drumbeat.

Soult swore as the images of dead Muslims were spread over the television. Some were burned, as if killed in an accident. But far too many had been shot, and there would be no doubt that it was French nationals who had done the shooting. Only the security agents had been permitted to carry weapons on the train. Only they could have opened fire.

"The Germans," he said.

"*Qué?*" Vasquez asked.

"This will galvanize them. Müller will not dare to contradict the mayor of Berlin now. Other mayors already follow his example. We will lose Germany."

"We cannot," Vasquez said. "Their economy…"

"Precisely," Soult said. "The loss of Germany would be a fatal blow to the EU. And every other country will know it."

Another image on the screen caught his attention, and he turned to look at it more fully. A country priest was descending from the remnants of the train, a sobbing young boy in a skullcap in his arms. Behind him came a uniformed EU security guard, unarmed. Such images were likely to kill all his plans if he didn't move swiftly.

"We need to move against Germany."

Vasquez looked at him. "You will have to justify it. The French government is willing to assist you, especially against Germany, but they say they need a diplomatic explanation. They do not wish to become the 'bad guy,' as the Americans would say. Especially since America has troops in Germany."

Soult pointed to the TV screen. "We will use that."

"How? It looks very bad."

"But now everyone will be expecting retaliation."

Vasquez nodded slowly. "Yes. We put out some warnings."

"Exactly. Say we have received threats because of this. It will then become necessary to protect the government of the EU, yes? From retaliation."

"Yes." Vasquez nodded in agreement. "So we protect this city with French troops."

"We create a *defense perimeter* around this city. Fifty kilometers."

"Which will extend into Germany."

Soult smiled and shrugged. "So it must."

"They will object."

"If we are fortunate, they will defend their borders."

The smile of understanding that spread across Vasquez's face said everything. "Brilliant."

"I did not become a general and then a president by accident, Hector."

"No, of course not." But then Vasquez paused, looking at the television, and the expression on his face became hard. "I want to command the defense force."

Soult lifted both eyebrows. "Why do you think you should do that?"

"Because I am in charge of the security forces. This will be an EU operation. The head of the Department of Collective Security ought to be in charge of it. And that is the understanding that we have with France. When acting under EU mandate, units will have EU leadership."

Soult's brows lowered, and his tone became eerily soft. "You did not make that part the EU agreement with them, did you?"

Vasquez flushed. "Of course. I am entitled, given my position and the purpose of this force."

"You are entitled to what I give you, and nothing more. Frenchmen will not fight under a Spaniard!"

"Monsieur President, may I remind you—"

"You may remind me of nothing!" Soult said. "Go see to the remaining plans, while I fix this mess you've made."

Vasquez hesitated, then nodded. As he walked out, both men looked as if they had just tasted something noxious. There had just been a rupture. The only question now was which of them would get the better of it.

Soult was sure he would. After all, he'd known Vasquez's usefulness was reaching an end. Soon, perhaps sooner, he would become nothing but a handicap.

Hector Vasquez was merely hurrying the inevitable.

Part III: *LA FLEUR DE GUERRE*
(French: *The flower of war*)

22

Berlin, Germany

The headlines shrieked from every newsstand: Massacre in Nice. Renate stood on the rain-dampened street before the vendor's stall, the night hazily illuminated by streetlights that only seemed to heighten the sense of quiet desolation. A horrific story. She had seen the video clips on the news, along with the strangely awkward reportage that seemed almost to dance around the entire event. As if no one wanted to face up to the underlying reality that had put nine hundred people on that train and sent them out to die.

The German government had already acted. Chancellor Müller had been on the news last night, ordering all local officials to suspend relocations in Germany. No sooner had he spoken than Soult had been on the screen, hinting that there had been a suicide bomber on the train, arguing that the hundreds of deaths were an unfortunate incident that could not be allowed to set back the plan that had, until then, been quieting the unrest in Europe. To stop the relocations was to give in to terrorism, he said. Then he had specifically challenged the Chancellor, stating that Germany was obliged to comply with EU mandates.

After her phone call that morning with Jefe, and the clear if circumstantial evidence that Soult was working through Vasquez to spread the very violence he claimed to be quelling, she no longer had any doubt where her duty lay. She was a German. First, last and always.

Annoyed and irritable, she turned from the mainstream press to the tabloid *Bild.* Germans joked that one should trust nothing one read in *Bild,* not even the date. Renate hadn't read the rag since her teens, when it had been a fun excuse to giggle with her friends.

But alone on a darkened Berlin street before sunrise, with no company save the occasional passing car and the vendor who sat in a corner of his stall smoking a pipe, she needed distraction. Things inside her were moving, shifting, trying to upend her in some way, and keeping her from sleep in the process. She felt awful, horrible, much as she had felt in the weeks following her death, when she had become Renate Bächle. Some major change was trying to take place.

Bild, with its usual disregard of events of current significance, was still harping on the riot that had resulted in Lawton's jailing. Photo of bomber! the headline shrieked. Unable to stop herself, she picked it up and paid for it.

A photo, even one from *Bild,* might provide a clue.

She was strolling away from the kiosk with the paper tucked under her arm because there wasn't enough light to study it on this wet, hazy night when her cell phone rang. It was an odd hour for a call, and at once her heart kicked into high gear.

The voice that spoke her name was utterly unexpected.

"Renate," he said. "Ahmed."

Ahmed. The Saudi who had helped them take down the cell in Prague. The man who called his organization the Sword of the East and claimed that all he wanted was to put the Muslim countries on an equal footing with the rest of the world. Put simply, he wanted the rest of the world to, as Lawton would say, "Butt out."

"What a surprise," she replied. They spoke in English, their only common tongue.

"I wish it could be a pleasant surprise."

"You read about the train?"

His voice was cold. "Read it. Saw it on TV. Already the photographs of the carnage are blown up as posters and plastered in cities across the Middle East, as well as in the relocation zones in Europe. It is a gift to the worst among us. I am told that boys and girls as young as seven or eight are flocking to the extremists."

"Tell me something I don't know."

"Renate, you must listen. I cannot say much. But I

will tell you this—*Saif Alsharaawi* will likely respond to this atrocity. And neither of us is going to like that response."

She didn't like what she was hearing. He was no longer in control of his own organization. After they disconnected, she quickly looked around to make sure she was not being followed, she hurried back to her hotel.

Her worst nightmares were coming to pass.

Béziers, France

"What feeling are you getting from the news over there?" Grant Lawrence asked her.

"It's been shifting even as I watch it," Miriam said. "The word *massacre* is being mentioned less, and there's more talk of a suicide bomber on the train."

"That's what we're starting to see here, too. Your impression?"

"It's being spun," she said. "It's a cover-up."

"You think the shootings were deliberate?"

"Not necessarily the shootings. But the evidence I've found here points to one place, and that place isn't in the Middle East."

"Miriam," Grant said, "what are you saying?"

"I can't say much, Grant. Not on the phone. But I have some sources who have been working this for a while. It looks like President Soult may be behind a lot of it. Like it's been orchestrated."

There was silence from his end. "What can we do?"

"Rice needs to let Müller know he has the support of the U.S. in defying these EU mandates. And Soult has to know it, too."

"I'll talk to him," Grant said. "So can I tell Terry you'll be coming home?"

"Not yet. There are some leads I need to follow up."

She hated to hold things back from Grant, but she saw no other option. There were too many leaks in Washington, even in the White House. She couldn't risk exposing Father Steve, or Lawton and the rest of Office 119. And she might have to do some things Harrison Rice could not know about.

"Okay. But keep in touch. I'll work on Rice to handle the diplomatic angle with Müller and Soult. You take the operations side." He paused for a moment. "Make things work out right, Miriam."

She disconnected. Grant had chosen his words well, with a clear subtext: *Do what needs doing, and don't leave our fingerprints when you're done.*

After she disconnected, she turned to Steve. "So what haven't you told me? Are you all right?"

"Honestly, no. My superiors attempted to have me followed. They still want the artifact I was sent to Guatemala to find. But it was stolen from me, and now they think I'm trying to get it back."

"Are you?"

He nodded, eyes hollow. "Miriam, I thought it was

merely a bit of text that might be embarrassing, but it's more than that. It is terrifyingly more than that."

"What?"

He shook his head. "You would never believe me. Suffice it to say that it is a powerful tool. A weapon. It killed Chancellor Vögel."

She hesitated, then said, "You know, Steve, if I can believe that much, I can believe a lot more."

His head jerked a little, but why she couldn't tell.

"You look awful," she said finally. "You haven't been eating, have you?"

"I've been busy."

"Well, you can eat and be busy at the same time. I haven't eaten today, so I'm going to call room service. What kind of food are you eating these days?"

A small smile leavened his face. "Anything that doesn't include a tortilla."

She chuckled at that, and reached for both the menu and phone. Before she dialed, however, she looked at him again. "I know we don't have much of a history, but what we do have was very, *very* important to me. You changed me, Father. Forever."

"The experience changed us all."

"No, *you* changed me. So let me make one thing very clear to you."

"Yes?"

"I don't have to believe every word you say in order to do everything within my power to help."

"What do you know about the Tablets of Thoth?"

Miriam frowned for a moment. Her initial impulse was to frown at words that sounded like ancient legend, but then an odd sense of rightness settled over her. "Nothing at all. Let me order, then we'll talk."

At Miriam's suggestion, Steve slipped out of sight when the room service cart arrived. If the waiter thought it at all odd that someone so slender should have ordered so much food, he never let it show. One advantage of a great hotel combined with generous tipping was the best service in the world.

When the waiter had gone, and the door was locked and chained, Steve joined her, and they sat down to a repast of duck, and an assortment of side dishes and desserts fit for a king. With an almost apologetic smile, Steve dug in like a starving man. Miriam smiled at his enjoyment. There was, she thought, genuine asceticism, and then there was foolhardiness. Steve's gaunt body worried her.

Finally his eating slowed, and he began to talk. "How much history have you studied?"

"That would depend on what kind of history you mean."

He smiled, and finally a bit of comfort stole into his expression. "The history of civilizations. Way back. The great architecture, the stories of gods, many things forgotten by most."

She shook her head slowly. "I've studied history, of

course, but my concentration was mostly on recent European and U.S. history. And for the past few years I've been delving seriously into Middle Eastern history and culture."

"Very typical."

He looked down at his plate as if surprised that it was still there. Once he'd eaten enough, apparently he'd forgotten all about the food.

"I'm trying to decide how to start. I don't want to bore you with a bunch of unnecessary information. I want to get to the point as quickly as possible."

"Take your time," she replied. Reaching out, she refilled their wineglasses from the bottle room service had brought.

"Did I tell you that the Church sent me to Guatemala to find something?"

"I think you mentioned something earlier."

"Did I tell you what it was? It was called the Red Codex."

"And the Church wanted it why?"

"Because it might establish that Jesus had married and had a son or grandson, who went to the Americas and became a teacher known as Kulkulcan, Quetzalcoatl, Viracocha…choose any of the names by which he's known."

"Yes," she said. "I remember you telling me this in Guatemala. It put the Church's knickers in a twist."

Steve chuckled and sipped his wine. With each passing minute he was looking better. "Apparently so. While the Church has no dogma on whether Jesus married, tradition has always held that he didn't. In the end, I suppose, it doesn't matter."

"It doesn't matter if Jesus married?"

Steve shrugged. "Why should it? He came here to be a man and die as a man to prove God's love for us. If he was a man, why should it appall anyone if he married and had children? That was certainly considered the right thing for a man to do in his time."

"But people would think they had been lied to."

"And that, I told myself, was probably the concern. Still, it remains that the Church says only that tradition and scripture say nothing of Christ having been married. If you press them hard enough, the answer will be that no one knows for certain."

Miriam nodded. "I can buy that."

"The worst that could be said is that there might have been some artful omissions from the gospels. That happened so long ago, it hardly seems to matter now, does it?"

Miriam pondered the matter. "I guess it wouldn't matter to me. I mean, I believe the teachings. I believe in the resurrection. If he had a wife, so what?"

"My thought exactly. Until recently."

"What happened?"

He sighed and shook his head. "Two things. One, the Red Codex exists. But it's not a book."

"No?"

"The other is... Suppose someone were to believe he was the descendent of Jesus. And just suppose he came into the possession of that codex, only the codex turned out to have...power."

Miriam was taken aback. "Are you talking about magic?"

Steve shook his head. "I'm talking about science. Extremely advanced science. The science that built the pyramids. There's an Egyptian legend that, in the earliest days of man, the god Thoth bequeathed an emerald tablet to men. This tablet revealed, to those who could see, some portion of the knowledge of the gods. There's a similar legend that traces back to a gift to Abraham when Enlil sent him forth from Ur of the Chaldees into Canaan."

"It sounds like the story of the Ten Commandments," Miriam said.

"A little." Steve shrugged. "There are similar legends in many cultures. The details differ, but in their essence they all describe divine knowledge being passed down to man in the form of some tangible object."

He shifted a bit in his chair and brushed a crumb from his lap. "Miriam, those legends are real. The Tablets of Thoth are real. But they weren't tablets."

"What were they?" Miriam asked.

"Perfect pyramids, carved of precious jewels," he said. "The Red Codex was carved of ruby. I held it in my hand, Miriam. And when I looked into it with light behind it, it was as if countless mathematical equations were dancing at its center. I'm no mathematician, and I couldn't make any sense of what I saw, but in the hands of someone who could interpret it and understand its meaning…"

"How does this relate to Chancellor Vögel?" Miriam asked.

"In a library in Toulouse, I found a diary," he said. "It was the diary of a woman who died here in Béziers, in the Albigensian Crusade. It spoke of a power being wielded by the crusader army. A power in the form of a pyramid. When the pyramid was lifted and words spoken, people inside the city heard the sound of trumpets, and the guards on the city walls suddenly began to gasp for air, choking to death for no reason anyone could see."

Miriam caught her breath. The reports of the security agents at Vögel's side had mentioned a hollow sound, like a distant trumpet, before the Reichstag dome collapsed and Vögel fell to the ground, gasping for breath. If this were the explanation, then a single man could be targeted. A terrifying possibility indeed.

"Unbelievable," she whispered.

"Is it?" Steve asked. "The Old Testament describes the battle of Jericho, where Joshua ordered his trumpeters to walk around the walls of the city seven times, blowing their trumpets each time. Then the walls collapsed and the city was taken."

"Are you saying Joshua had one of these pyramids?"

"Perhaps," Steve said. "Perhaps not. But if we are to believe the history of the campaign to capture Judea, he had some similar power. The herald trumpet is a common theme in scripture. The Jews still call together their people with the *shofar.* It is said that the archangel Gabriel will announce the return of Christ with the sound of the trumpet. Similar themes abound in other cultures. And I've held the Red Codex, Miriam. I know it exists. And whoever wields it now is a greater threat than you can possibly imagine."

Miriam reached into her briefcase and withdrew the sketch that Steve had e-mailed to her, along with the results of her search and the scanty information she had exchanged with Jefe in Rome, including the fact that the man in the photo had been killed a year earlier in Strasbourg. She did not mention that he had been killed by Office 119.

"And whoever killed him…they did not find the codex?" Steve asked.

"They certainly didn't mention it," she replied. "And I think they'd have said something about it. I'm not sure, though. They're a pretty secretive crew."

He regarded her warily. "Can you trust them, Miriam? Doesn't the world have enough secretive crews as it is?"

"Yes, I trust them, Father. And sometimes we need people who can fly beneath the radar. That's what these people do. But they do good work, Father. I know them."

He nodded. "In that case, we know who has the codex."

"Yes," she said. "The man delivered it before he was killed. And now Jules Soult has it."

"Even worse," Steve said, "he knows how to use it."

23

"In light of the bomb attack that nearly destroyed the Institutions Européens, the European Parliament must be able to protect itself," Soult declared, looking out at the bank of reporters and their television cameras.

It was a calculated risk. He had spent the last two days meeting with the French general staff, listening as they dusted off contingency plans that most had assumed would never be revisited. Even a year ago, the prospect of a major power war in Europe would have been laughable.

But Soult knew he could not allow Germany to lead Europe off the path he had set, and in the aftermath of the disaster in Nice, Chancellor Müller had made it clear that he would not enforce the removal laws. The Minister-Presidents of Baden-Württemberg and Bavaria had taken this as a cue not only to suspend removals in their regions but to return those who had already been relocated back to their own homes.

The German state of Baden-Württemberg lay directly across the Rhine from Strasbourg, and therein lay the germ of Soult's idea. He needed only to take a small, easy first bite to set his plan in motion.

"Because the European Union must be able to protect its capitol complex, today I have proposed legislation that would mandate our Muslim Protection Act in all regions that lie within fifty kilometers of Strasbourg. I am aware that this zone includes both French and German territory. And I have received assurance from the French government that the Muslim Protection Act has been and will continue to be enforced on French soil."

This next part was key, and he paused for a moment to allow both reporters and the television audience the chance to concentrate fully on his words.

"However, when I spoke with the Minister-President of Baden-Württemberg today, he made it clear to me that he would not comply with the removal legislation enacted by the *Bundestag* and signed by the German president. He has said that he will defy his Chancellor and the will of the German people as expressed by its legislature.

"As you know," Soult continued, "we have open borders within the European Union. Anyone can cross the Rhine from France into Germany or vice versa, at any time. And we are proud of our open borders, which have become a sign of international trust and cooperation. For France to close the Rhine would both interrupt the commercial shipping on that great river, and would send a sad and even dangerous message within the Union. We considered this option, but after discussions with both French and German leaders, it was not considered a viable solution."

Eyes widened as the implications of his plan began to settle into the minds of the reporters, and Soult took this as his cue to nod sadly, gravely, as if the weight of his decision bore heavily on every fiber of his being.

"Thus, I have no choice but to ask that our parliament declare the fifty-kilometer radius around Strasbourg as a security zone under the exclusive jurisdiction of the European Union. The President of France has assured me that, if this legislation is passed, France will cede its part of this region to the European Union. The Chancellor of Germany has said that he will not. And if he will not, the Union will be forced to assert its lawful jurisdiction over the area.

"We hope to resolve this peacefully. We pray that we can. But to Chancellor Müller, I say this. Do not test the will of the European Union. We must and will protect ourselves from terrorism. Stand with us, or stand alone and face the consequences."

For an instant the room was dead silent. Soult knew that his steely gaze as he read the final paragraph would leave no doubt as to the subtext. Not a single mind had failed to hear the unspoken words: Under the EU flag, French troops stood ready to move into Germany.

It was tantamount to a declaration of war.

Baden-Württemberg, Germany

Hans Neufel and his men had gathered around a portable TV, listening to Soult's speech with tightening guts.

"Stand alone and face the consequences?" Schulingen was clearly outraged. He stomped away toward the trees as if he could walk away from what they had all just heard.

They were on the move again but had paused for a meal, most likely, Neufel thought, because the lieutenant had wanted to hear this speech on his radio. So the panzer unit, stretched along a barely discernible cow path, had halted, eaten some of the horrible MREs their bosses bought from the Americans, and Zweibach had turned on his fancy new TV.

Now this.

Zweibach, just eighteen, looked up at Neufel, who was less than two years older, as if he were a wise man. "Why?" he asked.

It was a simple question, but a loaded one. Neufel hardly felt adequate to answer. This was politics, and he was still learning the ways of the army.

But his gut, clenched like a fist, gave the answer anyway. "War," he said.

Zweibach's eyes grew huge. Neufel ignored him and

went to stand facing the thick forest, looking away from his men. The test was coming, and fear slickened his palms and dried his mouth. Would he be up to it?

A half hour later his suspicion was confirmed when the lieutenant came up to him.

"You heard?"

"Ja."

"We are to move toward the Rhine. To the vicinity of Kehl. Be ready in twenty minutes."

And so it begins, Neufel thought numbly. With such simple words.

Berlin, Germany

Renate was distracted from the book she was reading by cries of outrage. She was sitting in the lobby of the Berlin jail, awaiting Lawton's release. At first she thought there had been another outbreak of violence, but when she looked up at the television firmly bolted to the wall, she saw the face of Jules Soult. The text crawling across the bottom of the screen explained the angry words that flowed around her like water.

Stand with us…or face the consequences?

Soult was threatening nothing less than war. If Herr Bundeskanzler Müller did not comply with Soult's demand to cede Germany's portion of the so-called "EU Security Zone," Soult would try to claim it by force. And Renate had no doubt that he already had troops at hand to send across the Rhine at the first opportunity. He wouldn't make such a threat if he hadn't already arranged to back it up.

"Herr Lawton Caine."

Renate looked up as the guard behind the counter called out the name. She rose and looked to the sally port, where moments later Lawton emerged with a surprised look on his face. Their embrace was brief and discreet, but warm nonetheless.

"What happened?" he asked.

"Not here," she replied.

He quickly retrieved his personal effects, and they stepped out onto the street. As they walked toward the U-Bahn station, Lawton seemed relieved simply to be free. She kept her silence for a few minutes, allowing him to experience the transition, before they finally took seats at the station and she turned to him.

"Thank God for *Bild,*" she said quietly. "And I never thought I would say that."

"The tabloid?" Lawton asked.

She nodded. "If they never again publish a true word, and they may well not, they justified their existence this week. Someone on the Oranienstraße had a camera and took pictures of the riot. *Bild* bought the pictures and, after the tragedy in Nice, published them under a shrieking headline about conspiracies in Europe. Most of their story was utter rubbish, but one of the pictures showed Paxti Lezeta throwing the firebomb."

"Even a blind squirrel finds an acorn now and then," Lawton said.

She looked at him for a moment, as she often did when he offered an American colloquialism. Finally she nodded. "Yes, that is a good description."

"What really happened in Nice?" he asked. "I saw some reports on the news, but I wasn't sure how much to believe. Some of the pundits were saying the security forces simply panicked, while others were talking about suicide bombers on the train."

"We don't know for sure yet," Renate said. "Margarite has been looking into it. So far there is no confirmed evidence of a suicide bomber on the train, but we have no evidence that it was a planned event, either. My guess is that it was an accidental fire that turned into a tragedy when the train guards lost their heads."

He shook his head. "That wouldn't be a surprise. Even if the guards were well-trained, everyone was nervous. If you put a handful of twenty-something kids with assault rifles in with a trainload of people they've come to see as potential terrorists, it's really not a matter of whether this is going to happen. It's just a matter of when and where and how often, and how many will die."

"*Ja, leider,*" Renate said. *Yes, sadly.*

They sat quietly until the subway train arrived, then settled into their seats. The train was crowded, and they were forced together in a way that Renate found both warmly comfortable and irritatingly distracting. She could not allow herself such feelings, and especially not for another Office 119 agent. But she did not resist when Lawton took her hand in his.

"I'm glad you were there when I got out," he said.

She noticed his hand was shaking a bit, and his eyes bore a faraway look. She sensed that there was more he wanted to say and gave his hand a gentle squeeze. She was aching, she realized. War lay just around the corner of the next few days or weeks, and before it came, she wanted to just be human. Not an agent. A woman. To toss off all the detritus of the past years and find that buried kernel of herself. Needing the same from him, she squeezed his hand again to encourage him to talk.

"I used to visit my dad in prison," he finally said. "I would try to cheer him up, and he would tell me it was all good. I knew it wasn't. But until these past few weeks, I really had no idea what he was going through."

"Did anyone mistreat you?" Renate asked softly. She knew that such treatment was not permitted in German jails, and especially not for those who were being held awaiting trial. She would find a way to have someone's head if he had been hurt.

"No," he said. "The guards were courteous. I had my own cell. The food was good enough. But still…"

His voice trailed off, and he stared out the window as the lights of the subway tunnel zoomed past. Renate gave him time, waiting for him to speak.

"I killed a man. There were times when even I wondered if I was sure he was the one who'd thrown that firebomb. I'd wake up at night, and I'd run that scene again and again in my mind. And sometimes it didn't look the same. Sometimes I thought maybe I'd seen someone else throw the bomb instead. I thought maybe I'd be convicted and end up spending years, or even the rest of my life, in jail. It was those times—the times I tried to steel myself for the worst possible outcome— when I understood how my dad had felt."

"You didn't think about...ending it, did you?" she asked carefully.

"I'm not sure you can be in that situation and not at least think about it," he replied. "You can't take a walk down the street and grab a sandwich. You can't think maybe you need a weekend off to sit on the beach, soak up some sun and let your mind wander. You can't pick up the phone and call a friend when you want to, or jump online to catch up on the baseball scores from the U.S. They treated me well, but I was still in jail. And suddenly all those things I'd taken for granted were gone, maybe for a little while, and maybe for the rest of my life."

"Das verstehe ich," she said. *I understand.*

"And yes, some part of you starts to think...what's the point? Why sit there, rolling through the same routine day after day, going nowhere, having no future except one more day of the same damn thing as yesterday? I couldn't tell you or Margarite that, of course. Just like my dad couldn't tell me that. He said it was all good. He kept right on saying it was all good. Then he found a way to kill himself."

"You couldn't have known," Renate said.

"Yeah," he said. "And I couldn't have known what my SAC had planned in Los Angeles. And I couldn't have known I'd break that guy's ribs when I tackled him. But at what point does 'I couldn't have known' become a meaningless phrase? How many dead before you decide you *should* have known…that you should have found *some way* to know? Nine hundred dead on that train in Nice, and I'll bet you someone said 'We couldn't have known.' He was my father, Renate. I should have known."

"Lawton, you're free now…."

He shook his head and continued. "I'm out, Renate. But I'm not free. My dad's still dead. Carlos Montoya is still dead. Lezeta is still dead. I'm still dead. You're still dead."

The ache within her overwhelmed her. Dead? They were not corpses rotting in a grave. Not yet.

They exited the train and rode an escalator up to the street. Renate's hotel was a half block away. Lawton was hurting, and she didn't know how to reach him. But one thing was painfully clear to her: She needed him back.

"We're not dead," she said as they stepped into her hotel room. "We're undercover, yes. Forever, yes. But we're not dead, Lawton."

"Aren't we?" he asked.

"We're standing here, talking to each other."

He let out a sigh and sat on the bed. "Yeah. We're standing here talking to each other. And when you need a release, you're fucking some Italian you met in a bar."

She studied him for a moment, trying to organize the thoughts that swirled through her. "Look, I'm sorry that...I didn't know it would..."

"And it shouldn't!" he said. "We both know that. We both know who we are and where we stand in life, what we can and can't do. I'm not stupid. You're not stupid. So I sit here and try to forget how Goddamned good it felt to step through that sally port and see your face, how good it felt to hug you and smell your hair, even if it smells like cigarettes, how good it felt to be squeezed next to you on that subway. I have to forget all that, because I'm dead and you're dead and dead people can't feel what I felt."

"We're not dead," she said, stepping closer, sitting beside him. "We're not, Lawton."

He moved away down the bed. "No. I don't want a mercy fuck, Renate. I'm not some desperate prisoner out of jail and looking for any pussy to feel alive again. And you're...you're too damn good to do that anyway."

"Yes," she said, closing the distance between them again. "I *am* too good to do that. I wouldn't give you a mercy fuck, as you called it. I wouldn't give my body to anyone that way."

"Unless he's Italian and in a bar."

"Stop it!" she said, slapping his face before she realized she had moved. "Oh, God. I'm sorry."

"No," he said, holding a hand to his cheek. "I deserved it."

"You did," she said. "But I'm still sorry, Lawton. That guy in the bar…that was scratching an itch. That's all it was. And you know what?"

She gave him no chance to answer. "I wouldn't do it again. It was going to scratch the itch, but I knew that was *all* it was going to do. It was not…like this…."

She leaned in and kissed him desperately. He didn't return the kiss, but neither did he resist it.

"Renate, we can't," he said, looking into her eyes.

"Yes, we can," she said. "Because we're *not* dead."

She kissed him again. This time he returned it, their lips caressing, exploring, parting for tongues to join in the dance. Her fingers wandered over his stubbly cheeks, the surprisingly soft skin at the curve of his neck, the gentle but firm curve of his shoulder.

"We're not dead," she whispered, a mantra of need, as he drew far enough away to cup one of her breasts in his hand.

"Not tonight, at least," he said.

He had just released the first three buttons of her blouse when the door burst open.

24

Berlin, Germany

Lawton and Renate were already rolling to the floor as the echoes of the splintering door frame had settled.

The metallic clicking of the bolt recycling, the thuds of rounds impacting on the mattress, were louder than the reports from the silenced handgun.

Lawton knew that neither he nor Renate had a weapon. Even if they had, there would be no way to reach it. While he had been lost in self-pity and lust and she'd been trying to pull him out of that pit, they had overlooked the basic rules of countersurveillance. They'd been followed. He hoped he would have the chance to kick himself for the mistake, but this was not that time. They had only moments before the gunman found them on the floor, sandwiched between the bed and the wall.

He gathered his legs beneath him, realizing even in that instant that he was stepping on Renate's knee. A distant part of his mind registered that a torn ligament was the least of their worries. Shutting his ears to her shriek, he pushed off, launching himself at the attacker who, even now, was turning toward them.

He saw the muzzle flash this time, and tried to block out the burning sting in his side as his momentum carried him into the man and against the dresser. The man let out a grunt as the breath rushed out of him, and for an instant Lawton thought back to the sounds he'd heard on the street outside the Centrum Judiciaum, but only for an instant.

It was an instant too long.

The impact of metal on his skull sent his vision into star-sparkled shimmers. His muscles wanted to give way to the pain, but he knew that could not happen. Curling his fingers into atavistic claws, he raked the man's face twice in rapid succession, grateful that he hadn't thought to cut his fingernails while he'd been in jail. He felt flesh give way on the first strike, and the second skidded over blood-slicked flesh.

That bought him the split second he needed to get his legs back under him, and he exploited the opportunity to the fullest, planting his right foot behind him, giving him a firm base to drive his forehead forward in a strike that would have made a soccer player proud. His next blow would not have, however, for he drove his left knee savagely into the man's groin.

He heard the clatter as the gun dropped to the floor.

They were on even terms now. No, more than that, because the other man's face was torn open, his nose broken, and Lawton could hear the high, keening sound from the man's throat as he tried to get his hands between his legs in that most automatic of self-protective responses.

They were not even. Lawton held the advantage, and he was determined to press it to the fullest. Shifting his weight onto his left foot, he drove his right heel down onto the man's instep, then snapped his knee up just as the man completed the autonomic reaction of doubling over. The knee caught him squarely under the chin, and Lawton saw his enemy's head snap up and back.

For the first time, Lawton saw the face of his attacker. The man's features were already slackening as he slid down the front of the dresser, eyes rolling back and up as he slipped into unconsciousness. The man had perhaps once been handsome, although the ragged tears from Lawton's fingernails and the mass of bloody mucous beneath his nose made it difficult to tell. European, definitely, although Lawton couldn't immediately pinpoint his origins beyond that. Close-cropped dark hair. A faded tattoo barely visible at the collar of his black sweater. The gleaming white furrow of a scar above his left ear, probably a bullet that had had the man's name on it, ever so slightly misspelled.

Lawton laughed at the thought, and the sound of his own laughter shocked him, even as the shooting pain made the room spin. The man's face was replaced by the ceiling, and then by Renate's as she stood over him.

"We have to get out of here," she said, wincing as she bent to pick up the man's gun.

"They misspelled his name," Lawton said, watching her swirl above him.

"What?" she asked. "What are you talking about?"

Lawton pointed to the scar over the man's ear, trying to collect thoughts into words, losing the battle as every breath seemed to drive a spike through his mind. Her face changed then, and she looked down at his side.

"You're shot."

"Yeah," he said. "They misspelled my name, too."

"Whatever," Renate said impatiently. "We've got to go, and we've got to go now, so you have to suck it up, Lawton. On your feet."

In a strange moment of clarity, he noted the hardness that had returned to Renate's face, so unlike the softness of the woman he had seen just before the door burst open. Then his brain spiraled away from coherency.

He tried to rise as she pulled his hands with surprising strength, but his legs wanted nothing more to do with anything his brain might be thinking. *Leave us alone and focus on the bullet in your side,* they screamed, then sulked into limp uselessness.

He tried to laugh as the thought flitted through, but that only reminded him of the burning pain. And didn't it just figure that his shock-weakened brain would tell jokes when he couldn't laugh at them? Life sure was a bitch.

He heard the slap before he felt it. He certainly never saw it, for his eyes shot open an instant too late. Renate's eyes had gone cold, hard, predatory. He knew that look. And she was directing it at him.

She'll cut her losses.

The whisper of thought tore away the fog in his mind like a hot desert wind, leaving him squarely and painfully in the here and now.

"Get up, Lawton," she snapped. "We have maybe thirty seconds to make it to the service elevator. Twenty-five…"

He nodded, taking her hands and pushing himself to his feet, ignoring the wet fire in his left side, letting her shepherd him out of the room and down the corridor. Already cautious heads were poking out of doorways.

"Herzattacke!" she barked. *Heart attack!*

He wondered if they believed her, or if they could see the blood on his shirt. Regardless, they ducked back into their rooms, good, obedient Germans staying out of the way. She leaned him against the wall of the elevator, stabbing the button for the basement parking level.

"I'm sorry," Lawton said with a groan.

"Later," she snapped, trying to keep her weight off her right leg. "Let's get out of here first."

"I'm all yours," he said, pressing on the oozing wound, fighting back the fog that threatened to return.

When she looked at him, a smile crept almost to the edges of her eyes. "Later for that, too."

Rome, Italy

Assif Mondi lay on his side beneath his desk, trying to draw a breath through the fear. He was not a field man. He'd received cursory weapons training, of course, first when he'd joined the Delhi Metropolitan Police and again when he'd been selected for the elite federal unit, the Central Bureau of Investigations. But his specialty had been such that neither he nor his instructors had worried all that much about his combat proficiency. His future lay in an anonymous, pale-green-walled office, in front of a computer screen, prying into the Internet communications of radicals who sought to overthrow the Indian government.

And there he would have remained but for the presence of Lashkar-e-Toiba sympathizers in the CIB. When he had broken into their communications network and informed his superiors of their involvement in the attack on the Indian Parliament, he had been swiftly targeted for death. He had known the assignment to the Kashmir region on the Pakistani border was intended to put him in a place where he could be eliminated. A voice on a telephone had saved his life in the minutes before the bomb exploded in his hotel room. He had "died" in that hotel room and then had been invited to move his talents to Rome.

But there would be no voice on a telephone to save his life tonight.

His ears still rang from the first blast, the one that had torn the warehouse door from its hinges. Now he heard the crackle of gunfire. God only knew how many of his colleagues were already dead or dying out in the front offices. He was alone in the computer center, unarmed. He might be the only one left. And he was terrified.

They would be thorough. Anyone capable of attacking Office 119 would send trained operators who would search every room, squeezing the trigger again and again until everyone was dead.

Everyone.

He could not simply hide beneath the desk. He had to move, had to find a weapon. The fire extinguisher on the far wall. It wasn't ideal. He wasn't even certain how to use it. But it was better than cowering under his desk and waiting to die.

He crawled out, slowly at first, then rose and ran as he realized there was nothing to be gained by stealth. He was alone in the room so far, and speed was what mattered.

The door burst open just seconds after Assif grabbed the extinguisher and read the operating instructions. He pulled the pin and raised the nozzle to blast the man in the doorway with a freezing spray of carbon dioxide when he recognized the man standing before him.

"It's me," Jefe said. "Are you okay?"

"What...?"

Assif stepped forward, looking past his blood-stained boss. Behind Jefe stood four slight Arab men, their hands at their sides, pistols pointed to the floor.

"They're okay," Jefe said. "We have good neighbors. Grab the laptops and let's go."

"I don't understand."

Jefe waited while Assif collected the computers he could carry and disabled the others, then led him out into the main office. He explained the bodies on the floor with a coldness that left Assif even more shaken than the attack itself. "It was a three-man team. Shock and speed. Blew the door and came in shooting. They hit her with the first volley. If they hadn't tripped the infrareds in the alley, they might have gotten all of us."

"Her?" Assif asked.

"They got Margarite."

Jefe's eyes were expressionless, yet Assif knew he must be feeling as shaken as he himself was. "Is she...?"

"Never had a chance," Jefe said, still walking toward the door with the four Arab men. He turned and touched a finger to his breastbone. "Three-shot burst. We'll deal with that later. For now, we have to leave."

"But where will we...?" Assif asked, hurrying to catch up as Jefe crossed the street outside the warehouse.

They walked two blocks before ducking into the small restaurant where Assif and the other Office 119 agents had often come for takeout. Grim nods greeted them. Everyone here knew what had happened.

"Upstairs," Jefe said, nodding to a stairway. "It's not a lot of space, four rooms, but it will have to do for now. Like I said, good neighbors."

The facilities upstairs were rudimentary at best, but they did have electrical outlets. Plenty of them. Assif assigned himself the task of setting up the laptops. One of the Arab men walked in with coils of T6 cable.

"You will need to network, yes?" the man asked.

"I…yes," Assif said. "Who are you?"

"We heard the first blast," the man said. "We came at once. I am sorry we were not in time to save your friend."

"Why did you come at all?" Assif asked.

"Because of Strasbourg," the man said.

"You're with *Saif Alsharaawi.*"

The man nodded. "A small cell. We have kept an eye on you since Strasbourg. We decided you were…doing good work. When this was made a relocation zone, we made sure you would not be disturbed." He sighed. "In that, we failed."

As he spoke, a series of powerful *whooshes* split the air outside, followed by a low rumble. Jefe had triggered the incendiary charges in the warehouse. What had been a state-of-the-art headquarters was now burning fiercely, its glow visible through the window.

"This is useless," Assif said, shaking his head as he

plugged in cables. "The data was on the mainframe. No way can we run on five laptops."

"You would want to connect to that port," the man said, pointing at the wall. He smiled an apology. "As I said, we kept an eye on you. We have been linked to your computers for months now. The pantry in our cellar stays quite cool."

"Sixteen degrees?" Assif asked, referring to the standard room temperature for a mainframe computer. Sixty-two degrees Fahrenheit, sixteen Celsius.

"Precisely."

"Good to know we were being watched," Assif said as he began booting up the computers. "It didn't help Margarite, though."

The man nodded sadly. "We were watching for agitators from our own community. We had circulated word that your office was not to be touched, but of course there were some who might get angry and look for any white face. We kept such people under a close eye. But they did not do this."

"Do you know who did?"

"No," the man said.

"We're going to find out," Assif said. In focusing his mind on hooking up the computers, shock had finally given way to anger. "And we're going to find out fast."

25

Béziers, France

Miriam had spent the day reading Father Steve's notes from his research at the library. She broke off to listen to Soult's speech in the early evening, and what she heard combined with Steve's research to give her a sick feeling in the pit of her stomach.

Nor was she surprised, shortly after the speech, to hear a knock at her door. Steve stood there, dressed tonight in a windbreaker, ballcap and ratty jeans.

"You heard?" he asked as he stepped inside.

"Every oily word."

He nodded toward the table where his notes were spread. "And those?"

"When I add them to the speech, I get sick." She closed the door behind him. "I may have trouble believing in this pyramid technology you're talking about, but I don't have any difficulty believing that man has de-lusions of grandeur."

"Delusions of entitlement," Steve corrected gently. "I'm afraid he believes he was born to be king."

"What scares me is that you might be right."

"What scares me more is that he has the pyramid."

Miriam still had difficulties accepting that a piece of ruby shaped like a pyramid could be as powerful as Steve's research indicated. But every time she started to dismiss the notion, she remembered what a ruby laser could do.

"I have contacts here in Europe," she said. "We're going to need them. There's no way you and I alone can move against that man."

"Certainly not." He dropped into a chair, resting his elbows on his knees. "For some time I've had the feel-ing that I'm walking a laid-out path."

"Destiny, you mean?"

He looked up, smiling faintly. "I don't have delusions of grandeur. But sometimes I feel as if no matter what step I take, I still get drawn in the same inscrutable direction."

"Like being caught in a spiderweb?"

He nodded. "Something like that. One thing I can as-sure you. There are many people who would like me to get this pyramid. And I can't say for certain what they want it for. The only thing I know is that they intend to take it from me."

"So why do you keep seeking it?"

"Look at the hands that hold it now. Can I leave it there?"

She sat on the couch, her lips pursing thoughtfully. "You're not going to give it to anyone, are you?"

He shook his head. "God willing, I can disappear with it and hide it forever. Unfortunately, according to the diary I read—you remember, the old woman I told you about who died during the attack on this city?"

"I remember."

"She mentioned there were at least three others."

"But it seems that for now no one knows where they are."

"Perhaps. I hope not. But absolutely no one is going to get that ruby pyramid from me."

"Where will you take it?"

He shook his head, smiling.

Miriam laughed. "You're right. I don't want to know. Oddly enough, if this pyramid is what you say it is, you're exactly the person I'd want to have it. But we're still going to need help from my friends."

"Where are they?" he asked.

"You're not going to like the answer."

He looked at her for a moment, then nodded. "Rome."

"We may not have to meet them there," she said. "I can get a message to them to meet us in Strasbourg."

"I don't think it matters, Miriam. No one will harm me until I possess what they want. Send your message, and tell them to meet us in Strasbourg if you prefer. I'll summon Miguel."

Berlin, Germany

It wasn't much of a plan, but it was the only plan Renate could form on the fly. She had to hope the young German doctor would remember having met Lawton and think of him as an ally to be protected rather than a suspect to be turned in.

They couldn't go to a hospital. That would involve the *Polizei*, and given that Lawton had only hours before been released from jail, another dead body at his doorstep would not be ignored. With everything else that was going on, they couldn't afford that kind of attention, nor the inevitable delay.

They made their way to the home of Frau Doktor Ulla Viermann and waited for her. A telephone call to the hospital, placed from a pay telephone in the guise of a friend confirming an evening at the theatre, had yielded the end of Viermann's shift. Assuming she had not been delayed by events at the hospital, or that she didn't pause to chat with a colleague or catch up on paperwork or any of a thousand other possibilities Renate couldn't predict or plan for, the *Doktor* should have been on her way home half an hour ago.

Lawton groaned quietly in the car beside her. She'd grabbed a handful of towels from the hotel laundry on their way out, and already one was soggy and heavy beneath her hand. Finally she saw Ulla Viermann walking up to her house, carrying a plastic bag with the bright blue, yellow and red logo of *Lidl,* a grocery chain. Another of the thousand possible reasons for her delay.

The *Doktor* was clearly tired, and Renate had circled the car and was already slipping her hands under Lawton's armpits before Ulla Viermann glanced over.

"I need your help. I can't take him to a hospital," Renate said quickly.

Viermann seemed suspicious for a moment, but the pallor of Lawton's face penetrated her caution. "Bring him. Quickly."

Lawton managed enough strength to moan, struggling to his feet as Renate pulled him from the car, and he leaned on her as they climbed the three steps into Ulla Viermann's house. The *Doktor* dropped her groceries on her sofa and pointed through a doorway.

"On the kitchen table."

Renate complied, explaining in brisk, clipped terms that he had been shot approximately one hour before, and had been slipping in and out of consciousness ever since. The strain of movement caused him to black out again, and he lay limp on the table. Ulla Viermann shook her head as she cut away Lawton's shirt.

"The deciding first hour has passed."

Renate knew she was referring to the critical sixty

minutes after a traumatic injury, when treatment was most effective. "I know. We had no choice."

"You are German," Viermann said as she wiped blood from the wound.

"*Ja.*"

"But you are not free to move openly in Germany."

"*Nein,*" Renate said.

"The wound is not so bad," Viermann said, probing it with a fingertip. "The bullet lodged in a rib. It was not very powerful."

That explained the near silence of the shots, Renate thought. The gunman had reduced the gunpowder load in the cartridges, both to dampen the sound and to reduce the risk of a round penetrating a wall. He was a professional. Or he had been, before she had fired the coup de grâce through the bridge of his nose before they'd left the hotel room. She'd quickly wiped down the weapon and placed it back in the man's hand. She could at least hope the *Polizei* would see it as a hotel burglary gone wrong for long enough to allow her and Lawton to escape Germany.

"He will be in much pain for several days," Viermann said, her eyes closed, her fingers working by feel alone, nudging the small bullet out of the wound. "And not fully healed for three to six weeks. He should not move much. But that will not be possible, will it?"

"No," Renate said. "It will not be possible."

Viermann dropped the bloodstained lump of lead into her kitchen sink. It was, Renate saw, a small caliber round. Probably a five millimeter, its tip flattened like a mushroom. A hollow-point round. Had it not struck a rib, it would have lodged in a lung. Or worse.

"I would like to ask what you are up to," Viermann said as she poured antiseptic powder into the wound and reached for a suture kit that she kept in a first aid box. "But I know you cannot tell me. Just please assure me that you are hunting the people who killed Chancellor Vögel."

"We are," Renate said. "You have my word."

The *Doktor* stitched quickly, her fingers moving with the speed and confidence born of years of experience. She glanced at Renate's face as she worked. "I believe you. If he will travel, I must stabilize his rib. Help me sit him up so I can tape it."

Lawton woke as Renate maneuvered him into a sitting position. She held his arms up as the *Doktor* wound cloth tape tightly around his chest. "Fuck, that hurts."

"Getting shot does," Renate said, trying to keep her voice light. "But it's a minor wound."

"Yes," Viermann said, picking up Renate's cue. "It is a minor wound, Herr Caine. It will hurt for some days, but you will live."

"I'm not sure I want to," Lawton said. "If I live, I have to breathe, and that's what hurts."

"The bullet broke a rib," Viermann said.

Lawton shook his head. "Oh, lovely irony."

"What do you mean?" the *Doktor* asked. Then Renate saw Viermann's eyes widen as she mentally connected Lawton to the dead EU agent on Oranienstraße. "That was you?"

"We need to get him out of Germany," Renate said, trying to force a smile. "Before there are no Germans left."

"The man who attacked you tonight was involved…" The *Doktor* seemed to answer her own question before she finished asking it. "Yes, you need to get out of Germany. A train would be best. I can purchase the tickets in my name."

"If you would be so kind," Renate said.

"Of course," the *Doktor* said. "I will call now."

Renate nodded. After Viermann had left the room, she whispered to Lawton, "We have another problem."

"What?" he asked.

"While we were waiting in the car, I tried to get through to Jefe, but no one is answering at Office 119."

26

Rome, Italy

The *Saif Alsharaawi* cell had indeed downloaded most of the contents of the Office 119 mainframe, but they had been unable to read most of the data because they lacked the decryption keys.

"So much for secrecy," Assif muttered as he checked things out to see where he stood.

The Arab who assisted him laughed humorlessly. "Nothing is secret, my friend. Nothing. We all try to prevent others from learning our secrets, but sooner or later... somebody finds out. Just as someone found out about the existence of your organization in order to attack you."

Assif lifted an eyebrow. "And I'm supposed to trust *you*?"

A smile. "What choice do you have? We saved your lives. We saved your data. We should work together."

Assif felt nearly violated. The computers were his sacred territory, and someone else had been mucking with them. Worse, someone had been mucking with them and he hadn't known it. He might as well have been kicked in the groin.

The Arab clapped a hand on his shoulder. "Don't feel so bad. We knew of your existence because we worked on an operation with you. We met some of your operatives. It was not as hard for us to find you."

Assif nodded reluctantly. "Which is probably how the others found us."

"Most likely. The question is, which of your agents made an unfortunate contact?"

Jefe entered the room just then. "Officially we're shutting down."

"What?" Just as Assif had begun to assimilate what had happened and was starting to think of ways to track the source of the attack, they were shutting down?

"I said *officially,*" Jefe repeated patiently. "At this time, anyone who knows of our existence will hear that we were wiped out. That will limit the threats against us while we get up and running again."

"What about Lawton and Renate?" Assif asked. "They're out there somewhere."

"For now," Jefe said, "they're on their own."

Berlin, Germany

Renate punched the end button on her cell phone and looked at Lawton. Ulla Viermann had put them in a tiny bedroom at the back of her three-story house. Like many European homes, it had been built upward, since land was so scarce, and the rooms were tiny by U.S. standards. Ulla's home had been inherited from her parents, not an unusual situation when it might take several generations to pay off a mortgage.

Lawton lay on a cot, gathering his strength before they set out again, but he was wide awake.

"Still no answer?"

"Not from anyone." Renate spoke calmly, but only someone who knew her as well as Lawton did would have realized that the situation had driven her back behind her barriers of ice.

He didn't need to speak the words, but he did anyway. Speaking something, anything, felt essential right now. "This is not good."

"No."

No one from the office was answering. Phones were ringing, but that didn't mean the phones still existed. The ring tone was provided by the cell company, not the phone being called.

Lawton pushed himself up on an elbow. "We've got to get back to Rome. Now."

She reached out and pressed gently on his shoulder. "We're not going anywhere until it's dark." She waited until he fell back on the pillow. "You can use the recovery time, and I need to think."

"Think about what? Something's wrong, but at this distance, we don't know anything."

"I know something. I know that Margarite went to meet a French contact a few days ago, and from there she returned to Rome."

He absorbed this. "Any idea who she met?"

"Of course not. But at this point, I wouldn't trust a Frenchman any further than I could...how do you say? Throw him?"

"That's it."

She smiled, but there was no warmth in the expression. "If she has leaked something that hurt the office, I will kill her."

Lawton looked at her. This was no idle threat. Renate intended to do exactly what she said.

Would he ever really know this woman?

Mannheim, Germany

The rabbi, the priest and the imam huddled together in the rectory of Liebfrauenkirche, sipping coffee in stony silence. Monsignore Veltroni sat with them, watching them, sensing their anger and distress as clearly as he felt his own. Action must be taken, but at this point he wasn't sure what to propose. And so far, despite repeated efforts, he had been unable to gain audience with the Pope.

Stoll spoke finally. "Monsieur Soult is claiming part of Germany for the EU."

The Imam Zekariah shook his head. "If it were only that."

Veltroni looked at him. "What do you think it is then?" Although he had his suspicions, he wanted to hear them voiced by someone else. Suspicions like this had to be confirmed.

"It is simple," Stoll answered. "The EU is being led by a Frenchman, and he proposes to use French troops, admittedly under the EU flag, to annex part of Germany. This will not be well-received. In fact, it will cause war, because our state, Baden-Württemberg, has refused to cede the land. How would Italy feel if Switzerland decided to take part of Italy as a buffer zone?"

"And no one else reacts," Rabbi Lev said bitterly. "The other countries say and do nothing, as if they are fools who cannot understand what is happening beneath their noses. Germany stands alone in resisting this act."

Veltroni spoke gently. "I think they are stunned. Events have moved swiftly."

"Not too stunned to agree to put my people on trains and buses. Not too stunned to put us out of sight like dirty dishes." The imam was clearly incensed, and Veltroni couldn't blame him.

"So now," said Stoll, "we face war. And we have no friends. Though why Germany should expect to have friends in war after the last century, I do not know."

Veltroni spoke. "The U.S. will stand beside you. Their President has said so."

Stoll shrugged. "It does not matter. It will be war, and we must *prevent* war. We *must*.

"I cannot believe this," Hans Stoll said. "Only a few short months ago, the future of Europe looked so bright. Now…now we may close our borders. We may stand alone against the EU. We may be facing war."

Ismail Zekariah, the imam, nodded as if his head were too heavy for his neck. "I know. I know. My friends, I grew up in this country. As you did, Hans. It has not always been easy for Muslims here. But still we persisted and were permitted to build our mosque. And bit by bit we have begun to feel more welcome here, at least in Mannheim. To us it has truly become our home. I cannot tell you how touched we all are that our friends here did not turn on us after the attack in Hamburg. We feared it. Indeed, we even expected it. It would have been understandable."

"But it did not happen," the priest said.

"No, it did not happen. Instead, the Germans who have accepted us with such difficulty now stand beside us in a way that takes my breath away. I would not have believed it possible."

Rabbi Lev looked down, a tear appearing on his cheek. "People can learn. If we could not, would not God have given up on us long ago? The Torah is full of stories of how my people have defied their God, yet again and again he has forgiven us. Because he believes we can be better."

Hans Stoll smiled faintly. "I have always thought the Old Testament was a love story."

"Love story?" The two other clerics looked at him.

"*Ja,* the love of God for his chosen people."

Rabbi Lev nodded slowly. *"Nu,"* he said. "It is so."

The imam agreed. "It is so."

"So far," the priest said, "many among our peoples have acted in God's love. So far."

"But," said Lev, "if there is war…"

He did not need to finish the sentence. They all knew that God's love too often fell by the wayside in time of war. *Turn the other cheek* gave way to *Kill or be killed.*

Ismail Zekariah sighed. "The consequences would be horrible. Everything Europe has striven to create for so many decades would vanish at the first gunshot. And there *will* be a gunshot. Germany will not tolerate French soldiers on German soil."

"Already," said Stoll, "we are positioning our defenses to prevent it. And have you noticed the convoys passing? The Americans are still here. They are not even telling their soldiers' families to go home."

"But many are going nonetheless," Lev said. "I have some in my congregation. American businessmen are growing anxious, as well."

"Everyone grows anxious," Stoll said. "Worse, the rioting in the streets has lessened since Nice, and Soult is citing that as evidence that he is right. And many in Europe believe him."

"What can we do?" Lev asked.

Zekariah thought for a moment. "Tiananmen Square."

Lev nodded, excitement creeping into his features. "Yes, I agree. We will stand together to block the tanks. But where?"

Veltroni drew a deep breath, watching these men come to a conclusion that might lead to martyrdom. Part of him wished to cry out that their lives could not stop the will of an army. Yet he knew, in the deepest part of his heart, that change begins with a single man willing to take the risk.

"Europabrücke," Stoll said at once. Not only was it a bridge between Strasbourg and Kehl, Germany, but it was a famous one. In the 1990s, the European cultural council, at the request of Kehl and Strasbourg, had undertaken a project to transform the bridge over the Rhine from a mere passage to an icon of unity. Along the bridge in illuminated panels were the words of forty famous European writers, all in their native tongues, speaking of unity and hope. Because of the brightly lit panels, many now referred to it as the Rainbow Bridge.

The site could not be more apropos.

"We will make our stand on the bridge," Stoll said.

Veltroni had visited Europabrücke, had stood in wonder as he considered the bright future it symbolized, a bridge of understanding, a symbol of peace.

Yet now it might be violated, painted in blood. "If you do this," he said finally, his heart and voice heavy, "you will not be alone."

Stoll looked at him, caught his meaning, and nodded. "The Stewards will help?"

"As many as I can find who are willing. And I will try to get back from Rome to stand with you."

Silence filled the room once again as each man searched his heart for the strength and faith to take this dangerous stand.

"We cannot count on them not wanting to hurt us," Zekariah said. "We must be clear that we may die on that bridge. If we are not willing to do that, then we must not go."

"I'm willing," said Stoll firmly, holding out his hand. Immediately three others clasped it.

It was settled.

For once in his life, Veltroni, the ultimate Jesuit, found no arguments against this action. For in his heart of hearts he knew: it was what Jesus would have them do.

Then the imam gave them a precious gift of laughter. Wryly he said, "Unfortunately, I do not believe I will be rewarded with seventy-two virgins."

27

Berlin, Germany

The explosion of a warehouse in the Muslim protection zone of Rome barely made a ripple on the tense surface of European news in the wake of Soult's speech. Even if it had been, as one reporter suggested, an act of terrorism, it appeared insignificant against the backdrop of the specter of war in Europe.

Most of the EU nations had fallen silent, their spokespersons refusing to comment until they had a chance to review the situation in depth.

Renate watched the television in Frau Doktor Viermann's small parlor, seated on a battered sofa next to the doctor. They sipped glasses of a perennial German favorite: *Apfelsaftschorle,* a combination of apple juice and carbonated water. The drink could be purchased ready-made, but many Germans still preferred to mix their own in varying proportions. Ulla clearly favored a larger ratio of carbonated water to apple juice. The drink bit the tongue.

"Everyone is afraid to speak," Ulla Viermann said. "They are afraid a single wrong word could trigger the war."

"*Ja,*" Renate agreed. But she hardly cared about that right now. The warehouse explosion story, as small as it was, had not escaped her attention. To an outsider she might appear riveted to the developments in Europe at large. Inwardly, she could think of nothing but the attack on Office 119. For although the stories were sketchy, they mentioned the location of the warehouse.

She wanted to be thinking coolly and logically about what she and Lawton should do next, but instead she was back in the *Schwarzwald,* driving home from Baden-Baden, where her father worked in a casino, with Karen, her best and only lifelong friend, hiding in the backseat. Despite the twisting mountain roads, Renate was relaxed. The car was handling well, and she and Karen were laughing, reminiscing about trouble they had gotten into as students.

It had felt good to laugh, for Karen was not only her friend but also a reporter for *Frankfurter Allgemeine Zeitung* or FAZ, Germany's equivalent of the *Wall Street Journal.* And Renate—then Gretchen Zeitgenbach—was feeding Karen information about the Frankfurt Brotherhood, information from an investigation she was conducting on her own, having been pulled off the case by her bosses at the BKA.

To this moment, Renate could not remember exactly what had happened that caused her to lose control and go over the embankment. But she *did* remember being thrown free and tumbling into the brambles that had stopped her fall. She did remember seeing her car explode, a sure sign that the gas tank had been rigged. Karen had died.

Then…nothing until she awoke in the hospital, battered but alive, and a stranger she later came to know as Jefe told her what had happened. She didn't even get to see her family. Jefe's organization had swooped in swiftly and efficiently. The charred body in the car—Karen's body—was reported as that of Gretchen Zeitgenbach. The woman in the hospital bed had a new name: Renate Bächle.

Jefe turned her world inside out. She was right. It had been no accident. Not only had the gas tank been tampered with, her brake lines had been punctured. Karen—in lieu of Gretchen Zeitgenbach—had been murdered.

Shock, then anger, had carried her through the next weeks. Then, as she settled into Jefe's organization, it had been replaced by the deliberate glacial calm that had become her trademark, a calm that had been broken only when her entire family was killed in one of the Black Christmas bombings, the only bombing that was not directed at a major cathedral. Her family had been the targets, murdered because somehow the Frankfurt Brotherhood knew that Gretchen, in the guise of Renate, was still alive.

The cool, controlled agent she had tried to become had retreated into the terrified young woman who realized that her personal crusade had brought her into the gun sights of ruthless and very powerful people, and had cost the lives of Karen and her family.

Now the years peeled away as if they had never been, and she sat rigid, silent and very much lost. The crisp, dry scent of the air in the *Schwarzwald*. The closeness of the trees. The confident thrumming of the car's engine as she changed gears. The sound of Karen's laughter.

Ulla spoke. "I knew no good could come from that man leading the EU."

"No," Renate answered automatically.

The sting as brambles pierced her coat and skin. Looking down as the car exploded in the gorge beneath her. Trying to free herself, to rescue her friend, but the brambles would not release their quarry.

The tangy, stinging scent of antiseptic. The bitter taste of guilt. Lying in a hospital bed. She should be dead, not Karen. *She* should be dead.

The flames shown in the brief snatches of video from the warehouse fire joined with the flames in her head. She wanted to scream. Everyone she had left, save for Lawton, would have been in that warehouse. The Brotherhood had tracked her to Rome after she had led a bank surveillance operation in Frankfurt. Renate had killed her would-be assassin outside the Rome train station. But of course the Brotherhood had not quit. Somehow they had uncovered the location of Office 119. And now all her colleagues were dead. All because of her.

"He was a general. A *French* general. Of course he would think in these terms." Ulla threw up her hands. "He knows nothing of diplomacy, nor would he care. Shoot, he thinks."

"Perhaps." Renate struggled to concentrate on what Ulla was saying. Flames. The clip was running again, and she stared at it, hypnotized.

"There is no 'perhaps' about it," Ulla said flatly. "A general thinks like a general." She snorted. *"Wenn du nur einen Hammer hast, sieht alles aus wie ein Nagel."*

"If your only tool is a hammer," Renate repeated the philosopher Foucault's saying in English, "everything looks like a nail." For some reason, English felt comforting to her now, as if everything German was a threat. But then, her German life had left her nothing but bitter ashes.

Ulla nodded with satisfaction. "That is what we have elected in Soult." She made a sound of disgust. "I have my doubts about that entire bomb incident that made him such a hero. How could a bomb explode and give him nothing but a few cuts? I am a woman of science. I cannot be fooled by a magician's trick."

Renate murmured agreement, struggling to yank herself out of the past and deal with the enormous complications of the present. Office 119 was gone. No one was left to answer her calls. Even if Jefe and the others had been fortunate enough to escape, protocols required them to instantly change every link in the communications network, to leave nothing of the past behind, so they could disappear again.

Agents in the field were on their own.

Digging her nails into her palms and forcing her gaze from the TV, she struggled back into the present. She and Lawton had been attacked in their hotel room. It had to have been the Frankfurt Brotherhood. Yes, some of Soult's operatives might want revenge for Lawton having killed one of their own, but that would be too high-profile a revenge to risk in these tense times. And if not Soult's people, then who would want to kill Lawton and Renate?

As it was so often, the calculus was cruelly simple: *Follow the money.* The Frankfurt Brotherhood had paid for the operation in Strasbourg that had catapulted Soult into political prominence. He was obviously their hand-picked leader for Europe, just as Harrison Rice had been their handpicked leader for the United States until they had overplayed their hand and Rice had thrown off their yoke.

Nothing else made sense. It must have been the Brotherhood. They'd tried to kill her. Again. And once again, someone had died in her place.

The critical question was where to go next. She could not stay in Germany. There were too many eyes here who would recognize a face from the past, whisper a word to a trusted friend and, wittingly or unwittingly, put Renate in the crosshairs again. And Ulla Viermann might well be the next person to die in Renate's place. As she looked over into the kind, intelligent eyes of the young doctor, Renate knew she could not let another life be lost on her account.

She had long since memorized the procedures for field agents to reestablish contact if the Rome headquarters was compromised. Orphaned agents were to place classified advertisements in *La Repubblica,* each as an owner looking for a lost dog named after a specific character in Charles Dickens' *Oliver Twist,* along with a contact number in Rome. For Renate, the designated pet name was *Schivare,* "Dodger" in Italian. Whoever remained of Office 119 would monitor the classifieds and contact the orphans as they surfaced.

But in order to carry out those procedures, she had to be in Rome. Could she get there undetected? How closely were she and Lawton being watched? Unanswered questions rolled around in her head as she fought her way out of the past and into the present.

"We've got to leave," she said to Ulla. "Now. I cannot endanger you."

"Endanger me?" The young doctor turned her attention from the television. "Why should you endanger me?"

She should not explain, and yet at this moment she had to. *Someone* had to know what was happening, if for no other reason than so her death—if that was what awaited her in Rome—would not be dismissed as just another tragic but inevitable blip on the radar of life.

"You see that burning warehouse they've been showing?"

"*Ja.*" Ulla nodded and looked at the screen. "The one in Rome."

"I worked there."

Ulla's jaw dropped a fraction. Then, in an instant, she diagnosed the situation and moved into action. "And already you have been attacked. This is why you need to leave Germany."

Renate nodded.

"You will need disguises," Ulla said, rising from her chair. Renate tried to object, but the young doctor was already in motion. "I have just the thing."

Minutes later, Ulla returned carrying black clothing on hangers laid across her arm and two crooked sticks.

"What are these?" Renate asked.

"My father and brother were both *Handwerksburschen*. Journeymen. Traveling carpenters. I have their uniforms and tools here. My father's will fit you, and I believe my brother's will fit your friend."

It was a medieval tradition that persisted even today. Upon completing their apprenticeships, carpenters and masons who sought master status had once been required go *auf der Walz,* to walk around Europe and even into Asia and Russia, working for various masters, learning different techniques. The minimum period of this work-study program was three years and a day, perhaps at first prescribed so that the local master would have time to recoup his investment in training the apprentice before the apprentice returned home and became a competitor.

Journeymen wore a specific uniform—black trousers, vest, coat and hat, a white shirt, and a pocket watch—and carried all that they owned, including their tools, in a cloth-wrapped bundle known as a *Charlottenburger.* They were held to a strict standard of conduct, were required to remain unmarried, and could work for no master longer than three months. Each master would stamp the journeyman's work record, and the journeyman often would add that city's coat-of-arms to his watch chain, a resume in cheap but treasured metal. During the three-year period, the journeyman was not allowed to work within fifty kilometers of his home. Having completed the three years of itinerant labor, and after passing his examination, he was recognized a master craftsman.

While the practice was no longer required, nearly a thousand journeymen still chose to take to the road, honing their craft, gaining experience, and working their ways across Europe and now even beyond, as far as Australia in some cases.

A number of women had, in these modern times, taken up the walk, as well, so it would not be remarkable if Renate and Lawton both wore the uniform.

And while *Handwerksburschen* were fewer in number than they had once been, they were still simply itinerant laborers, hardly worthy of a passing glance except by a potential employer or interested tourists. The disguises would render Renate and Lawton almost invisible. People would notice the uniforms, but not their faces.

Ulla smiled. "I have the *Charlottenburger*, as well. My brother has new tools."

"I can't take these," Renate said. "Ulla, they must be precious."

"They are precious to no one if they do no good. Take them. You can return them when you are done with them."

"I will return them," Renate said. "I give my word."

It was a promise she intended to keep. Even if it cost her her life.

28

Hans Neufel sat on the turret of his tank with his legs crossed and a notepad in his lap, looking down across the gently sloping fields at the city of Kehl and the *Europabrücke*. His platoon was positioned on the forward slope of a ridgeline between the villages of Querbach and Kork, seven kilometers east-northeast of the bridge itself. From his position, he could observe every vehicle crossing the bridge, as well as the French forces massing beyond it, south of Strasbourg.

Beobachten und berichten. Observe and report. Those were his orders, and he would carry them out.

On the surface, it felt like just another field exercise, complete with Leutnant Bräuburger's incessant pea counting. Perhaps if the four tanks of his platoon had been in hull-down positions back in the tree line, nestled into earthen berms that concealed all but their turrets, he could let himself believe that this was simply an exercise, rehearsing the field manual doctrines for defense against a river crossing.

But his platoon was three hundred meters in front of those positions, in plain view of the French observers, who were doubtless watching him at that very moment.

His platoon was not hidden because it was intended to be seen, men and steel spelling out an unmistakable message: *Germany will not be cowed.*

The weight of consequences hung over every moment of every day. Peter Schulingen, his loader, had joked that he would bare his heat-rash-reddened buttocks to the French, prompting laughter from Neufel's crew until he fixed them with an icy glare that killed the moment. In a situation like this, such a gesture could make the difference between war and peace.

Neufel had no desire to fire his tank's twelve centimeter cannon at a live target, nor to hide within his tank's fifty-five-ton bulk from bursting French artillery. Surely those in power would step back from the brink before the fighting erupted. Because once it did...

Neufel tried not to think about that possibility, yet he could not prevent himself. Those were real French tanks and armored personnel carriers on the plains south of Strasbourg. And from airfields farther west, televised reports showed real Mirage 2000 fighter-bombers, loaded with real bombs and missiles. All were manned by real French troops, men just like Neufel, men he might well have met during his NATO postings. Men who, if the orders were given, would be as intent on killing him as he would be on killing them.

And for all that his platoon's presence on this ridge was intended as a visible deterrent, Neufel knew that it was more than that. For while his platoon was in the open, the remainder of his company lay in carefully concealed positions in the fighting line to which he would retire if deterrence failed, part of a battalion-sized tripwire that would harass and delay any crossing until the rest of his brigade could deliver a counterattack.

Similar tripwires had been set up opposite the other Rhine bridges in Soult's declared security zone, but Neufel knew his battalion bore the greatest responsibility. The Europabrücke was adjacent to a rail bridge. That railway, along with the two highways that emerged from Kehl, would be essential supply arteries for a French force attempting to operate in Soult's fifty-kilometer zone. The attack, if it came, would have to come here.

But his battalion was not merely cannon fodder to be chewed up in the first hours of such an attack. It was not a suicide mission. For while Neufel was only a sergeant and a single tank commander, *Bundeswehr* doctrine was to brief all members of a unit as thoroughly as was consistent with operational security. He knew his battalion's task, and he believed they could carry it out.

The key to stopping any river crossing was to destroy the bridges. On the face of it, that was impossible, for to deploy pioneers onto the Europabrücke and prepare it for demolition would be far too provocative. It would almost guarantee the very war that Neufel and every sane German wanted to prevent.

However, two kilometers east of the Rhine lay the Kinzig, a smaller tributary that joined the main river at Auenheim. Both the highways running east into Germany from Strasbourg, as well as the railway, crossed the Kinzig north of Kehl. Crossing the Rhine would not help the French unless those bridges were also secured.

And they were already prepared for demolition.

If French troops began to cross the Rhine, the Kinzig bridges would be blown, trapping the French in the densely built-up triangle between the rivers. Neufel's battalion would pin them there while the Luftwaffe's Typhoon fighter-bombers pounded them. The rest of Neufel's brigade would then come up to deliver the coup de grâce, smashing Soult's notions of European empire.

"You worry too much, Neufel."

He looked down to see Leutnant Bräuburger beside his tank. Ordinarily he would have saluted the officer, but now he did not. To do so here, out in the open, would identify his platoon leader, whose tank would then become the first target in any attack.

"Perhaps," Neufel said. "Perhaps others do not worry enough, Herr Leutnant."

"Herr Kanzler Müller was a soldier," Bräuburger said. "He knows the risks."

"Monsieur President Soult was also a soldier," Neufel said. "Would this be the first time two old soldiers sent young soldiers to die?"

The lieutenant ignored the question. "How are your men, Neufel?"

"They are good." Neufel had not told Bräuburger about Schulinger's intended stunt, nor would he. As the tank commander, it was his responsibility to handle such matters. "I told them to get some sleep."

Bräuburger nodded. They had moved into their positions overnight, and the entire platoon was exhausted. Neufel had taken it upon himself to remain awake, watching the bridge, trying to calm his thoughts. He could not have slept regardless.

"You do not doubt them?" the lieutenant asked.

"No more than I do myself," Neufel said. "None of us wants war."

"No," Bräuburger agreed. "But we are soldiers."

Neufel nodded. "We are."

He looked across the river. A few small dust clouds signaled vehicles changing their positions, probably as much to keep the men sharp as for any tactical reason.

"I wonder if they are having these same discussions over there, sir."

"I'm sure they are, Neufel. But it is best not to dwell on such matters. If they attack, we cannot think of them that way. If we do, we will hesitate at the moment when hesitation could kill us."

That, more than anything, was what Neufel feared. He had no doubt of his own competence or that of his crew. They could follow orders quickly and efficiently. Nor did he doubt his weapon. The Leopard II was an effective main battle tank, capable of hitting a moving target on the first shot, while moving itself, at a range of nearly two thousand meters. His vehicle was in good working order; he and his crew took a perverse pride in the tedious routine of maintaining it.

He did not doubt his crew or his weapon.

He doubted his hate.

That would be the difference between hesitation and cold, calculating, deadly efficiency. He would have to hate the men across that river, to feel no pity as their vehicles exploded and the men within were burned alive or torn in two by the blasts. He would have to feel a brutal satisfaction as the Typhoons swept in, spilling death and destruction on the French trapped in that killing ground between the two rivers.

He would have to hate.

And he was not sure he could.

Béziers, France

Miguel joined Steve when he visited Miriam that evening. She hardly recognized the youth she had met in Guatemala, and spent a few moments holding him at arm's length and looking him over.

"You've grown taller," she said, having to look up at him now.

"Better diet," Steve remarked.

"And you've gained weight, as well."

"Pasta," Steve said, reaching for a piece of fruit on the room service table Miriam had ordered earlier.

Miguel chuckled, then reached out to hug Miriam. "Do you like my hair?"

"I liked it better Quiche style, but I can understand why you changed it."

Miguel's face darkened. "I'm sorry…."

Miriam shook her head, silencing him. "You were a boy. A very hurt boy. Let's put all that behind us. Apparently, according to Steve, we need to save the world."

There was no laughter.

Miriam's attempt at a smile died. "I can't reach my friend in Rome."

Steve looked up from the plum he was about to bite into. "No?"

"I've sent several e-mails and tried several times to phone the number he gave me."

"So something is wrong."

She nodded and sat on the chair at the suite's desk, near her computer. "I've always received prompt responses before. I have another friend who worked with this man, but he's…away right now."

Steve nodded thoughtfully and seemed to lose all interest in the plum. He placed it back on the table.

Rachel Lee

"Where does this leave us?" he asked. "I can't go back to the people who sent me, and your contacts are missing. We can't solve this situation alone." He did not mention the Guardians. He still had doubts about them.

"I have other contacts," Miriam said slowly. "The thing is, I'm reluctant to spread what we've learned when I don't know who all the players are."

"But what exactly *have* we learned?" Steve asked. "No one would believe in the existence of the codex, and the fact that I was pursued across the Guatemalan jungle by a man who was employed by EU security is hardly going to raise alarms. What we have are suspicions of Soult's imperial ambitions. I'm sorry, Miriam, but no one in your agency is going to worry about that."

"Actually," she said, "I know someone who might. And I should call him before we get any deeper into this mess, in case something happens and I can't tell him later."

"Do not mention the codex," Steve warned her sternly. "We don't need any more people trying to obtain it."

Miriam's smile was crooked. "I'd be a fool to mention it. I want to be *believed*."

She excused herself, leaving the two men to eat and drink in the sitting room, and took her cell phone into the bedroom with her. A few minutes later she was on a secure line with Grant Lawrence.

"How's it going?" he asked. "When can we expect you?"

"Not soon. Things are developing here."

"Care to tell me what things?"

"I can't tell you all of it, Grant. But there's one thing I'm sure of: Jules Soult is making a play to consolidate power. A lot of power. In himself."

Grant paused for a moment. "Lay it out for me, Miriam. I've got to go to the President on this."

"The plan seems to be to centralize power in the EU, far more than its charter and the current treaties would support. A source here referred to it as 'aspirations of empire.' People working for him may have been instigating a lot of the street violence he's now claiming to quell."

"Make them afraid and they'll grovel for security," Grant said. She couldn't tell if his voice was laden with sadness or anger.

"It wouldn't be the first time someone tried that plan," she said. "Here's the thing. Right now he has a lot of popular support. And we can't go public with what he's doing until we have the evidence nailed down. Even then, it would be better if the information came out here in Europe. Through the Brits, maybe. They're sitting on the sidelines so far."

"What do you need?" Grant asked.

"Get on the NSA," she said. "Get them into Soult's banking and business records. I think he started this by hiring private contractors, but he'll have done it through an intermediary. That man will be the weak link. We find his intermediary, we snatch him, and we squeeze him until he coughs up the details. Then we expose Soult and let the EU take him down."

"Will they do that?" Grant asked. "*Can* they do that?"

"If we can prove that Soult has been sponsoring criminal acts…"

She didn't need to finish the sentence.

"Okay," Grant said. "I'll get on the NSA, Treasury and anyone else we need to nail this down. It may take a while, though."

"I'm not sure we have a while," she said. "Things are getting dicey over here."

"I'll do what I can." He paused a moment. "Keep your head down, Miriam."

"I'll do my best."

When she hung up, she sat thinking for several minutes, trying to figure out her next moves. If only she had more to go on. At the moment, though, she knew of only one thing to do: head for Rome, which seemed to be at the center of at least some of this, and keep trying to find Lawton.

Slowly, feeling suddenly old, she returned to the sitting room.

"We need to move," Miriam said. "Staying in one place is never wise when you're hunted. So I suggest we start making our way toward Rome. A roundabout way."

"There is no need," Steve shrugged. "If my watchers discover me, they will think I am returning like a good priest with what they want."

Miriam frowned. "I'm worried about other watchers. Steve, you have some idea of how big this is. I seriously doubt the church is the only interested party."

"Of course not. But why would anyone else be seeking *me?*"

"That depends on who knows what. Let me introduce you to the shadowy world of intelligence, Father Steve. Invariably, there are multiple players. And the ones you need to worry about are the ones deepest in the shadows. If what you suspect about Soult is true, then there are people behind him. And those people aren't likely to have anything to do with your church, nor are they likely to have many scruples."

She looked at her computer again, but the e-mail screen offered no new information. "Circles within circles. And no one person knows where they all intersect. This game is growing deadly. We need to make a plan to go to Rome. Now."

Vatican City

Monsignore Veltroni listened to Hans Stoll's voice on the phone, his stomach tightening with each word.

"It is time," Stoll was saying. "We are leaving for the bridge."

The knot in Veltroni's stomach caused him to offer a last protest. "Hans, you will be standing between two armies prepared to fight!"

"We know that. And as *you* know, we are ready to face the consequences. Some of our flocks will accompany us."

"Hans…" Veltroni closed his eyes, incapable of speech. Hans Stoll was a life-long friend. Now the reality was here.

"We must stand up for what is right," Hans said. "We cannot stand by while people are persecuted for their beliefs. Nor can we stand by while a war is begun for no good reason. Maybe our deaths will shock the world into paying attention."

Veltroni doubted that anyone in the world who mattered was ignoring the present situation, but he knew what Hans meant. The Nice Massacre had succeeded in causing Germany to take a stand against the removals. A protest on the very bridge that was symbolic of the yearning for European unity might have an impact beyond imagining.

But still his stomach and chest ached with prescient grief. "I will call the others to support you," he said.

"The cardinal will not approve," Stoll warned him.

It seemed to Veltroni that Stoll was trying to protect *him* now. "Estevan isn't going to know until it's too late. But you will not stand alone, Hans. This I promise you."

"Do not come yourself, Giuseppe," Stoll said after a moment. "If we fail, your voice will be needed."

"I cannot come," Veltroni said, anguished. "Estevan suspects something, I think. And now I am getting hints that I may get my audience with His Holiness. I cannot afford not to be here if the opportunity arises."

"Good. That relieves me, my friend. Your presence in Rome will do more good than your presence here." Hans fell silent for a moment. "Send only those who are willing to face the consequences freely. And offer a Mass for us, *Monsignore*."

"I will offer a novena of Masses for you. And I will keep pressing to see the Holy Father as soon as possible."

"Perhaps what we do on the bridge will make an opening for you."

"But at such a cost!"

"The cost will be higher if we do nothing. History has taught us that lesson."

Hearing the resolve in Stoll's tone, Veltroni knew there was only one thing left to say. "*Dominus vobiscum*. The Lord be with you." Veltroni replaced the receiver in the cradle almost reverently.

Tears stung his eyes as he made his way to the kneeler in the corner and looked up at the wooden crucifix carved so long ago as a gift by a skilled carpenter in his home village. The corpus on this cross displayed all the anguish of a man dying for the sins of others.

And in that tortured face Veltroni suddenly saw the face of Hans Stoll. Bowing his head, he prayed fervently for God's help, begging for God's grace for them all, to guide them all correctly.

He didn't expect to like the answers to his prayers. God's will seldom led to an easy path.

All he wanted was to choose rightly in the hours and days ahead.

And to have the strength to bear the coming burdens.

Then, rising, he gathered himself to do something he had never dreamed he would do: call men and women to ask them to lay their lives down for a principle.

29

Strasbourg, France

"The German people will not allow this," Chancellor Müller said. "Even if it were not political suicide, I would not support it. The success of the removals is, at best, a temporary one. In the long term, they will create far more tension than they relieve. The violence will only explode in even worse form."

Harald Müller had flown from Berlin to Strasbourg to make a last, face-to-face attempt at a diplomatic solution. While he did not have high hopes, he was as familiar with the history and workings of the European Union as any man alive. He had no doubt that, if anyone could reach Soult, he would have to be the one to do it.

So here he was, sitting across the conference table from Soult. The two men were alone, each having shooed away a phalanx of anxious aides who wondered what their principals might say in their absence. God forbid that anyone should speak an impolitic truth, even when those impolitic truths were precisely what the situation called for.

Müller had resolved that he was going to tell the truth, so far as he knew it to be. Nothing less had any hope of penetrating the knot of war that threatened to entangle all of Europe.

"You must understand, Monsieur Soult," he continued. "I have a responsibility to my people and to history. I will not betray either. What you propose will not work. We—you and I—must find another solution."

"The European Union will not have policy dictated to us," Soult replied. "Not by Islamic fanatics, and not by American puppets in Berlin. Do not lecture me on what will work and what will not. Europeans—all *real* Europeans—will *make* this work."

"And who are the real Europeans, Monsieur President? You have already chosen to remove people who have lived among us for generations. Who will you remove next? Germany is not alone. The British have not yet decided on removals. Will you wage a second Norman Conquest, as well?"

"I will do what must be done to secure Europe."

Müller paused at that. Soult had used the verb *assurer,* rather than *protéger.* To make certain, rather than to protect. Make certain of what?

The conversation was trailing dangerously into an exchange of insults that would—to quote an American phrase—generate more heat than light. He decided to pull it back on track by an appeal to something that perhaps Soult would understand.

"Perhaps you do not see what this area means to the German people," Müller said. "The Rhine has been our shelter and our lifeline for centuries. It runs through our music and our mythology. You would go beyond even that. Your proposed zone would gouge a hole in some of the most sacred land in Germany, the *Schwarzwald.* The Black Forest is not simply 'in Germany.' It is *German.* It is part of our national identity. It would be as if France were asked to cede part of Paris."

"Pah!" Soult said with a sweep of his hand. "These lands are only yours because others in my government agreed to give them back after World War Two. Weak-minded men who foolishly believed that a united Germany would never again threaten Europe. And here you are, threatening to tear Europe apart *again,* for the sake of a handful of ingrates who would kill us all if we let them."

"I have threatened nothing!" Müller said. He took a breath, trying not to rise to the bait that Soult had quite purposefully dangled. A shouting contest would accomplish nothing. "Monsieur Soult, need I remind you that it is the French army that is poised to attack Germany and not the other way around."

"*Non!* It is a *European* army."

Müller sighed. "Do not take me for a fool, Monsieur Soult. That 'European' army is equipped with AMX ar-

mored vehicles and Mirage jets, manned by French soldiers and airmen, under French commanders. You may
announce that the Paris government has 'loaned' them
to the Union, but no one believes this. Certainly no one
in Germany believes this."

"It matters not what you believe," Soult said. "The
facts do not change. French army? European army?
There is no difference. Europe has spoken—*I* have spoken—and you will comply or face the consequences.
Need I tell you what your advisors undoubtedly already
have? We have three hundred combat aircraft. You have
one hundred eighty. And do not forget, we have nuclear
weapons. You cannot hope to prevail."

Soult was speaking not as President of the European
Commission but as a would-be Napoleon, Müller realized. And now he was threatening to use nuclear weapons against Germany.

"Germany will not be cowed, Monsieur Soult."

Soult's gaze was unbending. "Then let a united Europe be *la fleur de guerre.*"

The man was insane, Müller thought later as he
looked out the window of the *Konrad Adenauer,* the
Airbus A310-304 that was the *Bundeskanzler's* official
aircraft. Whatever glaze of normalcy had once shielded
Soult's ambitions had long since given way.

"Let a united Europe be *la fleur de guerre?*" Müller
asked himself. It was madness. The only flowers of war
were death, destruction and misery.

He climbed from his seat and walked to the secure communications center onboard the aircraft. "I need to speak to the Prime Minister of England, and then to the President of the United States."

"Yes, Herr Bundeskanzler," the man said.

Soult's nuclear threat left Müller no choice. He would have to ensure that he had allies. Allies who could not only match Soult's nuclear capability but overmatch it, to the point where Soult would not dare to deploy such weapons.

For beyond that door lay the end of Europe itself.

Rome, Italy

"What happened?" Renate asked as she and Lawton entered the small restaurant.

The journey to Rome had been painful. While the uniforms of *Handwerksburschen* had largely allowed them to travel undisturbed and unnoticed, Lawton's wound had not. Ulla Viermann had left specific instructions that were as necessary as they were agonizing.

A bruised rib could be a life-threatening injury. The temptation, born of long-evolved pain aversion, was to breathe shallowly, to minimize movement. But prolonged shallow breathing allowed fluid to build up in the bottoms of the lungs, creating the very real risk of pneumonia. Worse, the racking coughs caused by trying to clear the fluid could exacerbate the injury, and prolong the suffering and danger.

The only remedy, Ulla had explained, was for Lawton to perform regular deep-breathing exercises. Before their departure, she had gone to the hospital to purloin a small plastic instrument that measured inhalation. Lawton was to inhale deeply enough to push the counter to a minimum of seventeen-hundred-fifty milliliters. Ten repetitions, every five hours.

Every repetition was self-induced agony, as his rib cage expanded against the wrapping around his torso, compressing bruised and angry muscle and bone, eliciting groans that made Renate cringe. An old German woman riding beside them from Frankfurt to Mannheim had patted Renate's hand and offered an understanding, maternal smile. It was a small comfort, Renate thought, but at times those were the only comforts life offered.

They were passing through the Po Valley in northern Italy when the time had come for another set of exercises.

"Please, no," Lawton had whispered. The grayness of his face had worried her. Even the incredible smoothness of modern European rail travel must have been agony for him.

She had squeezed his hand, and the memories of what had nearly happened in the Berlin hotel room flooded in. She fought them down. It had been a mistake. A mutual mistake born of transitory need. Yet as she squeezed his hand and implored him to do the exercises, she could not forget the emotions that had surged through her, emotions she had buried deep in an icy glacier since coming to Office 119.

For those few glorious moments before the door burst open, she had been a woman again. A *real* woman. That interruption alone had been cause enough to kill the man who'd barged in.

"You must," she had said. "I will hold your hand."

And she had, trying in vain to close her mind to his groans and the way his fingers curled around hers, that most basic, childlike request not to be alone when the pain came. From midwife to mother, lover to friend, nurse to soldier and even to enemy, the impulse ran deep through the core of the human species. She could no more resist answering than he could resist asking.

And the pain of it chipped at the icy walls she had built around her heart.

Thankfully, after that he had slept until they reached Rome, husbanding his strength for the most difficult part of their journey, the part that, by dint of their disguises, had to be made on foot. For while journeymen might ride a train over a long distance, to hire a taxi would attract attention. It was a life of walking, and walk they must, whatever the pain that emanated from every step.

Finding quick and cheap lodging had been easy. They had simply followed along with four other journeymen who had also made the trip. The others were hoping to find work on the restoration of one of the city's many old and priceless buildings, learning a kind of crafts-manship that had not changed in centuries, skills that would set them apart as true masters when their time of journeying ended and they returned to their homes to set up businesses.

She had conversed little with them, and Lawton even less. His injury—incurred on a job in Hamburg, she'd said—made it difficult for him to talk. They had given nods of understanding, for theirs was a profession in which workplace injuries were not uncommon. It was the nature of working with one's hands, shaping wood or stone into form and structure and beauty.

The transient connection made, they had not objected when she trailed along in their quest for lodging. While she knew the city better than any of them, she and Lawton were still in disguise and could not shed the charade until they were alone. So she let the others guide her to a hostel where she and Lawton settled into a room that was ideally anonymous, if only passably clean.

Thirty-six tense, painful hours later, Jefe had answered her ad in *La Repubblica,* refusing to talk details on the telephone. Not until she entered the familiar restaurant and was directed to the upstairs room did she have any clue what had become of Office 119. The Muslims from whom they had often bought food now provided safe haven. Her heart jolted repeatedly as she helped Lawton up the stairs to find a small group of operatives working on computers and realized they were a *Saif Alsharaawi* cell stationed to observe and protect Office 119.

"We've confirmed that the bombers were working for Soult," Jefe said in response to her immediate question. "We think they latched onto Margarite when she met her contact in Paris."

Renate seethed. "I *told* her."

Jefe held up a hand. "Don't even go there, Renate. Whatever she did, she was one of us."

"Was?" Renate asked.

He nodded, his lips tight. "She was in the front office when they came in. She never had a chance."

Everything inside Renate froze. She wanted to feel anger. She wanted to offer some cutting phrase— "served her right"—or anything to wash away the kick that sent her stomach reeling.

Instead, she heard Margarite's laughter when Renate had strode into the office talking of her Italian lover, the excitement in Margarite's voice as they'd talked through the problem in Berlin. Even their last moments together, when Margarite had told Renate to give herself over to her feelings for Lawton.

Whatever she had done, whatever tradecraft she had overlooked in Paris, she hadn't deserved to be cut down by assassins, her body not even given a proper burial but instead reduced to charred ash as fire tore through an anonymous warehouse in a foreign land.

"Renate," Jefe said, reaching out to her, as if reading her thoughts.

She shook his hand away, collapsing into a folding chair, her lips white, her jaw screaming until she realized she was clenching her teeth to fight back the river of rage that threatened to erupt. Rage at herself. Rage at Jefe. Rage at Office 119. Rage at a world that bent and twisted every ideal, every notion of goodness and duty and honor, until the idealist was nothing but a disposable part in the evil machine that was life, a machine that ran on cross and double-cross, plot and counterplot, promise and betrayal and all too casual death.

It was Lawton's touch that pushed through the storm within her, a tactile lighthouse in the hurricane of her thoughts. It was Lawton's touch that brought the tears.

"What are we doing?" she asked between sobs.

"We're reorganizing," Jefe said. "Officially, we're closed down. They'll be working on a new site. Probably here in Europe, but we're not sure yet. In the meantime, we're working with *Saif,* piggybacking their infrastructure."

She had no desire to hear institutional jargon. "No. What are we *doing?*"

"We're tracing the money that bought the hit on the warehouse. We'll get them."

She pounded her fists on the table, drawing a curse from Assif as the laptops jumped. "No. You don't get it. *What. Are. We. Doing?* What is the point of all this, Jefe?

We swing at shadows, and the shadows swing back. Karen dies and my family dies, and Margarite dies, and when it's all over, where are we? What have we accomplished? *What. Are. We. Doing?*"

He didn't answer.

"I'll tell you what we're doing," she continued. "We're pushing at the ocean. And every time we push, the ocean drowns someone else. And it always will. I never dreamt I would see war in Europe, and it's going to happen, no matter what we do or anyone else does. Why? Because Jules Soult, and men in Frankfurt and Tehran and Washington and Darfur, want to fight to prove their manhood and enrich their businesses and prove that their race, their god, their economy, their belief, is superior to someone else's. We push against this ocean, day after day, week after week, month after month, year after year, and all we end up is awash in more bodies than we can count, piled up to the heavens and rotting with the stench of our hubris and our justice and our fear and our selfishness.

"So how many?" she pressed on, screaming now. "How many dead bodies is enough? How many dead friends and dads and moms and nieces and Margarites? How many do we need to stack one upon the other, until we can climb over them all the way to God and say 'I did my best'? *How many?*"

The room was silent as she sagged back into the chair. Ahmed Ahsami had come up from the restaurant below, a look of alarm on his face. Jefe looked as if he had been punched in the chest. Assif stared. Lawton seemed to be fishing for words and finding none.

"Give that speech," Ahmed finally said. "Give that speech in every town and every city in every country in the world. Maybe Allah will open their ears. But until he does, Frau Bächle, we are the levee between good people and the ocean of evil in the hearts of men. And we will never hold back the whole of that ocean so long as men's hearts turn to darkness. But if we allow ourselves to break beneath that ocean, what is left?"

She could not answer.

Ahmed held out a small cup. "It is good coffee."

She took the cup wordlessly. At that moment, good coffee was the best life had to offer.

"Thank you," she whispered, her voice hoarse.

He nodded silently, his eyes fixed on hers. They were the eyes of a soldier. Eyes that understood. "It is strong and good, yes?"

She followed his eyes to the cup in her hand and beyond it into the smoking landscape of her soul. She took a sip. "Yes. It is good coffee."

30

Strasbourg, France

"He thinks you are insane," Hector Vasquez said, sitting opposite Soult's desk. He had listened to the discussion with Chancellor Müller—the conference room was bugged, of course—and wondered if Soult had played his chosen role too well. "There is a fine line you must walk, Monsieur President. Are you sure you did not step across it?"

Soult was watching the television, where the news showed a gaggle of protestors gathering on the *Pont de l'Europe*. "I do not think I went too far, Colonel. Why do you suspect I did?"

"It was the mention of nuclear weapons," Vasquez said. "Chancellor Müller will doubtless carry that implied threat to London and to Washington. It will help him to gain allies at a time when we would rather he was forced to stand alone."

Soult nodded the colonel to go on.

"Our plans called for a skirmish with Germany, Monsieur President," Vasquez continued. "Not a long and destructive war that could cripple Europe and reduce us again to rubble. A quick, decisive skirmish will boost our war industries and energize our economy, making us ready to challenge the Americans for dominance. But a prolonged war will only leave us exhausted."

"I am aware of our plans," Soult said. "I helped to craft them, Colonel."

"Forgive me," Vasquez said. "It is simply that the mention of nuclear weapons makes it less likely that we can contain this skirmish. We knew the Americans would defend their bases. That is why we defined the borders of the European Zone to exclude those bases. So long as we do not threaten their bases, the Americans will only posture in support of Müller without actually giving him any material support. That posturing will work to our benefit, by drawing the rest of Europe to us out of their resentment for American bullying. So long as we can keep this war small and brief, the British and Americans will stand by impotently. But if there is a nuclear threat…"

"You think the British and Americans will commit their forces in defense of a small slice of southern Germany, when France has also ceded an equal portion of its own land to the Union?" Soult asked.

"No, of course not," Vasquez said. "But they *will*

promise to commit their forces if they think you may employ nuclear weapons. Their nuclear capability is far greater than yours. They know you cannot employ your weapons under such a threat. We will be back to the days of mutually assured destruction, hamstrung at the very time when you need the freedom to act."

"Perhaps you are right," Soult said. "I should not have mentioned the nuclear weapons."

"Alas," Vasquez said, "you cannot unring that bell."

"No, I cannot. What do you suggest, Colonel? Where do we go from here?"

"What is the Islamic population in the German part of the European Zone?" Vasquez asked.

"It is negligible," Soult said.

"So it is already secure, yes?"

Soult turned to him and smiled. "Yes, it is already secure, Colonel. So long as the Germans do not remove any Muslims into that zone."

"And Müller has already announced an end to the removal policy in Germany."

"Yes," Soult said. "He has."

"Then, while our troops must stand ready in case any threat should develop, there is no immediate cause to send forces across the Rhine."

"Unless we are provoked," Soult said, smiling.

"Yes," Vasquez said. "And if we are provoked, no one can condemn us for taking steps to protect ourselves."

"What do you have in mind?" Soult asked.

Vasquez walked over to the large-scale topographic map on the wall of Soult's office. "Allow me to show you."

Querbach, Germany

Hans Neufel had been watching the people arriving for hours now. From the French side, they came on foot. From the German side, a few were dropped off from buses, but many more had ridden the train to the city and walked from there. At first they were only a trickle, then a steady stream. Among the gathering crowd were men who wore the cassocks of priests, the dark hats and beards of Orthodox Jews, and men who wore the knit skullcaps of Muslims. The Muslims, he had noticed, were all old men, one with a walker, another in a wheelchair. Probably to avoid being mistaken for terrorists.

All day long the gathering had steadily been growing, and scouts had reported that religious and even lay people were arriving not only from Germany and France, but from other European countries, too. There were perhaps three hundred as evening gave way to dusk, but three hundred on the bridge was enough to draw the attention of the world.

Those who wanted to were sleeping on the bridge. Those who sought more comfortable lodgings would have no trouble finding them, for the citizens of Kehl and its suburbs had been packing their belongings and leaving throughout the day. The few residents who remained were mostly men and mostly armed with whatever they could find: rifles for hunting, pistols that were family mementos from past wars. All were committed to one thing: ensuring that the French did not cross the Rhine.

On the one hand, Neufel admired their courage, and that of the protesters. On the other hand, their presence complicated his mission. If the French rolled onto that bridge—no, *when* the French rolled onto the bridge—the situation would very quickly get out of hand. Having three hundred religious protestors squarely in his sights might make a gunner, or a tank commander, hesitate. And that moment of hesitation might get the tank destroyed and its crew consigned to ugly, fiery deaths.

Very quickly, Neufel was able to pick out three leaders among the protestors: a priest, a rabbi and an imam. That fact was not lost on Schulingen, who had christened them *der Vorsichtige, der Unschuldige und der Weise*—the cautious, the innocent and the wise—after the punchline to a common joke. The joke and the christening had sent echoes of laughter through the tank, and though Neufel knew he should scold his gunner for such humor, not even he could resist laughing.

Now, watching the clerics move among the ranks of the protestors, calming those who seemed at the point of turning peaceful protest to something else, Neufel realized he, too, was speaking of them in terms of Schulingen's nicknames.

In an odd way, it made Neufel feel as if he knew the

clerics. And that troubled him still more. For now, having named them, he would be even more likely to hesitate if the order came to fire.

He didn't know what he resented most: the clerics for being there, Schulingen for humanizing them, his fear that he might put their safety above that of his crew, or the insanity of a species and a situation that could set all of the above against each other.

If this was what it meant to be at war, he wanted no part of it.

Rome, Italy

It was a hunch. No, it was both less than that and more, Steve thought. It was a prayer.

Miriam had no real idea how to find the ultrasecret United Nations division called Office 119. Every previous communication, she had explained, had come through untraceable telephone calls or e-mails. Now they were not responding to e-mail, and she had no idea who Jefe was or where he might be.

But she had met Renate and, of course, Lawton. When she described them, Miguel remembered having seen them together, here in Rome. Steve had pressed Miguel for more details. It had been in a restaurant. A small restaurant. Just after the attack on the European Parliament building. Miguel and Steve had come in together. Steve had sat with his back to them, but Miguel had been able to see the woman. In fact, he thought, she might have recognized him.

"Yes, she did," Miriam had said. "She contacted me to let me know you were still alive. She recognized you from photos taken in Guatemala City."

"So they know I am still alive," Miguel said, sadness in his eyes. "I knew that eventually my past would come back."

"No," Miriam assured him. "It was a personal contact, not through official channels, and I didn't update the file. What you did was wrong, Miguel, but you don't need me to tell you that. You have already paid for it many times over. And you've done a lot of good since then. Now do more good. Where was this restaurant?"

And on that most slender of threads, they had come to this quiet and dark corner of Rome, never a tourist area, now one of the Islamic protection zones.

Much had changed in the weeks that Steve had been away. The poor who had walked these streets in hope that someone would take pity with the leftovers of a meal were gone, moved into housing formerly occupied by Muslims elsewhere in the city and its suburbs. The streets were cleaner, save for charred debris from a nearby warehouse that had burned. The scent of the fire still hung in the air, yet it was mixed with the tangy scents of food from across North Africa and the Middle East.

Yet much had not changed. Young men still walked along the streets in small groups, many with the shuffling stride of the unemployed, bored and dispirited. Others seemed more purposeful, slightly older, pausing to whisper a word to the loiterers, words Steve could not hear or understand but which set the younger men to small tasks. Gathering bits of rubbish into bins, or moving kiosks out of streets and against walls.

The older ones, Steve realized, were something of an unofficial police, shepherds to a flock of younger teens who might otherwise let idle hands turn to trouble. There was an order in these streets now. The *Polizia* were not in evidence, but neither were they needed. The young men of this neighborhood were policing their own, in their own language, under the rules of their own culture.

"That is the restaurant," Miguel said, nodding to it without pointing. "That is where I saw the woman."

"The odds of her being there again..." Miriam began, looking around, clearly uncomfortable in this neighborhood.

"They're at least marginally better than the odds of spotting her on some random street," Steve said. "It's the best we can hope for. And if I remember, the food in the restaurant is excellent."

Miriam nodded. "At the very least, we can eat."

As they entered, Steve made a point of nodding briefly to the Arab man behind the small counter. There were only a handful of tables, mostly unoccupied.

"*A'salaam aleikum,*" Steve said.

"Aleikum salaam," the man replied, with a courteous but cool smile.

Steve didn't offer a handshake in greeting, having read somewhere that it wasn't common between Muslims and non-Muslims. He did step closer to the counter, so that he could speak without being overheard. "We come in search of friends."

"Many search for friends in these times," the man said, his voice revealing neither hostility nor welcome. "Perhaps we should include friendship on our menu."

"If I remember, you already do," Steve said. "The food was excellent when I ate here before."

"Then sit, please," the man said. "And let us hope it is as good tonight as it was then."

Steve, Miguel and Miriam took a table away from the windows. A menu was brought to them, and they pretended to peruse it with great interest. When the waiter came to take their orders, however, Miriam looked up at him. "I seek the one called Jefe. I am an American friend."

The waiter looked at her, shrugged and pointed to the menu.

Steve could see that she was impatient, probably wondering if the man had understood her at all. He pointed to her menu. "Order, please, Miriam. Don't offend our hosts by refusing their hospitality."

She looked at him, skepticism writ large on her features, but ordered a lamb couscous with a double espresso. Once the waiter had taken their orders and left, Steve heard steps on a stairway behind him.

He turned and saw a Hispanic-looking man, accompanied by a striking blonde.

"You must be Miriam Anson," the Hispanic man said.

Miriam's eyebrows rose, and she turned in her chair. "Yes, I am."

The man extended a hand. "I'm Jefe."

"Have we met before?" Miriam asked, studying his face.

Jefe smiled and shook his head. "No, Director Anson. Even if we have, we haven't."

"Of course not," she said.

The blond woman nodded coolly. "Good to see you again, Miriam. What brings you to Rome?"

31

Rome, Italy

Miriam flinched when she saw the man she had once known as Tom Lawton. Lawton Caine was not the man who had once lived in her spare bedroom. And she wasn't sure she liked the changes.

"You look like hell," she said.

"I feel worse than that," he replied quietly. She reached out to hug him, but he backed away, lifting his shirt to show her his bandaged ribs. "I wish I could, but these wouldn't let me enjoy it."

"He got shot saving our lives," Renate said.

Renate briefly recounted the attack in the Berlin hotel room, and Miriam could tell she was leaving out part of the story. It was probably, Miriam thought, a part that had nothing to do with the workings of two undercover agents and everything to do with the longings of two human beings. While Renate's eyes were still glacial, there were things not even she could hide. She hovered over Lawton like a broody hen.

"I'll have to compliment the close combat instructors at Quantico," Miriam said with genuine gratitude to the men who taught hand-to-hand fighting at the Bureau's training center.

"Yeah, do that," Lawton said, trying to laugh and then wincing. "Damn that hurts."

"So sit down already," Renate said to him. She turned to Miriam. "He needs a mother."

"It seems he has one," Miriam said, smiling. She looked around the tiny space above the restaurant and the bank of laptops. "I expected...something bigger than this. For everything you do."

Jefe nodded at the window. "We had bigger, until a couple of nights ago. Soult's men hit our headquarters."

"The burned-out warehouse?" Steve asked.

"Yes," Jefe said. "Killed one of our agents. Assif and I got out—barely—with the help of our friends here. Assif grabbed what he could carry on the way out, and I set off the willy-petes. Woosh. This is what's left."

Miriam knew she'd recognized Jefe from somewhere, and the memory came back when he said *willy-petes*. John Ortega. He'd been in the Marine Corps before he'd joined the Bureau. She'd met him once or twice in passing, at training seminars. And he'd been killed in Los Angeles, on the operation that sent Lawton's career spiraling downward. Or so the records said. Another death that wasn't.

She turned her mind back to what he'd said. *Willy-petes* was military-speak for white phosphorous, a highly flammable compound used in incendiary bombs. The Office 119 headquarters had been pre-rigged for demolition, just in case. And "in case" had happened.

Miriam looked at the three Arab men in the room, two of them working at laptops with Assif, the other, the man who had been behind the counter when they'd come into the restaurant, standing next to Jefe. "Who are your friends?"

The man beside Jefe smiled. "Call me Ahmed."

"Okay," she said. It wasn't an answer. "So what's your horse in this race, Ahmed?"

He seemed to need a moment to figure out the metaphor. Then he said, "My people had worked with them before. Another operation. They were trustworthy, so we took it upon ourselves to look after them should the need arise. Sadly, it did."

It still wasn't an answer. She spoke to Jefe. "Look, I need your help, and it looks like you could use mine. I want our cards on the table. There are enough shadows out there without having them in here."

"I could ask the same of your friends," Ahmed said.

"I am a priest," Steve said. He turned to Miguel. "This is my friend and my bodyguard. We are on a mission for the Church."

Ahmed studied Miguel for a moment, seemingly looking for something he could connect to, and nodded.

When he spoke, it was to Steve. "That is fair." He pointed to the other Arab. "This is Reza. We are part of *Saif Alsharaawi*. In English, the Sword of the East. Our goal is to protect the interests of Allah, much as your interest is to protect the interests of Jesus Christ."

"An al-Qaeda look-alike," Miriam said.

Reza stiffened. "No. Do not dare to judge us. *Saif Alsharaawi* is committed to peace, to the true path set out for us by the Prophet, peace be upon him. We fight those who would oppress Islam, but we also fight those who use Islam as an excuse to commit atrocities. Justice cannot be purchased with the blood of the innocent."

"I'll vouch for them, Miriam," Lawton said. "They helped us track down a lot of the Black Christmas people. Out here in the field, you have to take the blinders off."

It was a subtle rebuke, but Miriam held her tongue. It *had* been a while since she'd been in the field, and maybe she had acquired some of the inside-the-Beltway mentality of us versus them. In Guatemala, she'd certainly had to deal with the vast gray murk of reality. The memories of the firefight outside Dos Ojos and her decision to conceal Miguel's survival were stark reminders of the times she'd had to walk both sides of the line between good and evil. In the field, that line was not simply blurry, it was often invisible.

"Okay," Miriam said to Ahmed. "If Lawton vouches for you, you're good in my book. My apologies if I offended you."

"In these times," Ahmed said, "no apology is needed. Had we met in other circumstances, I might well doubt the motives of the United States' intelligence czar."

"I doubt them every day."

Miriam let the statement hang there for a moment, then gave the barest flicker of a smile. Ahmed laughed, and the tension broke.

"We can work together," Ahmed said.

"And we must," Miriam said. She paused for a moment, considering how much to say. She couldn't reveal all that Steve had told her, but she also couldn't ask them to work in the dark. "Jules Soult is a dangerous man."

"Tell me something I don't know," Jefe said.

"He has an awful power," Miriam said. "A device he should not have. One of his agents stole it from Steve, in Guatemala. Soult used it to murder Chancellor Vögel."

Renate looked up. "How do you know this?"

Miriam nodded to Steve. He looked down.

"Well?" Jefe asked.

"It is an ancient technology," Steve said. "Some say it was handed down by the gods themselves, at the birth of mankind. That is legend, of course. What is not legend is what I have seen with my own eyes. I have held the device in my hands. It was hidden for centuries, buried deep in a volcano. It should have remained there. But I failed."

"What is this…device?" Lawton asked.

Steve shrugged. "Honestly, I don't know all of it. To look at it, it's a small ruby pyramid. It fits in the palm of a hand."

"Pyramid power," Renate said, shaking her head.

"Do not dismiss it," Steve said. "When I held it up to a candle flame, it seemed as if knowledge danced inside it. Mathematical symbols. I'm no scientist, so I couldn't make any sense of them. But if someone could...the device has terrible power. Imagine the walls of a city crumbling, soldiers on the ramparts choking on their own breath, dying under the sound of a distant trumpet."

"Oh, shit," Lawton said. "The Reichstag dome. The sounds reported by Vögel's bodyguards. This pyramid did that?"

"I believe it did," Steve said.

"We have legends of such a power," Ahmed said, nodding. "We always believed that the legends were exactly that, tales to be told to children to entertain them as they fell asleep under the desert sky. Or tales of merciful Allah's help when it was most needed."

"There are such legends in many cultures," Miriam said. "Apparently this one is more than legend."

Jefe made as if to speak, then paused. After a moment he looked at Renate. "It makes sense. It fits what you and Margarite were thinking. Soult's people instigate the street violence, which he then uses as an excuse for the removal program. He needed an 'other,' and the European Muslims fit. But the removal program is just a cover, a tool, a way to seize control of a European empire under the flag of the EU. Vögel opposes him, and Soult kills Vögel."

"He maneuvers to get Herr Müller the chancellorship," Renate said, nodding. "The bombing at the port of Hamburg seals the deal, and Germany goes along with the removals. But then comes the disaster in Nice, on the train. Müller rebels, and Soult is blocked again. Now we face war."

"And Soult won't hesitate to use the pyramid in that war," Steve said. "In the face of such power…"

"Germany would have no hope," Renate said. "Müller would be forced to sue for peace at once."

"A tidy little war to secure Soult's position," Miriam said. "A new Napoleon."

"Nein," Renate said. "A new Hitler. He has taken that path from the beginning. The attempted bombing of the European Parliament building was his Reichstag fire. The Muslims are his Jews, and the bombing of the Paris Mosque ignited his Kristallnacht. Now he proposes to annex a new Rhineland, in the guise of a 'European Security Zone.'"

"So assuming that's all true, we know his playbook," Miriam said. "We're in—when was the Rhineland…?"

"Nineteen thirty-six," Renate said. "But he's moving a lot faster than Hitler did. We don't have three years."

"No," Miriam said. "We don't have three weeks. I

need to call my boss. Congratulations, Jefe. You now have the power of the United States behind you."

Jefe nodded, but he looked skeptical.

Miriam looked at him. "You don't trust me?"

His eyes were unflinching. "I trust you, Director Anson. I just don't know if the power of the United States will be enough."

32

Querbach, Germany

Hans Neufel had watched through the night as the crowd of protesters on the Europabrücke grew. Part of him longed to be down there with them, to sit on the bridge in naive innocence, pretending that soldiers ordered into battle would not roll right over them, crushing them beneath the tracks of their armored vehicles. And perhaps, if those French troops were ordered forward, they would pause for a moment before driving through the protestors.

But only for a moment, Neufel feared.

He had tried to sleep in the wee hours of the morning, but sleep had eluded him. Every time he closed his eyes, he saw the French tanks rolling forward, saw himself peer through the targeting rangefinder of his tank, heard his voice give the order, felt the iron behemoth around him buck with the concussive force of propellant burning and the armor-piercing, discarding-sabot round shooting forth from the gun barrel, smelled the bitter tang of cordite, all in the instant before the target in his rangefinder exploded as the penetrator burned a thumb-sized stream of molten metal plasma into and through flesh and fuel and ammunition.

It was what he had trained to do. It was what he hoped he would never have to do.

Neufel held no comfortable illusions that he would simply be destroying an enemy vehicle. Emergency bailout drills and first-aid training films had made clear what would happen to the men inside an armored vehicle when it was struck by modern ammunition. The fate of the men inside would have given Dante pause.

As the darkness weaned into dawn, Neufel considered whether he should ask Leutnant Bräuburger for permission to visit the battalion *Militärpfarrer.* Perhaps a priest could quiet the turmoil in his soul. But even to ask would be to admit to his platoon leader, and to his crew, that he had doubts about his ability to perform his duty. He would be showing weakness at a time when his crew needed to see strength and resolve. He would lose his position as tank commander. Any thoughts he might have had about a career as an officer would be dashed forever.

No. He would not risk his men. The other three soldiers in his tank relied on him to remain cool. He had to put his emotions aside and focus on his duty.

"Waffen- und Ausrüstungskontrolle," he called out on the intercom. It was time to wake his men and ensure that his vehicle was fighting fit. *Weapons and equipment check.* "I will inspect in ten minutes."

His order met the usual groans as brains fought their way up from sleep and into the rigors of another day. Men whose bodies needed to urinate and take a swirl of water in their mouths put off those needs as they turned to their assigned tasks. There would be time to care for themselves after the inspection.

Neufel turned on his rangefinder and selected a small truck crossing the secondary highway bridge north of Kehl. He already knew the range to the meter, and the rangefinder read accurately. He toggled the targeting button, and the turret of the tank turned a few degrees, the huge gun barrel depressing slightly, until the gun was aligned with the rangefinder.

Had there been a round in the breach, Neufel would have needed only to depress the trigger. The computerized fire control would have done the rest, turning what looked to be a bakery truck into a pile of smoking, twisted metal.

But the truck exploded anyway.

No, not the truck. The bridge beneath it.

Moments later, the main highway bridge, as well as the railway bridge, began belching flame and smoke as charges rattled along their lengths. The concussive *pop-pop-pops* echoed across the valley and up to Neufel's position, a sound like thick canvas being ripped apart. The bridges disappeared behind dense clouds of smoke.

Stunned, Neufel continued to watch through his range-finder, switching to infrared mode without conscious thought, allowing him to look through the smoke as the white hot pinpoints of melting steel and burning concrete twisted, then buckled, then dropped into the river below.

Who had ordered the bridges destroyed?

Had the war begun already?

He looked across the Rhine at the French encampment. The distance was too great to make out individual faces, but Neufel still saw shock and surprise in the way the way men scrambled from latrines and mess tents, running for their vehicles.

They had not been forewarned. It was obvious.

Neufel keyed his radio. *"Rot-Eins-Sechs, Rot-Eins-Zwei, Ende?"* Red-one-six, red-one-two, over?

Bräuburger's voice on the radio crackled with tension. *"Rot-Eins-Zwei, Rot-Eins-Sechs.* Damn, what is going on down there, over?"

"I don't know," Neufel said.

"Get down there and find out. Now!" Bräuburger replied.

"Ja, Herr Leutnant," Neufel said. Later, he might be surprised that he hadn't stopped to question the order. Instead, he switched to the intercom frequency. "Driver, forward!"

His driver responded immediately, and the fifty-five ton Leopard II began to roll.

Rome, Italy

Television cameras recorded the event in painfully sharp detail. The picture bounced wildly as cameramen struggled to take in all that was happening. But in the very center, one thing was clear: Three bridges over the Kinzig River, two kilometers east of the Europabrücke, were burning. The metal twisted and flamed in a way that, to Miriam, suggested magnesium bombs or shaped charges, the only implements that could have melted metal so quickly.

She stared at the television, her heart stopped in horror. No one in the room moved. The only sound issued from the phone pressed to her ear. "Miriam," Grant Lawrence was saying. "Miriam, are you watching?"

"Yes," she whispered.

Now a tank moved down from the woods above Kehl, the cameras zooming in to capture the slow movement of the Leopard II, its turret tracking back and forth as if in search of prey. Another camera showed a French encampment that appeared to have been taken utterly by surprise.

"The Germans started this?" she asked with astonishment.

"It looks like it," Grant said. "But Müller told the president that he wasn't going to initiate anything. I'm guessing they had the bridges wired, intending to blow them if the French started their attack over the Rhine. Maybe it was an accidental detonation."

"What a time for a fucking accident," Miriam said.

"You'd almost think the Guy Upstairs is rooting for Soult."

"The President is trying to get through to Berlin now," Grant said. "With Soult's threat to go nuclear, there can't be even the appearance of German provocation. And blowing bridges, even your own bridges, in the face of the enemy…that's provocation. I don't have to tell you what the comms are like now."

"And Müller has his hands full right now," Miriam said. "He has to be as stunned as the rest of us."

"So let's focus on what we *can* do," Grant said. "You're sure about Soult?"

"You can't take it to court yet," Miriam said. "What's more, right now he's untouchable."

"Because of that pyramid device?" Grant asked.

"That's what I'm being told," Miriam said, despite the skepticism she heard in his voice. "Look, Grant, I know it sounds nuts, but these are good people I'm working with. Solid people. One of them held this pyramid in his own hand. All the pieces fit, including how Vögel died, and that's the first good explanation we've had for that. It explains how Soult survived that bomb in Strasbourg."

"So what's your action plan?" Grant asked. "And what can we do to help? The President wants to move on this. We have a lot of people in Germany. We can't look as if we're abandoning them."

"Tell him to keep the military on standby," she said.

"Keep that as a last resort. How fast can you get a snatch team here on station?"

"Hold on," Grant said. She heard a muffled exchange. Apparently he was in the situation room. The Joint Chiefs were probably right there beside him. "Okay, special ops has a team with the Sixth Fleet, in the Med. Tell me where you want them. They can be there in three hours."

"Hang on," Miriam said. She put a hand over the mouthpiece and turned to Jefe. "I can have a special ops team here in three hours."

"Do it," Jefe said. "I have an operations group, but they're all over hell and gone, and with my communications still screwed…"

"Here in Rome," Miriam said to Grant. "I'll meet them at Gaeta. And, Grant, make sure they're guys who don't mind working with…an international group."

"Gaeta is a two-hour drive," Reza said after Miriam had disconnected.

"Do you have a car?" she asked.

He nodded. "Of course. I will take you."

"While you're gone, I'll work up a target profile on this Hector Vasquez," Jefe said, then briefly explained the Hitler-Röhm-Soult-Vasquez. "Renate's right. He'll be Soult's weak link. If we can turn him, Soult's house of lies will collapse."

"You know what they'll need?" Miriam said.

Jefe nodded. "The same thing my people would. I'll get it together."

"Quickly, please," Miriam said, looking at the television screen. "This is building fast."

The Bridge of Europe

Monsignore Giuseppe Veltroni stared in horror as the explosions erupted. His cell phone was already ringing. When he picked it up, he could barely make out the voice of Hans Stoll—the priest from Mannheim—above the shouts of panic and confusion.

"They're blowing the Kinzig bridges!"

"I see it on television," Veltroni said. "Is everyone there okay?"

"For the moment," Stohl said. "But we are now cut off. Even if we tried to flee, we could get no farther than Kehl. And my country's troops are all on the far side of the Kinzig. They had no intention of trying to hold the village."

"Why would the Germans blow the bridges?" Veltroni asked. "It makes no sense."

"They want the French held here," Stoll said. "They will make of this place a killing ground."

"What do you mean?" Veltroni asked. "How do you know this?"

"Let me give you to my friend, Rabbi Lev," Stoll said. "He can explain it."

Veltroni heard a muttered exchange, and then the rabbi's voice came over the phone. "In my youth in Russia, one could not avoid serving in the Red Army. I was always a gifted student. I was sent to our staff college, where we studied Western doctrine and tactics."

"And?" Veltroni asked.

"And if you cannot stop a river crossing on the far bank, the best time to strike is when the enemy army is divided by the river," Lev explained. "With these bridges destroyed, the French can get into Kehl but no farther. Not until they can force crossings on the Kinzig. And they cannot prepare those crossings until they are east of the Rhine. And the EU zone gives them no other choice but to cross here. This will present a window of opportunity."

"My God," Veltroni said. "The German army would bomb its own territory?"

"It makes sense, yes?" Lev said. "If the battle is fought east of the Rhine, Germany has not attacked France. In terms of world opinion, this is a very important point. Would you not sacrifice one small city to save a nation? Most of the residents of Kehl have already evacuated east of the Kinzig."

"I see," Veltroni said, thinking through the options in his mind. "Yes, it makes sense. Soult would clearly have attacked Germany, but his forces would be stuck for some time on the east side of the Rhine. Easy targets for bombers. And Germany would not have attacked French soil."

Lev sighed. "We are at ground zero, *Monsignore*. The battle will happen here. And now we cannot escape it."

Not that they had intended to flee, Veltroni thought after disconnecting the call. They had intended to stage a Tiananmen Square protest. But unlike the Chinese students in that square, these protestors had nowhere to run.

He looked back at the television and asked himself whether Germany had declared war. Lev's analysis held a cruel but irrefutable logic. There was no way for Germany to put a strong enough blocking force at the Rhine itself without creating a propaganda opportunity for Soult, who would claim that Germany was massing to attack. But the terrain had yielded another option: defend at the Kinzig, destroy the enemy in Kehl.

This meant Germany had blown the bridges. Not an overt act of aggression, for the bridges were on German soil, but an unmistakable signal that there would be no more talking. They were going to war.

His heart sank into his belly.

They had only hours left to act.

Part IV: *LO OD*
(Hebrew: *Never Again*)

33

Monsignore Giuseppe Veltroni was a desperate man in a sea of desperate men. The cloud of war hung over Europe like the smoke that rose from the three bridges in Germany, three bridges whose names were unknown only an hour ago and were now on the lips of men all over the world. In every world capital, men and women were scrambling to organize a response on behalf of one side or the other, most of which would be only empty words. It was no different here in the Vatican, where well-meaning experts were huddled, waiting for their chance to brief the Holy Father.

Empty words would not be enough this time. Twice in the past century the Vatican had been silent as Europe erupted into spasms of death. Whatever the reasons those Pontiffs may have had—and Veltroni had no doubt of their good intentions—tens of millions had bled and died from Madrid to Moscow, Narvik to North Africa.

Veltroni had seen this coming and felt as if he ought to have been prepared for it. Yet it had still come with a suddenness that left him feeling as if he had been kicked in the stomach. It had seemed as if there would be time to plan, time to organize, time to think through details and options. Now there was no time left.

He had to see the Holy Father. And he had to see him immediately. Before those well-meaning advisors counseled him into empty words.

But he never got that far. Once again he was blocked by Cardinal Estevan, keeper of the gate by way of his influence over the Stewards and his long friendship with the Holy Father.

"Giuseppe," Estevan said quietly, "you would meddle in things you don't understand."

"I understand war. I understand racism. I understand that the seeds of genocide are being planted all over Europe. Will we stand aside as we did before?"

Estevan shook his head and reached for a goblet of wine. His ruby ring sparkled in the lamplight, seeming to shoot an angry beam straight at Veltroni. Over the top of the goblet, he stared steadily at Veltroni for long silent seconds.

"*Monsignore*," he said finally, "for a man who has spent most of his priestly life in the Vatican, you are rather impatient."

"More people may die!"

"Of course they may. It will be as God wills. But you are missing my point."

With difficulty, Veltroni maintained his silence.

"Here within these walls, as you should well know by now, we have a longer view of history. We are aware, as few others are in the world, of the importance of any steps we take now, because they will affect the future of Mother Church for centuries to come. We and our flock live with mistakes for a long time, Giuseppe. The papers may forget them by next week, but God will not."

"God cannot possibly want to see a war break out."

Estevan shrugged. "My dear *Monsignore,* that is kindergarten logic. Only consider the times when God sent his chosen people into battle."

Veltroni wanted to scream. Instead, as calmly as he could, he said, "God does not wish such things."

"You would dispute the Bible? You would dispute the doom that the Lord laid on the cities when the Israelites triumphed, causing them to slaughter every man, woman and child?"

"It is not God placing this doom, Eminence, it is man." He was beginning to wonder if he'd ever known Estevan at all.

Surprising Veltroni, the cardinal suddenly smiled. "You are a passionate, moral man, Giuseppe. Go to bed with an untroubled conscience, for the Church will do what is right."

He wished he could think of a way to question the

cardinal further, but instead he suffered the man to press a goblet of fine Italian wine into his hand.

"The Church is eternal," Estevan said, striding slowly around his office, his cassock skirt swinging with every step. "The actions that the Church takes must be taken with an eye to eternity. God will restore our temporal power one of these days, *Monsignore.* You will see it, because it is God's will."

"It is?" Veltroni wondered if Estevan were going round the bend.

"Yes, it is." Estevan paused and faced Veltroni, smiling. "You may not see it yet, *Monsignore,* but the pieces are moving into place. The things that are happening in Europe right now are creating a vacuum of moral and political power. You will see."

"And then?"

Estevan shrugged and smiled, then drained his cup. "Pax Romana was a good thing in many ways. Too bad it's gone."

Walking back to his chamber a short while later, Veltroni felt unease crawling up and down his spine. Then he forced himself to shrug it off. There was absolutely no way that anyone could restore the Holy Roman Empire, not even the Pope.

Not even Cardinal Estevan.

Neumühl, Germany

"Driver, halt," Hans Neufel said into the intercom.

He climbed out of the turret of his tank, which had

stopped on the eastern approach to the now-destroyed railway bridge. The air reeked of molten metal and dust. To his right, lying on its side in the fast-flowing Kinzig, was the shattered remains of the bakery truck, its driver hanging half out of the cab, limp and still.

There was a certainty in that stillness. It would be pointless to dive into the river and try to save the driver, whose only crime had been to begin his day as he always did, delivering bread to local markets, crossing a bridge he had probably crossed a thousand times before. He was beyond salvation.

The railway bridge had stood between the two highway bridges. It was the obvious place in which to position the pioneer platoon. Although Neufel could not yet see those positions, the absence of movement did not give him a feeling of confidence.

Neufel shrugged into his field harness and climbed down from the tank. He pressed the transmit button on the shoulder microphone. "Red-one-six, red-one-two, over?"

"Red-one-two, send your traffic."

"I am approaching the railroad bridge. I see no movement."

"Understood, red-one-two."

Neufel found the pioneers' position among some small trees on the embankment. It was a six-man position, which should have been adequate to man the demolition switches and protect itself against infiltration. There was no concealed route of approach. Had they followed standard watch procedures, they should have seen anyone approaching them in plenty of time to respond and defend themselves.

But Neufel knew how difficult it had been to get his own crew to maintain a twenty-four-hour watch over these past days. There was nothing more draining than the ennui of standing watch when there was nothing to observe. Men wrote letters to girlfriends, smoked a cigarette, read a book or magazine, listened to an iPod or simply rested their heads on anything convenient and snatched a few minutes of precious sleep.

As he pressed a finger to the cold throat of one of the men, he reasoned that whoever had been on watch in this position had done what men will do. Once the adrenaline high of moving into the position had given way to the daily routine of manning it, he had grown careless and inattentive.

That carelessness had killed him, and his comrades.

"Red-one-six, red-one-two. They are all dead, over."

The chatter on the frequency came to a complete stop, as if the air had been sucked from the lungs of every man listening.

"Say again, red-one-two."

"Alle sind tot." All are dead.

"Understood." Braüburger's voice was leaden. "Secure the scene and wait for me."

"Understood, red-one-six. Red-one-two, out."

Neufel switched to his tank's intercom. "You heard

the lieutenant. We secure the scene. Schulingen, load smoke. Sanger, in my seat and sweep the area. Do not fire without my order."

"*Ja*, Herr Stuffz."

A smoke round, Neufel reasoned, could be used both to warn and to mark a target without actually opening hostile fire. He saw the Leopard II's turret begin to slowly swing back and forth as Sanger, his gunner, scanned the area through the rangefinder's optical and infrared sights, the gun barrel like an angry pointing finger.

Feeling somewhat more protected as he waited for his platoon leader, Neufel turned to the task of examining the pioneers' position. Only one of the six men had his rifle at hand. Its butt lay on his chest, its barrel near the toe of his boot. He had been the man on watch, probably resting his rifle barrel on his foot and his head on its stock. Probably asleep.

While he had been hit first, the rest had been hit almost at the same moment, each dispatched with what looked like a three-round burst in the center of his chest, before he could even shrug off his field blanket.

Neufel looked back up to his platoon's positions on the ridge to the east, thinking back to what he had seen and heard through the night. He had slept hardly at all, and never deeply. While he'd had no clear line of sight into the pioneers' positions, he'd been able to see the area around them. He should have seen muzzle flashes. And even if his eyes had been closed, or he had been looking in another direction, he should have heard the crackle of small arms fire.

He had seen nothing. He had heard nothing.

The attackers had used silencers. And they had been inside the pioneers' bunker before they fired.

He studied the terrain immediately around him, looking for any shallow fold that might yield dead ground, a place that could not be observed from this position.

And there it was. Invisible unless one was actively searching for it, looking out from this place—or looking for a way into it.

It was too shallow to be called a ditch. A trough, barely a twenty-centimeter depression etched over the years as rainwater found its way down the embankment and into the river below. The pioneers had established this position in daylight, when the trough would have seemed insignificant. Anyone approaching through it would have to belly crawl, and even then, the crest of a helmet or pack would have been easily seen in the daytime.

But at night, under a cloudy sky that shrouded the moonlight, with no light to silhouette the movement, a team could crawl through that trough, their sounds masked by the sounds of the river, undetected by any but the most alert sentry, until they were but a few meters distant. Even had the man on watch not been asleep, the likelihood that he would have seen the enemy approach was minimal.

After that it would have been fast and deadly. The

first silenced shots taking out the man on watch, and then the quiet thudding of boots as the team burst into the small bunker.

When he looked out toward the ridgeline again, he saw that Bräuburger's tank had joined his, coming to rest on the other side of the railroad line, maintaining the proper spacing of vehicles that prevented a single enemy round or bomb from taking out two targets. The lieutenant climbed out of his tank and joined Neufel at the bunker entrance. He looked in for only a moment before he turned to Neufel.

"Gott im Himmel."

"Ja," Neufel said. *God in heaven,* indeed.

He explained his theory of how the enemy had approached and how the attack had been carried out. The lieutenant nodded his agreement. "That's how they did it."

Bräuburger relayed the information on the battalion command frequency in terse, carefully chosen words. The French had destroyed the bridges. They likely had thought to destroy only the railway bridge, as a provocation, not knowing that the other two bridges were wired to the same circuit. The smoke and dust had concealed their escape, perhaps across the river, but not likely. More likely they were still in the immediate area, hiding, waiting for an opportunity to exfiltrate.

"Find them," the battalion commander ordered. "Find them quickly."

"*Ja,* Herr Oberstleutnant," Bräuburger said. He turned to Neufel. "Leave Sanger on overwatch. Tell your driver and loader to take their personal weapons and join us."

Bräuburger looked at Neufel for a moment, and Neufel realized that, in his rush to get down to the bunker, he had not grabbed his MP7 machine pistol. Neufel told his driver to bring it.

"*Wir sind jetzt Infantrie,*" Bräuburger said.

We are now infantry? Untrained infantry, Neufel thought, hunting for what were obviously skilled special operations men. Men who had executed six soldiers without a second thought, and who would not hesitate to kill again. It was not a comforting prospect.

"*Ja,* Herr Leutnant."

Strasbourg, France

"Brilliant, Vasquez," Soult said, watching the news coverage from a mobile command vehicle near the French army command post. Clearly, the media were saying, the Germans had chosen to destroy the bridges to prepare for war. "We will be on the right side of history."

"Perhaps," Vasquez said, his voice troubled. "But my men are on the wrong side of two rivers. It will not seem weak for you to take twenty-four hours to mull over this new provocation before launching our attack. This will let my men escape during the night."

"*Merde!*" Soult said. He slammed a fist into his other

palm. "The moment of action is now! How long before it is discovered that the German engineers were killed in their bunker? You see those two tanks and the men moving about? They know already. How long before the bodies of the dead are on television and public opinion shifts to Germany? Can you guarantee this will not happen in the next twenty-four hours?"

"No," Vasquez said. "I cannot guarantee that. But we can shape the story, issue denials."

"Denials will mean nothing next to pictures of dead German soldiers with bullet holes in them. Denials will be useless when forensic experts identify the ammunition. Denials are words, Vasquez. We will issue our denial with action!"

"There are still protestors on the bridge," Vasquez said. "Priests and nuns and rabbis. What of them?"

"Fools," Soult said. "Fools begging to their gods. Fools on a fool's errand, awaiting a fool's end. And we will give them that end."

Soult picked up the olive green field telephone.

"No, *mon général*," Vasquez said, stepping forward. "Give my men a chance."

Soult ignored him and spoke into the phone. *"Commencer Forêt Sombre. Je répète, commencer Forêt Sombre."*

Commence Dark Wood. Vasquez shook his head as he walked out of the command vehicle. His men would be killed, if not by the Germans then by the French. Good men. Men who had served well and deserved better.

But there was no stopping Monsieur Soult now.

34

Auenheim, Germany

Hans Neufel held up two fingers and pointed across the street. They had been at it for an hour now, moving house to house, a slow and dangerous progression where each knock on a door carried with it the possibility of a reply in the form of nine-millimeter bullets cutting through the air.

The saboteurs' most logical hiding place would be near the east end of the Europabrücke, so they could slip into the ranks of the French as they crossed the river. After a brief radio conversation, Neufel's battalion commander had sent a platoon into the village of Neumühl, a collection of shops and homes on the eastern bank of the Kinzig across from Kehl. Bräuburger and Neufel were left the task of clearing Auenheim, a smaller village to the north, at the junction of the Kinzig and the Rhine, in case the saboteurs had gone that way instead.

This gave Neufel a clear view across the open ground north of Kehl to the Rhine and the Europabrücke itself. As he cleared each building, he found himself glancing back over his shoulder at the bridge, to see whether the French had begun to move. It was not his job to keep watch on the French across the Rhine; Sanger, his gunner, was watching from his tank. Yet Neufel did not want his first warning of danger to be a panicked call over the radio or, worse, the crack of the tank's twelve-centimeter cannon as Sanger opened fire.

Later, Neufel would be unable to recall whether he had been looking at the bridge when the radio call came in, or whether the radio call had drawn his attention there. He would only remember the sinking feeling in his stomach as he watched the French infantry form up and march onto the bridge, and his anger that this war could not be stopped.

Rome, Italy

Veltroni stared in horror at the scene unfolding along the Rhine. The instant he saw French troops marching onto the bridge, he ran from his Vatican apartment and grabbed a cab to the Trevi Fountain. There, he prayed, God would have Nathan Cohen waiting.

While he rode in the cab, he dialed the number of the cell phone he had given Steve, a cell phone that only he and Steve knew about. So far he had never used it, but now he needed to talk to the young priest.

The answer was surprisingly swift. "Steve Lorenzo."

"Steve. My son! Have you seen what is happening in Strasbourg?"

"Yes."

"We need to do something. I cannot think what, but this cannot go on. And I cannot reach the Holy Father."

"I know what I must do," said Steve. "Believe me, Giuseppe, I know what must be done. But you must not call me again. I will meet you soon to brief you. What I do now, no one can know."

"All right, all right. Just stay out of the line of fire."

Veltroni snapped the cell phone shut and closed his eyes tightly. He had sent those people to that bridge. He had called upon the Stewards to go there. He had not truly believed that anyone would move against them.

But it was happening. Good men and women were about to die, and much of it would be his fault.

God forgive me.

The Bridge of Europe

The French infantry came forward in riot formation, two columns of twelve abreast, assault rifles held at port arms. As they neared the protestors, the command was given to march in riot step, each man lunging forward on his left foot as he pushed out with his rifle, then bringing his right foot up behind the left.

Even though the protestors had linked arms, they stood no chance of stopping the onslaught. Neufel imagined that the riot step might look harmless enough on the television cameras, but the impact of a FAMAS G2 assault rifle, driven into the ribs by the full body weight of a trained soldier, was anything but. A nun fell and, as an imam bent to help her up, one of the soldiers crushed him to the ground with a savage butt stroke.

Oddly, it was those who fell to the ground, more than those who stood in defiance, who did the most to disrupt the attack. The French soldiers were reluctant to step on the bodies, and their ranks broke open as men moved around the human obstacles.

Now anger surged through piety, and Neufel watched in horror as some of the protesters tried to storm into those gaps. As closed ranks opened, the disciplined riot control maneuvers gave way to individual combat, rifle butts driven into stomachs and backs and faces, officers yelling vainly to regain control, angry words hurled in French, German, Hebrew and Arabic, pained grunts and soft, fluttering sighs as priests and nuns collapsed under the assault.

Neufel couldn't bear to watch anymore.

Nor could he afford to, for he was engaged in a deadly game of cat and mouse that required his full attention. He and his men could not use standard urban assault tactics—throwing a grenade into the room, then following after its explosion with guns blazing—because there were still civilians in the town. Forced to yell *"Raus! Raus! Raus!"*—Out! Out! Out!—at each door, lest they burst in firing on an innocent family, they sacrificed any hope of tactical surprise.

They worked in teams, Bräuburger and his two men on one side of the street, Neufel and his men on the other.

Schulingen had just kicked open the door of a tiny chocolate shop when Neufel heard the ragged clatter of distant rifle fire. For a moment he wondered where it was coming from, for it was too faint to be here in the village. He looked first up the ridge to his platoon's positions, but there was no visible activity there.

The Europabrücke.

It was not an organized volley, not on order. It was, predictably, born of a series of accidents: a safety turned off in the push and pull of the fray, a trigger depressed without intent. But once the sound of the first shot rippled through the melee, the door of carnage swung open.

He stepped out into the street, looking toward the southwest. There were French troops on the bridge. And they were shooting protestors. His heart sank as he saw that the column of tanks at the far end of the bridge was already advancing, their turrets sweeping back and forth. Between the French tanks rolling onto the west end of the bridge and the infantry nearing the east end

lay the crumpled bodies of dead and wounded protestors. Some were crawling. Many were still.

The tanks would crush their bodies to pulp.

The thought enraged him. The French soldiers could
have avoided that. Common decency called for moving
the dead and wounded aside.

Neufel had wondered if he could hate. He did not
wonder now. He pressed the transmit button on his intercom microphone. "Sight on the lead French tank. Fire
smoke. If they do not stop, load sabot and engage."

"*Nein,* Herr Stuffz," Sanger said. "The battalion commander has forbidden it."

The battalion commander had forbidden them to engage? Were they to simply sit and watch the French kill
civilians on the bridge?

It was Schulingen's startled cry that broke through
his sense of helplessness. He turned in time to see his
loader slump to the ground, his black tanker coveralls
wet with blood. His driver had plastered himself to the
outside wall beside the doorway, his eyes on Schulingen's body, his face frozen in shock.

"In there!" Neufel shouted, pointing as he sprinted
toward the doorway.

He could not avenge the dead priests and nuns on the
bridge. But he could avenge Schulingen. He thumbed
the MP-7 to full automatic and rammed the short barrel through a window beside the door, squeezing the
trigger, watching as flame and lead spurted from the ma-

chine pistol, emptying the thirty-round magazine in a single two-second burst, not caring as the kick made the weapon climb in his arms, driving his hands onto the jagged glass above.

Bräuburger's team crossed the street just as Neufel pulled back from the window. His driver, jarred from the shock of seeing Schulingen fall, burst through the doorway with Bräuburger's men, four automatic weapons firing in unison, a crackling cacophony of death.

The room reeked of cordite as Neufel came in behind them, having loaded a fresh magazine, ready and eager to join in the killing.

But there was no one left to kill.

Four men in black sweaters were sprawled behind the counter, their bodies shredded, one still clutching his silenced weapon. They were all dead, as were the man and woman who were bound and gagged in the center of the floor.

Neufel would need no pathologist to know who had killed the couple. They were squarely in his line of fire from the window.

As he sucked in air, he found another scent beneath the cordite.

Chocolate.

He bent over and vomited.

35

Rome, Italy

Miriam Anson climbed the stairs to the crowded office over the restaurant. She knew exactly what she would find. Since the French had moved onto the Bridge of Europe and killed demonstrators, the streets outside were full of people crying for blood from one side or the other. She had listened to them as she and Reza had returned from depositing the special forces operatives in a safe location nearby. She had seen the television footage before she stepped into a quiet alley to call Grant Lawrence from her satellite phone.

Reza had stood back, keeping an eye out for trouble as she talked with Grant.

"The Germans want to move," Grant had said. "The President is doing his best to get twenty-four hours, Miriam."

"That's all?"

"I doubt he can get any more. He'll be doing well to get that, after the slaughter on the bridge. Especially since the German army has confirmed that the bridges were detonated by saboteurs, most likely working for Soult."

Miriam bit her lip. "It's not a lot of time."

"It's all you've got."

So she was hardly expecting the cacophony of voices from above as she ascended the steep creaky steps. She wasn't surprised to find at least three conversations going on while televisions displayed the ugliness in three versions: Al Jazeera, CNN International and Deutscheweld. Nor did she need an interpreter to tell her which broadcasts were pushing which agendas.

Fatigue nearly hit her between the eyes. She wouldn't have believed that these events could leave her feeling as if she'd run a marathon while fighting off the flu. She dealt with crises every day on her job. But this one…

The sight of those poor people on the bridge, flashing again and again on the screens, was too much to bear.

Slowly the room fell silent as her return was recognized. Renate was the first to speak. "How bad is it?"

"Not as bad as it could be. The President is asking the German chancellor to hold off for twenty-four hours."

Renate blanched. "That's all?"

"That's all."

Needing suddenly to escape for a few minutes,

Miriam took the next set of creaky stairs up to the roof. The sky was clouding over, as if readying for the coming storm. She gripped the stuccoed half wall that provided protection against a fall from the flat roof and stared heavenward. She supposed she wasn't alone in her horror at the turn events had taken. These were not events she had ever thought to see in her lifetime. Elsewhere, yes, but not in Europe.

"Miriam?"

She turned at the sound of Renate's voice. Sometimes she hated the other woman's icy calm. "Yes?"

"We need to get things together quickly, yes?"

Miriam nodded, but she didn't move. After a moment Renate joined her at the wall, looking out over rooftops, which stretched back so far in time that they reminded Miriam that some things could be nearly permanent. The blackened mess that had once been the Office 119 warehouse was on the other side of the building, mercifully concealed.

"I hate this job," Renate said.

"I can imagine a million reasons why. I'm not too fond of mine at the moment, either."

One corner of Renate's mouth lifted. "You carry a huge burden."

Miriam managed a shrug. "Others carry bigger ones."

But not many. Renate pulled out a pack of cigarettes and lit one. "I started smoking again in Berlin. Usually I quit when I leave Germany. This time…I cannot."

"After this is over, maybe."

Renate nodded. "Maybe. If it is ever over. It is so good for Lawton to see you again. Most of us never have the opportunity to see old friends."

"That must be hard."

Renate blew a stream of smoke and didn't answer directly. "Lawton is managing this very well. This is a life better suited to men, I think."

Miriam turned to face her. "Is your biological clock ticking?" As she had hoped, Renate smiled.

"No. I never wanted children, for some reason. But I had other dreams." She sighed and puffed on her cigarette again. "This is not a job for a woman," she said finally.

"No."

Their eyes met, and understanding passed between them.

"But it's our job, anyway," Renate said. She dropped her cigarette and ground it out beneath her heel. "You cannot come on this mission, Miriam. You understand why."

Miriam nodded reluctantly. "If the Director of National Intelligence for the U.S. were to be found to have participated in a military operation on foreign soil…"

"The consequences would not bear thinking of. Come, we must prepare."

Ahmed Ahsami and Sheik al-Hazeer watched the flat screen TV in the sheik's opulent Rome hotel suite.

Ahmed felt penned in, watched at every moment, first by Abdul and now by the sheik. Why was he suddenly so distrusted? Why had al-Hazeer come to Rome? He seemed to have nothing of import to convey. Certainly he had not summoned Ahmed simply to watch TV with him.

Had al-Hazeer in some way changed *Saif's* original agenda without telling him? Ahmed began to fear this was so. Consequently, he had only half his attention on the unfolding events in Europe near Strasbourg. The other half was focused squarely on the sheik, who nibbled on dates and sipped expensive bottled water from France.

"This Soult," al-Hazeer remarked. "I do not like this man."

"I don't, either." Ahmed tried again. "We should be offering all those Muslims homes in Arab countries."

Al-Hazeer frowned. "Too many of them are Shi'a, the curse of the Arab lands. Let them stay."

Ahmed, too, had grown up in a strict Sunni faith, but education had tempered that. Since living in the United States and Europe for his undergraduate and graduate degrees, he had decided the conflict between Sunni and Shi'a was hardly any different than the conflict between Catholics and Protestants, and they all managed to live together.

But the most fundamentalist of the Sunni populations believed the Shi'a weren't even Muslim. Wahhabist Sunni clerics tried to block the Shi'a from making the

Haj, the required pilgrimage to Mecca. In a region comprised of near theocratic dictatorships, the Shi'a had no voice in government save in Iran and Iraq, despite being nearly half of the population in the Middle East. And as if by a cruel twist of Allah's will, the Shi'a were a majority wherever there was oil: in Iran, Iraq, Bahrain and eastern Saudi Arabia. Political power commensurate with their population would put the Shi'a in control of the world's oil supply.

Ahmed rubbed his chin and studied al-Hazeer. "So you would let our fellow Arabs die because many are Shi'a?"

Al-Hazeer frowned at him. "Heretics who spit in their food. What is wrong with you, Ahmed? You know they are an abomination before Allah."

Ahmed nodded, though he did not agree. "But still, they are our people."

Al-Hazeer shrugged. "We would be better off without them. All of them."

The way he said that chilled Ahmed's spine. After what he considered to be a safe amount of time, he rose. "I must get back, if you want me to keep control of our part of the operation away from the Europeans."

Al-Hazeer waved him away without even looking at him. That as much as anything solidified Ahmed's sense of foreboding.

Al-Hazeer's voice stopped him at the door. "Do not get too close to these Europeans, my friend. They are tools, nothing more."

* * *

Renate pointed to a series of pictures, maps and diagrams that she had taped to one wall. The room above the restaurant—Office 119's temporary headquarters— was tightly packed with Office 119 personnel, operatives from *Saif Alsharaawi* and the American special ops team that had been sent to lend their expertise.

Renate's finger tapped the map, drawing everyone's attention. "Colonel Hector Vasquez has an office in the Parliament building, but we can't get in there. Not in strength, anyway. The entire complex is crawling with French and European security right now, and they're on high alert. But here—" she pointed to the map of Strasbourg "—is his apartment on Rue Twinger. We take him there."

Renate and Jefe had spent the past six hours making contact with an asset in Strasbourg and convincing the man—a mid-level administrator in the European Union—that this was more important than whatever Jules Soult had his office working on at the moment. Jefe had finally turned the screws on the man, threatening to expose the second mistress the man was keeping. His wife might not have minded the first mistress, but one of those two women would certainly mind the third.

The man had relented, developing a sudden stomach virus that gave him a reason to leave his office and spend the day chasing down the information that Renate was now presenting to Miriam and the Americans.

"You made arrangements for helicopters, yes?" Renate asked Miriam.

"Yes," Miriam said. "They're UH-60s…Black Hawks."

"Do they have the range to make the trip?" Jefe asked. "We're not going to be able to refuel in France."

"We won't need to," Miriam said. "We fly Rome to Aviano and refuel the birds there. Then through the Alpine passes to Mulhouse, south of Freiberg. That will be our P-N-R. After that, it's a half-hour hop to Strasbourg."

"P-N-R?" Renate asked.

"Point of no return," Miriam explained. "We'll need two birds for the mission. One for the insertion team at Rue Twinger, and a second to drop Steve and Miguel at the Parc de l'Orangerie and then cover the extraction at the primary target. We're leaving with three, but things can go wrong. Mulhouse is our P-N-R. If there's a problem, that's our last chance to abort."

"Flight times?" Renate asked.

Miriam looked down at a page of notes. "Two hours to Aviano. Two and a half to Mulhouse. Then a half hour into Strasbourg."

"Six hours, including refueling," Renate said, adding the numbers in her head.

"No, that included refueling times," Miriam said. "I'm sorry. I didn't make that clear. Five hours total."

Renate nodded and looked at her watch. Twenty-two hours left of the twenty-four that Herr Bundeskanzler

Müller had finally promised to President Rice. "We must work fast. I want to be in the air in two hours."

"Agreed," Miriam said. "Tell us more about the flat on Rue Twinger."

"It's a second-floor flat," Renate said, pointing to a poorly composed photograph. Their asset had obviously been in a hurry and was not an expert photographer. "The one on the right—here."

"That's the third floor," one of the Americans said.

Renate looked at him, confused, until Jefe spoke. "In Europe, there's the ground floor, then the first floor and so on."

"Ahh," the man said. "Understood."

"The roof is flat and mostly clear," Renate said. "You can rappel onto it, yes?"

"We can fast rope onto a kitchen table if we have to," the man, obviously the leader of the special ops team, said. "But it would be nice if we weren't trying to dodge power lines on the way down. We need a photo of the roof."

"I don't have one," Renate said.

"We need one by the time we get to Mulhouse," the man said. "That's go-no-go intel."

"What Major Conrad means," Miriam said, "is that they need to know what the roof looks like, so they can make their final briefing. They don't want to be landing on the wrong roof, and, as he said, they don't want to be swinging around between power lines. Without that intel, we'll be forced to abort at Mulhouse."

"We'll get it," Jefe said.

"What about extraction?" Conrad asked, stepping up to the map. "We can fast rope in, but we can't fast rope out. That street looks awfully narrow. What about here, at this intersection?"

Renate looked where the tip of his finger was resting. There was a large open area where Rue Daniel Hilz, Rue Trubner and Rue Massenet merged. It was less than one hundred meters from the target building. "Yes, that is good."

"Yes," Conrad agreed.

He looked at the photos and maps for a moment, as if calculating times and distances, the very same thing Renate was doing.

"Ten minutes on the ground?" Renate asked.

"I make it twelve," Conrad replied. "One minute from insertion until entry. Two minutes to subdue Vasquez. Six minutes for the document team to grab his computer's hard drive, cell phone and desk files while we're getting him to the extraction point. Two minutes for them to meet us at the birds and load up. We'll be skids up within sixty seconds after that."

"That close to the European Parliament complex," Renate said, shaking her head. This was the same area of the city where they had worked before. It looked larger on the photos than it was on the ground. "Twelve minutes..."

"Yes, we'll get resistance," Conrad said.

Resistance. Such a sanitary term for French police and European security agents rushing to the deafening *thwap-thwap-thwap* of American helicopters in the streets of Strasbourg, the rotor wash throwing up debris and tearing off roof shingles, door gunners ready to lay down a deadly hail of lead from miniguns.

"The second bird should be a distraction," Renate said, thinking aloud. "After they drop Steve and Miguel, they'll stay here at the park. Close enough to cover the action at Rue Twinger if needed, but in clear view of the Parliament building." She tapped the map. "They'll go here, to the park, to what they can see. Our primary team will be five blocks away. By the time they figure out there's another bird in the area, the primary bird will be on the way out."

"So we shouldn't have to do any shooting?" Miriam asked, thinking of the repercussions if they did.

"Not if everything goes right, Ma'am," Major Conrad said. He shrugged. "But life being what it is…"

"Something will go wrong," Renate said, nodding.

"Yes, Ma'am," Conrad said.

Something always did. The question was not whether but what and when. And when it did, would they incite the very conflagration they were trying to prevent?

"These guys are the best in the world at what they do, Renate," Miriam said, as if reading her thoughts. "And we have very tight rules of engagement."

"Yes, Ma'am," Major Conrad said to Renate. "We're not cowboys. None of us wants to shoot anyone."

"I understand," Renate said. "But I'm still going to worry until we're back in Germany."

"So will I," Miriam said. She turned to Steve. "You have somewhere you need to be, and not much time."

Steve nodded, rising from his chair. "I'll be back in an hour."

"Don't be late," Renate said.

She wasn't entirely comfortable running two separate, concurrent operations. She was even less comfortable not knowing what Steve and Miguel were going to do. But Miriam kept Steve's confidences as tightly as she herself kept Lawton's.

She looked at the maps on the wall, and the complex series of lines and arrows detailing the operations.

Oh, yes, she thought. Something would go wrong.

Walking back from al-Hazeer's hotel, Ahmed was stopped by Hassan ibn Hassan, the doctor he had put to work helping the relocated Muslims. The man was clearly full of fury and in no mood to be deterred by mere words.

Ahmed smothered a sigh. "What is wrong, brother?"

"They are moving us."

Ahmed froze, astonished. "You are already in a zone."

"There are too many of us, they say. So I and my family must once again move, this time taking a train to Fiorenza tomorrow. They are madmen! And my son Ali is so angry right now I fear he will think about doing something he should not."

"I will speak to someone," Ahmed said, though he was not certain to whom. "I will do something."

"You can do nothing," Hassan said bitterly. "I demanded an explanation, and they tell me only that Rome is too crowded. Too crowded! I have lived here all my life. Of course, it is only too crowded for the Shi'a."

So that was it, Ahmed thought. The Shi'a community within the protection zone was being broken up and sent to various other cities. In Fiorenza the Hassan family would know no one. They would truly be alone. Ahmed wondered if al-Hazeer or men like him were behind this move to break up anything resembling community among the Shi'a.

He drew a deep breath, and reminded himself that matters could be worse. Far worse. He had seen the news out of Strasbourg before he had set out that morning. Yes, matters could be far worse.

He clasped Hassan's shoulder, more worried than he wanted the man to know. "Go, my brother. Go as they tell you. Tell Ali that I will need his help in coming days, so he must be patient. Tell him to do nothing stupid. I will need him very much." It was not true, but he would think of something.

Hassan nodded. "Thank you, brother." His voice still trembled with anger. "I cannot go home until I am calm. I will walk around, yes?"

"Yes. And I'll find a way to fix this. *In sh'Allah*."

"In sh'Allah."

He watched Hassan stride away, then turned to go to the restaurant. Matters were growing worse by the second.

36

Rome, Italy

As if by magic, Nathan Cohen walked up to the Trevi Fountain just as Veltroni and Steve arrived. Veltroni didn't want to think about what that might mean. In fact, for years now, he'd resolutely avoided thinking about it. This man found him every time Veltroni wanted to see him. That meant a comprehensive body of intelligence that Veltroni found too troubling to ponder.

"Father Lorenzo," Cohen said, nodding first to Steve and then Veltroni. "It is good to see you."

"I didn't realize the two of you were acquainted," Veltroni said.

"It's recent," Cohen said. "When you were worried about him in Guatemala, I checked on him."

Steve nodded, but Veltroni thought there was something awkward in his face. There was a connection between Steve and Cohen that Veltroni had not anticipated.

Perhaps that was the source of Cohen's bafflingly complete knowledge of the Stewards? At some level, and to his surprise, Veltroni found that thought comforting. For he could not find it in himself to distrust Steve Lorenzo.

Steve glanced at his watch. "We don't have much time. I will be leaving in forty minutes to retrieve the codex."

"You have found it?" Veltroni asked.

Steve seemed to fumble for a response. "I have. And, I am sorry to say, I do not feel I can turn it over to the Church. Please do not ask me to explain, *Monsignore*. I beg you to trust me in this."

Veltroni studied Steve's eyes, then looked over at Cohen. Steve's face was dark with worry, but the Israeli could have been choosing a loaf of bread at the market for all that his face revealed.

Veltroni had known this moment would come. Moreover, he knew what decision he had to make. "Steve, you must do what you think is right."

"Thank you, *Monsignore*," Steve said. "And now you must speak with Mr. Cohen. I must go."

"*Shalom,* my friend," Cohen said, shaking Steve's hand.

"It would be nice to know peace again," Steve said, sadness in his eyes. Then he turned and embraced Veltroni. "Perhaps one day we will."

"You will not be returning to Rome, then," Veltroni said. It was not a question, for his heavy heart already knew the answer.

"No, *Monsignore*," Steve said. "Not for a time."

"Go with God," Veltroni said.

"And you, my friend," Steve said.

Veltroni drew a ragged breath as Steve strode away. He felt as if he might weep. Once again, his friend was walking into a darkness from which he might not return. Only Cohen's hand on his shoulder brought Veltroni back to the moment.

"He is a faithful servant," Cohen said.

Veltroni nodded. "He is too good for this world. I have spent nearly three decades keeping secrets, dealing with the holy and the venal, whispering in the shadows of the saints. But I have known no other man like him."

Giuseppe Veltroni lost his struggle against the tears. In his heart, he knew that he would never see Steve Lorenzo again. He had just said his last goodbye to the only son he would ever have.

He looked at Cohen. "You will keep him safe?"

Cohen's lips tightened for a moment. "I wish I could promise that, *Monsignore.* We must trust He whose hands are greater than our own. In the meantime, there is something you are to ask of me, yes?"

Veltroni studied Cohen. He knew so little of this man, and yet now he had no choice but to trust him. "Yes, there is. I need to see the Holy Father. Tonight."

Cohen's head tipped for an instant. "And how can I help you with this?"

"There are many who seek the Holy Father's ear," Veltroni said. "And some who would monopolize it.

You have a talent for…being where you want to be, when you want to be there. I have need of that talent."

He watched as Cohen processed the information behind the words. Finally Cohen nodded. "Yes, *Monsignore,* I can help you do that. May I ask what you intend?"

The die was cast. Cardinal Estevan would doubtless remove him when this was over. But he saw no other choice.

"The Holy Father is a good man," Veltroni began. "The world needs the voice of a good man."

Querbach, Germany

It was madness, Hans Neufel thought. From his position on the ridge, he could clearly see the French pioneers laying the heavy pontoon bridges across the Kinzig. He had taken their precise coordinates, using his tank's laser rangefinder. Yet no artillery was falling on the bridge builders. No Typhoons swept in to bomb them. He could only watch them work.

"Once the bridges are finished, they will pour across the river," he said.

"*Ja,*" Leutnant Bräuburger said. "Yes. But we have our orders."

The platoon leader was nearly as angry as Neufel was. Schulingen's death had shaken both of them. While it had been Bräuburger's duty as an officer to write a letter of condolence to the family, he had turned to Neufel for help in drafting it. Neufel, in turn, had asked the other men in his crew to add a few words. Yet they all knew that not even their combined efforts could frame an adequate tribute to a lost comrade and son.

Neufel had a new loader, a man named Schiffer who, until the day before, had been cooking in the battalion mess. Neufel had no doubt that Schiffer was a better cook than he was a tank loader, for he could not be worse. If Bräuburger's information was correct, Schiffer's former tank commander had worked at great length to get the young private out of his tank and into the mess tent. Neufel could well understand why.

It was not that Schiffer was incompetent. He could perform the task of loading the tank's twelve-centimeter cannon adequately when he felt motivated to do so. But to motivate young Schiffer was a task that would have frustrated Job. The fact that he was replacing a man who had been killed in combat seemed to lend no sense of urgency to his actions. Quite simply, Otto Schiffer did not want to be a soldier, and he did everything within his power to avoid his duties.

"He will get us killed," Neufel said.

"Who?" Bräuburger asked.

Neufel realized he had begun speaking in the middle of a thought, as if his lieutenant could follow the thought with no need of context. It was the kind of mental error he had made increasingly often in the past two days.

"Schiffer," Neufel said. "He does not belong in the army."

"Perhaps not," Bräuburger said. "But Schulingen's ghost still sits in your loader's seat."

"*Ja*," Neufel said.

Perhaps that was it. His crew and Bräuburger's had gone into combat together. Men with whom he had once joked now had the hard eyes of men who knew what it was to kill and to see one of their own killed. The other tankers in the platoon looked at them differently, almost with a kind of reverence. In those few terrifying hours, Neufel's and Bräuburger's crews became the *alte Hasen,* the old hares, men who had been where the rest had not. How could Neufel expect Schiffer to fit in immediately?

And yet there would be no time for Schiffer to ease his way into the crew. In hours, perhaps, they would be in combat again. Would Schiffer do his duty? Or would he pause for the critical second that would mean death for Neufel and the others?

"Why are we waiting?" Neufel asked, looking down at the French pontoon bridges. "Do they think it will be easier to fight the French on this side of the Kinzig?"

Bräuburger looked at him, his eyes hard, his face unyielding. "It would be better to spend your time training Schiffer rather than asking questions for which there are no answers."

"*Ja*, Herr Leutnant," Neufel said.

Bräuburger climbed off of Neufel's tank. As he began to walk back to his own position, he turned. "And, Hans, try to get some sleep."

As if that were possible, Neufel thought. He would sleep when he was dead.

Göschenen, Switzerland

Renate looked out between the pilots as the Alps swept past the helicopter. Despite the headphones, the noise in the helicopter was almost deafening. "How much longer to Mulhouse?" she yelled.

"Forty minutes," one of the pilots replied.

Forty minutes. She looked at her watch. They had fifteen hours left. Every second seemed to pass in slow motion. During their stop at Aviano, the U.S. Air Force briefing officer had told them that the French had finished bridging the Kinzig River east of Kehl. They would surely try to begin the crossing tonight.

She wondered if they were already too late. Surely no one could expect the Germans to hold their fire all night and all day tomorrow as the French infiltrated their positions. The *Bundeswehr* was disciplined, but there was a limit to discipline. Her helicopter and the two beside it were racing against that limit.

At least the operation had gone smoothly thus far.

The thought had no sooner crossed her mind than she saw a red light begin to blink on the cockpit panel. "What is that?"

"Oil temperature warning," the pilot said.

"Is it serious?" she yelled.

"We should make it to Mulhouse," he said.

Should? Renate bit her lip, picturing the maps on the wall back in Rome. They were over neutral territory, and so far as she knew, they had not secured overflight rights for this operation. Putting down between here and Germany could get very awkward. Questions would be asked, not only of the pilots but also of Renate and Lawton. Questions neither of them could answer.

"We must make it to Germany," Renate said.

The pilot nodded. "Then maybe you should let me focus on flying, ma'am."

"Of course," she said.

She changed back to the rear bench, where Lawton was holding his seat belt with both hands, his knuckles white. The pain on his face was evident whenever the helicopter banked to follow the twisting Alpine passes.

"Are you hurting?" she asked.

"I'll live," he said. "I just hate helicopters."

"You shouldn't have come. I can do this part alone."

He shook his head. "I need to be in Mulhouse."

That was as much as they could say here, where the helicopter crew could overhear. The rest—the next mission that Jefe had given her, a mission she both loathed and needed in a way that made her hate herself—was restricted information. Office 119 only.

So far as the others knew, she was riding along to begin the interrogation of Vasquez. She would begin it on the return flight to Mulhouse and pass the information they gained on to Steve Lorenzo's contact at the Vatican.

And she and Lawton *would* do that—first.

But they would not be returning to Italy with the rest of the task force. The rest of their mission awaited in Paris. Jefe's sources had confirmed that Michel Sedan had betrayed Margarite, and that betrayal had led to the attack on Office 119 and her death.

She tried to pry one of Lawton's hands from the seat belt, but his fingers were clenched tight. She forced a smile. "The pilot said we should make it to Mulhouse."

"He said *should*," Lawton replied. "I don't like that *should* part."

"They're excellent pilots," Renate said.

Lawton nodded. "I'm sure they are. And it's a good aircraft. And blah, blah, blah. I still don't like that *should* part."

"You are a strange man," she said. "I would not have thought you were afraid of flying."

"I don't mind flying," he said. "It's crashing that scares me. Helicopters do that way too often."

"Yet you will chase down a man who throws a bomb, or fling yourself at an assassin with a pistol."

"Can do," he said, smiling weakly. "So long as they're on the ground."

Renate laughed.

"And listen," he added. "When we get there, we don't do anything extra. It's just another mission."

Just another mission. No, it was more than that.
She was going to commit cold-blooded murder.
She would pay her debt to Margarite. In full.

37

Strasbourg, France

Renate tried not to think about her lurching stomach as the helicopter rose and dipped and banked its way into Strasbourg after leaving Mulhouse. They were flying NOE—nap of the earth—less than one hundred feet off the ground and well below the coverage of French radar. Because of that, every hill, tall tree or building was an obstacle to be avoided or, if that was impossible, to be hopped over and then ducked behind.

She looked at the special ops team around her, all dressed in dark street clothes: blue jeans, dark sweaters looking bulky over body armor, knit caps now turned down into balaclavas and black poly-cotton gloves. They wore no dog tags and carried false French identification papers. All spoke fluent French. If anything went wrong, they could vanish into France and make their separate ways back to Italy without anyone ever knowing that the

United States military had made an armed incursion into an ostensibly allied nation's territory.

And armed they were, with Heckler & Koch MP-5 submachine guns, flash-bang grenades and black ceramic combat knives honed so sharp they could slice through human flesh as if it were water. More than that, they were armed with finely tuned combat instincts, born of exacting training and perfected over dozens of covert missions around the world.

The pilots, who served exclusively with the special operations teams, were equally at home with the difficult task of ducking along river valleys at two hundred knots, watching the terrain flicker past through the pale green glow of night-vision goggles.

Apart from having to leave one helicopter at Mulhouse due to mechanical problems—and they had planned to bring only two helicopters to Strasbourg regardless—it had been a seamless operation.

So far.

Tension drew every muscle of her body taught just short of cramps. Her heart raced hard enough for her to feel its rapid beating in her chest. Her palms sweated as if the day were tropical, and her stomach was a knot.

The helicopter seemed to stand on its side as it rocketed into a tight turn, and Renate felt her stomach roll again. The men around her seemed calm and relaxed, as if this were just another training mission in Georgia or California. She wondered if that seeming relaxation was real or feigned. The only clue came from eyes that flicked over the city like the eyes of hawks, searching out danger, searching out prey.

"Two minutes to target," the pilot announced.

The target. A rooftop among thousands of similar rooftops. Glancing out the window beside her, Renate wondered how they would ever be able to find the right one. A sea of rooftops filled Strasbourg and its environs. True to his word, Jefe had provided them with photographs of the roof they sought, both as seen from neighboring buildings and from high above in satellite images that were available on public web sites. But looking out, Renate had no idea how the pilots could pick that one rooftop out of the maze below them.

"Thirty seconds. Ropes at standby," the pilot said.

The two men of the Black Hawk's cabin crew stood, their torso harnesses hitched to safety lines, their legs flexing to absorb the pitch and roll of the aircraft, and secured the ends of two-inch-thick black nylon ropes to the booms that extended out above the helicopter's side doors. The rest of the ropes lay coiled at the crewmen's feet like sleeping serpents, almost invisible in the darkness.

Suddenly the helicopter flared, its nose rising, its engines straining against inertia as it came to a halt in midair. Renate felt as if she were going to fly out of her seat and gripped the restraining strap. The men, however, simply leaned into the g-force, moving their weight onto the balls of their booted feet.

"Ropes out!" the pilot called.

"Ropes out!" the two crewmen answered in unison, flinging the heavy coils out the doors.

In moments **the** ropes seemed to dance under the tension of their own weight. The six assaulters were already on their feet, in two lines of three.

"Go! Go! Go!" the crew chiefs yelled, signaling out and downward with their hands.

The second "Go!" command had not left their lips before the first of the assault team grasped the ropes tightly in their gloves, clamping them between their boots, and disappeared into the night. Six seconds later, the last of the team had left the aircraft.

The crewmen released the ropes from the booms, and then they, too, dropped onto the rooftop below. The pilot pulled pitch, and the massive Black Hawk reared away, throwing Renate back into her seat. She keyed her radio mike.

"Adder is on the ground."

Five blocks north, over the Parc de l'Orangerie, Steve heard the radio call. He glanced at his crew chief, who nodded confirmation. The primary strike team had begun its assault. Now his helicopter turned into the park, dropping quickly, then slowing in the instant before he felt the shudder of the skids impacting the ground.

Despite the preflight briefing and the reminders during the half-hour flight from Freiburg to Strasbourg, Steve hesitated for a moment. But Miguel was already up and reaching for the buckle of Steve's harness.

"*Vamanos,* Padre," Miguel said. *Let's go.*

The rotor wash was both deafening and disorienting, and Steve let Miguel guide him away from the helicopter alongside their two companions from *Saif Alsharaawi.* Steve had objected to their presence, but they had insisted on participating in the operation. Now, on the ground, preparing for a kind of activity he had never undertaken before, he was glad to have them along.

"We will stay in the woods as we cross the park," Miguel said. "But we must move quickly."

Despite the friendly lights along pedestrian paths, the woods were dark, nearly dark enough to cast Steve back into the mountainous jungles of Guatemala and the terrifying memory of being hunted. Seconds stretched to eternity as his heart hammered loudly. His feet knew an aching desire to glue themselves to the ground, but Miguel's hand on his arm prevented him from showing cowardice.

Shortly, however, saliva returned to his mouth and his feet moved more easily. He had a job to do, as important a job as any he had ever done as a priest. Fearing death was hardly cowardice, but it was certainly a waste of energy.

Death inevitably came, and beyond it lay union with God. If tonight carried him into the arms of his savior, he could count himself a lucky man.

But first the job. First the pyramid.

His step grew surer as he darted along with his companions, staying in shadow as much as possible, stopping abruptly at each noise. As each sound was identified and determined not to be a threat, they dashed again, feet silent on soft grass, toward the building where Soult presided over the mess he had created.

A flicker of anger lit in Steve's stomach, burning hotter with each step. While his eyes remained attentive to the world around him, his mind served up a repulsive smorgasbord of recent events, of removal trains, of the Nice massacre, of the wounded and dead at the European Bridge, many his fellow believers.

Abomination, he thought, the anger surging through his muscles. Abomination.

With his final breath, he would fight it.

Sixty seconds, Major Peter Conrad thought, watching his men affix their rappelling ropes to the parapet of the rooftop. The noise and vibration of the Black Hawk's rotor wash must have roused everyone in the building, but they would have awakened in a state of shock and confusion. The goal was to make entry and seize the target before he could recover his senses. Sixty seconds.

The Black Hawk was rearing away above, its huge engines straining, adding to the vibration, making the rooftop a swirl of dust and deafening noise. Like his

men, Conrad had long been inured to that effect. They
had done this countless times, until the brutal, hellish
combination of shrieking wind, biting sand and
thundering noise was simply their normal operating
environment.

His own rope fixed, Conrad gave the signal to his
men, and they kicked out over the side of the building,
quickly dropping the eight feet that placed them immediately above the windows of Vasquez's apartment.
Leaning back into his rappelling harness, he pulled a
flash-bang grenade from his belt and tore the pin free.

Two of his men had done the same, and now, in unison, they reached their arms back and hurled the grenades down and through the windows, the shattering of
glass quickly lost in the ear-popping *cracks* and blind-
ing blue-white flashes of the trio of explosions.

Moving as one, the six men again kicked away from
the wall, dropping only five feet this time, arching backward in their harnesses, feet together, knees flexed, and
letting gravity and the pendulum effect of the rappelling
ropes propel them through the windows, eyes closing
at the moment of impact and then opening an instant
later when they were clear of the glass.

Conrad pulled the quick-release on his harness and
curled his body forward as he passed through the window, letting his legs fold under the impact with the floor
of the apartment, rolling smoothly in a somersault that
bowled over a small side table and left him on his feet,

hands already clutching the grip of his machine pistol and turning it to follow his line of sight.

He had entered the dining room, exactly as planned, and he now looked down as the terrified face of Hector Vasquez briefly poked above the corner of the dining table. Conrad placed his left foot against the table and pushed through it with his entire body weight, toppling it and driving it across the floor, revealing his quarry.

"Haut les mains!" Conrad bellowed. *Hands up!*

Vasquez seemed to ponder the command for an instant before his eyes fixed on the barrel of Conrad's MP-5. He lowered his head, arms up, and Conrad moved in from the side, grasping Vasquez's right hand with his left, then driving his boot into Vasquez's shoulder, taking him to the floor with his twisted arm up behind him. Instinctively, Vasquez fought against the pain, and Conrad seized the man's thumb and twisted it over and behind his wrist, adding to the tension, as his boot slid up to the side of the Vasquez's neck.

"Ne resiste pas ou je vais vous blesser!" Conrad yelled. *Do not resist or I will hurt you!*

The combination of noise, aggression, pain and a clear command cowed Vasquez, and Conrad felt him go limp. Conrad twisted the man's hand into the small of his back, folding a thigh around it to secure it, then grasped the other hand and brought it back, as well. In less time than he needed to think through the maneuver, he drew a nylon flex cuff from his belt and encircled Vasquez's wrists, pulling the end, hearing the harsh *zip* as the metal tooth passed over the grooves of the nylon, holding it tight in the man's skin.

As he drew a black woolen capture hood from his belt and prepared to pull it over Vasquez's head, he saw movement in the doorway. He looked up just as a man raised a pistol and aimed it, not at him, but at Vasquez.

"Door! Door! Door!" Conrad shouted, but the man beside him had already reacted.

Gunfire echoed in the tiny room.

38

Querbach, Germany

Hans Neufel listened to the crack of gunfire below him. French reconnaissance units had crossed the Kinzig and were infiltrating the villages of Neumühl and Auenheim, hunter-killer teams moving house to house in search of German observation points and sniper positions. Through his infrared sight, he could watch the battle in the darkness, glowing forms moving in threes from doorway to doorway like ghosts on the prowl.

But these ghosts were far more deadly than any apparition. In this kind of fight, quarter was neither sought nor given, for the moments one might use to invite surrender would be the same moments one's enemy would use to locate, sight and squeeze a trigger. Nor was there time to distinguish between soldiers and civilians who had remained behind in their homes. To move was to kill or to be killed, and already there were fading forms visible in streets or through windows, images turning paler as bodies cooled in the crisp nighttime air.

"What's happening, Sergeant?"

It was Schiffer, his voice rising in pitch. This was not the army that young Schiffer had had in mind when he had signed his enlistment papers. It was not the army Neufel had had in mind, either. But it was his world now.

"War, Schiffer. War is happening."

Strasbourg, France

Steve heard the distant *pop-pop-pop* of gunfire. It came not only from the east, across the Rhine, but nearer and from the south. The soldiers attacking Vasquez's house were taking fire.

He and Miguel picked up their pace as they moved through the darkened woods, ignoring the stinging cuts of branches snapping across their faces. Miguel, like the two Arabs flanking them, moved with the silence of a cat, his hands comfortable on the grips of his assault carbines, his eyes sweeping the darkness as if he were an owl. But Steve was not a trained soldier, and he heard his every footfall as if it were the crashing of a clumsy giant.

He whispered a silent "Our Father" as they jogged, repeating the verses again and again, letting them lull his mind into something approaching calm, his body responding to the rhythm with the smooth stride he had once used in his daily jogs in Savannah.

A lifetime ago.

Our Father, who art in Heaven. Left foot, right foot. *Hallowed be Thy name.* Left foot, right foot.

The time seemed to pass in slow motion, and he found himself wondering how long it had been since Miguel had all but pushed him out of the helicopter. He took inventory of his body, his lungs still comfortable, his legs not yet tingling with the exertion. Surely, his inventory said, they had not yet been running for even five minutes. Yet it seemed as if they had been in these woods forever.

The trees thinned, no longer the nearly random placement of the hand of God, now spaced in the geometric lines of the hand of man. That made the running easier, but Steve knew it also made detection more likely.

No sooner had the thought entered his head than he felt Miguel's hand grasp his back, pulling him to a stop. Steve held his breath, listening, as one of the Arab men slipped a few yards farther into the darkness. Moments later, a muted *oof* crept through the night air, followed by an almost silent, gurgling hiss. Steve's feet detected the vibration of a body crumbling to the ground just before the Arab reappeared, his knife glistening black.

A man lay dying, Steve thought, still hearing the fading gurgle of the victim trying to draw precious breath through a throat laid open by a knife he had never seen. Every fiber in Steve's being ached with the need to go to the stricken man, to give him the last rites, to grant him absolution, to care for a stricken soul. But Miguel's grip on the back of his shirt left no doubt that that would not be possible. At this moment Steve was a soldier and not a priest.

The thought crushed his heart like lead.

Minutes that felt like hours later, they were at the west edge of the park, looking across the street at the Tour de l'Européens. The sculpture at its entrance, of a couple in a heart-shaped embrace of peace, seemed wholly at odds with the war that now threatened Europe. A war that could only be stopped by exposing the madman at its heart.

And that man was protected by the codex, an awful power he had already used to deadly effect.

This thought kept Steve moving. Yes, a man lay behind them in the woods, eyes fading into an eternal gaze, his soul now committed to the mercies of a God he might or might not have believed to exist. But if Steve and his colleagues did not press on and retrieve the codex, more would die. Countless more.

Steve watched as Miguel and the two Arabs worked the bolts on their weapons, preparing to kill or die in a quest that, if legend were to be believed, was born in the power of the gods and the evil of men. Steve wasn't sure if the pyramids were indeed the gifts of the gods, but he had no doubt as to the evil of men.

"Ready," Miguel whispered to the two Arabs.

"Ready," they whispered back.

Steve felt his weight shift onto the balls of his feet,

muscles twitching like those of a cat preparing to pounce. And that, he thought, was what he had become on this night. A predator, in the company of predators.

Lead me not into temptation, he whispered as they set off across the street. *And deliver me from evil.*

General Jules Soult watched the men sprint across the street. He had been awakened by the rumbling *thump-thump* of the helicopters over the city. Had the Germans dared to launch an airmobile assault? But as he had shaken himself into full awareness, he realized he could hear only one or perhaps two aircraft, far too small a force for a full-scale attack. That meant they were coming for him.

They were in for a surprise, he thought, as he turned from the window and walked to the wall safe. He twisted the dial quickly, feeling the solid, satisfying *thunk* as he turned the handle and the case-hardened steel bolts released.

Soult reached inside and picked up the soft leather pouch that held the ruby pyramid. He had spent many hours alone in his office, pondering its secrets as he gazed into its crystalline red depths. While he was no mathematician, he had studied calculus at university, and with the help of academic Web sites, he had begun to plumb the knowledge that danced within this small pyramid. He had not learned all its secrets, not by any stretch of the imagination. But he had learned enough to end the life of Karl Vögel.

Just as he would end the lives of the men who were, even now, coming to kill him. Men who had no idea of the power Jules Soult could wield…men who were preparing to kill a mere mortal and not a god. For that was what the pyramid made him, he knew. And a vengeful god, at that.

Who had sent these assassins? Who had dared to challenge him?

The question answered itself almost as quickly as it arose, for only one group would believe it had the power to threaten him. The bastards in Frankfurt. The men with their hands on the throat of the world, choking it for every percent they could squeeze out, never having the courage to seize power openly, instead seeking to control and harness those who did.

He knew they were furious that he had threatened the use of nuclear weapons. Well, let them quail at this new weapon he possessed.

Soult lighted a candle and held the pyramid in front of it, reminding himself of the mathematical sentences that expressed the deepest truths of the universe. Truths that only he knew.

Truths that he would use to kill.

Oh yes, he would kill these assassins. And then he would go to Frankfurt and kill them all.

Hector Vasquez struggled to keep his feet beneath him as two men walked him down the stairs and out into the street. Or at least he assumed that was where he was being taken, for after the burst of gunfire in his apartment, a heavy hood had been pulled over his face and tightened at his throat. He could breathe, but the man holding the drawstring of the hood left no doubt that breath and life could be snatched away in the twist of a wrist.

The last thing he had seen was his bodyguards, assigned by Monsieur Soult, standing in the doorway. But his guards had not been preparing to protect Vasquez from the men who had crashed through his windows and interrupted his late dinner. No, his guards' pistols had been pointed squarely at him.

Vasquez had no difficulty imagining the orders that Soult had given. Protect Vasquez if possible. And if not, kill him.

In that instant before one of the attackers had cut the bodyguards down with a three-round burst, Vasquez had seen the truth he had avoided these past months. For Jules Soult, loyalty was a one-way enterprise. And Vasquez was nothing but a tool to be used and then destroyed.

The hands gripping his arms tightened as he heard the rumble of helicopter rotors swell. Yes, they were out in the street now. And judging by the way the roar grew with every step, he was being steered toward the aircraft.

These men had not come to kill him. They had come to capture him. And they would interrogate him, of that he had not the slightest doubt. Moreover, they seemed to know their business, which meant the interrogation, when it did happen, would be brutal and effective.

Except that Vasquez had no intention of resisting their questions. No, that fire had been extinguished in the instant he had looked into his bodyguards' eyes. He would tell his captors everything. Not to save his own life—he had no doubt that it was forfeit no matter what—but simply because Jules Soult had become a monster.

But not an omnipotent monster.

And Vasquez knew more than enough to push that monster out of the darkness and into the cold light of the day for all to see, for all to know in its true form.

The rotor wash tore at his clothes as they neared the helicopter, and then Vasquez felt himself hoisted inside, wincing as he was thrust into a seat, pinning his bound hands behind him.

"Doc team is still working," a man's voice said.

"Tell them to hurry," a woman replied.

They were speaking English, with plainly American accents, except for the woman. Yes, Vasquez thought. It would be the Americans. Once Soult had issued the threat of nuclear weapons, he had touched a lighted cigarette to the tail of the python that encircled the world. The python had responded immediately, and with crushing force.

"You are American," Vasquez said.

"Shut up," the woman said. Then, a moment later, "Viper is in the bag."

"I demand to know who you are."

"I said shut up."

"But surely you want to know what I know," Vasquez said. "That is why you are here, yes?"

"We'll get to that," she said. It was the voice of someone who was not reluctant to issue orders. And it was the voice of someone who expected obedience. "But not here, and not now."

There was a tension in her voice, as well. American soldiers were in France. Certainly they had no invitation to be here. She wanted to get out of here, he thought, and quickly. Which gave him the leverage he needed.

"Your men are searching my flat," he said. "I can save them time."

There was a pause before she spoke. "I'm listening."

"First remove the hood," he said. "It is difficult to breathe. And I wish to look into the eyes of my captor."

"No way," she said.

"Very well," he said. "But the information you want is not information your men have the time to discover for themselves."

Seize the initiative. He had been taught that from his first days in the army. It was especially important if you were captured. Keep the enemy reacting to you, rather than reacting to them. Whatever opportunities might arise, they could only arise for the man who was alert, aware and in control of himself.

Vasquez needed an opportunity. Just a sliver.

Then he would escape. And he would do what he should have done months ago.

He would kill Jules Soult with his own hands.

He felt the drawstring loosen in the instant before the hood was yanked off his face. He looked into the eyes of his captor, eyes hard and cold like glaciers he had seen in the Alps. He did not doubt this woman's ability to kill.

"All right," she said. "Talk."

"My hard drive is reformatted weekly," he said. "You will want the flash memory sticks I use for backup."

"Where are they?"

"Tell your men to look on the bookshelf. The bound edition of *Don Quixote*."

"Don Quixote," she said to the other man in the helicopter, who relayed the information over the radio. She turned to Vasquez. "You like hopeless causes?"

"There are no hopeless causes," Vasquez said. "There are only people without hope."

39

Strasbourg, Germany

The keycard was, as promised, barely hidden beneath a layer of soil at the base of a tree. The individual pass code that matched the card was written on Steve's palm in waterproof ink that had not smudged despite his sweat. As he retrieved the pass code, Miguel and the two Arabs swept silently onto the two guards at this private side entrance, felling both with swift and silent butt strokes from their assault rifles. Moments later Steve slid the keycard through the reader and punched in the pass code.

They were in.

Third floor, the source had said. Steve thought back to the confusion at the briefing in Rome. The third floor would be the third above ground level. The stairwell was ten meters to their left, as promised, and they took only a moment to gather themselves, communicating in silent looks, before moving up the stairs as if they were four fingers of the same hand.

Steve wondered why men could rarely harness this same sense of oneness toward good ends. Men would sacrifice their own interests, even their own lives, welding themselves together with bonds that far surpassed ordinary life, toward the purpose of killing one another. But when it came to creating beauty and life and love, too often men were left to act alone, their every act weighed against self-interest and simple inertia.

If men were as good at creating heaven on earth as they were at creating hell, it would be a very different world. But, Steve thought, that was not the way of the human species. It was into that weakness that God had planted the grace of His Son. And even that grace all too often seemed to fail.

Perhaps the next twelve hours would be different.

They paused at the third-floor landing, and Steve found he already had the pouch of white powder in his hand. He must have withdrawn it from his pocket while his mind was wandering on the nature of humanity. He could not let that happen again. There would be time to ponder the deep issues of life later—or maybe there would not. But if he did not stay focused on the task at hand in these next minutes, there *surely* would not.

He took a pinch of the glistening powder in the palm of his hand, wet the tip of his finger with his tongue and touched his skin to the *mfkzt*. The manna that had sustained the children of Israel in the desert would now sustain the children of Ishmael. One by one, he touched a dab of the powder onto each man's tongue, before finally placing a dab on his own. He saw surprise in the Arabs' eyes as the fatigue of their exertions faded, their minds and bodies refreshed.

They opened the door and moved down the hallway with supernatural silence and grace, as if the manna had given them wings, turning ordinary men into avenging angels.

Steve found that thought comforting as they paused for the briefest of instants outside Soult's office.

Avenging angels come to seize from a madman the power of the gods.

"Found them," the voice crackled over the radio. "I count six flash memory cards."

Renate turned to Vasquez. "Six?"

"Yes," the Spaniard said.

If he was lying, he was a very good liar. She keyed her microphone. "That's what we want. Get out now."

"Roger," the leader of the doc team replied.

"They are encrypted," Vasquez said. "It is very, very good encryption. The American NSA could break it, of course, but not for several months. I think you do not have that much time, yes?"

Vasquez was trying to play her. Renate studied him, trying to determine if this man was friend or foe.

If he could be turned into an asset, he could be very useful. But, having seen her, he could also be very dangerous.

"Madame," he said, "Monsieur Soult would have me dead at this moment rather than permit me to be captured. As your friend will attest, my own bodyguards were prepared to kill me only a few minutes ago."

Renate looked at Major Conrad, who nodded.

"I have no loyalty to a man who has none to me," Vasquez continued. "And especially not to a madman who sees nothing but his own ambition, his entitlement to be the sole ruler of a new European empire. Everything you need to prove a case against him is on those memory cards in far greater detail than I could remember in questioning. I can give you the encryption keys."

"And in return?" she asked.

"Let me kill the monster," Vasquez said. "My people made him. We should also be the ones to unmake him."

"Simply killing Soult will not be enough," Renate said. "The French would assume that he was killed by German agents. It would only inflame the situation."

"And for that you have the evidence on the memory cards," he said. "Surely you had some plan to put forth that evidence to the world? Surely that is why you came here for me?"

Renate nodded. "Yes, we do."

"Then you simply proceed as you had planned," he said. "Your agents found the memory cards in my flat.

I had been careless and written the encryption keys in my journal, and thus you were able to read the evidence so quickly. But as for me, I was not at home. These things happen, yes?"

Renate considered the proposal for a moment. Through the door of the helicopter, she saw the doc team emerge and begin to run down the street. Once they were on board, the pilot would take off. If she wanted to use Vasquez, she must decide now.

"And what happens to you after?" she asked.

"I make a public resignation," Vasquez said. "I am ashamed of Monsieur Soult and had no idea he was using my security men as agents provocateur in his insane scheme to take over Europe. Still, I cannot continue in my post, not knowing which and how many of my men were—perhaps still are—loyal to Monsieur Soult's vision. With great regret, I must leave the cleaning of the house to my successor. It is a story people can be allowed to believe."

"And then?" Renate asked. "I don't see what we gain from this, Colonel Vasquez. You get to kill a rival. You escape prosecution for capital crimes. And we get?"

"A source," Vasquez said. "A source inside an organization that you would otherwise never gain access to. And this organization will not end with Monsieur Soult. We have been here for two thousand years, handpicked men whom you would never otherwise compromise. We will continue. Surely it is better that you can know what we are doing and with whom we are working?"

The doc team was almost at the door of the helicopter. She had perhaps ten seconds to decide. Vasquez had ordered and orchestrated violence that had killed thousands across Europe and displaced tens of thousands more. And yet he was still deeply connected to an organization that would indeed continue to operate, whether she released him or put him on trial. The question was whether she would be in a position to anticipate what his group would do or whether she would be forced to react.

In the end, the calculus was simple and direct.

"Cut him loose," she said to Conrad. He gave her a look of disbelief, but she shook her head. "You heard me, Major. Cut him loose. We have what we need. Besides, the colonel cannot afford to disappear into the woodwork, not if he is to be useful to the people he works with. If he should be so foolish as to cross me, he knows I could find him quickly. And I'm sure he knows I would not hesitate to do so—with a *gravely* different outcome."

The threat was clear and unmistakable. Vasquez simply nodded. "My life is in your hands."

"Yes, Colonel Vasquez, it is. Forever. And don't you dare forget that fact."

"I will not," he said.

"Cut him loose, Major," Renate repeated.

Conrad nodded and snipped the flex cuffs with his

combat knife, then touched the knife to Vasquez's throat. "Don't doubt what she said, Colonel. I would kill you myself without a second thought."

"I do not doubt that, Major," Vasquez said. He looked to the door of the helicopter, careful not to move. "But if that time comes, it will not be tonight, yes? You and your friends need to leave."

"First the decryption codes," Renate said, motioning Conrad to keep his knife close to Vasquez. She pulled a pad and pen from a trouser pocket and passed them to the Spaniard. "These had better work. If they don't, you're dead in forty-eight hours."

"They will." Vasquez scribbled quickly and passed the pad back to Renate.

She scanned the pad and found the writing legible enough. She nodded to Conrad.

Conrad lowered the knife, and Vasquez scrambled out of the helicopter, almost falling into the stunned arms of the doc team. Conrad nodded to his men, and they parted to let Vasquez disappear into the swirling night. The doc team climbed aboard, and Conrad patted the pilot's shoulder.

"Adder is away," Renate said as the helicopter rose into the night. "I say again. Adder is away."

"You have Viper?" Miriam asked over the radio.

"No," Renate said. "We thought we did, but it was just a bodyguard. Viper wasn't there. But we got what we needed. We got his computer files."

Freiburg, Germany

Several hours later, Miriam prepared to leave Mulhouse with her team. Vasquez had been released. There would be no interrogation. She was shaking hands with Lawton and said quietly, "She lied about Vasquez."

"You'll just have to trust her judgment, Miriam. I do."

Miriam stared at him in the poor light, clearly wondering who he had become. "She should have consulted me."

"The way you consult us on every action?"

He was right. They might work together in certain things, but the United States and Office 119 would never completely trust each other. It was the way of the world in which they lived.

After a moment she turned away and walked to the waiting helicopter. No hug for him this time. She did not really know him anymore.

As the copter lifted with a deafening roar, Renate came to stand beside him.

"There is no reason to wait now," she said, raising her voice to be heard. "We will conduct no interrogation, so we are not needed here. We can leave for Paris."

"Yes," Lawton said, not moving. "We can."

"You do not have to go," Renate said. "I can do this job on my own, if you do not wish to be a part of it."

"It's not that," Lawton said.

"What, then?" she asked.

"Office 119 doesn't exist," Lawton said. "Margarite

Renault was already dead. For that reason, there is no way to prepare a case against Michel Sedan. No such case could be presented in any court without exposing all of us."

"I know this," Renate snapped.

"That's why we're going to kill Sedan," Lawton said. "Not out of simple revenge, but because it is the only way we can bring him to justice. If there were another way, I would have argued for it with Jefe. I don't like what we have to do tomorrow. But it's the only option we have."

"And you think I feel differently?"

He nodded. "Yes, I do. No, check that. I *know* you feel differently. And I don't like it. Renate, if you let yourself feel what you're feeling right now, then we're no different from them."

"Guess what?" Renate said, shouldering her bag. "We *are* no different from them! Are you coming, or do I leave you here?"

He rose from his chair.

"I'm coming," he said. "Not for Margarite. Not even for Office 119. I'm coming for you. Because...I..."

Renate stepped forward, her face only inches from his, her voice harsh and cold. "Don't you dare finish that sentence. Not tonight. Not ever."

Lawton's mouth snapped shut. For a moment he studied her, as if trying to determine whether the deadly intent in her voice was real. It was, and she knew he could see it.

"Fine," he said. "Let's go do this."

Strasbourg, France

Jules Soult held the codex, mouthing the words he had memorized, as the men burst into his office. An American, he guessed, along with a smaller man who might have been Spanish, and two Arabs. The bankers had assembled and sent an international team. How symbolic. How useless.

He held up the codex, watching its inner glow rise to a flaring red light, the hollow, piercing sound of a horn echoing in his office, shattering windows and causing the floor to shudder.

But when he looked at the assassins, they were not choking and gasping for breath. How could this be?

The American stepped forward, his face full of wonderment and, even more so, of resolve. "Give me the codex, Soult."

"Do you think your gunmen frighten me?" Soult asked. "You know they cannot kill me."

"No," the American said, reaching into his pocket. He took out a small, weathered leather pouch. "But I can."

"It is impossible!" Soult said. "I am protected by the power of the gods!"

"Perhaps," the American said, shaking a tiny pile of glistening white powder into his palm. "But even the gods tremble at the voice of the One True God."

Like iron fragments drawn to a magnet, the white powder began to sift out of the American's hand and fly toward the pyramid. As more of the powder accumulated on the codex, Soult felt a tingle in his hand that grew into a burning.

Back when he was a young officer, he had impressed his soldiers by holding his hand over the flame of a cigarette lighter, shutting out the pain, demonstrating that a true soldier must have the self-discipline to endure any agony to accomplish his mission. More than once, the battalion surgeon had called him a fool while treating the blackened and blistered skin. But Soult had made his point. His men had feared him and tried to emulate his iron resolve.

What he felt now, however, was not the flame of a cigarette lighter. There was no flame at all, and yet the burning seemed to claw from the nerve endings in his palm up his arm and across into his spinal cord, spilling from there through his entire body, like a million ants eating him from the inside out.

His iron will fought against a will far beyond his own, and he found himself on his knees, still trying to clutch the pyramid, his fingers growing numb.

"I will take the codex now," the American said, stepping forward, hand extended.

Soult's hand opened, and the pyramid fell into the American's hand. In an instant the burning stopped, though his muscles still quivered with remembered agony.

"Thank you," Steve Lorenzo said, dropping the codex into the pouch. He had what he had come for. And that thought terrified him beyond words as he looked down at Soult's spasms. He turned to Miguel and the Arabs. "We can leave now."

One of the Arabs raised his assault rifle, taking aim on Soult. "No, we must finish him."

"He is already finished," Steve said, reaching out to push down the barrel of the man's rifle. There would be no more bloodshed on this night. Not if he could prevent it. "He is nothing more than a cruel, ambitious man now. A man whose ambition will never be fulfilled. My friends will soon see to that."

The Arab paused for a moment, then finally nodded.

Then he turned and pointed his rifle at Steve. "In that case, you will give me the codex."

Steve took a step back, stunned. "No. I will not."

As casually as if he were tying a shoe, the man aimed his rifle at Miguel's chest and squeezed the trigger. Steve's breath caught in his throat.

"Give me the codex," the man said, "and I will let you care for your friend. Your manna can save him, if I do not shoot him again. But I will, if you do not give me the codex. I know I cannot kill you, but I can make you watch this man die."

"*Padre,* no," Miguel whispered, looking up at Steve. "I am ready to face God."

Perhaps Miguel was ready to die, Steve thought. But he wasn't ready to watch it happen. He looked up at the Arab and had no doubt of the man's willingness to do exactly what he said. And something deep in Steve's soul told him that this was not the time for Miguel to fall into the arms of God.

With a sad, bitter sigh, Steve took the codex from the pouch and handed it to the man.

"You will keep that pouch closed until I have left the room," the Arab said. "My colleague will be here to ensure that. I do not wish to experience what happened to Soult."

"You have my word," Steve said. "And unlike yours, my word means something."

The man smiled. "My word means a great deal, priest. But my word is given only to Allah and his servants. Take care of your friend."

The man left, followed thirty seconds later by his partner. Steve waited until he heard no more footsteps, then pulled the pouch open and began to sprinkle the white powder on Miguel's wound.

"Stay with me," Steve said, turning Miguel's face to his. "You're not going to die tonight, my friend."

"You should not have given him the codex," Miguel said. "You should have let me go to God."

"No," Steve said, shaking his head as he worked the white powder into Miguel's chest. "You are not going to die tonight. Not if I can help it."

Steve was still working on Miguel's wound when the small Spanish man walked into the office. The man gave Steve and Miguel only a cursory glance before he looked over at Soult and leveled a pistol.

"No," Steve said. "He must be exposed."

"He will be," Colonel Hector Vasquez said. "But he must also be purged."

Vasquez squeezed the trigger four times, each crack causing Steve to flinch. So much death.

"We'll leave him for the cleaning crew," Vasquez said, holstering his pistol. He looked at Miguel. "Let us get your friend to a hospital, yes?"

Steve nodded. "Please."

Please, God, let Miguel live.

40

Paris, France

The streets outside the hotel room looked inviting, but Renate ignored them. Lawton moved around behind her, gathering the last of his belongings. Today, she thought, and summoned the memory of Margarite's face. Today.

But mostly, as she checked her SIG-Sauer P-226, she thought about the final preparations they needed to make for this mission. Working the slide repeatedly to make certain it was smooth as silk and unlikely to jam, she paused for a moment to sight down the barrel. A beautiful piece of equipment, probably the best pistol available in the world.

Grabbing a clip of fifteen nine-millimeter rounds, she tapped it against the outside of her hand to ensure that the cartridges were seated evenly, then used the heel of her palm to ram it into the grip. If there was any complaint to be made about this weapon, it was the possibility of putting in a clip wrong, in which case the world's best pistol might as well be a water gun.

She grasped the slide between her thumb and the knuckle of her forefinger and pulled back, chambering a round, careful to keep the safety engaged, then released the clip and worked the slide again to eject the round in the chamber, snatching it out of the air in a smooth, graceful motion. Each time she repeated the act, she felt another part of her shutting down. Like the petals of a rose bitten by frost.

"You've done that a few times," Lawton said.

"Yes, a few," she said. "My father was a member of a shooting club. He taught me from age six."

"Is there anything about you that you learned from your mother?" Lawton asked.

The question caught her short, and she realized that, indeed, most of what she had shared about her childhood involved her father. He had seemed full of exciting ideas and challenges to meet, while her mother had been the oasis of quiet strength in the family, keeping both Renate and her father grounded in the basics of life. And perhaps the answer to his question lay there.

"My reserve," she said. "It was always difficult to know what my mother was thinking, save for one fact. We always knew she loved us."

Lawton studied her for a moment. "I'm sorry, Renate."

"Let's have this conversation another time," she said.

This was not a time to think about her family or the calm life she had once enjoyed. A life probably much like the one Margarite had experienced as a girl in Paris. A time when the world seemed fresh and bright with possibility, and the prospect of true love and happily-ever-afters. A time before the ugliness leapt out of the television and came, front and center, into their lives and hearts.

A time before an old and trusted friend would betray you to your enemies, safe in the knowledge that he would not have to watch the breasts in which he had once sought comfort be shredded by a hail of bullets.

Renate could not remember when she had last felt innocence. Worse, though, she could only dimly remember when she had last felt guilt.

She sighted down the barrel of the pistol again and imagined Michel Sedan's head, felt her finger gently squeeze the trigger, imagined the kick as the hammer struck the primer cap and eight grams of smokeless powder ignited, propelling the round with over five-hundred joules of energy. Upon contact with the base of Sedan's skull, the hollow-point round would mushroom to more than twice its size, a ragged, two-centimeter lump of lead tearing through bone and brain tissue, turning out—in an instant and forever—the light of life in a man who had called that darkness down on her friend.

She ought to feel guilty about such thoughts. She was, after all, going to kill a man in cold blood, with premeditation and, she assumed, without remorse. She had felt no remorse when she had killed the assassin at the train station in Rome, and none when she'd finished off the one in the Berlin hotel room. But in both those cases, the enemy had been actively trying to kill her, and she had acted in self-defense.

This was different. Sedan was not actively trying to kill her. He probably had not intended to kill Margarite. Instead, he had betrayed her to Soult, who had ordered the attack on the headquarters in Rome, which had killed her. And for that, she and Jefe had decided that a message must be sent, a cautionary message to anyone who might think of playing both sides in this game of shadows.

Those who betray us will die.

When she had joined Office 119, she had not imagined that the group of dedicated law enforcement professionals would become another dangerous cabal living in the dark corners of a dangerous world. Nor had she imagined that she could become an instrument of that darkness.

But she had.

She put the pistol down and looked over to Lawton. "Let's go over the plan again."

Rome, Italy

Ahmed Ahsami helped Hassan ibn Hassan and his family onto the train. He wished desperately that he could find a way to prevent this man from being removed yet again, but he had been forbidden to take any action that might draw attention to him or *Saif*.

Hassan looked at the overhead bin for a place to put the last of his bags. Ahmed helped him. They were allowed two bags each—a total of six for Hassan, his wife and his son—but already the bins were full, even in the private compartments. Of course, some had brought more than they were allowed, arguing that a bag of food to be eaten along the way should not count, for example. Over the objections of the porter, Hassan found a way to rearrange the packed bin to make room for Ali's suitcase.

Ali's face was dark as Hassan sat. "This bin should not be full, father. It is our cabin. You paid for it."

The boy was not truly angry about the luggage bin, Ahmed knew. That was merely a momentary focus for his feelings. They were leaving their home, and everything that had been his life, for a new place where he would know almost no one and where his life would be turned upside down. And all because they were Muslim.

Just this morning the news had reported that Jules Soult had been assassinated in his office. Of course, the murder had been blamed on Islamic terrorists, because two Arab-looking men had been seen in the vicinity. The eyes of the train guards were taut and angry today, and even in the faces of ordinary people at the station, Ahmed saw rage and suspicion.

Hassan, he thought, had never committed a violent

act in his life, yet he was being treated as a criminal. In the wake of the tragedy in Nice, security was especially tight, and every Muslim passenger was subjected to pat-down searches for weapons, even women and children. It was a cruel religious violation, for it was forbidden for any man but her husband to touch a woman. Hassan had had to hold Ali back while the guard's hands roamed over his own wife, probing every possible place where she might secrete a weapon, save for that most intimate of places. It had looked to Ali—and to Ahmed—like something barely short of an act of rape. Yet to resist was to risk worse for them all.

Now Hassan held his wife's sobbing form against him, cooing gently to her in Arabic, reassuring her that both Allah and he understood that she had not violated any law or vow in permitting the search, that he still loved her, that this was for the safety of everyone on the train, so that no one would open fire and risk the lives of all, begging her to forgive him for permitting the search.

Every word burned in Ahmed's ears and in his soul, but he listened to Hassan offer them with every ounce of feeling he could draw from his wounded heart. She needed to hear them, and he needed to say them, however hollow they might sound.

When her sobbing finally stilled, Hassan looked over at Ali. His son's eyes filled with tears. But in that moment, for the first time in what seemed like months, they were not tears of rage.

"Ali," he said softly, "it will be all right."

"Does Allah still love us?" Ali asked. "How could a god who loves us permit this?"

Ahmed had more than once asked himself that same question. In what ways had he turned from the will of Allah? In what ways had he abandoned the words of the Prophet, blessings be upon him? How had the followers of Islam sinned so greatly that they deserved such treatment?

In the end, he could find no answer. He had tried to live a faithful life. So had Hassan. Hassan's family had performed the *haj* just two years ago, an experience he had described as the most beautiful of his life. He said the daily prayers. He treated both family and stranger with peace and justice. And while Ali had been drawn into the wrong crowd of young men and had committed some minor acts of vandalism in recent weeks, surely Allah would not trample Hassan's family for the common misdeeds of youth?

"Yes, Ali," Ahmed heard himself say. "Allah still loves us. Even the Prophet was reviled by some. The greatest of the Shi'a saints, after whom you are named, was murdered by enemies. Did Allah not love him and welcome him into heaven?"

"I...I do not want to go to heaven yet, Ahmed."

Ahmed watched as Hassan opened his other arm, inviting his son—once an infant whom he cradled, now a young man—to join in the embrace. "*In sh'Allah*, Ali.

It will be as Allah wills. Let us pray that His will is merciful. But we must accept that it may be otherwise."

Ali crossed the small compartment and sat between his parents, his breath ragged, his fists clenching both his father's robe and his mother's, as if searching for some stone of stability in the raging sea that had enveloped them.

"I am sorry, Father."

"Shhhhh," Hassan whispered. "You need not."

"I am sorry to Allah for my sins."

"I know, my son," Hassan said. "And Allah knows this, as well."

"Please forgive me?" Ali whispered.

"You were always forgiven," Hassan said. "Allah is merciful. I can be no less."

Ahmed turned away, feeling the tears sting his eyes. *Allah is merciful.*

Did he still believe that?

Paris, France

Renate watched as Michel Sedan had a leisurely lunch at *La Rive Gauche* café. He was sharing his last meal with a woman. She knew—both from their behavior and from the photographs she had committed to memory—that this woman was not Sedan's wife. Yet it was obvious that Sedan had designs on her.

It was obvious in the way his hand rested on hers, in the way his eyes met hers, in the subtle smile that he let filter through at random moments. While she could not hear their conversation over the chatter of the car radio, even a blind man could have seen that Sedan hoped to take this woman to bed.

Just as he had done with Margarite.

Don't do it, she thought. *Don't fall for the wiles of this viper.*

Just as those liaisons had led to Margarite's death, this woman would die if she decided to join Sedan in a *pied-à-terre*. Renate was going to kill Sedan. If the woman was with him, Renate would kill them both. It was not that she held any ill will for the woman. It was simply that she could not risk leaving a live witness.

"She's pretty," Lawton said.

"Is she?" Renate asked.

"Renate, you can't."

"He may leave us no choice."

Lawton sighed. "There are always choices, Renate."

She looked at him. "Michel Sedan must die."

41

Neumühl, Germany

Hans Neufel performed a final inspection of his Leopard II tank. Every link of track had been checked, every fitting sealed, every vision port and sight lens cleaned, every round of ammunition counted and stacked. The vehicle was fully fueled and ready for combat.

And, save for young Schiffer, so were his men. They had turned to their duties with a quiet precision, showing none of the bravado, none of the dark humor, that had been their former norm. They knew what lay ahead, what it would mean to kill. They had faced the threat of death, and while they were still afraid, as any sane man would be, they simply refused to let that fear control them.

Save for young Schiffer, who sat in his loader's chair, eyes wide, palms sweaty. For a moment the young soldier's posture reminded Neufel of how he had felt the first time he had seen a dentist, and he fought down the urge to laugh. Laughing at Schiffer would not make it better. His fear was both real and rational.

"*Wir werden* okay," Neufel said, patting Schiffer's shoulder. *We will be okay.*

"Are you sure, Sergeant?" Schiffer asked.

The question was both sincere and absurd. Of course Neufel could not promise the young man that he wouldn't die on this day. The platoon was preparing to assault the village of Neumühl to drive out the French infiltrators. The attack would be preceded by a series of air strikes that, the battalion commander had assured them, would paralyze the French. The air strikes would be followed by several salvoes of the battalion's artillery, fifteen-centimeter howitzers firing ICM—Improved Conventional Munitions—shells that would burst apart into bomblets as they neared the ground, each bomblet then exploding and sending fiery metal fragments tearing through flesh and bone, multiplying the terror of the air strikes.

Only then would Neufel's tank roll forward, blasting apart strongpoints with its cannon, dealing death to the exposed enemy from its twin machine guns.

It was a small village. The attack should take less than an hour. And, if the Typhoon fighter-bombers and the artillery were accurate, if the timing was perfect, if the French had not brought forward antitank guided missiles or heavy armor that German intelligence had not yet seen, if, if, if...

If a million "ifs" had been met, and if they were

lucky, then yes, Neufel could give the guarantee Schiffer wanted. The problem with war was that all those "ifs" were never met. Young Schiffer knew all too well that he was sitting in a seat formerly occupied by a dead man.

But Neufel could not allow Schiffer to be overwhelmed by such thoughts. Fear was contagious in battle—and deadly. Neufel needed Schiffer to be confident, not only for his own safety but for the safety of the crew and the platoon.

To tell Schiffer the painful truth, that there was no way to guarantee his survival, would serve no purpose. So Neufel lied.

"*Ja,* Schiffer. I'm sure."

Schiffer paused for a moment, then nodded. "I trust you."

Neufel nodded and looked into his weapon sight, not because there was anything to see, but simply so Schiffer could not see the pain in his face.

Rome, Italy

The buzz spread through the crowd, and Veltroni watched as the people parted. It was not for himself that they parted but for the German who stood beside him, a man whose face was fixed with a determined gaze.

The Holy Father. At a train station.

Normally such an appearance would have been scheduled weeks in advance, the crowd carefully searched, barricades manned by Vatican guards, an elegant podium erected from which the Pontiff could offer blessings at a safe distance. In the wake of the attempted assassination of John Paul II, security had become a major planning function of any papal appearance.

But not today. Today the Pope had traveled to the train station not in the Plexiglas-enclosed bubble of what was commonly known as the Popemobile but in a common sedan driven by Veltroni himself. The Holy Father swept aside the objections of both cardinals and security men who claimed that the danger was too great. In the face of war, the danger was too great for anything else.

The Pope reached the edge of the platform, directly in front of the removal train into which Italian Muslims were still being packed, and lifted a bullhorn.

"Stop!" he commanded.

Every face—Muslim, Christian, citizen and guard—froze in an instant. A palpable silence swept through the crowd, as if the air had been taken away, leaving each of them to hold his breath.

"The Torah prescribes an eye for an eye," the Pope continued. "Yet as Mahatma Gandhi said, if each man takes an eye for an eye, the whole world will be blind. We must now choose whether to live in blind darkness or in light. Here and now, at this station, with these people, we must choose whether to extract an eye for an eye, or to forgive, as our Savior commanded, seventy times seven. We cannot avoid a choice. Each of you will choose how to act. Each of you will decide to forgive...or to be blind."

Paris, France

The woman had not accepted Sedan's invitation, and now the French policeman strolled along the Left Bank, perhaps disappointed, perhaps wondering what else he could have said so that he might now be in her arms rather than alone.

Or perhaps he had already forgotten her.

Renate neither knew nor cared.

Fifteen meters ahead, Sedan would turn down a quiet street, one that bent sharply to the left and offered no clear lines of sight from the more traveled avenues. When he did, Renate would quicken her pace, nearing to within a meter or two as he made the left turn. She would lift the SIG Sauer that now rested in the cloth shopping bag hanging from her shoulder. At that range, she would not need to take careful aim. She would not miss.

Rome, Italy

Ahmed opened the window and leaned out, only meters away from a man who, until that moment, had been only a face on the television or in a newspaper. A man to whom Ahmed had given little thought, the leader of another faith whose history was interwoven with his own and yet was as alien to him as the far side of the moon.

"The same God created all of us, did he not?" the Pope was asking the crowd. "Did not Christ pray on the cross, *'Eloi, Eloi, lama sabachtani?'* My God, my God, why have you forsaken me? Do you not know that 'Eloi' was but the Aramaic pronunciation of the Arabic word 'Allah'?"

Ahmed drew a breath. Had he heard this man correctly? On the platform outside the train, others seemed to be asking themselves the same question.

"Yes, it is true," the Pope continued. "Christ prayed to the same God as our Muslim brothers and sisters. And if Christ were standing here, watching this, he might call out again, 'Allah, Allah, *lama sabachtani?*' Why have you forsaken me? For as I watch this, as I have seen the rise of hate and killing in these past months, I must wonder if God has forsaken us. If God has left us with nothing but the will to kill each other, in ones and tens and hundreds and thousands, until the dead number in the millions for a future generation to mourn in disbelief. Will this be the legacy of our generation? To recreate the most heinous sins of the past? To leave our grandchildren shaking their heads at our cruelty? Has God forsaken us?"

Ahmed found himself squeezed between Hassan and Ali. They were not alone. This holy man was asking the same question Ali had asked, the same question Ahmed had pondered in these dark days.

Had Allah forsaken them to their own evil?

Paris, France

Lawton barely heard the Pope's words, broadcast on the car radio, as he followed behind Renate. Ten meters and Sedan would turn down the alley to his death. Yet something in the words penetrated his concentration, the translator's voice following the rhythm and pitch of the Pontiff and, somehow, carrying Lawton back to a small parish church in Michigan, where he had sat impatiently through sermons, waiting for the Mass to end so he could go home to eat his lunch and watch football.

He hadn't thought any of what he had heard from the lectern had broken through to a young mind bent on food and pondering whether the Detroit Lions might win that week.

But it had, he realized.

His entire life had been dedicated to intervening in the cycle of violence that was the human existence. He was not an avenger. He sought no eye for the eyes taken, save for the blind eyes of Lady Justice, her judgment to be administered equally to all with dispassion, reason and, yes, mercy.

Renate, too, had committed herself to that ideal, vain though it might seem at times. For the alternative was, as the Pope had quoted, an eye for an eye until all were blind. There was no guarantee that they could purge the darkness in the world. But they need not become it.

He eased down on the accelerator and rolled down his window. He must stop this. This was not justice. This was simple murder.

Rome, Italy

Cardinal Estevan stood in the crowd, in mufti, watching the Pope. The German was giving a good speech, Estevan thought. He was now laying out in detail the evil behind Soult's plans, the dark machinations that had led to this moment on a train platform in Rome, the way the people of Europe had been manipulated into hatred by a man bent by and toward cruel ambition. Fact piled upon fact, detail upon detail, until they reached a critical mass that did not rely on the documentation the Vatican would doubtless produce later that day. The case was made in the hearts and minds of the people listening.

They had been lied to in the cruelest of ways, led into the most horrible of crimes.

Every eye at the station was riveted, every mind captivated. That, Estevan realized, was power. The power to seize every mind and bend it to his will. It was a power he would now have, save for the bungling of Veltroni's priest. Still, he would have it soon.

He looked across the platform at the young man in a gray windbreaker, mere meters from the Pope, to the side and behind. He had chosen the man carefully. This was too important. The man looked at Estevan questioningly, but Estevan shook his head.

Not yet.

Paris, France

Renate heard the car accelerate. What was Lawton doing? Sedan was a traitor, but he was a policeman. He would certainly notice a car following on his heels. He would turn, here on the busy street, where Renate would have no opportunity to complete the mission.

Renate put a hand behind her back, palm open and pushing away, signaling Lawton to slow down. She could not take her eyes off the target now, could not know whether Lawton saw the signal. Surely he must have, for his role was to watch her rather than the target. Yet still he drew nearer. She could see the tension rising in the muscles of Sedan's neck, his subconscious mind reacting to a danger he could not yet articulate.

But he turned down the alley regardless.

Perhaps he ignored the niggle at the back of his mind. Perhaps he was still distracted by thoughts of the woman he had hoped to bed.

It did not matter, Renate thought. Whatever his reason—fantasy, inattention or sheer habit—Michel Sedan had sealed his fate.

She quickened her pace, rising slightly onto the balls of her feet, the soles of her jogging shoes rolling smoothly and silently over the pavement with each step. Almost without thinking, she thumbed off the safety on the pistol.

Now only two meters ahead, Sedan followed the left-hand bend of the narrow street, and Renate lifted the bag that concealed the pistol.

Her right foot swept over a piece of broken glass, a faint but discernible *crunch* that finally drew Sedan's mind into the present, the final present he would ever know. He turned and looked at her, looked at the raised bag, the form of the pistol clearly visible through the thin fabric, his eyebrows arched in a question.

"For Margarite," Renate whispered.

She squeezed the trigger. Once. Twice. Then again.

He crumpled to the pavement, two holes in his chest, a third between eyes that would never again see a dawn.

Renate took her hand from the bag and backed out of the alley, forcing her posture to be that of a confused woman moving away from some unknown danger, lest anyone take a passing glance in the moments before she climbed into the car.

As she reached the end of the alley, she kept her focus on the car, not wanting to arouse suspicion by looking around for witnesses. She opened the car door and climbed in, dropping the bag to the floor between her feet, closing the door, fastening her seat belt, as if Lawton were picking her up from a trip to the grocery.

* * *

Lawton didn't notice her at first, focused as he was on the Pope's speech.

"We must choose life over death, light over blindness," the German pontiff said, his voice rising in a firm crescendo. "We must stand now and say, in the Hebrew, *'Lo od!'* Never again!"

The history was not lost on Lawton. For the Pope— a German—to speak that admonition in Hebrew left no doubt what he meant. Fourteen million massacred, and Europe on the brink of repeating that tragedy.

Never again.

Yet what was it that Stalin had said? A single death is a tragedy; a million dead, only a statistic. What of the single death? What of Michel Sedan?

"It's done," Renate said. She reached across and turned off the radio. "Come on, Lawton. Let's go."

He looked at her face. His thoughts died stillborn as he saw her eyes.

"Renate…" he began.

"No," she said. "Just drive."

Rome, Italy

"Lo od!" the Pontiff repeated. *"Lo od!"*

Ahmed watched as the crowd picked up the chant. Soon, impossibly, he heard himself speaking the language of the Jews. *"Lo od. Lo od."*

Hassan, too, mouthed the words. He rose with his wife and son and left the compartment, holding their hands, repeating the words. They stepped onto the platform, man and wife and son united with thousands around them in a moment that said Allah had indeed not abandoned them. Ahmed followed.

"Lo od! Lo od!"

The chant was flowing freely through the crowd now, and Ahmed watched as the Pope lowered the bullhorn to the pavement and climbed down onto the railroad tracks. The priest beside him followed, and they lay on the tracks in front of the train, a tangible expression of defiance that hurried television crews captured and broadcast immediately across the world.

"Lo od! Lo od!"

Hassan looked at his wife and son. He did not need to ask the question. They nodded and walked to the front of the train, preparing to climb down onto the tracks.

A man in a gray jacket stepped forward, as if to join them, then stopped at the edge of the platform. Ahmed watched in disbelief as the man drew a pistol from his jacket and aimed it at the holiness beneath him.

Ali had seen the man, too, and he tried to pull his hand from Hassan's, already moving forward. But Hassan clearly saw that his son would be too late and held firm.

The bodies of the Pope and the priest twitched as the bullets struck.

* * *

Veltroni could not bring himself to feel disbelief. He had known this might happen. Instead, he felt only an awful pain in his chest as he tried to draw breath, and a deeper pain in his soul for the dying man beside him. A holy man. A holy father.

As his strength ebbed, his eyes fell upon another father on the platform, clutching his wife and son in his arms, staring down in disbelief. Muslim, Veltroni saw.

The man's eyes met Veltroni's. *"Lo od."*

Veltroni nodded. This, too, was a holy father. He drew a final breath and whispered, *"Lo od."*

Ahmed saw the life slip from the priest's eyes.

Security men, a step too late, tried to tackle the man in the gray jacket. Before they could subdue him, he turned the gun on himself and pulled the trigger.

Hassan and his wife sobbed, but Ahmed did not hear it. Their sobs were lost in his own.

"What now, Father?" Ali asked.

Hassan turned to Ahmed for an answer. It was a plea Ahmed felt in his own heart, a plea for which he had no answer that could give justice.

"Now we go home," he said.

Epilogue

With camera flashes going off from every direction, Hans Neufel studied what had become of the world's most recognized faces. Bundeskanzler Harald Müller, as the story was told, had shown the new face of Germany: strong and willing to defend herself, yet also willing to pursue diplomacy even in the face of an armed attack on his country's soil. Now the chancellor was reading a citation acclaiming Hans Neufel.

But Neufel's thoughts wandered, as they seemed to do often these days, over the recent events that had brought him so close to war, then had yanked him back from the precipice.

Television had covered the events Neufel had missed while in the field, constantly replaying the Pope's final speech, the near breakdown of peace at the Rhine and Soult's part in it all.

In his mind's eye, Neufel remembered the German Chancellor's speech decrying the horrible events that had swept over Europe, and his determination to maintain peace at any cost. Even when the now-dead Pope had stood at a train station in Rome to deliver the stunning indictment against Jules Soult and his policies, including evidence that proved Soult had ordered the assassination of Bundeskanzler Vögel, Müller had not loosed the dogs of war.

Indeed, Müller had canceled the attack that would have sent Neufel and his platoon sweeping into Neumühl, and ordered the Bundeswehr and Luftwaffe to stand down. Neufel felt a surge of pride in his country and his chancellor as he recalled Müller's repetition of the Pope's cry: *Lo od.*

Then Müller had fallen silent, to allow time for the inevitable fallout from the Papal indictment to make its way across the European political landscape.

Soon the news had become full of the European Council. Like dreamers awakening from a nightmare, the national leaders of the EU member states had dismissed Soult's Commission, calling for new elections, the withdrawal of EU troops from German soil and an end to Muslim pacification policies. A new tide had risen in Europe, a tide of revulsion at what they had almost done.

The resignation of Colonel Vasquez sealed the fate of Soult's legacy. Vasquez produced the documents that showed the world how Jules Soult had circumvented him and manipulated the EU Department of Collective

Security to instigate the very violence Soult had promised to end.

The war had been stillborn, the press had written,
dead before it began. And, perhaps, through the long
lens of history, that was how it would appear.

Hans Neufel knew otherwise. The stand-down order
had come in time for his crew to take a two-day leave
to attend Schulingen's funeral. Then he had returned to
his post, to attend memorial services for the civilian
dead in Kehl. An historian might count those deaths
moot in the larger scene of an aborted war in Europe,
but Neufel had watched many of those men die. They
had died in war, whatever the pundits now and the his-
torians later might say.

"*Danke,* Herr Bundeskanzler," Neufel said, after
Müller had finished draping the *Bundesverdienstkreuz*—
the Federal Service Cross—around Neufel's neck.

"It is my great honor," Müller replied.

The citation said much, and yet it said nothing. It said
that Herr Neufel had shown exceptional courage, discipline and leadership during the "difficult events" at the
Kinzig River bridges. Leutnant Bräuburger had received
a similar decoration moments before, though it was a
grade higher, due to his officer status. Bräuburger's eyes
met Neufel's for an instant, the same question running
through each of their minds: *How should I feel?*

In truth, Neufel thought, he had not done anything
that ought to be deemed extraordinary. He had followed

his orders as best he was able, relying on his training and the competence of his men. His battalion commander had written in glowing terms of how Neufel had sacrificed for his men—ensuring that they ate and slept first—and how his firm hand had forged his crew into a perfectly integrated team, one that could strike with decision and still exercise restraint in a situation where lesser men might have lost their heads and precipitated a wider conflict. Herr Neufel had acted in the highest traditions of the Bundeswehr and the German people.

The flowery words made no mention of the doubts and fears, the moments of cold, dark hate or the physical revulsion at the scent of chocolate, that would haunt him for years to come. Neufel hardly recognized the man his commander had described. That man's deeds bore only the slightest resemblance to Neufel's own memories.

Insofar as he had been able to form conclusions, and there were many that he thought would forever elude him, the war had taught Neufel two things. First, that the fortunes of war turn on the smallest of things—an unseen drainage ditch on a bridge embankment or which man goes to a given door first. And second, that he could not return to a civilian world that took no account of such things.

He had applied to the Universität der Bundeswehr at Hamburg, and on the basis of his high school grades and the medal he was now receiving, he had been accepted into the German military academy. Leutnant Bräuburger had written a personal recommendation, including—to Neufel's surprise—testimonials from the men of Neufel's crew.

The most touching of those testimonials had come from the most unlikely of sources, Otto Schiffer: "Herr Neufel was our father."

Neufel looked out at his own father, sitting in the front row, eyes misting with tears.

"Danke," Neufel mouthed silently.

His father nodded. And that nod said more than any medal ever would.

Riyadh, Saudi Arabia

Saif Alsharaawi had scheduled a meeting for Sheik al-Hazeer's house. Ahmed Ahsami had not been invited.

But Ahmed heard about it and extracted a promise from Karim—his friend since the cradle—to tell him all that happened. Karim was a small, wiry man, a distant cousin. The two had been raised together, and together they had gone abroad for education. They had shared much, in the way of friends, including the now shameful night when both had lost their virginity with London prostitutes. They had come a long way together. But now, far enough.

"It is as you feared," Karim said, then accepted the tea offered to him by Ahmed's sister and spent a moment in idle chat about her two children. Then the woman properly withdrew, leaving the men to their work.

"How so?" Ahmed asked.

"Al-Hazeer would turn *Saif* into the sword it was named for. His first act will be to rid us of the Shi'a. This he has vowed. He intends to do it."

Ahmed looked down, thoughts flying around in his head like angry locusts. "This is impossible, Karim. The Shi'a are nearly one-half of the population in the Middle East."

Karim nodded. "He says we will purge the heretics from our midst, especially in the oil fields. 'They will never again stain Islam with their spittle,' he said."

"Genocide."

"He did not say that."

"He doesn't have to," Ahmed said. Despair stood before him like a seductive mistress. It would be so easy to step into that void, to tell himself there was nothing he could do. He looked out the window, filled with night, and prayed for strength. Then, straightening, he looked at his cousin. "We must stop him."

Karim nodded. "But how? He has a new weapon."

"What weapon is so powerful?" Ahmed's words were biting.

Karim shrugged. "The weapon that killed the German Chancellor from several hundred miles away. The weapon that brought down Jericho."

"Is that what he says?"

Karim nodded and leaned forward, lowering his voice. "He says it was once in the Ark of the Covenant."

"And you believe him?"

"He used it while I was there. I believe him."

Ahmed closed his eyes. Now two dark maws gaped open before him. The first was despair, and the second the near impossibility of defeating al-Hazeer. The first was easy, the second likely fatal.

"We will need help," Ahmed said.

"Who will help us now?" Karim asked. "Sheik al-Hazeer watches us too closely for us to make contacts here and your friends in Europe believe you betrayed them."

"I did not!" Ahmed said, slamming his palm on the table, then catching himself. He had not sanctioned the betrayal in Strasbourg. But he could not deny that it had been *Saif* operatives who had carried out that betrayal. To his former allies, the truth would seem obvious. "I am sorry, my friend."

Karim shook his head. "There is no apology needed."

"You are right in one thing," Ahmed said. "My friends in Rome cannot trust *Saif Alsharaawi*. But perhaps they can still trust me."

Karim thought for a moment; then his face sagged as realization dawned. "You cannot. What of your family?"

"You must keep them safe, Karim."

"This is a dangerous gambit you propose," Karim said.

Ahmed nodded. "It is. But it is the only gambit left open to us. Can you make the arrangements?"

Pain was etched on Karim's face. But beneath the pain was something else. Hope.

"Yes, my friend. I can. The sheik will believe me."

"Then it is decided," Ahmed said. He would miss his sister, and his wife and two sons. But there was no other way. "I must die."

"Yes," Karim said. *"In sh'Allah."*

"In sh'Allah," Ahmed repeated.

As Allah wills.

"But for tonight," Ahmed said, grasping his friend's hand, "let us remember our days in London."

Karim blushed and shook his head. "Not London."

Ahmed needed to remember a better time, even if it had been a time when youth strayed from the path. A time when anything seemed possible.

"Yes, Karim," he said, smiling. "London."

Vienna, Austria

Renate had paused in front of the bank of television monitors, watching the news clip of two German soldiers receiving medals for their actions on the Rhine.

Lawton watched her, hurting in ways he hadn't hurt since he had looked into the betrayed eyes of a drug-dealer's daughter.

What he saw these days in Renate's eyes was not betrayal. It was worse…an icy emptiness, a barren emotional tundra, stark, forbidding and terrifying. Even when they had first met and he had first looked into her cold blue eyes, there had been life behind them. Now there was none. Something essential in her had died, and it tore his heart apart.

He cleared his throat. "You must be very proud of your people."

She turned to stare at him. Her eyes could have been those of a corpse. "I have no people."

He pressed his lips together for a moment, forcing himself to remember who she had been and who she might someday be again. "You have friends."

But she gave him no quarter. "I have no friends. *We* have no friends. We have duty. And that is *all* we have."

She had become what she most feared. Aching, he stared back at her, refusing to look away. Like a grainy newsreel, a memory played in his mind, a memory of a hotel room in Berlin and the woman she had almost become in his arms. He didn't argue with her. Argument wouldn't work. But he would find a way to bring her back.

Somehow, some way, he would bring her back to life.

Authors' Notes and Acknowledgements

The Jericho Pact—and the Office 119 series—is a bigger story than any one person can tell. As always, we are indebted to many people who helped in the research for this novel. Of course, any errors are our own.

As always, we are indebted to our agent, Helen Breitwieser, and our editor, Leslie Wanger, for their encouragement and forbearance in the times when it seemed this book might never see completion.

Our research assistant, Rolf Winkenbach, was tireless and resourceful in locating and translating European source material, as well as in answering our seemingly endless questions and requests. His personal visits to several of the settings in this novel—and the dozens of detailed photographs he provided—enabled us to describe those settings with confidence. Rolf also corrected our German diction and spelling, introduced us to the culture of the journeymen, and in general allowed us to look far more expert than we are. *Danke*, Rolf!

We would like to thank Kathryn Marie Engst, M.S., R.N., for carefully describing the danger of adjacent rib fractures, and for providing the details of emergency room treatment procedures.

We are grateful to Frau Hella Mewis—owner of the Galeriecafé Silberstein in Berlin—for permitting us to use her establishment as a setting in this novel.

The story of the Battle of Jericho can be found in Chapter Five of the Book of Joshua. The interpretation implied in this novel is a complete fiction.

Information about the Reunification of Germany and its aftermath was drawn from several sources, including *Der Spiegel, www.germanculture.com* and *www.wikipedia.com.*

Information about cyanide poisoning and its treatment was drawn from the Centers for Disease Control, as well as *http://www.aahealth.org/physicianslink/bioterrorism_cyanide_overview.asp* and other sources.

The causes and course of the Cathar Crusade and the destruction of Béziers were derived from many sources—some factual, others speculative—but the specific events described in this novel were fictionalized. Additional information about Béziers was taken from *www.beziers.fr* and *www.beziers-tourisme.fr.*

Information about the Port of Hamburg, its security

and the effects of nitric acid clouds were drawn entirely from public sources.

Information about the Mannheim Mosque and the Liebfrauenkirche in Mannheim was found at *www.goethe.de*, *www.moschee-mannheim.de* and *http://www.marktplatzkirche-ma.de/gottesdienste/liebfrauen.html*.

The delightful *Le Rive Gauche Café* can be seen at *www.fotosearch.com*.

Information about the Sunni-Shi'a conflict in Islam was taken from Vali Nasr's *The Shia Revival,* as well as Dr. Nasr's presentations to the Council on Foreign Relations, which can be found at *www.cfr.org*. Other perspectives were provided in personal interviews with gracious Muslims—both Shi'a and Sunni—who for their own reasons prefer to remain anonymous.

The Bridge of Europe, spanning the Rhine between Strasbourg and Kehl, is an actual structure. Its history can be found at *www.cultureroutes.lu*. It is our fervent hope that this beautiful bridge will never see the kind of carnage described in this novel, and that it will forever be a symbol of European unity.

Finally, we would like to thank our children—Aaron, Heather, Andy, Matthew and Holly—who somehow manage to not only remain sane amidst the insanity of having writers for mothers, but also keep giving us hope for a better and brighter future. It is to them—and to all of the world's children—that this book is dedicated.

New York Times bestselling author

SUZANNE FORSTER

Alison Fairmont Villard wakes in a hospital bed with a
face she doesn't recognize and a husband she doesn't
know. Andrew Villard, a self-made millionaire, has a bright
future but a shadowy past. When he tells Alison the details
of their life together, she has no choice but to believe
him—and to accept the shocking proposal he offers.

When the veil of amnesia lifts, it's too late. Alison is caught
in a web of her own making....

The ARRANGEMENT

"Strongly recommended."
—*The Mystery Reader* on
The Lonely Girls Club (starred review)

*Available the first week of May 2007
wherever paperbacks are sold!*

MIRA®

Enter a new reality in this sexy thriller
by acclaimed author

GENNITA LOW

Chosen to be the ultimate secret operative, Helen Roston
has become the most dangerous woman in the world.
Two years of training and she's now ready for the final phase, a
risky combination of virtual reality and a mind-altering serum.

Helen's final test is a challenging mission, picked by the other
government agencies whose candidates lost out to her.
To succeed she has to put herself completely in the hands of her
mysterious and faceless "trainer," a man she's not sure she can trust.
But all of COS Command are counting on her. She cannot fail.

VIRTUALLY HIS

"A gritty, powerhouse novel of suspense and intrigue."
—Merline Lovelace, *USA TODAY* bestselling author
on *The Protector*

Available the first week of May 2007
wherever paperbacks are sold!

Journey back to Valhalla Springs with
a new comic romance mystery by

SUZANN LEDBETTER

Halfway to happily ever after...probably.

Hannah Garvey, the resident manager of Valhalla Springs, an
exclusive retirement community, is convinced she has this love
thing all sewn up. She's engaged to David Hendrickson, the hunky
Kinderhook County sheriff, and thinks the future looks pretty
rosy—until one of Sanity, Missouri's most esteemed citizens
becomes the county's latest homicide victim.

Meanwhile, Delbert Bisbee and his gang of senior gumshoes
are driving Hannah nuts, digging dirt where they don't belong.
Literally. And no matter what they unearth, there's just no
halfway about it...life has a funny way of happening when
you're making other plans.

Halfway to Half Way

"A crowd-pleasing, lightweight whodunit filled with
unabashedly wacky characters."
—*Publishers Weekly* on *Once a Thief*

Available the first week of May 2007
wherever paperbacks are sold!

REQUEST YOUR FREE BOOKS!

2 FREE NOVELS FROM THE ROMANCE/SUSPENSE COLLECTION PLUS 2 FREE GIFTS!

RACHEL LEE

MIRA®

www.MIRABooks.com   MRL0507BL